BLACK RAIN

MATTHEW B. J. DELANEY

Text copyright © 2016 Matthew B.J. Delaney
All rights reserved.

Published by 47North, Seattle

www.apub.com

Amazon, the Amazon logo, and 47North are trademarks of Amazon.com, Inc., or its affiliates.

ISBN-13: 9781503937017
ISBN-10: 1503937011

Cover design by Kirk DouPonce, DogEared Design

Printed in the United States of America

County Council

Libraries, books and more.........

WHITEHAVEN

−5 DEC 2018		
1 2 MAR 2019		
3 0 APR 2019		
2 1 MAY 2019		
2 3 OCT 2019		
31/10		

Please return/renew this item by the last date due.
Library items may also be renewed by phone on
030 33 33 1234 (24 hours) or via our website

www.cumbria.gov.uk/libraries

Cumbria Libraries
CLIC
Interactive Catalogue

Ask for a CLIC password

ALSO BY MATTHEW B.J. DELANEY

Jinn

BLACK
RAIN

CHAPTER 1

The security men had advised against it. Or at least Greeley had. But Greeley advised against most things. Like taking walks, sitting by open windows, and eating in restaurants. He'd be against meltwater, Synthate shopping, and visiting pleasure parlors, if he thought anyone would pay attention. The secret to getting along with Greeley was to listen to his advice, nod, then do whatever it was you planned on doing. Only do it when he wasn't looking.

Greeley wasn't looking now, so Martin Reynolds slid his hand around Betsy's waist.

"Don't!" Her hand met his. "You'll crush my wings."

"I'm sorry, my angel."

Her wings were little lacy ones, extending out from the back of her tightly fitted white dress. Reynolds slid his arm down the side of his wife's thigh instead. The big clock on the wall chimed eleven, barely audible over the sound of the band.

What Greeley had advised against was Seeks. A silly game, really, Reynolds thought. An adult version of hide-and-seek. One that rich people played at the lavish parties Bruce Livingston had been throwing inside his Fifth Avenue mansion for years.

Reynolds had known Livingston since undergrad. Livingston had gone on to become a senator, while Reynolds had become a molecular geneticist specializing in DNA recombinant nanotechnology for Genico Industries, a job description that made most people fake calls on their syncs just to avoid small talk with him.

Livingston addressed the crowd. "In a few moments we'll start the Seeks. At the stroke of eleven thirty, half of you will be given twenty minutes to hide anywhere on these premises. The other half will then be given the opportunity to find those hidden. Last couple not found wins a six-month-long domestic Synthate lease. Now, each couple received a card in an envelope at the door, so please open it now."

Betsy opened her purse and produced the white envelope. Slipping her finger under the flap, she tore it open. A red letter H was printed on the card inside.

"Looks like we'll be hiding."

Reynolds was used to Livingston's idea of entertaining. Once the ballroom had been the scene of a female bodybuilding contest. Another time, a hundred little people had reenacted the Battle of Hastings. The columns claimed that not a single invitation had ever been refused. Nor was any member of the media ever allowed to attend.

Tonight, the forty people standing around created that fantastic, almost surreal environment produced by only the most opulent costume balls. An African warrior stood by the bar talking with Al Capone and a NASA astronaut while Hermes danced the waltz with Mother Teresa around and around the floor.

It was absurd, really, which was why Reynolds wore only his old green hospital scrubs, untouched since he'd been a resident.

The clock neared 11:30.

Livingston was traditionally referred to as old mao. And more than that, he was old, political mao, which, before the Chinese currency crisis, would have been old money. Which was the best kind. He had access to more touch bucks in one finger than entire honeycomb blocks of the conurb.

"We'll head for the library," Betsy whispered. "I know a place we can hide. It's where Livingston takes those young female interns he enjoys mentoring."

"Who told you that?" Reynolds asked.

"The senator's wife."

Reynolds looked around the room again. He had the uncomfortable feeling he was being watched. And he was right. In the corner stood a man in a long black robe. His face was covered by a leather plague mask with a long, protruding nose and two perfectly round black eyes.

The masked figure turned toward Reynolds. Reynolds looked quickly away.

The clock sounded the half hour. A cheer rose from the partygoers and the band struck up a brisk rag. Greeley headed out the door toward the front lawn. Henry VIII and Cleopatra and the others headed for the hallways and hiding places beyond the ballroom.

"Good luck, everyone!" Livingston called out. "Let the Seeking begin!"

Betsy took her husband's hand and led him toward the rear of the ballroom. She checked her watch. "Twenty minutes to get ourselves in place. Let's hurry."

They left the ballroom and quickly made their way down a long hall. Reynolds glimpsed strange sights as they passed rooms. Wyatt Earp and a Catholic schoolgirl trying to squeeze inside a closet. A clanking knight and a French maid pushing themselves underneath a bed. Husband and wife reached the foot of a wide staircase and immediately headed up. Betsy seemed to know exactly where she was going. After a bit more walking, they came to an abrupt stop.

They stood before a beautiful library. A marble fireplace was cut into the wall on their left, the stone glowing from the light cast by two red-shaded lamps. An Oriental rug, its background the same faded rust color as the bindings of the books (actual paper, what a novelty!) covered the floor. Windows looked down on the Central Park contaminant dome. And reflecting the room's interior was an enormous mirror on the back wall framed in heavy gilded wood.

Betsy walked over to the mirror. First she inspected the trim, then she cupped her hands against the glass and tried to peer through it.

"What are you doing?" Reynolds asked. "It's not fluxglass?"

"Give me a minute."

When the competitive spirit seized Betsy, small talk was of little interest. A black remote sat on a nearby chair. On a whim, Reynolds pressed the power button. The wall clicked and the mirror slid outward. Betsy took hold of the frame and the whole piece swung into the room like a giant door.

Beyond the mirror was a small room with a bed, lamp, and a wooden bureau. A bottle of wine sat on the bureau, which made Reynolds think Betsy might have had this planned from the beginning. She was a very resourceful woman at times.

He slid out his father's old Glock handgun from the pancake holster attached to his belt. He placed the gun on the bureau.

She raised her eyebrows. "Still afraid?"

"Still."

She kissed him hard. Her hands wrapped around his back. He was still afraid. But the gun was more magic amulet than useful tool. He doubted he could actually pull the trigger. But he liked the feel of the metal against his skin. The weight of it on his belt. He hoped just having the weapon was enough to keep away whatever was out there.

Whatever they might send for him when the time came.

A single window looked down on the dark expanse of the rear garden. There Greeley burned a smoke stick as two shapes moved quickly past him, a billowing white ghost accompanied by a witch, her face painted green.

The library clock chimed midnight.

"Well, let the games begin," his wife whispered.

The mirror door was still open, showing the view into the rest of the library and the hallway at the far end.

"Shouldn't we be closing that?" Reynolds had the remote in his hands.

"By all means."

She took hold of the mirror and slowly swung it shut. There was a click as the frame locked into place, sealing them inside the small room. The glass was one-way reflective, allowing them to look out into the library and see anyone approaching. Without the remote, no one could get into the room short of breaking the glass.

Through the one-way panel, Reynolds watched the empty library. Next to him, Betsy's wings glittered and sparkled as she moved about the room. The clock chimed a final time, after which the sound slowed into a long dying tone before finally rolling out altogether. Then silence. Now, somewhere below, the Seekers would be coming for them.

Reynolds experienced an instant of stomach butterflies, like the giddy excitement of kids at play. The feeling was similar to another, more adult sensation he'd experienced many times in the presence of women, except that dose of excitement usually happened a good foot or so below his stomach. Betsy must have intuited this, because she was looking at him, her hip cocked slightly forward.

Reynolds's heart skipped with surprise. Someone was staring at them.

Betsy frowned. "What is it?"

"Someone's out there."

It was the man in the plague mask. He stood in the doorway of the library, eyeholes directed at their hiding place. Reynolds reminded himself that the fellow couldn't see them through the mirror. Betsy appeared to have come to the same conclusion.

She moved closer to Reynolds. The bells on her wings jingled. "Just ignore him."

He allowed his gaze to flick back at the mirror. The man was still there, head cocked to the side. Listening.

"Shh, shh," Reynolds whispered, grabbing hold of his wife, keeping her costume still.

"What's wrong?" she asked, looking vaguely annoyed.

"I think he's listening."

She pulled herself away, straightening her dress. "Who is he?"

"I saw him downstairs."

"The mirror is closed, right?"

"Yes . . ."

"So who cares? Let him listen. He can't get in here, anyway."

His wife had always been the adventurous one. Reynolds went to the window and looked out again. The garden stretched before him, glowing in the moonlight. Greeley had vanished. Then from the darkness came a sharp, piercing cry.

Betsy grabbed his arm tight. "What was that?"

He knew what they'd heard had been a scream.

But had the sound been real? Livingston might be up to some kind of trick. Turn out the lights, then try to scare everyone. Exactly his idea of a joke. On the other hand, the scream had struck him as authentic. So either Livingston had brought in a very motivated and talented actor for the part, or . . . or what?

Or, Reynolds thought, it was genuine. In which case . . .

From the other side of the mirror, out in the library, came a dull thump. He turned quickly from the window and looked through the mirror. The plague doctor had vanished, but Reynolds had seen something move. Gone in an instant behind the doorframe, beyond their line of sight. But in that moment, Reynolds had registered two feet, limp, dragging as someone out of sight pulled along the body of their owner. Something that caught the light had congealed on the floor, there at the rug's edge. Reynolds pressed his face against the glass and strained to see.

Was that blood?

"What is it?" Betsy asked. "What do you see?"

"I don't know," Reynolds replied. Then he surprised himself by saying, "But stay here. I'm going to go look."

Did I really just say that? Martin Reynolds by no means considered himself brave. He'd flushed a rabid raccoon out from underneath their porch with a 7-iron once last summer, but this was a far cry from that. Any other time, he would have stayed safely hidden with his wife behind the mirror. But something about the feel of his wife against him had gotten Reynolds's testosterone going and he suddenly felt that most dangerous of all male emotions, the need to prove something.

The Glock sat silent on the bureau, its black metal bursting with the possibility of violence. He thought of sliding it back into his holster, but he was a coward at heart. And cowards did stupid things when it came to guns. He didn't want to shoot someone accidently, some poor domestic Synthate or, even worse, one of the other guests. Better to run than fight. That was his way.

Reynolds pressed the remote and the mirror swung slowly open, an effect akin to breaking a seal. Suddenly he could hear all the lower-register noises that had been inaudible inside the sealed room. The tick of the clock in the library. The hum of the lamp. And in the far distance, he heard a door slam.

"Stay here. Keep quiet," Reynolds said. "I'll be back."

Unarmed, he stepped out into the library. The room was empty. Behind him, the mirror swung back into place. Now nothing but his own reflection showed in the glass. Betsy was suddenly invisible. Pausing, he listened. Nothing. He peeked around the door. The hall was empty in both directions.

Turning his attention to the floor, he saw a dark streak along the carpet. He bent and touched the stain. His fingers came away red. Blood. No doubt. He remembered the man in the mask. And the feet being dragged. He should call the police.

But Livingston was a strange man. The entire evening might be just an elaborate bit of theater. If Livingston knew where the Reynoldses were hiding, he could have staged a series of scenes on the other side of the mirror, intending to frighten his old college buddy. Such actions seemed implausible and made no sense, but Reynolds wouldn't put it past him.

The bloodstains streaked down the hall before turning right and disappearing around a corner. If Livingston *was* playing a trick, he was certainly going to a lot of effort. And if Livingston was trying to frighten his guest, it was starting to work. Reynolds's heart thumped rather painfully in his chest while a slow chill crept the length of his neck. Suddenly he was aware of how alone he felt in the big old house. But he pushed forward, not wanting to give Livingston the satisfaction of winning whatever little game he was playing.

"I'll track you down, old friend," Reynolds said to himself as he began following the wet stains. "We'll see how this turns out."

Blood streaks wound back and forth along the carpet like the marks of a snake over sand. At the end of the hall, he turned and tracked them to the end of a second corridor. There was no sign of other Seekers.

The streaks proceeded on and on. The blood pooled on marble floors and beaded on parquet. Livingston was ruining parts of his house with this little joke.

Then the streaks disappeared.

The marks led to large, closed double doors, vanishing beneath them. End of the line. A single beam of light shone through the keyhole below the brass knob. Quietly, Reynolds crept up to the door and placed his ear against it. From inside he heard footsteps. *Livingston, I've got you now.* Slowly he lowered himself into a crouch, then put his eye against the keyhole and peered inside.

It wasn't Livingston.

The room was a study. Bookshelves lined a back wall, against which a shadow suddenly fell. A man stood, his arm upraised. Reynolds followed the source of the light. A lamp on an end table. The plague doctor was there, blocking the light from the lamp. He held a long, curving sickle. Greeley was there, too. The security man lay half propped up on the wall, the red stains ending at him, blood pooled all around his body. The sickle was lacquered in dripping blood. The costumed figure looked down at Greeley's body, tapping the sickle against his leg until blood seeped into the fabric of his robe.

Reynolds fell forward slightly, in shock. His forehead hit the doorknob and the metal rattled. The plague doctor spun toward the sound. Listening and still tapping the sickle against his leg, he moved toward the door.

Reynolds pulled back from the keyhole. He had a strange urge to stand in place. Wait for the double doors to open and see what came out. Or at least bend down before the keyhole again, his rational side telling him to make sure he'd really seen what he'd seen and that the whole thing wasn't just some fantastical delusion wrought by the circumstances. No. There was a better solution.

Turn and run.

He headed back down the way he'd come. Behind him he heard the telltale sound of doors opening, then footsteps across the marble floor. He ignored what he heard. Ignored the hideous evidence of somebody chasing him. *Keep moving.* Now the final stretch was in front of him. He moved quickly, his pursuer climbing the stairs after him.

As Reynolds entered the library, he slipped open his sync. The mirror beckoned at the far end and he sprinted for it. He pulled hard on the gilded frame. Nothing happened. He pulled again in a panic. His sync slipped from his hand and skipped across the floor. The mirror was still shut tight. The footsteps in the hall were loud now, the terrifying figure getting closer and closer. *Dear God.* The pounding of Reynolds's heart seemed to him as loud as the approaching footfalls.

All at once the mirror slid open and his wife's hand pulled him into the secret room. The mirror shut behind him and locked. There in the darkness, trying to control his breath, his heart continued to ripple painfully. He turned and looked out through the glass, back into the library.

Empty.

"Jesus, what happened?" Betsy hissed. "What's wrong?"

Reynolds shook his head. "Quiet. He's coming."

He kept his eye on the library's doorway. Watching. Watching. Then a figure appeared. The terribly long nose, the black eyes of the plague doctor. He stopped for a moment in the doorway, then turned and kept walking, disappearing from view. What was happening in Reynolds's chest felt like a heart attack. But then the pain dropped so hard into his stomach he felt he was going to be sick.

"Who was that?" Betsy asked, her eyes wide and scared.

"Call the police." Reynolds's voice wavered and Betsy froze. "I dropped my sync. Call the police now!"

She looked around, thoroughly frightened by the tone of his voice. Obediently she dialed the numbers. "Where's yours?"

Reynolds looked out and saw his sync on the library floor. He stared hard at it, attempting to somehow will it back into his possession. Betsy handed her sync to Reynolds. The operator's voice picked up after the second ring, curt and impersonal.

"911, what's your emergency?"

Forced to speak, Reynolds breathed deeply and tried to gather his words. "We need help, there's someone here, there's a man, trying to kill us. I'm at 578 Fifth Avenue, the townhouse, fifth floor."

"You need the police?"

"Yes . . . please . . . right away . . ."

"Stay on the line, sir," the operator responded.

Betsy pressed hard against Reynolds, her mouth very small and tight as she stared at something through the glass and into the room beyond.

"What is it?" Reynolds asked.

"He knows."

Reynolds knew they had come for him. They had found out about his work. He had done his best to keep it secret, but he had always known this moment would come. He had just hoped it wouldn't be when he was with Betsy. Reynolds reached into his waistband. They had left him no choice.

The 911 operator came back on the line. "Are you there, sir?"

"Yes." Reynolds whispered. "There's been a murder. He's here now. I'm looking at him."

"Where are you and your wife hiding?"

Reynolds opened his mouth to respond, then a warning flashed in his mind. Something was not right. "What did you say?"

"Where in the house are you and your wife hiding?"

My wife. I never told the operator I was with my wife. His mind moved sluggishly. The voice on the sync. Someone who had seen him at the party with his wife. Someone who knew who he was. Someone who couldn't be a 911 operator.

"Why do you want to know where we're hiding?" Reynolds asked.

Pause.

Click.

Reynolds felt suddenly calm.

There would be no more waiting. No more secrets.

He lifted the old Glock 9mm handgun from the bureau. The weapon felt strange in his hands. Betsy stared at him, her eyes wide. "What are you doing with that?"

"They found me out."

"Who found you out?"

"Who do you think?" Reynolds tried to remember how to flick off the safety on the weapon.

"Oh God. Where is it?"

"Hidden," Reynolds said. "Safe for now."

In the library, the masked figure stopped and stared down at Reynolds's sync. Slowly he bent down, picked it up, and inspected the screen. He pressed the device with his thumb, then seemed to wait.

Reynolds suddenly knew what the man was waiting for, but he was too slow to react. In his hand, Betsy's sync came alive and a shrill ring filled the small space. The man's head slowly swiveled toward the sound as Reynolds's sync fell from his fingers.

He approached the mirror and stared at it. Up close, Reynolds could see flecks of blood on the leather mask. Only feet from them, the man ran the point of the sickle over the glass. His wife pressed herself against Reynolds again. The little bells on her wings tinkled. The blade on the mirror screeched. Reynolds's adrenaline surged as his focus narrowed to a single smudge on the unblemished glass. A fingerprint.

His own that he had left behind.

The man in the mask saw the mark at the same time. The movement of the blade stopped. Slowly, he lifted the sickle, then the blade hissed down. The glass shattered and the man stepped through the broken frame, gripping the blade in his hand.

Reynolds closed his eyes, his finger tightening on the trigger, and fired.

CHAPTER 2

The black unmarked rolled up on the park side of Fifth Avenue, directly across from the Livingston townhouse crime scene. The front curb was still crowded with marked police cars, and uniformed cops milled around with their hats on, playing on their syncs and waiting for somebody to let them go home. Crime scene pulses sectioned off the townhouse, while on the far sidewalk a crowd of people in costume stood together, some of them crying.

Detective Charles Arden sipped cherry meltwater. Arden was a big man, wide across the chest, but now growing soft, a former athlete past his prime. His body spread across the center line of the car, encroaching on the passenger seat where his partner, Detective Dwayne Sanders, sat. Sanders had a runner's build, tall and slim, the kind of perfect mannequin frame that made even off-the-rack suits look perfectly tailored. He watched NY1 on his sync: the New York Braves had overrun Los Angeles in the invasion of Normandy, the crushers had expired three Synthate rebels in the Brooklyn conurb, and tomorrow's rain would be six percent acidic.

Arden studied the containment dome that covered the lower portion of Central Park, which had become a tangled mass of overgrown vegetation. Eight years had passed since the dome's construction by the genetic conglomerate Genico, and the covered area was still too radioactive for habitation. Too expensive and dangerous to ever fully decon, the dome kept the contaminants in place and turned the most expensive real estate on the planet into an overgrown wilderness.

Ahead of them, news trucks lined the block. Sanders flipped off his sync. "Ever get this much coverage in the Synthate Zone?"

"Kidding me. Synthate gets expired, just roll the body up and call the crushers."

Sanders nodded toward a fat man in a musketeer outfit. "Recognize him?"

"That would be Senator Livingston. Pulled him out of enough midtown pleasure parlors to know." Arden pointed out another man dressed Gordon Gekko–style with slicked hair and suspenders. He stood away from the crowd, a massive security-model Synthate behind him. "And that's Harold Lieberman. Number two guy at Genico."

"How do you know that?"

"Genico built half the Synthates in the Zone. You get to know who owns them. Doesn't look like he was at the party, though," Arden said. "Must have come after."

"Wonder why."

Senator Livingston's residence took up the entire corner of the block. Two emergency service trucks had erected light towers at the edge of the park while crime scene units unpacked gear from the back of their vans.

The interior foyer of the townhouse featured pink-and-white marbled floors and columns amid fluxglass 3Deeing Venetian carnival scenes. Detective Rojas, assigned to the Crime Scene Unit, waited for them in front of an oil painting, some sort of large castle with a lightning bolt overhead.

"That painting would look great in your living room," Arden said.

"It would really complement my da Vinci."

"Someone's been studying their art history." Arden and Sanders both shook hands with Rojas. "What do we got?"

"Three dead naturals." Rojas led them toward a waiting elevator. "Two were a married couple, both hacked up, name of Reynolds. The third was security. Guy named Greeley."

"Sounds pleasant."

The elevator carried them upward. Arden's sync chimed a reminder that it was time for his daughter to take her meds. He would call his nanny, Pisces Flyer, when he was done here.

"Some sort of costume party going on at the time," Rojas continued. "Like a hide-and-seek sort of thing. Around forty guests. Some security people. And maybe fifteen or so maids, chefs, etc., all Synthates. So far they've been a little hesitant to talk to us. But their bioprints are all pretty calm. Oceans. Rainbows. Shit like that. I think we can eliminate them as suspects."

"Maybe. Lot of Synthates learning to control their bioprints, though," Arden said.

"I say we just pin it on a Synthate and call it case closed." Sanders looked bored. "Grab one of the usual suspects."

For many in the squad, that had been an easy way to close open cases. Grab a Synthate with a record and pin whatever had gone down on him or her. The department wanted homicides solved, and Synthates couldn't defend themselves. You just had to pick one up, call the crushers, and throw some evidence around. Worked out for everyone. Except, of course, in high-profile cases. When the public inconveniently demanded the real killers be brought to justice.

The elevator doors opened to a floor crowded with more uniforms. The trio walked down a long hallway that ended in a luxurious private library. The room had twenty-foot-high ceilings, a gilded fireplace on one wall, and a chandelier the size of Arden's kitchen table. Windows looked down on Central Park, the abandoned zoo visible through the dome, rusting and overgrown.

A gorgeous brunette natural in a tight calfskin dress with a feather in her hair sat crying in the corner of the room, being comforted by a man in a tricornered hat and breeches.

"Who's she?" Arden asked.

Sanders snapped his fingers and pointed at the girl. "Pocahontas next to Napoleon."

Rojas shook his head. "No, no, no. You're way off. It's Sacagawea and Thomas Jefferson."

"No, I meant, who is she? What's she doing here?"

"Oh," Rojas responded. "Synthate found the bodies initially. But these two were the first naturals afterward. She and Betty Boop were hiding in the study next door. Thomas Jefferson is—"

"Napoleon," Sanders interrupted.

"Whoever." Rojas looked annoyed. "That's her husband. He was in the billiard room at the time."

"See anything?"

"Aside from the two dead bodies? Nah, she didn't see anything."

Arden studied the room. Opposite a wall with a grandfather clock, broken glass lined the floor. A smaller room was also visible, recessed from the library.

"Looks like our two victims were in some sort of concealed back bedroom. Apparently there was a mirror with one-way glass on the bedroom side. It opened with a remote." Rojas raised his eyebrows. "Whatever that was about. Anyway, the two victims were found inside there. Some shell casings. Looks like some shots were fired. No weapon recovered, though. Help yourself."

The Evidence Collection Team, or ECT, was already on scene. One of the officers crouched down as he placed a yellow marker over what appeared to be a shell casing on the floor.

"I suggest it was Colonel Mustard, in the library, with the revolver," Sanders said as they stepped over the broken glass and into the once-hidden bedroom. The bed's comforter was pulled back and bloodied red. The body of a man in surgical scrubs lay sprawled facedown on the floor. On the bed was a woman dressed as an angel.

"Detectives Arden and Sanders," Rojas said. "Meet Dr. and Mrs. Reynolds."

"Doctor?"

"Yeah, Dr. Reynolds. Had a Genico lab identification card in his pocket."

"What'd he do over there?"

Rojas grimaced and looked at his shoes.

"What?" Arden asked. "What's with the glum look?"

"Synthate design work. He was also in charge of the Black Rain program."

"Oh." Arden exhaled, then scuffed the ground with his shoe. "Well, I guess this guy won't be coming up with a cure anytime soon."

Inside he felt familiar disappointment take hold of his chest, like some predatory bird digging into his heart with talons. Arden looked away from the crime scene to compose himself. Finally, he turned back to the detectives and cleared his throat, flustered. "What . . . uh . . . did you get someone to come down for the ID?"

"Yeah, we did."

Arden looked back at the bodies. "Good."

Arden bent down over the corpse of Dr. Reynolds. Outside the room, Sanders and Rojas both studied their syncs. The rest of the crime scene team was in the library. Nobody was paying attention to him. Arden slipped out a biomimicry hacker from his pocket and slid it over his hand. He then pressed the device against Dr. Reynolds's right finger. The DNA hacker beeped, then glowed green. Arden slipped it back into his pocket, then stood.

There were blood spatters on the inside of the mirror.

"How many shell casings?" Arden asked.

"Five," Rojas said.

"How many bullets did we recover?"

"Only two. Buried near the bookshelf."

"So where are the other three?"

Rojas shook his head. "Maybe we haven't found them. Maybe they're in our perp."

Arden turned his attention to the dead woman. "Broken fingernail here," he said, then turned to one of the evidence collection guys. "Can we get a DNA read on this?"

"Yeah, sure." The evidence collection officer bent over the female vic's broken nail. The DNA scanner hummed to life, and he inserted her finger into the machine. There was a whir, and a flash of blue light, then the machine beeped. The ECT officer pulled out the recorder chip and dropped it into a brown paper evidence bag.

The scanner 3Deed a small, rotating DNA image in midair over the victim's body. The machine had isolated two separate DNA components beneath the vic's nail and was now sequencing the profile to construct a visible image of both.

The image on the left quickly began to take form. First, a silhouetted figure appeared, then the figure was given long hair, the universal symbol for female. After a moment, the hair was colored in blond, and the skin turned from dark silhouette to white. Caucasian female. Blond hair. The machine continued to work, isolating and expressing each segment of the DNA. The female's eyes turned blue, her facial features shaping, until Arden stared at a likeness of Mrs. Reynolds.

If one set of DNA components belonged to the victim, then there was a good chance the other belonged to the perp. Arden watched patiently as the machine went to work deciphering the second set of DNA. The machine blinked once, and the words "Segment Unreadable" appeared and floated in midair.

"Segment Unreadable. What happened?" Sanders asked.

"It can't sequence the DNA," Arden said.

"Why not?"

"Because the DNA segments have been blocked off."

"By whom?"

"By whichever company designed the Synthate that did this. All the major Synthate manufacturing companies block off their Synthates' DNA. Protects against genetic pirating by other competitors."

"So it *was* a Synthate who did this?" Sanders asked.

Arden stared at the late Dr. and Mrs. Reynolds. "Looks like. The Synthate who found them?"

"Downstairs," Rojas said. "One of the domestics. We're holding her."

CHAPTER 3

Domestic Class Synthates were generally genomed to be of average appearance. Of all the classes, they spent the most time living among the naturals, and companies found that no natural wife would want a beautiful Synthate around her husband every day.

Rojas had detained the Livingston Synthate in the kitchen, where she practically stood at attention before an industrial-size stove, two crushers on either side of her.

She was a flat-faced woman, with thick legs and arms and broad hands. Her uniform was a light gray, the name "White Moonstone" stitched onto the front. She pulled down her uniform and exposed her shoulder bioprint, a sleeping cat curled up before a fire.

Arden held out his Synth scanner. "White Moonstone?"

"Yes, sir."

"Touch here, please."

She reached out and touched the scanner. The device glowed green and 3Deed White Moonstone's image and all her fabrication specs. She was a three-year-old Genico Domestic Class Synthate from the Roosevelt Island grow garden. No insub history or run-ins with the crushers.

"Where's your residential pod?"

"Midtown Synthate Zone."

"And your employer?"

"I've worked domestic service for Mr. Livingston since my harvest date."

"Do you like working here?"

She looked uncomfortably at the crushers on either side of her. "It's not my place to like or dislike it."

Arden sighed, then turned to one of the crushers. He was a burly natural in black body armor. A stun stick hung from his hip. "Can you give us a minute?"

"Why?"

"Because you're making everyone uncomfortable. Take a walk."

The crusher sulked, but slowly he and his partner left the room. When they were gone, Arden put his hand on White Moonstone's shoulder. "It's very important that you be honest with us."

"Yes, sir."

"We're not the crushers."

"Yes, sir. You're natural police."

"We are. Do you like working here?"

White Moonstone hesitated, then said, "I don't mind it. Mr. Livingston doesn't mistreat us. We do our work. He visits the pleasure parlors so he doesn't expect us to do anything more than clean his house."

"Fair enough. And you were working tonight?"

"Yes, sir. I was cleaning the exhalation condensers. The exhalation moisture from the party had filled the aqua receptacles, so I was moving the water to storage."

"Did you serve at the party at all?"

"No, sir. I was tasked to only clean."

"Did you see anything unusual?"

"Well . . ." She hesitated again, shifting uncomfortably on her feet. "I was on the basement level finishing a condenser when I heard footsteps and saw a man in a mask."

"A mask?"

"Leather. With a long nose."

"Had you seen this mask before?"

"Back when the Black Rain attack hit. Lots of people wore them. I saw them on TV. Protesters."

Memory glimpses of packed streets filled with protesters came to mind. After the attack, the city was in chaos. Lots of people took to wearing plague doctor masks. At that point, nobody knew what was making people sick. Hysteria gripped the city.

"Was this man in the mask a guest?" Arden asked.

"I thought so at first, but as he passed by me, he didn't say anything. But he . . ."

"What?"

"Nodded in my direction. Like he was saying hello."

"And that's unusual?"

"Naturals never say hello. Never acknowledge us. This man, he actually reached out and touched my shoulder. His shirt was ripped and that's when I saw the edge of a bioprint on his shoulder."

"What of?"

"A lightning storm over a farmhouse."

"So he seemed angry to you?"

"His bioprint indicated his mood was aggressive, yes. But he didn't speak. He was limping, too. Like he was injured. Sort of holding his stomach."

"Could he have been shot?"

"Maybe."

"And then what happened?"

"My sync notified me the library condenser was full, so I went upstairs, and that's when I found Dr. Reynolds and his wife. Dr. Reynolds was . . ."

"Was what?"

"Still alive."

"What did you do?"

"I went to him to try to help him. He reached out and took my hand. I could tell he was dying."

"Did he say anything?"

"He said, 'The pain passes, but the beauty remains.'"

The pain passes, but the beauty remains. What the hell did that mean?

"Do you know what he was talking about?" Arden asked.

The Synthate shook her head. "No. Then his eyes kind of went funny. And he died. So I synced my master and waited."

"Did you see anything unusual in the room?"

"No, sir." Her eyes began to water, and she swiped at them with her thick fingers.

"Are you crying, White Moonstone?"

"Yes, sir."

"Why?"

"Dr. Reynolds was very kind to me once."

"You knew him?"

"He designed my specs. So I guess one might say that he was as close to being a father as a Synthate can have. On the day of my harvest, I was in the awakening phase, still covered in amniotic, and he welcomed me to the world."

"Welcomed you?"

"Yes, sir. We were in a group of a dozen Synthates. All Domestics. And he wished us all well and said he would do his best to find us good placements. And then he gave us each a present."

"What did he give you?"

From the pocket of her uniform she pulled a small black spray bottle. Skin spray. The spray was used to treat wounds and burns. Arden had never heard of it being given to a Synthate before. He asked her, "Do you know what this is?"

"Skin spray," she said. "He told us that it was genomed to our exact skin tone. If we were ever in trouble, it would help us." Her hand went back into her pocket and she pulled out a 2Dee photograph on static print paper. In the photo, White Moonstone stood next to Dr. Reynolds, the grow garden on Roosevelt Island in the background behind them. "He took this 2Dee with me on the last day of my training. I knew he would be at the party tonight, so I brought it with me. Maybe to show him in case he remembered me."

"Is this something he did with everyone?"

"All the Synthates in my harvest. He spent a minute or two with each of us. I never forgot his kindness." She wiped again at her eyes. "I hope you find who did this."

CHAPTER 4

Arden and Sanders drove south on the FDR. The East River flickered with the lights of wave power farms and, beyond that, the thin strip of Roosevelt Island, the Genico Synthate Factory visible at the southern tip.

"That the grow garden?" Sanders flashed an image on his sync.

Arden navigated around an acid scrubber. "One of them."

"So why did Dr. Reynolds have such a special interest in Synthates?"

"Pride in your work. Get attached. I don't know."

They exited the highway near Wall Street. Ahead the great sky turbine structure of Genico slowly rotated in the wind. Most of the lights were off this late at night. They pulled along a front lined with Synthate shops and were met by a woman in a white lab tech coat. She had an identification tag clipped to her front pocket.

Elsie Woods, Genico Laboratories.

She shook their hands, then led the detectives toward the Genico building. Above them came a low rumble as the Maglev train sped by on its return trip from Bloomberg Island. Arden watched as the cars streamed by, fifty feet above them, passing directly through the center of the Genico building.

"I'm sorry for your loss, Ms. Woods. Dr. Reynolds worked for Genico?"

She nodded, a tissue pressed against her nose. "Synthate design and some of our viral programs."

"He worked on Black Rain?"

"He was working to find a cure for Black Rain; that's right."

There was a long pause. Arden felt the old disappointment creep in on him. Another bad luck hand. In this life, the house won every time.

"Was there anyone who might wish to harm him?"

Elsie Woods shook her head. "No. Everyone loved Dr. Reynolds. He was a brilliant man," she added. "Working on some of the toughest DNA puzzles in the field."

Arden wondered if that was how all scientists thought of their work, as puzzles. Put a piece here. Try this there. Nope, doesn't fit. Start over. A puzzle made it sound fun. Something an American family once upon a time might have done together, listening to the radio on a wintry night. But his daughter wasn't a puzzle.

And Reynolds had to go and get himself murdered. Arden didn't know the man, had never even heard of him, but whoever had taken his life had interfered with finding the cure for Black Rain. After the dirty bomb in Central Park, and the explosion on the Brooklyn Bridge, the Black Rain fallout was the worst terrorist attack in the city. Arden couldn't help but feel angry.

"You wanted to see his office?" Woods asked as they entered the Genico lobby.

"That's right."

They passed the front security desk and proceeded into the wide open foyer. Around them, volumetric displays projected into space, silently flashing colorful images. A Synthate cleaning house. A perfect blue-eyed five-year-old doing calculus. An old man playing racquetball like a teenager. Genico offered dreams of different lives. Lives free of chores. Free of failure. Of old age. Of pain.

Genico. Live Your Dreams.

"When my father was a kid, life sucked, and everything was about sweat and hard work," Arden said.

"It's the traditional method of living," Woods said as she tapped the elevator wall and the doors opened.

"So maybe that's how it supposed to be?"

"If our technology never evolved, we'd still be living in caves, dying from smallpox and trying to catch food with our bare hands. So, surely, you'd admit that a little change is good."

"Never have an argument with a scientist. They're smarter than you and have had more practice," Arden said.

Woods smiled. "What wise man told you that?"

"My mom. She worked for a pharmaceutical company."

"Does she still?" Woods asked.

"She's dead." Arden followed her out of the elevator. "Father, too."

Woods looked genuinely sad. "Oh, I'm sorry."

"Not your fault," Arden said, without turning to look at her. "You didn't blow up the Brooklyn Bridge."

"She died in the attack?"

Arden nodded. It wasn't something he cared to talk about. It wasn't something he even cared to think about. He winced and rubbed his forehead.

"We have Samps that can help you," Woods said, her voice syrupy and well meaning.

"How's that?"

"Our Amnease Samp. Modifies the Tet 1 gene responsible for memory. Can help reduce some of the pain."

"What, so I don't remember my parents anymore?"

"You won't remember the pain of loss. The trauma of death."

"But that's all part of it," Arden said, feeling angry that he was even being forced to talk about this. "My parents lived and were taken away from me. So not only am I supposed to lose them, but also lose the memories?"

"Just the selected memories. The painful ones."

"The pain is how I honor them. I would never let that be taken away."

Sanders quietly stepped forward, placing a hand on Arden's shoulder. "Hey, man, let's be cool." Sanders was always cool. And Arden loved him for it. But Sanders hadn't known pain like Arden had. He hadn't known the threat of loss.

Woods pressed her lips together awkwardly. "I'm sorry. Of course. You're right."

They continued to move through the building. The floor was dark, but at the far corner, a single light was on. Someone working late.

Woods walked directly toward the lit office and pushed open the door. Inside, a man was bent over a desk. He whirled around to face them. He was in his early thirties and handsome, sporting a pink shirt with slick hair. The man looked up, startled at the sudden intrusion.

"Oh, I'm sorry, Phillip," Woods said apologetically. "I didn't mean to . . ." She paused, then blurted out, "Dr. Reynolds was killed tonight."

The man named Phillip stiffened in his seat and leaned back, quickly composing himself. Then he said, "How? What happened?"

"I still don't know. He and his wife . . ." She looked toward Arden and Sanders. "These are the detectives investigating the case."

"Oh," Phillip said. There was a long pause. Manners might have dictated that Arden now introduce himself. But he stayed put. Awkwardness was a detective's best friend. People said stupid things to fill the silence.

Finally, Phillip got up, stepped forward, and offered his hand. "I'm Phillip Saxton. Senior Broker, Genico Trading. George Saxton is my father." Up close, Arden could see he was high on euphoria. His eyes looked like watery radishes, and he kept running his tongue over whitish lips.

"Well, that's tragic news," Phillip said to Woods as he headed for the door. He suddenly turned to the detectives. "Of course, if there's anything you need . . ."

"You're Phillip Saxton. Senior Broker, Genico Trading," Arden cut him off. "I'm sure I can find you for help."

"Right, well . . ."

"Did you and Dr. Reynolds have an appointment tonight?" Sanders asked.

"I came down to check on a research project file."

"Like the cure for Black Rain?"

Phillip laughed. "I wish there were one. One day maybe."

"Right," Arden replied. "One day."

Phillip left and Arden turned back to inspect the office. It was small, with a view out toward Bloomberg Island, just above the Maglev track. The space offered a simple desk with an eyeScreen, a small garbage bin with fifty trash credits, and some kind of ergonomically designed buoyancy chair.

Arden turned back to Woods and pointed at the chair. "These as comfortable as everyone says?"

"I guess so."

Arden eased himself onto it. "Nice."

He spun himself once around, then knocked against the eyeScreen terminal. The screen flashed to life, the desktop 3Deeing in front of him, the touch screen security preventing access.

"Oops," he said.

"Oh, um . . ." Woods began. "I think that's confidential."

"Sure. Of course it is," Arden said. He could probably get a judge to sign off on a warrant to access Reynolds's files. But then again, maybe not. Big firms like Genico had powerful enough attorneys to hold up access to proprietary corporate files for months. Even in a homicide investigation.

"So tell me more about Dr. Reynolds and the Black Rain program," Sanders said.

"After the attack, Genico began research on developing Samps to combat the pathogens. Then, when people started getting sick, the research program was accelerated. He was working toward a cure. Why? Do you think that might have something to do with his death?"

"We're looking into all possibilities."

Somewhere a sync rang. Woods held up a finger. "Would you please excuse me?"

"Of course," Arden said.

She turned and left the office. Arden turned toward Sanders. "Hey buddy, keep an eye out."

"What are you doing?"

From his pocket, Arden produced the biomimicry hacker, then with a quick look toward the office door, he tapped the hacker against the eyeScreen. The eyeScreen read the Dr. Reynolds DNA signature and flashed on. Images illuminated the glass in rapid succession as the hack downloaded the contents of the doctor's eyeScreen.

Search warrants could be so inconvenient sometimes.

"She's coming back," Sanders said.

The hack ended and Arden slipped the device back into his pocket just as Woods rounded the corner.

"I'm sorry," she said. "Where were we?"

"We were just finishing up."

She looked disappointed, but nodded. "Of course."

Arden moved to leave, then Reynolds's last words occurred to him. He turned back. "Does the saying, 'The pain passes, but the beauty remains,' mean anything to you?"

She thought for a moment, then shook her head. "I don't think so. It's a nice thought, though."

"I guess it is," Arden said. "Comforting. Thank you for your help."

CHAPTER 5

A thin morning rain fell and the pavement began to glisten. The algae fins of taxis splashed water onto the curb, while the mass of kebab vendors and Africans selling Luis Venetion purses and Rolex watches rushed to put up striped umbrellas. Phillip Saxton checked the care label of his Caraceni suit, scanned the sidewalk for any female strong buys, then hurried out of the parking garage. From what he remembered, it rained more now than when he was a kid. But at least since the citywide acid scrubbers had been installed, the sky had stopped drizzling bursts of pepper spray.

His brain, however, still drizzled the lingering effects of Club USA. A dull pain roosted like a gargoyle over his eyes and he thought he detected a note of derision in his liver. He chewed two aspirin, then downed a Vicodin with the remains of a bottle of meltwater. Phillip thought of the cop last night in Reynolds's office and his headache grew worse. Time to push reality away. The sidewalk was packed with the Wall Street crowd headed into work, and somewhere a sync rang. After a moment, Phillip realized it was his.

"You coming in?" an apathetic female voice asked.

The voice belonged to his secretary, Amy. He checked his watch. Ten minutes late. He walked faster. Phillip had slept with Amy a total of twelve times. The exact number of Durex in a box. Neither one of them could muster the enthusiasm necessary to make the required additional thirteenth purchase.

"Yes, I'm coming in right now."

"Long night?"

"Club USA is always a long night." Ahead, the Genico sky-scraper slowly rotated like a giant Rubik's Cube, each floor its own wind-powered turbine. Four Synthates who looked like male models cleaned the windows. Phillip paused, stared at his reflection and gently patted the curve of his hair. "Anyway, I'll be up in a minute."

"Good, the natives are restless."

The models finished cleaning the windows and in unison moved toward the new Synthate retail shop that stretched along Financial Plaza. Synthate boutiques had sprung up quickly across the country. As ubiquitous as cell phone stores had once been, each offered consumers the ability to design their own genetically engineered humanoid beings.

In this way, thousands upon thousands of unique Synthates had been fabricated and shipped to keep homes clean and gardens trim, babysit children, and become personal trainers, cooks, and massage therapists. For anything the consumer demanded, there was a Synthate to be supplied. And conveniently located at a mall or shopping center near you!

Phillip clicked off the sync and turned his attention toward the feeling of warmth the Vicodin had begun to spread through his abdomen. He preferred the old drugs. Phillip was a senior broker at Genico Trading. His was one of the more important names flanking the multitude of cubes spanning the massive open floor plan. Each cube was hooked to a sync, all of which rang and rang, driving the firm like the firing synapses of a hungry, pulsating brain.

He nodded to the company doorman, James Wilson, a retired New York City sanitation worker, sixty-nine years old, with a wife and a son.

Wilson's son was born deaf, and the doorman had been able to secure a patent for the gene Connexin 27, the fragment of material linked to deafness in naturals and isolated in little Jimmy Jr. Connexin 27 later became Connexio, a Samp that cured deafness and added seven more zeros to the Wilson family checking account.

James Wilson was the new American dream. Father a genetic defect. Isolate the gene. Become a millionaire. The doorman currently had these funds foolishly squirreled away in bonds (such a waste!), each earning around two and a half. He also possessed a genetic predisposition toward Alzheimer's and a deluded belief that opening doors was a noble profession.

Know your customer, the SEC's golden rule.

Not that many years ago, James Wilson would have begun the slow descent into Alzheimer's, gradually deteriorating into a human vegetable without the memory capacity necessary to follow the plot of *Knight Rider*. But now, with his millions, and the help of someone like Phillip Saxton, this ordinary doorman could invest in his own future. Could save himself the indignities of old age. Could net for his broker a Van Gogh worth of commissions.

"Hey, Jimmy," Phillip said. "When you gonna come see me about opening an account?"

This was a routine that they went through every morning. Something to fill the void while Phillip waited for the elevator. The Maglev train whirred by overhead as it cut through the Genico lobby, the light green of the algae fin visible as it sped into the distance.

"I don't know, Mr. Saxton."

"You forget? Is that Alzheimer's kicking in already, or did you take some Amnease?"

"No, no," Jimmy said quickly. "I'll see you sometime soon."

"Jimmy, you're killing me. You've been saying that for three years now. You still have my card? Your kid didn't miss out on *The Sound of Music* so his old man could wear burgundy suits and flag down cabs. You look like a blackjack dealer at Mohegan Sun."

"I still have it."

The doors pinged and Phillip stepped inside.

"Call me," he said through the space between the closing doors. And then Jimmy was gone, but not before Phillip caught the doorman shake his head and mutter "asshole." Phillip *was* an asshole. And he was fine with that.

The elevator ascended rapidly. Inside Phillip was barraged with news. A volumetric display of CNN filled the elevator's space. Another Synthate terror attack in San Francisco. The heat wave continued in Alaska. More violence in the African nation of Ituri. Phillip sipped his meltwater as an Ituri village burned. Horrible. Really, horrible. He checked his watch. Running late.

As the doors opened onto the chaotic swell of the brokerage floor, the congregation was in an uproar. The ring of syncs, the shouting, the swearing, the sweating of the eighty-ninth floor all bled together into one beautiful mess. Phillip stepped out of the elevator and took it all in, like the pope at St. Peter's Square, arriving to meet the faithful.

Size mattered, and Genico was the biggest swinger in the industry. The floor stretched out before him, a massive space surrounded on all sides by giant windows. Rows of cubes divided the floor, pockets of honeycomb filled with industrious bees. The walls were barely waist high. Each cube had a sync and an eyeScreen.

The bees themselves, who shouted and cursed into their syncs, were the chosen few. They had been harvested by the biggest trading firm in the world and sown into neat little rows. The old-boy warriors of the eighty-ninth floor went for what they wanted: the mao, the women, the drugs, the cars . . . God, the cars alone. The parking lot reserved for the eighty-ninth brokers could have been a showroom straight from *Automotive Digest.*

Phillip let the amazing hum of the room flow over him.

A Bentley Continental was standing up, squeezing an exercise handgrip. "I'm telling you, people are fucking dropping like flies from this. It's big mao for us . . ."

Across from him, a Jaguar S-Type was pacing back and forth, frantically swinging a golf putter while he yelled, "Bone cancer? I don't know, is that even fatal? What the hell is the survival rate on that? If it's over fifty percent, I don't want to go near it! Get me some fucking research on this. Jesus!"

"Ulcerative colitis? I don't deal with digestive disorders!" cried an Aston Martin Volante, loosening his necktie and staring hard at a 3Dee Synthate in a bikini dancing on his eyeScreen.

They were all bachelor cars. Meant for you and whoever your strong buy party girl Italian model friend for the evening was. There were no hatchbacks, no minivans . . . if you wanted a family car, you wouldn't be wanted at Genico.

And everyone here wanted the same thing.

Like Scarface said, *"The world, chico, and everything in it."*

Phillip breathed it all in and he loved it.

He was one of them, these financial warriors. Each morning they woke, the scent of battle in their noses, like the smell of gunpowder at the Games. This was pure. No bullshit and only one rule: You're making mao or you're wasting time.

"Phillip!" Amy waved to him. She was one of the last natural secretaries. Her dating profile: With the body of a Social Class Synthate, she cardio kickboxed five nights a week, or whenever she wasn't pulling all-nighters in the office. She had just bought a top-floor condo; Tribeca, pretty hot :) She loved fast cars, and a man who gave it to her real.

She lowered her voice as he approached her desk. "Pancrease took a drop today."

Pancrease had been last week's IPO of Nucleotech Pharmaceutical and Development, a genetic treatment designed to limit and prevent pancreatic cancer in men. The ticker symbol, PCR, had gone through the roof on its release, going from an IPO mark of 19 all the way up to 97 1/3 on the first day of trading. Last Phillip had heard, it was trading just above 130. Without treatment, pancreatic cancer had a survival rate of less than ten percent, bad news for people diagnosed with the disease, but great for the business of making profit.

Phillip had made sure to invest for his clients as heavily as possible.

"What?" He frowned. "How much?"

"Six mao a share."

Phillip's heart skipped. "Six mao? Jesus. How the fuck did that happen?"

"What do you want me to tell you?" Amy shrugged and inspected the tips of her nails. Phillip turned to look back across the floor. The clamor had taken on a distinctly ominous tone now. He thought of the packet of Mama Blanca in his desk just waiting for his attention. At least that would sustain him through the morning.

"Where's the old man?" Phillip asked.

"He's doing an interview on *Samp Watch* until nine thirty, but he'll be around after that."

Phillip checked his watch. A little over an hour to set this right. The Hallucion that Phillip took on the ride to work had kicked in and made his mind very foggy. Nothing made sense.

"Did you hear about the new Starbucks promo for Mommy Mocha? You get a free prenatal genetic screening with five cups," Amy asked, mumbled something else, and then said, "Or was it a free gift card?"

Phillip was suddenly filled with anxiety. He opened his mouth to speak. "No . . ." Then he slowly backed away from Amy's desk, like a cartoon character tiptoeing away from a ticking bomb.

"Hold my calls," he said. He turned away, stepping up his pace until he was almost running down the line of desks toward his own office. He could fix this. He just needed some Mama Blanca to set his mind right first. Mama would tell him what to do.

His office, at the far corner of the floor, had a view over the Hudson and into New Jersey. 2Dees hung from the wall: Phillip in the Hamptons, Phillip in Paris, at a polo match, in Turks and Caicos. He collapsed into a chair, checked his Rolex again, then slid open the desk drawer. Inside, next to a roll of Certs, a few paper clips, and a bottle of Hallucion, was a small, clear, glassine envelope. He opened it, dumped the contents onto his desk, then with his trash bucks card he carved up little white lines.

Last year it was all about the synthesized drug Paradise. Everywhere Phillip went, people were popping those little blue pills. Chelsea gallery openings. Blue pills. Upper West Side bar mitzvahs. Blue pills. Tribeca model shoots. Blue pills. But Paradise was definitely over, or at least done only by the bridge-and-tunnel set.

Euphoria, a nice little red pill, wasn't so bad. Nice mellow high. Long lasting. Engineered in Russia. Good for corporate attorneys. The occasional actor. But Wall Street guys had to kick it old school. Strictly cocaine. The same drug that fueled the 1980s was the only real choice for today's power broker.

A shrill ring interrupted his focus and an image of Charles Mazomba appeared on the sync. Phillip checked his watch. Almost one p.m. in Ituri. Lunch time in much of Africa. He was familiar with Mazomba's schedule. Morning was for raping and burning. Next, hacking children to death with machetes. Then lunch. And the afternoon was usually reserved for machine-gunning women. After which came a nap. The civil war there was completely out of control, but fortunately the chaos allowed for a lax level of human rights restrictions that benefited Phillip's plans. He sighed, took a yearning look at the little lines, and answered the call.

Immediately, General Charles Mazomba appeared in a small window just below the Bloomberg Stock Ticker on his monitor projection.

He had a salt-and-pepper beard and was dressed in a military green shirt, bands of decoration hung like party streamers over his left chest. Behind the general was a bookshelf, the green-and-blue flag of Ituri, and a white marble bust of Mazomba himself.

"How do, general?" Phillip asked.

Mazomba looked annoyed and tapped his fingertips on the surface of the polished oak desk in front of him. "I seem to remember a conversation we had when I was promised an amount of a certain one of your products."

"I remember that conversation, and I will, in fact, be delivering said product."

"Yes?"

"Indeed, and in payment, all I am requesting is—"

The general held up his hand. "I know what you are requesting. And it is easily accomplished. We have many Butu refugees who will suit your purposes. This is not the problem."

"Then we have no problems."

Mazomba leaned back and flashed Phillip his famous smile. As an indication of thought, the general's smile was somewhat ambiguous, seeming to roughly translate that he liked you, but perhaps also indicating that he was about to behead you gleefully. Both were scary propositions.

"Do not fail me on this. I am a happy man now, but if I find you are lying, well, you will not find me cheerful." The general took up a pen and paper and placed them on the table. "I would like to send you an official invitation to my country. Where is it that you live?"

Phillip felt the sudden urge for a strong sell. Not a chance he wanted the African warlord knowing where he lived. The butcher didn't show the local pit bull how to get into the meat truck. "Send it to the office," Phillip said. "I'm here most of the time, anyway."

The African leader shook his head in displeasure but wrote down the address Phillip gave. Then the man's image flashed away. Phillip exhaled, reminding himself to upgrade the alarm system. The general was a means to an end, but his constant demands became tiresome. He acted like a Roman emperor, not the self-appointed military despot of a country that hadn't existed a year ago and would probably cease to exist a year from now. The only things the general had that were of interest to Phillip were a large number of diamonds, a fierce civil war, and an almost inexhaustible supply of naturals.

He pondered Africa, until thinking became too much work and he bent down for a spirit boost from Mama.

The sync interrupted him again with the name George Saxton hovering on the monitor, more menacing even than a General Mazomba smile. He debated ignoring the call, but his father would only keep trying again and again. The old man was a genetic disorder with no Samp. A second later, Pop's image appeared on screen. He was calling from his own green room up on the penthouse floor as he was being prepped for an interview with CNN's genetic news studio. A makeup girl bent over him to put on a finishing tan, then quickly whisked away the tissue-paper neck bib tucked around his collar.

His father turned toward the camera lens. "What's the story, Phil?"

"Nice to see you, too, Dad. How are you?"

"This isn't Sunday dinner, it's business. It doesn't matter how I am."

Phillip knew exactly why his father was calling. Better bite the bullet. "Pancrease?"

"What's going on with the drop?"

"Jitters, nothing important, just a market correction," Phillip said as he called up the Samp's numbers onscreen. Share price had fallen another fifty cents, half a mao. Mama Blanca whispered to him from the desk. His throat was dry and he looked toward the minifridge next to the scale model of Alinghi, last year's America's Cup winning yacht.

His father sighed, then looked at himself in the makeup mirror. "What's our holding on this?"

Phillip paused, stalling. "Uhh . . . I'm checking."

Phillip didn't have to check. He knew exactly how much was at stake. Alarm bells clanged inside his head.

"Solution?"

"I'm working on something."

"Something? That's rather vague. When will I see this something?"

"Within the week," Phillip said vaguely. "Or two."

"I've got CNN in five minutes. How's this make my credibility look?"

"I know." Phillip eyed the cocaine again.

"I look like an amateur." George shook his head, looked off camera, then spoke loudly to someone else in the room. He looked back at his son. "All right, I'm up."

"Okay," Phillip said. "Wait, Dad."

"What is it?"

"Martin Reynolds was murdered last night."

George Saxton look annoyed. "It's taken care of. Lay off the drugs. I'm running a brokerage company, not a nightclub."

George's image flashed off and the AT&T logo appeared in its place, 3Deeing over his desk. Phillip stared thoughtfully at the insignia, then bent down and pulled two lines of white powder into his nose.

He crumpled up the empty envelope, then touched his trash bucks card to the garbage can beneath his desk. The can blinked green, opened, and deducted two credits as Phillip tossed the envelope inside.

Unbidden, the eyeScreen glass on the windows flashed to CNN's *SampWatch*, where George Saxton appeared behind a panel desk, the panoramic view of the Hudson River behind him. A balding man in an arrow-collared shirt and suspenders was interviewing him. Phillip flicked off the sound of his father's voice. He leaned back and regarded the city thoughtfully. So many lives below him, so much sickness, so much pain and suffering. And so much mao to be had.

The old man had created Genico, but Phillip wanted more. He deserved more. And why shouldn't he? He had the greatest motivator ever invented working for him. Fear. People feared what gave them pain. They'd pay anything, any amount of mao to stop that fear. And those that couldn't pay? Well, Phillip thought, their deaths would only motivate the rest of the pack.

The income potential was limitless.

Genico was the largest and most powerful genetic firm in the world. Genico Investments pioneered OTC trading of Samps and was the first to capitalize fully on the most important aspect of the scientific breakthrough of DNA research.

Making mao.

The markets were waiting. They just needed Genico to provide them with cures. The revenue market for asthma was six to seven billion. For HIV/AIDS, four billion. Diabetes, seven billion. And the champion of them all, cancer, an astounding twenty-seven billion and climbing. If the old Deep South had cotton, Genico traders had cancer. And from now on, Cancer Was King!

The Genetic Samp Exchange traded cures like the NYSE traded stock equities, genetic trading being the buying and selling of gene therapy samples, or Samps. Each Samp was the equivalent of a share of stock, with a fluctuating price that rose and fell according to market conditions. The difference was, instead of representing a piece of a particular company, a Samp represented a discrete amount of therapeutic DNA. Each Samp could be redeemed for a single sample of a therapeutic gene that could be delivered into a patient's cells.

Dying of lung cancer? Buy a portfolio of a hundred Samps to receive the cure. Born a hemophiliac? Seventy-five Samps would eliminate symptoms.

That these diseases could actually be cured was an astonishing revelation. No more would the goal be remission or the diminishment of pain to the point of livability. Now chronic and sudden illnesses could be wiped out. What would people pay for that?

In the 1980s, an enterprising trader named Lewis Ranieri working for Salomon Brothers had created the mortgage bond market. Some years after the decoding of the human genome, and following the model Ranieri had set up, Genico created another sort of market. The first international exchange for cures: the Genetic Samp Exchange.

Greed was back.

This was the world Phillip Saxton had inherited. He swiveled his chair to look out across the city. A solar island floated just over the Hudson. Further to the north, the Central Park dome glittered in the light, but his eyes fixed on a video billboard, a smiling blond woman holding an infant in her hands, a twirling strand of DNA rotating around them.

Genico. Your Baby. Only Better.

Phillip buzzed his secretary. "When my brother gets here, tell him I want to see him."

CHAPTER 6

Breathe.

Jack Saxton slowly opened his eyes. He took in the feel of the room.
By the bed, a glass of water stood on the nightstand next to an empty
plastic skin spray bottle. A Van Gogh print 3Deed on the wall. Two
windows looked out across the Brooklyn conurb, the clack of a trash
grinder audible from the street below. A plant died slowly on a bureau.
A terrible wave of dizziness overtook him. The same dizzy sensation he'd
experienced when he was younger.

A woman lay in bed next to him. Her eyes were open. A door closed
somewhere.

"Hi," she said. "Remember me?"

"Of course. You're my wife."

Dolce smiled, looking relieved. "I thought you might have
forgotten."

"I'm sorry. I haven't been around much. Work."

Dolce wore jeans and a T-shirt. She reached out and touched his
face. "Please, stay with me."

"Why are you wearing clothes?"

—〰—

An hour later, Jack Saxton navigated his mountain bike down Broadway through the constantly shifting phalanx of cabs and solars. He slowed at a red light and watched the mass of crowds pass by on the crosswalk. Early '90s grunge rock played to his left, and he turned toward a woman in an open jeep solar. Her hair was pulled back in a ponytail and she wore shorts and a small tank top. She was drinking coffee, and she lowered the mug, smiled at Jack, and turned down the radio. "Number thirty-four," she said. "Miami."

"You know your players."

"Only the good ones." She tilted the mug toward him to show the familiar orange-and-green University of Miami logo. "Cheerleader for three seasons. Go, 'Canes."

Jack laughed. "Long way from Florida."

"You too. How about I give you a ride? We can catch up on old times."

"Wish I could."

Ahead of them the light turned green. A solar honked.

"Married?"

"Something like that," Jack said.

She shook her head. "Too bad for you. You don't know what you're missing."

More cars honked behind them. "I'm sure I don't." He nodded toward the light. "It's green."

"Bye now."

The jeep solar accelerated with the flow of traffic. Jack bore his weight down and the bicycle moved forward. He turned off Broadway onto Murray Street, the gleaming Genico tower rotating ahead of him. He was still recognized for his time at Miami. As the years passed, though, he was remembered less and less. Which he was glad about. He'd never loved the spotlight as others did, but he did miss the game days. That was a rush not easily found again in regular life.

Jack pulled the bike to a stop, hoisted it to his shoulder, and moved up the plaza stairs into a volumetric display ad 3Deeing a beautiful Synthate at the casino in Necropolis. Nearby, four male Synthates in window-washer overalls stepped out from a Synthate boutique, separated, and walked quickly away. They moved easily through the crowd of suits thronging along Financial Plaza.

The explosion came seconds later.

The Synthate retail shop stood for a moment in perfect testament to all-you-need retail genetic consumerism, before glass and metal twisted violently outward in a raging torrent of heat. People screamed and collapsed onto the sidewalk as a powerful wave of invisible energy pulsed against Jack and knocked him backward.

He felt a hand on his arm. The Genico doorman, James Wilson, looked down at him. "Are you hurt, sir?"

The strangely formal tone seemed at odds with the chaos of the scene. Jack needed a moment to put the man's words together into something that made sense.

"I'm fine." Jack stood up carefully, propping himself with his bicycle. Traffic had screeched to a halt along the plaza and people who'd not been knocked to the ground stood there and surveyed in horror the burning store. The blast had been contained inside, and aside from a few cuts and faces darkened by smoke, Jack could detect no serious injuries along the street.

Already, sirens could be heard in the distance. Above, the Maglev train passed through the lobby, flames reflected against algae fins.

"Another Synthate attack?" Wilson asked.

"You can't enslave a population and expect them to be happy about it. Sooner or later they'll get tired of doing our laundry."

"And then what?"

Jack felt the heat from the burning store. Overhead, a Synthate Fugitive Unit helisquall skimmed low over the street, its rotators churning the smoke.

"I don't know what happens then," Jack said. "But this isn't over."

Pushing his bike through the Genico lobby, he entered a waiting elevator. As he was carried upward, news images 3Deed inside the car. The project to rebuild the Brooklyn Bridge had stalled under fears of another Synthate attack. This morning would only make things worse.

Jack could hear the roar of the eighty-ninth floor through the closed doors as the car moved upward. That was Phillip's world. Jack's own was something different entirely.

The elevator stopped one floor above his brother's turf and the doors opened.

After the economic collapse, excess moved toward extinction. The American addiction to easy mao and fast living had depleted the supply of its pleasures, but, as natural resources vanished and the Earth warmed, green markets offered new avenues for profit. Consumers preferred to drink expensive coffee harvested by fair-wage farmers in Costa Rica or purchase flimsy shirts made of recycled materials than contribute to the degradation of the oceans or the extinction of the Mexican gray wolf.

There was a superficiality to such behavior that Jack recognized and hated. And yet, if making the Mexican gray wolf the new cause célèbre meant the species could be saved, Jack was ready to endure the smug self-righteousness of the eco-correct.

Unlike the level below, the ninetieth floor housed Genico's Corporate Social Responsibility Department. Its denizens were ex–Peace Corps types, vegetarians who walked to work, burned biofuel, gave mao to Greenpeace, adopted strays, and wore hemp. Jack did his work here.

"Hey, handsome," Cindy Smith, the floor coordinator, said as Jack wheeled his bike out of the elevator. She was small, her body coiled with energy. On her head, she wore a floppy brown fedora. "What happened down there? We heard a big explosion. People are like really freaked."

"Looks like another bombing."

"Awful. Anyone hurt?"

"I don't think so," Jack said. "Should be coming up on the vid-Screens soon."

"Your brother's looking for you." Cindy rolled her eyes. "He wanted you to see him in the den of sin."

"Money is pretty good there. Maybe I should make a move."

"If you ever left, I'd keep everything of yours and take it out once a week to remember you."

Jack knew how most of his coworkers felt about his brother and the other traders. The reality of the situation, however, was that without them, there was no Genico. And with no Genico, there was no Corporate Social Responsibility Department, and without that department, Cindy and everyone else would be back working office temp jobs, living off their parents and planning backpacking trips to Thailand.

Jack knew his brother's floor was driven by greed. But he was a realist. There was a cost to doing good. As he descended the stairs, Jack instinctively reached to cover his ears at the approaching clamor. Even the bombing below affected nothing going on there. Business as usual. Traders screamed into syncs while ticker symbols 3Deed around the room.

Many years ago, investors bought up shares of General Motors and Coca-Cola. Now it was high blood pressure and diabetes. And at every step there were brokers like Phillip Saxton, standing by with their razor blades, ready to take a little sliver of each and every trade. The brokering of life and death.

Inside his brother's office, an attractive young woman floated on a tesla buoyancy chair before the New York Harbor view. Her attention was carefully focused on the man behind the desk.

"Do you want me to stay?" she asked Phillip.

"For a minute."

Phillip leaned back in his chair, one hand obscured in the pocket of his suit jacket. "How you doing, brother?"

"Good, fine."

Phillip eyed Jack for a long moment, then finally said, "That's good."

"Something wrong?"

"No, no." Phillip smiled at the girl. "Take off. I'll meet up with you later."

She was perfect in design, Synthate definitely, and Jack felt sorry for her. Women like her were made for only one purpose. Jack pitied any Synthate who came within his brother's reach. For Phillip, everything was tradable.

The girl winked at Jack as she passed. Her bioprint tattoo showed beneath the strap of her top, a farmhouse far in the distance, darkening cloud cover overhead.

"Who was that?" Jack asked.

Phillip dropped something heavy and metal into his desk drawer, then poured himself a glass of something amber colored. "That? Oh . . . a distraction. So fucking boring without them."

"So how goes things in the world of a high-powered trader?"

"Well . . . for starters, I lost an Andy Warhol amount of mao today. I won't frustrate myself with the details." Phillip sighed, then pushed the tesla chair in a drift across the floor toward Jack. "Have a seat."

The chair rose up beneath Jack and he sat. Phillip sat on the edge of his massive cruise liner desk. "One of our employees was murdered last night."

"My God, who?"

"Martin Reynolds. Know him?"

"Of course. Nice guy. Worked on the Black Rain project."

"Yeah. He was a nice guy."

"Do the police have any leads?"

Phillip laughed strangely. "Probably not. Do the police ever have any leads?"

"Maybe it was connected with the store explosion this morning? That seems like a clue."

"A clue? What are you, one of the Hardy Boys? It's the Synthates. They need to learn their place. This world is for naturals. Shame, though. Reynolds was a huge art collector. Lot of cash in that art. He had an original Renoir. Donated it to some museum. Total waste."

Jack was in no mood to argue. There was a long pause before Phillip finally asked, "How's business?"

"We're looking into—"

Phillip held up his hand and interrupted. "It was a polite question. And while I'm sure your answer is entirely fascinating, I didn't bring you in here to talk about sustainable chicken farming or whatever it is you do upstairs."

"So what am I here to talk about?"

"Africa."

His brother's pharmaceutical habits frequently led to cryptic conversations. "Is there more to that, or am I supposed to guess?"

"Have you ever heard of Ituri?"

"An African nation that annually tops the charts as one of the biggest human rights violators on the planet. The civil war waged by General Mazomba has claimed thousands of lives and displaced almost a million people, while making the general himself one of Africa's most feared men. And one of the wealthiest." Jack shook his head, then added dryly, "No. What's Ituri?"

"No reason to look so smug," Phillip said. "Just a simple question."

"Asking me if I knew Ituri would be like asking you what a Zagat guide is. Aside from the nuked-out radiation zones of Pakistan and India, Ituri ranks as one of the world's most critical humanitarian and ecological hotspots."

"Okay, okay, calm down. Don't get your recycled boxers all in a bunch."

"What about it?"

"I'm planning a trip there," Phillip said. "My little friend you saw leaving just dropped off my personal invitation from General Mazomba himself. I need you to sign some footballs for me. He's apparently a big fan."

Jack laughed. "You? Why? Last I heard there was no Ritz-Carlton Ituri."

"That's unfair, little bro," Phillip said. "Sometimes I also give back to the world."

"I'm waiting for the punch line."

"And General Mazomba happens to be ready to make a rather large investment in Genico."

"And the truth shall be revealed," Jack said. "So you're willing to invest in the most corrupt regime in Africa? Doesn't that hurt your conscience at all?"

"Did you just use the 'C' word in front of me?" Phillip asked. "Conscience? Listen, I'm the owner of a lonely heart. And I'm sorry you seem to forget that the point of business is to stay in business. Genico is in the business to make mao, mao, I might add, that'll continue to pay the salaries of your little granola group upstairs."

"Touché. So it's a bribe, then?"

"Something like that."

"Sure," Jack said. Befriending General Mazomba might eventually open the country to accept humanitarian aid. That would be worth a few footballs.

"Good," Phillip said as he stood up. He rubbed his temples. "Headache?"

"Pounding. I feel like there's a Culture Club concert inside my skull right now," he said. "I'm taking Vicodin like crazy. No effect anymore. I think I'm evolving into a new species."

Jack looked at his brother with concern. "You going to be all right?"

Phillip flashed him his best plastic smile. "Excess is our friend, right?"

"Well, if you ever want to detox, you're always welcome upstairs," Jack said. "I'll see you tonight."

CHAPTER 7

Back in his office, Jack skimmed the *USA Today* illumipaper. Eddie Marquis, the popular NFL star, 3Deed a touchdown run while the blurb described his positive test for genetic modification. Since the advent of genetic testing, key professional players in all sports had tested positive. Over the years, steroid use had all but been replaced by genetic doping, meaning athletes sought to change their own genetic makeup to make themselves faster and stronger.

Eddie Marquis was one in a series of sports figures who had been implicated in genetic modification scandals. No natural-born athlete could ever compete with one whose coding had been modified. The result of thousands of hours in the gym and on the track could be instantly produced by simply moving a few codons around. After several seasons of dramatically increased results on playing fields, league officials had grown wise to the practice and started blanket testing programs. Any modification got you banned for life. Too much modification, and they might not even classify you as a natural anymore.

Someone knocked on the door and Jack looked up. As he did, the pictures and print on the illumipaper faded away to the pale blue sky of the screensaver.

Cindy appeared in the doorway. She had taken off her hat, and her hair was a wild nest of greasy-looking strands. "Your father's done with his interview. He wants to see you."

Jack studied her hair. "You okay?"

"Oh." Cindy suddenly grinned and pointed to her head. "My hair. I've given up all cosmetics, detergents, shampoos, and conditioners. I switched to olive oil with a little warm meltwater. Just like the Romans."

"Looks . . ."—Jack struggled for the word—". . . natural."

"Thanks!"

Happy, Cindy disappeared back down the hall. Jack tidied up his desk, then took the elevator to the top floor of the building.

The Genico penthouse was reserved for the founder of the company, the creator of the Samp exchange and one of the minds instrumental to the creation of Synthates. He was also Jack's adoptive father.

Jack's mother had met George Saxton at a benefit two years after the death of Jack's biological father. His mother had been a Genico biotech scientist who worked closely with the Synthate development programs. She'd married the elder Saxton when Jack was three years old, and Phillip, then five, was suddenly given a kid brother.

George Saxton had always been a disciplined, methodical scientist, and he applied those same traits to being a dad. After Jack's mother passed away from cancer, two years before the Samp was invented, George Saxton, with help from Synthate nannies, raised both children.

Throughout Jack's youth, his father was a flickering presence in the household. Appearances here and there. Always seeming on the edge of vanishing entirely.

The penthouse felt like a museum. The floor was polished hardwood that stretched out like an oil slick. A conference room took up the far corner, a long boardroom table visible through fluxglass. The kitchen was stocked with bottles of meltwater and some actual spring water. A massive 3Dee of Venice filled one section, evening lights shimmering over the canals.

Near the elevator were long glass cases filled with historical weapons. Swords and axes and knives sparkled under the overhead light. Jack was never sure where his father's fascination with weaponry had come from.

Outside through the glass, Manhattan glittered in the fog. A pillow and blanket lay bunched up across the cushions of a sofa while 3Deed Samp numbers floated overhead.

Jack saw Pancrease had dropped again.

A great brown-and-white hooded falcon sat on a wooden perch, shifting its weight back and forth nervously as Jack stepped toward his father. George Saxton appeared from the conference room. He was a slim man of immense presence with a face composed of angles; the sharp line of his nose, the jutted edges of his cheekbones, and the square shape of his jaw came together to form an appearance that seemed created by architects. His thick, sculpted mustache punctuated his features, while his eyes were the most alive part of him, black, holding the morning light.

Regal Blue, his father's bodyguard and helper, followed close behind. One of the earliest designed Synthates, he was hulking and muscular, with a brooding face and a thick, sloping, Neanderthal forehead. His right eye was blind, a useless milky jewel that floated beneath a bushy eyebrow. He'd lost it in the Games. Saxton could have had the eye repaired, of course, but Regal Blue wanted it left alone. A reminder of where he had come from.

Regal Blue acknowledged Jack with a slight bow. He wore an old-fashioned tuxedo, his left hand sheathed in a thick buckskin falconry glove.

George Saxton shook Jack's hand firmly, then led him toward his work desk, a massive wood affair that rose from the floor like the deck of a ship. Always the handshake formality. Jack was never sure if he was saying hello to his dad or greeting the prime minister of Japan. His father's desk was clear except for a few family images. The first was a

2Dee of Jack's mother. The second a volumetric display of Jack in his University of Miami football uniform breaking tackles, then skirting the sideline for a touchdown against Boston College. There was nothing of Phillip.

"Slept here last night?" Jack inspected the sofa with a frown. He didn't like the old man shutting himself up in the office like this. The lifestyle of a recluse wasn't healthy.

"Just a nap." His father looked tired. He seemed suddenly older, and that scared him. "Long days. How have you been?"

"Good."

"And how's Dolce?" His father tapped the top of his desk with a knuckle. He was the product of a centuries-old lineage: Since the first Saxton male had set foot in the New World, none of them had ever expressed a human emotion unless it was pried out like a decayed tooth. From the stilted, awkward conversation, Jack knew something was bothering his dad.

"Everyone is fine," Jack reiterated, waiting.

"Good, good . . ." His father's voice trailed off. Remaining quiet for a minute, he finally brought himself to the point of speaking. "There was a murder last night. A Genico scientist. Dr. Martin Reynolds."

"I've heard."

"He worked on our Black Rain program. It's a loss for the scientific community."

"Are there any suspects?"

"The police are investigating now," his father said. "I've heard it might have been a Synthate. But who knows. First the bombing, and now this. Things are going to be difficult for Synthates."

"Sounds like you pity them?"

"How can one pity something so perfect?" There was silence for a moment, then he continued. "Dr. Reynolds was working on something else. A private project. Just for me."

George waved his hand and the Samp numbers on the eyeScreen vanished. Technical specs for a Synthate line appeared, an image of a muscular Synthate with a war hammer bioprint 3Deed in space.

"How much do you know about Synthate design?" his father asked.

"Just the basics. I never agreed with the program to begin with," Jack said.

"Synthates fall into four design categories. Social. Domestic. Industrial. Guard." His father, never missing a chance to go over genetic design with his son, indicated the 3Deed Synthate that revolved in the center of the room. "This specimen here is from the Guard production line. Designed for security, like my friend Regal Blue. But also constructed to fight in the Games. Stronger. Faster. Modified with increased aggression. They are synthetic humans, share the same genetic composition as naturals, just upgraded."

"I've seen the Games."

"Then you know how they can feel pain. Can die. Just like naturals," his father said. The Synthate on display changed to a beautiful woman. "This is a typical Social Synthate production line. Every pleasure parlor in the city has a handful. Disease resistant. Emotional downgrade." The eyeScreen projected two more types of Synthates. Thick legged. Hardy looking. "These are our Domestic and Industrial lines. Synthates used for factory work. Construction. Nursing. Domestic servants. You were raised by one of the first productions of Domestic Synthates."

Jack remembered the two grim-faced nannies who had cared for him as a child. Synthates were different back then. More primitive, somehow. Their personalities not fully articulated.

The eyeScreen flashed a series of Synthate bioprint tattoos. Snow-covered woods. A thunderstorm over a city. A desert.

"As Synthate development improved," his father continued, "it became more and more difficult to differentiate between natural-born humans and Synthates. We experimented with different ideas. Giving them green blood. Changing the tone of their voice. But in the end we found that naturals were most comfortable around Synthates that looked human. So we developed the bioprint."

"A modification to the genome that created color patterns on the skins of Synthates."

"Biological tattoos. Each Synthate has its own unique moving bioprint genomed on the body. It serves as differentiator between naturals and Synthates. But even more, the bioprint is tied to the emotional core of each Synthate, and the image the bioprint can morph to reflects the Synthate's mood. A sunset can change to dark clouds to show a dangerous feeling."

His father put an arm on Jack's shoulder and guided him out through the glass doors and onto the terrace beyond. The sky was overcast, a mass of fog obscuring the buildings on the New Jersey side of the Hudson. Regal Blue silently followed them, coaxing the falcon off its perch and onto his gloved hand. The bird reacted as it felt open air, shifting back and forth, its hooded head bobbing up and down.

"Before his death, Dr. Reynolds was doing work that would change everything," the elder Saxton said as he slipped on one of the heavy leather gloves. "The genetic industry has been overwhelmed by greed. We have the ability to help millions, but we don't. Why? Because there's no profit in it. This is not what I intended. But apparently, it's what I've taught one of my sons."

"Phillip is trying," Jack said. "I think most times he just wants to please you."

His father stroked the falcon's back, then offered his gloved hand up beneath the bird. The falcon's talons clamped down on the glove.

"My son is so caught up in the pursuit of profits he's failed to see how his actions affect lives. And his failings, I fear, are mine to share."

"He's still a good man," Jack reassured him.

"Is he?" his father asked. "I'm not sure anymore."

Deftly removing the hood from the falcon, he then held up the gloved hand and uttered a command. The great bird's wings beat the air as it soared up and away from the terrace. All three of them watched the creature catch an updraft and soar between the skyscraper peaks, passing the kite wind turbines and descending into the valleys of Financial Plaza.

His eyes still on the falcon, George said firmly, "When I step down, I want you to take my place."

Jack laughed, then realized his father was serious. Of course his father was serious. He never joked about business. Words left his mouth with the solidity of a chisel striking stone. Jack glanced at Regal Blue, but the milk-eyed giant stared straight ahead. Finally, he looked back at his father. "Me? No, you don't know what you're saying."

"I do know. It must be you." He turned his attention away from the falcon and acknowledged Jack with a nod. "It has always been you. For reasons you can't possibly understand now."

Jack envisioned his brother. He was the one who craved control of Genico, and this would devastate him. But for a moment, Jack allowed himself to consider the possibility of running the company. Of molding it into something good. And he felt ashamed. Ashamed that the same news that would hurt his brother so much made him feel hopeful. Still, there were doubts. "I don't know how to run this place. I wouldn't know where to begin."

"You can learn," his father replied. "There are decent men and women on the board. Not everyone, but there are a few. You can learn from them."

"I'm reformer, not a businessman."

"This is why you must take my place. Genico must become what it was originally intended to be, a mechanism to help people, all people, to bring change to their lives."

Surprise and excitement flared in Jack's chest. He had never imagined himself part of the Genico machine, and certainly not its leader.

In the distance, the falcon soared across the jagged landscape of lower Manhattan. Jack turned his attention to the east. A decon bot drifted down the East River beneath the wrecked structure of the Brooklyn Bridge, harvesting plastic from the water. The sun glinted on the river and the rows of wave farms, and beyond that, he could see out across to what must be a million lives in the Brooklyn conurb, each one filled with wants and needs, desires and hopes. Genico could help these people. All that was needed was someone to lead the company in that direction.

But Jack still wasn't sure he was that person.

"Phillip cannot run Genico," his father said. "He will eventually become a man of enormous wealth. Of great importance. But he is not a leader, not in the right way. He's controlled by pride and greed."

His father held up a gloved hand, and with a rush of air, the falcon returned to its master. George cooed to the bird as he slowly replaced the hood over its head. He stroked its wings, the feathers damp from fog. "You two have always been close. You must make him understand the reason for my decision. He will accept it eventually."

"And if I refuse?" Jack asked.

"You won't. In your heart you know this is best."

"Can I have some time to think?"

His father passed the falcon to the gloved hand of Regal Blue. "Of course. I intend to announce my decision to step down at the next board meeting. One week from today. I hope to name my replacement at that time as well."

"I understand."

Regal Blue opened the glass door for them, and Jack followed his father back into the office. The Synthate carefully placed the falcon back on its perch, then reassumed his position in the far corner of the office, silent and unmoving as the rest of the furniture.

George lit a cigar he pulled from his inside suit pocket. "I want you to go to the next Games."

"That's not really my thing," Jack said. He hated the Games. They were a barbaric relic of ancient times that had no place in civilized society.

"Many important people will be there. People from Genico. And I think you should be seen by them. It's safer that way."

"Safer?"

"You're about to take over the largest genomic research company in the world. You don't want to be perceived as favoring Synthate rights. That would cost quite a few naturals a lot of money. So you will go to the Games. And you will not voice anything negative about our Synthate programs. You speak for the company now. Not just yourself. I left touch stubs for you at my apartment."

"If that's what you want." Arguments with George Saxton could not be won. In the midmorning light, Jack could see his father's age. The man who had created the genetic industry had refused to take a Samp his entire life. He preferred to let nature take its inevitable course.

"I have one more favor to ask of you." Jack's father lowered himself into his desk chair. "I won't be around forever."

"Don't say that. We have Samps . . ." Jack began, but his father held up a hand to interrupt.

"I believe we should live as God created us. No regrets. I started this business to do a small part to alleviate suffering, not to extend my span on Earth. Life is fragile. Delicate. So easily subjected to the whim of fate. When I'm gone, there may come a time when you find yourself in trouble."

"What do you mean, trouble?"

"You'll know if the time comes. There's a deposit box held in an account at the Bank of New York at the Wall Street branch. If you ever find yourself in a tight situation, I want you to go and retrieve it. I left something for you there."

Jack sat forward, intrigued by the secrecy. "I'll find it."

"The box is already coded to your touch. No one knows about this. Not your brother. Not Dolce. No one. You and I are the only two people, and you must always keep it that way."

"I will."

"Promise me. I almost lost you once already."

"I promise, Pop. Now try and relax, okay?"

Relieved of the burden, George leaned back in his chair. The Synthate specs vanished from the eyeScreen, replaced by a 3Dee of the Redwood Forest. And in that second, any moment of intimacy that they might have shared as father and son was gone. The falcon beat its wings, and Regal Blue stepped forward to tend to the bird.

"Pancrease keeps dropping," George said. "My son acted stupidly."

CHAPTER 8

Just after three a.m. in the Palladium, Phillip stared at a Jean-Michel Basquiat painting while a freestyle dance-rock version of Laura Branigan's "Gloria" blared in the background. On the wall of monitors that rose over the dance floor and winked like fifty eyes, a tree swayed back and forth in perfect time to the beats while the blue-and-red cubed walls flashed in synchrony. Phillip turned back to the Basquiat, a particularly disturbing image of two yellow-and-red scratched-out figures on a stark black background.

Someone slid by on roller skates. The line out of the bathroom snaked toward the dance floor. A bartender lit a drink on fire. Hello, world. Say no to drugs.

A strong buy sat on the sofa next to Phillip; a blond natural with thigh-length black boots, a short skirt, and a ponytail. She had a hand on Phillip's knee, and in some distant realm, Phillip was aware of this pressure, this transference of heat from her palm, through his linen pants, to his skin, but now he was so focused on the Basquiat that everything else seemed secondary. The girl's hand. The man in the violet Calvin Klein briefs dancing near the Andy Warhol. Drought in the Sahara. The encroaching hour of work.

The Palladium was filled with strong buys tonight. Beautiful naturals and Synthate pleasure workers filled every crevice of the dance floor. Phillip smacked his lips together; his mouth felt filled with sand. His throat burned with a thirst strong enough to draw his attention away from the painting. On the table was a small green vase filled with orchids. He grabbed the vase, held the edge to his lips and drank. Water and orchid stems fell against his body. Jack appeared from the men's room and tugged on Phillip's shoulder.

"Move out to the moon!" Jack screamed over the jungle beats.

Phillip reared back with alarm, a frightening image of his Upper West Side loft honeycomb suddenly transported to the lunar surface, the Earth a distant ball of bluish light visible through his floor-to-ceiling windows.

"What?" Phillip screamed back, a hand cupped to his ear.

Jack spoke again, this time slower and clearer, the words thankfully taking on a less foreboding meaning. "I said, YOU'VE GOT WORK SOON!"

"Oh." Phillip looked at his watch. It was now 3:30 a.m. The last half hour had evaporated somewhere into the smoky club past. Phillip was losing the battle with time. He stood suddenly.

"I need to be at work," he said sharply as his mind snapped into focus.

"Your nose is bleeding."

Phillip touched his upper lip and his finger came away red.

"You should go home, go to sleep."

"I feel fantastic, buddy." Phillip patted Jack's arm reassuringly. "I just . . . need . . ."

Phillip paused midsentence as something caught his attention. He watched, horrified, as the Basquiat moved on the wall. The yellow man opened his mouth and spoke to Phillip in a stream of color. "Analysts recommend a strong sell on . . ."

"I need . . ." Phillip pushed away from his brother. His foot latched on to the edge of a sofa that had not been there ten seconds earlier and he stumbled backward. "To get to work . . ."

Jack reached out and caught his arm. "Easy there, brother."

Feeling a sudden burst of efficiency, Phillip turned and strode off. His mind was clear now. He rampaged his way through the crowd, knocked a strong buy waitress over a table, pushed a Boy George looka-like into the wall. There was no time to waste. Someone, somewhere, was trading something. There was mao to be made.

On the street he flagged a taxi.

"My watch to take me to the Genico building," Phillip said as he dangled a Blancpain Villeret Ultra-Slim watch to the driver. "In under ten minutes."

"No . . . no . . . I cannot do this," said the driver, a South Asian natural with a turban and thick black beard, shaking his head.

"Ten minutes. And the watch is yours."

"No, no."

"What is so complicated? You worship the elephant with ten fucking arms! How can you not understand what I'm saying?" Phillip pressed his fingers on the touch bucks screen. The screen thanked him. "Fine. Touch bucks. Just drive."

The cab lurched forward, and Phillip held on as they sped down the empty, shabby streets of the Synthate section in Midtown. Phillip's sync vibrated. He picked up the call.

"What are you doing?" His brother sounded almost petulant. "Tell me you're going home."

"Negative. The Hang Seng is trading. Everything is a strong buy now," Phillip gushed. "I need to go to the gym. The rupee is overvalued. I'll make a million mao before breakfast."

"Whoa, slow down," Jack said. "I think somebody did too much Euphoria tonight."

The taxi pulled up in front of the slowly spinning Genico sky tur-bine. Without a word to the cabbie, Phillip was out of the car. He sprinted toward the front doors, the sync still pressed to his ear.

"Please tell me you're not going to work like that," Jack said.

"Correction," Phillip said as he banged on the glass doors to get the guard's attention. "I'm already at work."

The security guard, a bruising Synthate whom Phillip had never seen before, opened the door cautiously, and Phillip blurted out, "I'm Philip Saxton. My father owns the building. Reporting for work."

The security guard eyed Phillip's clothes. "I know who you are, Mr. Saxton."

"Good. How's your portfolio?"

Phillip rushed past the guard to the elevator. He waited impatiently for the doors to open. His sync rang again, and he saw his brother's name on the projection. Without thinking, Phillip threw the sync and watched as it sailed, still ringing, across the building lobby. The Maglev train whirred by overhead.

The elevator opened.

The eighty-ninth floor was black and empty. He sprinted down the long rows of cubes, past darkened monitors. The motion-sensitive lights flashed on behind him as he ran, like the strobe of runway bea-cons urging him forward, faster, faster. He pushed open the glass door to his office. Syncs beckoned him. His computer called to him. Behind the glass case, the scale model of the Alinghi seemed to ride along the fluid wave of his desk.

Warm wetness broke from his nose. He dripped sweat. It was all too much.

"The Samp Market is bearish. We recommend a strong sell."

Phillip staggered a few steps forward. The world turned. The market closed.

CHAPTER 9

Jack found his brother facedown in the middle of his office. Phillip still wore the clothes from the Palladium, a white linen suit with a peach-colored undershirt. His head was turned to the side, a large wet spot of drool visible on the carpet.

Jack squatted and rolled his brother onto his back. Slowly Phillip's eyes opened and he groaned. His pupils dilated, then focused. Turning his head, he looked up at his brother.

"What time is it?"

"Eight thirty in the morning."

"Perfect timing," Phillip said as he licked the white crust from his lips. "Just came in to do a little work last night."

Phillip sat up, steadied himself, then stood. Making a face, he buzzed his secretary.

"Rough night?" Jack asked.

"I've had rougher."

"Right. Anyway. As stimulating at this conversation is, I've got to get upstairs and check in."

"Ecology emergency?"

"Actually, we're putting together a protest in support of Ituri human rights."

Phillip's eyes widened. "What? Hey . . . whoa . . . slow down." Phillip's mind snapped to attention. "What does that mean?"

"The country has no potable water, electricity, or food, the stuff of basic existence. And that's all because General Mazomba has kept a civil war going to consolidate his corruption of power."

"Whatever you may think, protesting is not a good idea," Phillip said. "In fact, it's a very bad idea. I've got a major deal going with this guy. How does it look if my own brother attacks his policies?"

"My name won't be on anything. Your profits will be safe."

Phillip shook his head, looking sober for the first time that morning. "I'm serious. Don't rock the boat. I need this to come together. It's important."

"How much time do you need?"

"There are a million people starving, or dying of AIDS, or whatever. Plenty of causes to wave your biodegradable flag at without getting involved in mine."

"These people need help."

Phillip sighed. "Always trying to save the world, brother."

"Sometimes I think I'm just a caricature to you."

"It's too early in the morning for such long words."

"You've got a busy morning." Jack checked his watch. "I have to go upstairs now."

Phillip smiled. "I'll remember to recycle."

CHAPTER 10

The ring of the sync startled Phillip. An image of General Mazomba appeared.

"Coming, coming," he said aloud to no one as he carefully dripped Visine into each eye. Dropping the bottle into his desk, he coughed to clear his throat, smoothed the front of his suit, and answered the call.

"Good morning," Phillip said.

The general did not look pleased. He pressed his fingertips together. "I am wondering why my people here are telling me that your brother was asking questions about our refugee population."

Phillip kept his face impassive. "Go on."

"I am one of your brother's biggest football fans. But what you need to know is that your brother's activities are highly displeasing to me."

"Everything is under control," Phillip said reassuringly.

"Why should I believe that? Because you tell me it is?" The general's tone was scathing. "If you want this deal to go through, I must not have such problems."

"I assure you, there will be no problems."

"I have a lot of mao invested with you," the general said. "Don't make me regret my decisions." Something that sounded like gunfire cracked in the background. There was a click, then instrumental music played as Phillip found himself on hold.

Somehow, once again, Phillip thought to himself, Jack was in his way. Casting a shadow over him and all his plans. And it wasn't fair. His kid brother had an advantage no one else had. His *secret* was what gave him the edge. And if people only knew, they'd understand why things were so much easier for Jack.

His eyeScreen chimed. Pancrease had fallen another two points. Somewhere, someone was probably dying from pancreatic cancer. Wasting slowly away, his or her body sickened from chemotherapy. And somewhere a loved one spent sleepless nights, sorting through old sync images, up late worrying. But Phillip wasn't that guy. He was on the other side, the guy in the expensive suit, with the Cuban cigar clenched between his teeth. Phillip was the fellow who was about to make a fortune off pancreatic cancer.

Only not now, because the Samp didn't work.

The sync clicked again, and General Mazomba appeared once more. Two beads of sweat had formed down the side of his cheek.

"If your brother shames me publicly, if these things happen, I can only blame you for them. You understand this?" General Mazomba paused, staring thoughtfully at Phillip. "So maybe it's time to do something about it."

CHAPTER 11

The deceased, Dr. Martin Reynolds, had lived in one of the newer con-urb apartment complexes in Battery Park City. The doorman, a burly Synthate in a black suit, had the touch key and let Arden and Sanders into the space. The place was large and looked barely lived in. The condenser was half full of clean water. A vidScreen 3Deed a vintage image of the Golden Gate Bridge while through the fluxglass, the recycle stations in New Jersey burned gas flames.

Arden turned toward the doorman. His bioprint flashed to an image of an abandoned house. "Did the Reynoldses have many visitors?"

The Synthate shook his head. "Not many, sir. They were quiet. Well liked."

"Anyone suspicious ever hang around the building?"

"Guy came by, maybe a week or so, wandered into the lobby high on something. Euphoria, probably. Had to kick him out."

"What'd this guy look like?"

"Natural. Broker-looking guy."

"Did he say anything?"

"Not really. Just Euphoria crazy talk. Knocked over one of the plants out front. Said he was meeting a friend. Wouldn't say who. Kicked him out, he never came back."

The Synthate shut the door as he left and the two detectives began an inspection of the apartment. Sanders stopped to watch a 3Dee of Reynolds and his wife at a grow garden, a line of Synthates at attention behind them. They were a handsome couple, like models from a skin spray vidImage.

"What are you hoping to find here?" Sanders asked.

"Don't know." Arden ran his fingers over the smooth glass edges of a liquor cabinet. He found a highball glass and poured himself something to tide him over. He downed the liquid in a gulp and turned back toward the living room. "Maybe nothing. He doesn't seem like the type to bring his work home with him."

The view through the bedroom window was blocked by a slow-moving wind power farm. The five diamond-shaped kites slowly slid south while 3Deeing ads for a Governors Island pleasure parlor. A buoyancy bed floated in the corner. Some clutter lined the top of one of the dressers. An open perfume bottle, crumpled Kleenex with lipstick marks, some loose change. Over the mirror, someone had written "Memory Core?" in black Sharpie ink.

"Memory Core?" Sanders said. "What do you think that is?"

"No idea."

More vidImages 3Deed on the wall, most of them of the Reynoldses with various important people.

"What do you make of this one?" Sanders indicated an image of Dr. Reynolds standing next to a square-jawed man with a thick mustache, a backdrop of laboratory equipment behind them.

"Let's take a look." Arden touched the image and enlarged it until it 3Deed almost life-size in the center of the room.

Sanders studied the image. "The guy with the 'stache is George Saxton, right?"

"I think so."

"What do you make of the lab behind them?" The space behind the two men was crowded with genetic recombination equipment. "Look at the floor. That doesn't seem like a Genico lab."

The floor was constructed of what appeared to be broken cobblestone. Arden indicated the bottom edge of the image where a rusted metal rail was barely visible. "What do you think that is?"

"Looks like a train track."

"What's a train track doing in a Genico laboratory?"

Something else caught Arden's eye. In the far right of the image was a bronze plaque affixed to a crumbling brick wall. Arden focused in on the section. There was writing on the plaque, barely visible under layers of dirt.

"Can you make that out?" Arden indicated the image.

"Looks like numbers."

Arden rotated the image in midair, and the plaque suddenly came into focus.

A.D. 1870

"This definitely isn't in the Genico building," Arden said. "Wherever it is, it's underground and very old."

"Why would Genico have a lab somewhere like that?"

"They would if there was something they wanted to keep secret."

"Like what?"

"Reynolds would have known."

"Maybe that's why he got killed."

Arden scanned the vidImage to his sync memory. If this was some kind of secret off-site lab, he doubted anyone at Genico would ever tell him anything. But there was definitely something that Genico wanted to keep hidden. Arden waved his hand and the image of Reynolds and Saxton shrank back down to frame size.

Sanders casually poked through an immaculately folded stack of clothes in one of the Reynoldses' drawers. He pulled out a diamond necklace and fingered it thoughtfully for a moment before putting it back in the drawer. "How much do you think old man Saxton knows?"

"Probably everything. We'll never get to him, though. Real question is, how much do you think his kids know?"

"Don't know," Sanders said. "This guy Saxton looks old school. He's probably a keeps-his-own-counsel type. Kids might not know anything."

The window power farm had moved off to the east, exposing the view through the bedroom window. Arden looked out across the city of lights, all the way north to the blackness of the Synthate Zone and Central Park beyond. This place was beautiful, something Arden couldn't have afforded even with ten years' salary.

"Why give all this up?" Arden waved his hand toward the view. "Reynolds had a pretty good life here. Beautiful wife. Great apartment. Lots of cash in the bank. This wasn't just some random jacking in an alley somewhere in Synthate town. Guy was assassinated. But for what?"

Sanders shook his head. "Something must have been important enough."

Arden thought back to the Black Rain attack. Lot of people got sick that day. Lot of people died. That might be important enough to cause waves. Maybe that's what got Reynolds killed.

"Hey," Sanders said. "Look at that."

Sanders pointed back to where the vidImage of Reynolds and Saxton in the laboratory had displayed near the bed. The 3Dee was gone, replaced with a generic view of the Rocky Mountains. Arden moved quickly into the kitchen, just in time to see the vidImage of Reynolds and his wife in front of the grow garden vanish from the refrigerator, replaced by a display of a kitten dozing on a pillow.

"Someone accessed the Reynoldses' home network," Sanders said.

"Looks like they're cleaning up," Arden said. "Someone's got something to hide."

CHAPTER 12

Phillip stood in the threshold in the York Conference Room of Genico. The York looked like the smoking room from an Agatha Christie novel with its overstuffed leather chairs and great stone fireplace. Framed portraits of the Genico founding board members hung from the wall.

The biggest painting of them all was placed just over the fireplace. On the canvas was a tall, broad-shouldered man. The bulges of muscle on his chest and arms made him look more like a soldier than the head of the Genico brokerage department.

This man was Harold Lieberman.

Lieberman himself had a Synthate party girl bent over the conference table, fucking her from behind. She was beautiful, straight black hair, her green eyes blank. A bioprint of a vacant house trembled on her shoulder. Lieberman's hair was slicked back from his forehead and shone in the lamplight. He possessed an olive complexion, with thick eyebrows and dark eyes. In the corner stood a hulking Synthate named Rasputin. He stared hard at Phillip.

"Please," Lieberman said, "have a seat." He waved to one of the leather chairs as he continued with the girl. "I'm almost done." The girl let out a final cry as Lieberman grunted and finished. Then he pulled away. Rasputin handed him a handkerchief and a bottle of water. The head of trading wiped the sweat from his forehead, then sipped the water. "When I was on Wall Street, we used to hit the rub and tugs downtown on lunch. Now I just don't have the time. You want some?"

"Water?"

"No, the girl."

Phillip shook his head. "No, thank you, sir."

The girl pulled down her dress, then quietly left the room through a side door. Phillip sat and Lieberman belted his pants, leaning against the table, sipping his water. "My father worked in the meat markets. He was a butcher. It's easy to defy expectations when nothing is expected of you. A rich man's son can have a lot to live up to."

Phillip desperately tried to push the image of the naked old man from his mind.

"I've looked at your trading record. You are an average trader, and, until now, your sole distinction that I'm aware of is that you are losing an inordinate amount on Pancrease." Phillip opened his mouth to protest, but Lieberman held up his hand. "I don't give false praise. But don't worry. Your father has ensured your future. Had you been born the son of a lesser man, you might have actually had to work for your success."

Phillip was starting to become tired of the insults. "Where is this conversation headed?"

"How'd you like to distinguish yourself?"

"What do you mean?"

"You live in a kingdom that soon will be looking for a new successor," Lieberman said. "Your father intends to step down."

"What?" Phillip asked, genuinely surprised. The old man had said nothing to him.

"Such a moment is always a dangerous time for a kingdom. The turning over of the reins. Ideas that have been in favor, the people implementing them . . . suddenly men of our kind find themselves facing opposition, having to justify themselves . . ."

"But Samp trading drives this company. And you made this place with my father. The two of you built Genico together."

"Of course. I've known your father for a very long time. We go way back. He's a good man. But, alas, good men are not well suited for this line of business."

"I don't understand."

"Your father has chosen your brother, Jack, to succeed him."

"My brother?"

"Actually, your stepbrother, if I'm not mistaken."

"Yes, yes . . . he is," Phillip said, distracted.

Lieberman studied Phillip with a careful eye. "You aren't pleased."

Phillip snapped to attention, a warning alarm sounding in his head. "Just surprised."

"Perhaps you'd thought there might be a different successor? Perhaps you had thought it might be you?"

"I wouldn't be so presumptuous."

"Then you would not be the man of conviction that I thought you would be. It's only natural for a prince to want to become king. Perhaps this prince feels the same?"

Phillip was quiet for a long minute, and then said, "Help me out. What's your angle?"

"The obvious one. I know about your brother. He could destroy this company."

"What are you saying?"

"I'm saying that perhaps it's time for you to become king."

CHAPTER 13

There was a note 3Deeing in Jack's office. Jack would meet Phillip and Dolce on the roof. Phillip collapsed into a chair and studied his surroundings. The room was a monument to adventure. 2Dees showed Jack posed in front of the Great Wall, on the stone steps of Machu Picchu, near the edge of the Tannhauser Gate.

In the corner a small gray packed parachute and yellow helmet, a souvenir from Jack's base-jumping days, sat on top of some kind of leather strapped West African drum. Phillip's eyes flicked to a 2Dee of Jack in his Miami Hurricanes uniform during the Orange Bowl victory. Taken on the field, it showed Jack grinning happily, holding his helmet in one hand while hugging a radiant looking Dolce with the other. Behind him was the mass confusion of the rest of the jubilant Miami players.

"Cheers to you, mate," Phillip said. Bending over, he snorted some powder into his nose from a little Ziploc he always carried with him. Mama touched him immediately, and the wave pulsed from his nose down through the rest of his body. Phillip sat up in the chair and stared at the football 2Dee again. He moved toward the image and took it down from the wall.

Jack the star. Dolce beaming up at him. Overhead, ticker tape fluttered down, frozen in its timeless fall. Almost lost in the background, Phillip could see his father giving a rare smile and looking prouder than his biological son had ever seen.

He focused again on Jack and slowly brought the picture up toward his eyes. The details faded out of focus, and Phillip moved the image closer still, until he could see each individual pixel of color among the thousands. Here, lost in the pixelated world, things began to make sense. Each pixel played its part in obscurity. Each was nothing. Just like every other pixel. And each easily removed.

"I know your secret . . ." Phillip whispered to the photograph.

A sharp knock on the door surprised him. The pixels disappeared as he focused for a moment, then turned toward the doorway. Dolce stood there, annoyingly beautiful as usual. She owned a yoga studio in Soho and taught classes a few times per week. Breathe through your eyes, eat lots of broccoli, read Alan Watts. She was that type of person. Part philosopher, part athlete.

While she and Phillip had grown up being close, Dolce had always been closer to his brother. The two of them had kept their relationship secret for years until it became too obvious to hide anymore. Phillip had feigned happiness, or maybe indifference, but inside he counted another resentful strike against Jack. She was the ultimate symbol of success before they even knew what success was.

"That's the Orange Bowl, right?" Dolce breezed into the room, looking at her sync. "He played well in that game."

Phillip hung the picture back on the wall. Jack had a record game that day. Phillip turned toward her. "Jack lived lucky. Death can't even touch him."

Dolce looked up. "You mean the accident?"

"T-boned by a truck at seventy miles an hour. Didn't work out so well for James Dean. Jack Saxton wakes up in the hospital without a scratch."

"God chooses a path for all of us in life."

"And that's who you think chose Jack's path? God?" Phillip tested.

"I believe God to be a divine force in all of us. The essential spark of life. However that spark came to be, yes, I believe that to be God's hand at work. So if Jack lived when he should have died, if his spark continued, then God made that happen. Whether we understand or not. God is everywhere. And in everything."

"God always seems to have Jack in the palm of his hand. The rest of us are on our own. Jack's always walked a higher path."

"It's not a higher path, but it's how we choose to walk it. We all have our own gifts, or circumstances that we're brought into this world under. Look at Synthates. Destined to be slaves from the moment of their creation. So what does that say about how the naturals perceive God? If God is the creator of life, and naturals are the creator of Synthates, we've certainly chosen to model our behavior in a selfish way. Our one creation we force into slavery. If your God complex is one in which you seek only to gain and never to give, you'll always look at the success of others with resentment."

"You think I resent my brother?"

"Of course I do," Dolce said. "You always have. Even when we were little. And that's blinded you to how fortunate you really are. You're born into wealth and privilege. You've been born a natural. That alone is winning the genetic lottery. I love you, Phillip. Your father loves you. Think about that, and not how much better you think someone else has it, and you'll go a long way to finding your happiness."

Phillip studied her, then sighed. "It's too early for philosophy. Jack said he'll meet us upstairs."

The roof of the Genico building offered an exclusive perspective, seen by the privileged few. To the west rose the peak of Nucleotech Pharmaceuticals, with its diamond-shaped point. The asset-rich genetic pharmaceutical company had developed the first combat line of Synthates. To the north appeared the distinctive black glass towers of DNA Design, the corporation that controlled the market on the Synthate Social class, the girls and boys that filled the pleasure parlors. Including Genico, this trio of skyscrapers made for a beautiful display of capital. The advances they symbolized were what people would remember a thousand years from now.

The day had turned overcast, with a feel of rain in the air. Dark clouds blotted out the surrounding towers until it seemed Dolce and Phillip were alone in the sky. Sir Edmund Hillary on the peak of Everest, nothing visible for miles except the endless white of cloud cover. Then somewhere in the white, the elevator pinged, and there was Jack.

"I'm glad you're both here," Jack said. He seemed unusually eager today. Like some freckled kid in the 1950s getting his first paper route. "It's important that we have each other. Especially now that we're going to have to deal with change. Big change. But more like evolution than revolution."

Phillip knew what was coming.

Jack looked steadfastly at him. "He gave us the company."

"Us?" Phillip asked, surprised

"Well . . . me . . . at least on paper." Jack paused. "My idea is we'll run it together."

So that old bastard Lieberman had been right, Phillip thought. Everyone seemed to know except for Phillip. *We'll run it together!* There was always only one king. Phillip looked over the edge of the railing, down the sheer side of the high-tech mountain obscured by fog. He imagined a village below, with little monks in crimson robes. Nepal, or was that Tibet? Phillip wasn't sure, but what the hell was the difference? He was on top of the mountain. What did it matter to him what people did on the bottom?

"Well, looks like, again, you've outdone me," Phillip said coolly.

"You're my brother. It's not a competition." Jack's expression was concerned.

"Limited resources. Everything's a zero-sum game."

"What are you talking about?"

"You know, those pictures in your office. I was just looking at them. You always made Pop proud," Phillip said. "Now the legend continues."

Making a mock bow, he turned and walked toward the elevator.

"We'll run the company together!" Jack called out behind him. "Genico needs both of us."

Phillip stepped into the elevator and turned to face Dolce and Jack.

"I could see how someone like you might think that was possible," Phillip said to his brother. Then the doors closed and he disappeared.

CHAPTER 14

Jack didn't move for several minutes. He'd expected his brother to be taken by surprise and thought he'd be upset. But although Phillip had been angry, he hadn't seemed surprised. Someone must have already broken the news to him. Jack wondered who.

Dolce tugged at his arm. "Come on. This way."

They walked along the edge of the roof. A helisquall skimmed through the evening air before heading north. She kissed him roughly on the mouth. "How are you feeling?"

"Fine." Jack smiled and took her hand. "Everything is fine. What's wrong?"

"Nothing. I'm just . . . I don't know. Your brother brought up your car accident today."

"That was a long time ago."

"I thought I lost you," she said. "And that changed things in me."

"Changed how?"

"The fear of losing you again. Sometimes I wish I could go back to before the accident. When things were simpler. I wouldn't have this . . . fear . . . all the time."

"Dolce, I was sixteen years old. A kid. Driving stupid. You don't have to worry, I'm . . ."

"I'm pregnant," she blurted out.

Jack stared dumbly as he took in the sense of her words.

She watched him gravely with perfect awareness of his thought process. Dolce knew him better than anyone else ever could. But he doubted she could know how afraid he felt in this moment. A fear that rose to border on panic. The new unknown stretched before him and it was going to be a wonderful, amazing adventure, but the road had just taken a sharp bend, and he had no idea what was ahead.

From her pocket, she pulled a small, cross-shaped locket and held it out to him. The locket was tarnished silver, suspended from a length of leather braid. Jack took the cross from her. "What's this?"

"Inside that locket is your son's complete genetic code. Eyes. Hair. Anything you want to know," she said. "Or if you're in an old-fashioned mood, it can be a surprise."

He slipped the locket over his head and around his neck. The leather was coarse against his skin. He was having a son. The thought overwhelmed him.

"Will you always love me?" Dolce asked, unusually serious.

Surprised by her tone, Jack looked at her. "Of course."

"I mean, what if you found out things about me? Things you might not like?"

"There's nothing I don't know."

She shook her head. "I don't think two people can ever really know each other. Some people live their whole lives never even knowing themselves."

"What are we talking about?"

Dolce looked at him intently. Then she began to cry. She threw her arms around him. He hugged her back. "What is it?"

"I wish we could go back to when we were kids. Remember what that was like?"

"Of course I do." He rubbed her gently.

"I don't know. Everything is different. There's so much happening, I can't take it all in sometimes."

"Everything will be fine. I promise."

Movement caught his eye, and Jack saw his father's falcon cut through the cloud cover, soaring on a burst of air before disappearing behind distant metal peaks.

CHAPTER 15

Danny Flynn of the NYPD Grid Crime Unit turned away from his eyeScreen as Arden came up behind him. Flynn was fortyish with long, salt-and-pepper hair and a scruffy goatee. He and Arden had been partners years ago, back in their Midtown North patrol days. They'd walked a foot post together, when the first Synthates were beginning to move into the neighborhood. Now Flynn was a detective specializing primarily in grid fraud and DNA hacking.

"I need a big favor," Arden said. He pulled the hacker from his pocket. "I need you to take a look at this and tell me what's on it."

"Where'd you get it?"

"From a mainframe at Genico Laboratories."

Flynn leaned back in his chair and looked confused. "They let you scan one of their eyeScreens?"

"Not exactly."

"Ah . . . okay, forget I asked." Flynn rolled his eyes. "Give it to me."

"You're a good man," Arden said as he slapped the hack into Flynn's palm.

Flynn touched the hack to his own eyeScreen and began checking over the contents. "What am I looking for exactly?"

"Anything unusual. The guy who owned the eyeScreen where that came from was working on a cure."

"Cure for what?"

"Black Rain."

"Oh." Flynn looked uncomfortable. He knew all about Arden's daughter. "Let's get some answers then," Flynn said, now fully focused. Folders 3Deed over his desk, opened, then moved to the side as Flynn expertly navigated file after file.

"Hmm . . . coming out with a new cure for obesity," Flynn said.

"What's that? Stay away from the peanut butter cups?"

Flynn patted his own rounded belly and said, "It's a hereditary disorder. You wouldn't blame an alcoholic. It's a disease."

"Actually I have a solution to that too. Stop fucking drinking."

"When did you become Mr. Empathy?" Flynn said, then paused. "Hmm."

Two folders hovered over his desk.

"What is it?"

Flynn opened the folders and flipped through them. "You said this guy was looking for a cure for Black Rain?"

"That's what the Genico people said."

"Well . . . according to this, he already found it."

Arden looked up sharply. "I'm sorry?"

Flynn pointed to some lines of text. "Right here. Says they have a cure for Black Rain already. They discovered it months ago."

CHAPTER 16

Phillip sat at a decent table at Harry's with Todd Miller, Michael Gorfinkle, Pierce Sullivan, and someone from the bonds department. In a private back room, Lieberman was having a steak with members of the board. At Phillip's table, the topic was the baldness Samp, set to IPO next week. Sullivan claimed that ever since that movie had come out with that sexy bald actor, baldness was marketable again. The IPO was going to be flat and nobody died from male pattern, and that was why Genico had downgraded the IPO.

Gorfinkle spread Coronas around the table. Phillip pushed his lime down into his bottle and stared, transfixed as the green wedge sank slowly through the amber-colored liquid, a mist of bubbles rising up around the edge of the rind. The lime hit the bottom of the bottle and came to a rest on its side, like the hull of some miniature ship hitting the ocean floor.

Someone snapped his fingers.

"You with us, Sax?" Sullivan asked.

"Yeah. Why?"

"The boss is looking for you," he said, nodding toward the back room.

"Who?"

"Who do you think? Lieberman. He's been waving his arm for ten minutes, trying to get your attention."

Phillip turned and saw Lieberman wave again. He waved back, drained his beer in three long gulps, and slammed the empty bottle back down on the table. He stood, slowly buttoning his sport jacket. "Gentlemen."

The rest of the table stared at him jealously as Phillip walked across Harry's and stepped into the legendary back room. This sanctum was where the genetic trading industry was really run, and the walls were hung with 2Dees proving it. Among the seminal moments recorded were the merger of JP Morgan Genetic and Deoxy Group, the day after the heart disease IPO.

"Have a seat," Lieberman said, motioning to an empty spot at the table. Rasputin and another Synthate guarded the door. Phillip sat and Lieberman motioned to a short, heavyset man with thick jowls that made him look like a man-bull terrier mix. "This is Johann Woerner, chairman of our board. I believe you've met before."

Lieberman turned to a much slighter second man. His face was scrunched together, as if a black hole had formed somewhere in its very center and was slowly pulling his features together. "This is Alexander Nicholson, senior advisor to the board, and founder of Synthate Design."

Phillip shook Nicholson's cold hand.

"I've heard of your work," Phillip said. "Modification and training of Synthates. The bioprint system. Industry standard."

Nicholson slowly let go of the handshake. "You may not yet know, but we've been manipulating the Synthate aging process to extend their expiration date."

"You mean when they die," Woerner said before he took a large gulp of whiskey.

"That's another way of putting it."

"Might as well say it like it is. These aren't cartons of milk. We built these things to be human, and humans don't expire. They die."

"They are not natural," Nicholson said quickly. "They're biological mechanisms, nothing more. The International Religious Council already ruled, as did the Supreme Court, that Synthates are not human. They do not have souls. And therefore they do not die like we do. They simply expire."

"As you can see," Lieberman said to Phillip, "there are some disagreements about the future of the industry. But there's one thing that we're all in agreement about. Your father is leaving the company and he has chosen your stepbrother to take control."

"That's very bad news for us, very bad for shareholders," Nicholson said.

"He would certainly change the focus of the company," Woerner added.

"Jack has discussed it with me already," Phillip said. "He wants us to run the company together."

Lieberman shook his head. "That's just what he says now. What sort of guarantees do we have? Genico's future is far too complex to be based on the intentions of one man. Our mutual benefit depends on what happens in the next few days. We're overseeing a business, not a forum for social change."

"You're right, of course. My brother's vision isn't mine. Nor is it yours."

"He will destroy this company," Nicholson said.

"Oh, I don't know, maybe we could use a little more compassion," Woerner replied.

Nicholson shot Woerner a harsh look. "You have as much invested in this as we do. We are an industry that feeds on the greed and laziness of the naturals. Do we really want to go back to taking out our garbage? Cleaning up our streets? Compassion will bankrupt this company."

Lieberman turned toward Phillip. "What my associates are saying is that we're entering into a most delicate time during this change of leadership. I'm hoping you follow me."

Unsure, but determined to keep his options open, Phillip nodded.

"We wouldn't want any mistakes to be made. The least error in judgment has enormous potential for lasting harm. And we believe your brother might make such errors."

"Stepbrother," Phillip corrected.

"Family can be very important," Lieberman tested gently.

"So is business," Phillip said firmly.

CHAPTER 17

Jack's father lived in a triplex in The Paris Hotel at the southeast corner of Central Park, near the edge of the dome. It was one of the few apartments left in the city, the rest long since divided into smaller honeycombs or pods during the population boom. The view swept across the abandoned section of the park and then veered south across the darkened Synthate Zone, reaching as far as the Genico tower at Manhattan's lower edge.

The touch stubs were stored on an eyeScreen table in the living room and Jack pressed his fingers against the glass to retrieve them. He wandered into the kitchen, poured himself water from the exhalation condenser, and stared meditatively at the Central Park dome.

Someone knocked on the door.

A woman was outside.

She was tall and slender, the kind drawn on the cover of dime detective novels from the 1940s; the young woman with pouty lips and wide eyes tucking the nickel-plated revolver into the band of her garter belt beneath a bold graphic reading, "Danger Lurks Behind Every Corner." She was beautiful in a way that reminded Jack of old Hollywood starlets from the black-and-white film days.

He opened the door.

"Hey . . ." she said slowly, her lips spread over white teeth. "You busy?"

"No. No, I'm not."

"Can I come in?" she asked.

"I'm sorry." He experienced a flicker of hesitation, the bombing and the murder of Dr. Reynolds having made him cautious. He paused. "Who are you?"

"A friend of your brother's," she said. Then seeing Jack hesitate, she added, "It's okay."

Jack opened the door wider, allowing her to step past him. She pulled an object from her bag and held it out to him. The object rang and politely she stepped back, lowering her eyes and staring at the floor as Jack took the call. The device was an old cellular phone, no eyeScreen, but of course Jack recognized the voice.

"Hey, little bro," Phillip said. "I'm sorry how I acted on the roof earlier. Just been tired, I guess."

"Apology accepted."

"Wanted to make it up to you. Her name is Night Comfort. She's a friend of mine, now a friend of yours."

"I don't understand."

"Yes, you do," Phillip replied. "Nobody needs to know, mum's the word."

Night Comfort had her eyes still lowered. If she heard what the man was saying, she gave no indication. On her shoulder, her bioprint was of a single leafless tree.

Jack stepped a few feet away from her and cupped his hand over the receiver. "Did you send a prostitute to Dad's house? Are you kidding me?"

"Come on, watch the language. A prostitute is some skank natural hooked on Euphoria walking the strip on Times Square at three a.m. offering twenty-buck head. Night Comfort's a pleasure parlor girl. You don't want her, send her out, your choice . . ."

Jack began to argue, but his brother had already clicked off. He slid the phone shut and held it out to the woman.

"Are you finished, sir?" Night Comfort slipped the cell back into her bag. She looked at him. "So where do you want to go?"

"For what?"

"For me to help you relax."

For me to help you relax. Jack was surprised by how casual she sounded. He wasn't used to Synthate socials, and her seeming submissiveness made him uncomfortable. They were designed entirely to entertain naturals. He could take her now, fulfill his every dark sexual desire, and she would never complain. Never talk back.

"I'm sorry. There's been a mistake," Jack said. "I'm not going to need your services."

Without seeming to hear, Night Comfort slung her bag back over her shoulder and walked slowly toward the guest bedroom. He watched her walk away, her dress tight against the curve of her hips and back. Someone had designed her perfectly. A male fantasy brought to life. She paused at the doorway, then turned back toward him.

"Please, come this way, sir."

When he entered the room, she stared at him as she slowly undid her top. Her breasts were perfect, of course. He thought of Dolce, then thought of all that this girl was programmed to do. The continual degradation. Built only to satisfy.

"Whoa . . . wait . . ." he said, holding out his hand. "Please."

"What's wrong?"

"I can't do this. I, um, I'm with someone."

She frowned slightly, her hands paused around her waist and the strap of her dress still half off her shoulder. The bioprint of the tree slowly morphed to a cloud. "Don't you find me attractive?"

"Of course I do." He was surprised she'd even think that. "I'm just . . . I'm with someone."

"Are you serious?" She asked as if she had never heard those words arranged in that particular combination before.

"I'm sorry. You're welcome to stay, though. Or sleep here, spend the night. However it works," Jack said, feeling ridiculous, but also sorry for this girl. She was a living thank-you card.

"Oh." She smiled for the first time, a faint half smile. Her bioprint became an empty chair drawn Van Gogh-style. "I have to be here for an hour. Is that okay?"

"No problem."

They sat in the living room together watching the news. DNA Design had released a new antiaging Samp. Rain, acidity five percent, was expected later in the day. New York was to fight Green Bay in Operation Desert Storm. Another terrorist group had attacked a genetic sorting facility in the Bronx and freed over twenty Synthates.

Jack could almost sympathize with their cause. Hundreds of years ago, another group of armed activists had rebelled against unfair governmental treatment. And the United States had been born.

But still, he could never support the violent acts committed in the name of Synthate rights.

"Those attacks get them nowhere," Jack said as they watched a video of the burning facility.

"What should we do?" Night Comfort asked sharply. "Nothing?"

"To sin by silence, when we should protest, makes cowards out of men," he quoted, remembering something he'd once heard.

"Who said that?"

"Don't remember." He laughed. "Of course they should speak out. But peaceful protest, that's the only way."

"And why do you say that?"

"Because terrorist acts make Synthates the enemy. When, every day, naturals turn on the news and Synthates have blown up some new target, the result is they demonize themselves."

"The use of violence as an instrument of persuasion is therefore inviting and seems to the discontented to be the only effective protest," she said. A stylized wave curled across her shoulder and slowly became a sword. "William O. Douglas. Benefits of a self-education."

"Naturals will only give Synthates their civil rights when they don't fear violent uprisings. Look at Martin Luther King, look at Gandhi. Peaceful protest. It's the only way."

"Look at the French Revolution. Look at your own American Revolution. For every instance you give of peaceful protest, there are ten more where armed revolution accomplished the same goals. Martin Luther King was a great man for his time, but his tactics won't work for Synthates."

"Why?"

"Because Synthate grievances are too great. We aren't fighting to not sit in the back of the bus. To not have to drink from separate fountains. The violence against naturals during the Civil Rights Movement, even at its worst, was nothing like what we face. Every day hundreds of us are dying. In the Games. In mines. In brothels. We don't have the luxury of peaceful protest," she said. "I don't want to take away from men like Martin Luther King and suffragists like Susan B. Anthony, but their difference from Synthates is enormous. They were naturals. Before anything else, their blackness, femaleness, they were acknowledged as humans. Synthates don't have that right yet."

Jack looked at her in surprise. He had never heard a Synthate talk this openly about their feelings, about their grievances, about anything. Synthates were to be seen and not heard. This conversation would be termination for her if the wrong person heard it. He wondered why she trusted him so much. "Who did you say you worked for again?"

"Yeah . . ." she said more carefully. "Sometimes I get carried away."

"It's okay. It's a difficult subject. And I don't have all the answers. But I just don't think such extremism is going to accomplish what Synthates want."

"Why don't we see what else is on," she said, changing the subject by reaching for the eyeScreen remote. She found a program about sport fishing. Two men in a boat off the Florida Keys were pulling in marlin.

"You seem tense. How about a massage?" Night Comfort said. She reached for his neck.

Jack pulled away from her. "For a minute there, I was actually sitting next to you. The real you. Now you're playacting again. But you're someone else, really. You don't have to be with me."

She looked at him thoughtfully. "It's a dangerous world I live in. You have no idea."

"You're right. I probably don't."

On screen, a beautiful marlin broke the surface of the waves, flashing marine blue in the sun before it crashed back into the water. Her eyes were fixed out the window. A commercial airship passed by, floating low over Central Park, projecting an image of a new type of shampoo; soon an ad for a more effective toothpaste took its place. Wash your hair. Brush your teeth. Rinse. Repeat. Spit. Ignore. Question nothing.

He thought of her words. They made sense to him. The Synthate movement had always made sense to him. From his early childhood, taken into a family that wasn't his, he'd always felt himself to be an outsider. Different, somehow. And that sense of his separateness had fostered a kinship with Synthates. Their anger touched a corresponding place inside him.

"What's it feel like to be a Synthate?" Jack asked.

"It feels like . . . have you ever been to the beach, and picked up one of those shells that make noise when you put it up to your ear?"

"A conch shell."

"Yes. A conch shell. Anyway, it's like that. You can put this conch shell up to your ear and hear this whole world inside, the sound of the ocean on the beach, waves crashing. But, in truth, the shell is empty. There's nothing inside. It's just an illusion."

She watched the commercial craft hover slowly across the Manhattan skyline, its robotic eye driving it forward. Her bioprint was a long stretch of desert.

"Yeah," she said finally. "That's about the feeling. Like you're empty inside."

When the hour was up, she excused herself to change. Through the window, Jack watched the stream of traffic along the FDR, the red tail-lights of solars slowly winding their way through the curving exit ramps. To the west, the Central Park dome shimmered for a moment, like a ripple of water. Strange, Jack thought. But then Night Comfort came out of the bathroom and he turned his attention from the window.

"So we're all right here?" she said, pulling her hair back into a ponytail.

Jack felt the strangeness of the moment. The intensity of emotion they had felt, now put behind them. "Sure."

"Because I have to get going."

"Where?"

"You don't want to know."

"Oh," he said. "Do I . . . owe you anything?"

She laughed. "We didn't do anything."

"For your time, you know."

She smiled, shaking her head. "Thank you for the thought. But you're all taken care of. I was instructed to . . . be aggressive with you."

"Instructed by who?"

"I never know. But I was told to do whatever it took to get you to fuck me," she said. "You're married?"

"Yes."

"Affairs make great leverage," she said before bending down and kissing him on the cheek. "But you've been a good boy tonight."

She turned, pulled her bag up over her shoulder, and walked out of the bedroom.

CHAPTER 18

Back in Brooklyn, jazz played inside Jack's high-rise honeycomb. Swing jazz. Glenn Miller's "In the Mood," to be exact. The music came from behind his bedroom door, where Dolce was getting ready.

Through the outside window, he could see evening was beginning to take over, blackness moving across the sky from the east. The door was half-open, and Jack slid through. Standing in front of the wall mirror, Dolce was focused on a stray eyebrow hair, which she attacked with a pair of tweezers.

"Everything okay?" She barely looked up.

"Sure. Why?" Jack was faithful, but being caught alone with a Synthate social was a difficult position to defend. He should never have allowed it to happen and, looking back, it seemed quite strange that it had.

"Your brother called, looking for you," Dolce said. "I told him to try your sync."

Affairs make great leverage. Jack thought about what Night Comfort had said. She'd been told to seduce him. Jack knew his brother was jealous, but was he ready to believe his brother would try blackmail? To what? Poison Dolce against him? To undermine his authority? To force him from the job he'd been promised? Jack dismissed the thought. His brother wasn't *that* far gone. They were family, after all.

—◊—

Jack sat double-parked in his 1988 Chevrolet Callaway Sledgehammer Corvette and waited for Dolce to come down. The vehicle was the one real luxury he permitted himself. Over the last twenty years, all new cars had become self-powered, run by fins of colonized algae that edged the roof and trunk using sunlight to produce biofuel. The Sledgehammer was a pure gas-guzzling, ass-kicking machine. One of the last remaining. Sometimes the guilt was worth the reward.

Jack hated the Games. He'd never been entirely comfortable with the concept, nor could he reconcile himself to the sight of so much bloodshed. Tonight was different, though. Genico's fortune had been built in part on the backs of Synthates. His father was right. To not have the stomach to attend the Games might signal weakness to the board of directors, and, unfortunately, Jack needed the current board.

Until he could find more humanitarian replacements.

The car door opened and Dolce joined him inside. Her face had its usual look of amusement as she surveyed the beautiful black interior of the Sledgehammer.

"Problem?" Jack asked.

"I always would have figured you for a biofuel or a solar." She smiled. "Who even has gas cars anymore? This thing is an antique."

He grinned at her. "Buckle your seat belt. We'll see what this antique can do."

Bloomberg Island had been specially constructed in the harbor just off the southern tip of Manhattan. Jack punched the accelerator, weaved around traffic, and didn't let up for some time, barely slowing as he crossed the long, cabled bridge. They drove under an enormous lit arch proclaiming: "Bloomberg Island: Home of the New York Braves." Cars were backed up along the bridge, so they parked and walked. Spanning the arch, a massive, neon-lit tomahawk rose and fell in strobic motion. "Go Braves!"

A large line crowded the executive entrance, where a gorilla-like Synthate with a shaved head stood guard. Jack heard someone call his name. He looked up and saw Phillip wave to him from the open doorway.

"Waiting in line? Who won the Cold War? This isn't Communist Russia." Phillip wore a powder blue Lacoste shirt, white slacks, alligator loafers, and a wristband. He pulled them past the front entrance into a large nightclub crowded with people.

"You know alligators are an endangered species now," Jack shouted over the pounding rhythm of the Pointer Sisters.

"Not at Prada they're not. For twelve hundred bucks, you can get as many as you want."

They followed him down a long central hallway, past strobes and granite walls lined with 2Dees from the Games, then up a private elevator and through soundproof doors. The deafening music died off. They were in the familiar Genico VIP area with its deep leather sofas and battalion of white-suited Synthate waiters parked helpfully behind buffet tables heaped with delicacies. The far wall was windowed and looked out over the playing field.

Phillip winked and then disappeared in the direction of the nearest bathroom. Jack walked to the windows and looked out. As always, the stands stretching below were a mass of moving bodies galvanized by fierce anticipation.

The organism, the living creature composed of three hundred thousand people, was separated from the fields by a barrier of impenetrable Plexiglas that rose up as high as the stadium and stretched for three-quarters of a mile, the length of the seating. Through the clear wall, the fields stretched out, an eight-acre expanse of grass and roads cut by rough fences and thick trees. Small stone cottages dotted the landscape, tiny trickles of smoke rising up from their chimneys.

"Tried the foie gras yet?" a voice said from behind.

Jack turned to see Harold Lieberman and his massive Synthate Rasputin.

If Jack lived in ancient Transylvania, he would have put a wreath of garlic and a crucifix around his neck. As far as Jack was concerned, the head of the board was the undead.

"I look forward to the Games," Lieberman confessed. "Though I'm hardly alone in that." He waved his hand at the crowd. "You?"

"Not as much." Jack's tone was guarded.

"Don't have the stomach for it?"

"I think it'd be better if Synthates were never born than put them through this."

"Born?"

"What?"

"You just said better that Synthates were never born."

"Did I? Oops."

"Ah." Lieberman held up a warning finger. "Synthates are an integral part of our economy. Slips of the tongue like that could be bad for business. Pretty soon you'll be wanting them to vote." Lieberman laughed. "Where would Genico be then?"

"Right." Jack was relieved to see his brother returning. Phillip's eyes glittered and his gait was jittery as he grabbed Dolce in a surprise embrace. She broke free an instant later. Lieberman stared hard at the three of them.

"See you later," Lieberman said. "Enjoy the Games." Rasputin, as ever, was silent. They moved off into the room.

Phillip shook his head and then hugged Jack hard.

"Whoa!" Jack laughed, patting his brother on the back.

"I always wanted to be you," Phillip said, then kissed him on the cheek. Pivoting, he too left them as he pounced back into the crowd and headed for the rear doors toward the nightclub.

"That was strange." Jack looked at Dolce.

"He's always had his moods."

Something about his brother's behavior was different, though. He was used to the energy, the cryptic remarks, the sarcastic cynicism, but the outburst of emotion he'd just seen was unlike Phillip. And it was especially troubling after Night Comfort's visit. Now a disturbing, hostile energy seemed to emanate from him.

Jack and Dolce's conversation was interrupted by the shriek of fighter jets in perfect formation over the stadium. The world around them went black. Time stretched out dramatically in the darkness. Suddenly, bright circles of light cut back and forth across the field before they targeted the concrete ramp on the far side.

"And now, ladies and gentleman . . ." cried the announcer. Steam rose from the illuminated ramp and rolled across the edge of the field. "Please welcome your very own New York Braves!"

A metal barrier on the far side of the field lifted. The clatter of hooves could be heard, and the crowd reacted, rising from their seats in an outburst of cheering. Up the ramp pranced a tightly reined stallion carrying a war-painted Native American. Mist rolled away from the giant animal in waving billows.

Up from the stadium's depths came one hundred Synthate soldiers, their long shadows cast across the rising mist. Wearing Union-blue cotton uniforms and black caps, they were led by their head coach, Samuel Sharp, a thick natural in a Braves hat and headset, his crimson red parka tight over his large form.

CHAPTER 19

Arden remembered the third nuclear weapon used on civilians in the history of the planet had been detonated by Pakistan three years earlier just outside Mumbai, India. Four days later, an Indian-made nuclear weapon detonated inside a school bus parked on a crowded street in Islamabad. The combined attacks claimed the immediate lives of approximately seventeen million people and created the largest mass movement of refugees in history.

Within two weeks, the first wave of Indians arrived in New York City. Not wanting to become further involved in the war between India and Pakistan, the United States declared itself unable to give permanent shelter to any refugees displaced by the attacks. Instead, the refugees were placed into camps inside the highly secure Synthate development on Governors Island. Already populated by thousands of registered Synthates, the island soon became an overcrowded slum. Existing side by side were homeless Hindus, Parsis, Sikhs, and Jains, whose encampments covered every inch of ground and whose neighbors could easily be Synthate terrorists. All of them a few hundred yards from Lady Liberty herself.

The place was a fine disaster, Arden thought, as the ferry tugged through the harbor and the profile of the island quickly approached. From across the water, he could see throngs of people packing the walkways and ferry landing. Time had reversed on the island until the place resembled the sepia-toned 2Dees of the immigrant tenement neighborhoods of nineteenth-century New York.

The ferry pulled along the edge of the wharf, and immediately a crowd of natural and Synthate beggars crowded around the gangway. Arden stepped from the boat and pushed his way through the crowd.

And then he saw her, as beautiful as he remembered. Night Comfort stood at the far end of the pier. She waved and smiled. She walked toward him and gave him a hug. Damn, she felt good.

"Charles," she said, her arms wrapped around his back, "so good to see you."

Night Comfort had a micro-pod inside one of the old military barracks that dotted the island. There was a twin bed, a nightstand, plain white walls, and a 2Dee of Arden's daughter. He lifted the frame from the nightstand and studied it. His daughter before she became sick, laughing on a long forgotten summer day.

"I didn't know you kept this," he said.

She smiled.

Arden turned his eyes to the ground, suddenly ashamed of the micro-pod, the bare walls, the crowded squalor that Night Comfort endured every day. After his wife left, he had hired Night Comfort as a nanny. For five years she had lived with him. His daughter loved her. And for Arden, well, when you hire a Synthate, the manual tells you everything except how to feel around them. But she occupied a separate plane of existence.

She was Social-class Synthate. For that reason, her world could never align with the naturals, even after five years of living in the same house, breathing the same air, eating the same food, and loving the same daughter.

"Can we get out of here, go somewhere to talk?" Arden asked. He couldn't endure a moment more in her tiny room. Her eyes traced the contours of his face and seemed to look straight through him. He felt sick that she lived here, ashamed that he'd driven her from his house and reduced her to this.

"Sure," she said. "The walls close in on you pretty quickly. I'm working on a painting on the roof."

Outside, Arden breathed deeply. The roof of her building looked out across the bay, the Statue of Liberty incredibly close and shining in the afternoon sun. Beneath them, Indi-pop music blared from a food stand while a group of kids ran along the sidewalk screaming and laughing as they followed a team of Synthate Guard class jogging in a tight group. The air smelled of spices and the harbor's salty tang.

Near the edge of the roof was an artist's easel, a half-completed canvas propped on it. A familiar image covered the top portion of the canvas. Night Comfort had painted Renoir's *Dance at Bougival,* masterfully recreated, every detail and color perfect. On the canvas, a couple whirled in motion. The bottom portion of the canvas was blank, like the progression of a copier that had been turned off midway through a job.

"I didn't know you painted," he said.

"It's mechanical. Something I got when I was created. It's always this painting. I can't get it from my mind. Probably just a whim of some Genico designer. So what brings you to our lovely island?"

"There was a murder," Arden replied. "A natural."

"I see. And you think it was a Synthate who did it?"

"Maybe. The victim was a scientist at Genico. Working on the Black Rain project."

"So this is a personal case?"

"My daughter is dying. Yeah, it's personal."

"Normally I wouldn't help a natural murder investigation, especially if the victim worked at Genico. I think you know that. But because it's your daughter . . ." She paused and looked out across the bay. "You should talk to Benny Zero."

"The Synthate dealer?"

Night Comfort's eyes narrowed in anger. "He's a pimp. And a slave trader. Nothing more. But he's gotten involved in moving violent Synthates. If it was a Synthate who committed your murder, there's a good chance he'd know about it."

Arden knew Benny Zero, a true scumbag. Most people looked at Synthates and saw a human face, a human body, and gave them a certain amount of respect. But men like Benny were Synthate abusers and traffickers, preying on them with only profit in mind. Benny Zero was the worst of a despicable bunch.

"You've got all sorts of Synthate informers, any one of whom would have been happy to drop Benny's name. Why come here?"

Arden felt a twinge in his chest, the familiar tightness around his heart that he'd carried with him since the day she left. The feeling had later turned to anger, and only recently had he begun, finally, to forget. But now the old feelings had returned.

He said nothing. Instead his eyes searched her face for some sign of hope. There was none.

She looked away. "I respect and cherish you for all the good things you've done for me. And I understand why you did the bad. But I truly wish my feelings for you extended beyond friendship."

"Maybe over time, friendship, respect, this is a basis for . . ."

"For later resentment," she interrupted him. "When feelings of love aren't returned."

Arden held up a hand to silence her. "I know your feelings. I wish I didn't. But I didn't come here to convince you. I just came here to . . . I don't know . . . to see you again."

"You don't want me, Charles. I'm a Synthate, you're a natural. I can't have children. I can't have the family you want."

"I never asked you for those things," Arden said.

"But you did ask me to leave your home," Night Comfort returned sharply.

"That was a mistake. After the attacks, I blamed you for things over which you had no control. I know it wasn't you or your people."

"When you kicked me out, I was just another Synthate. You have no idea the things *your* people made me do." She looked angry. "What I was forced to do to survive until Alphacon found me. Things that would make you think differently about me. And my people, we never resorted to violence. Ever. We never hurt naturals. While they hurt us every day."

"I know that now and I'm sorry."

From his pocket, Arden revealed a handful of DNA ID rings. They had been taken during a raid on a Chinatown storage center last month. The Chinese had become skilled in fabricating knockoff ID rings which, when scanned, provided legitimate natural ID. The rings were sold to Synthates to provide them with fake identification.

"What's that?" she asked.

"Had a few of these lying around," Arden said. "I figured you could use them."

Night Comfort paused, still uncertain. "You'll be arrested for treason if they find out you gave me those."

"I know what you're involved with," Arden said. "I know what it means for you and I understand why you do what you do. Maybe this will keep you from getting caught. Because the crushers *will* come after you."

"Thank you," she responded as she took the fob from him. She studied the painting. "I can recreate almost any masterpiece. Van Gogh. Degas. Even Andy Warhol. But I just can't seem to paint my own original. I don't know why that is. It's troubling. I thought the mastery of art would prove the existence of a soul. But I'm a good forger. Nothing more."

"You're a beautiful artist," Arden said, the conviction of his voice surprising him.

Night Comfort gazed off across the water. "No. But when I look at art, touch art, I feel better about myself. Closer to something good." She turned her attention from the harbor and looked at him. "You said they will come for me. What about you?"

"What about me?"

"Will you come after me, too?"

"I'm no crusher." Arden remembered their time together. "But I will always come after you."

The boat ride back was slow, the diesel engine fighting the current all the way up the East River to the South Street Seaport. Everything Synthate was still powered by the old means, gasoline or diesel. A water taxi carrying naturals cut through the river past them; a biofuel-powered catamaran, its top decks were scattered with men in business suits relaxing on comfortable cushioned chairs, drinking coffee and watching syncs. Arden studied his surroundings. The Synthate ferry was a relic, an antique craft that looked like it had been pulled from a nautical museum after being dredged up from the bottom of the ocean following a shipwreck. The deck was crowded and dirty, the air thick with diesel smoke, and there was no sign of a life preserver anywhere.

No wonder Synthates felt the way they did, Arden thought.

Now it was only a matter of time before the rebellion. The Brooklyn Bridge had been only the beginning. We naturals had been shocked at the attack. The Synthate Domestic who watched our kids while we were at work, fixed our lunch; the Synthate Industrial who paved our road, took out our garbage, all with a smile; was it possible these friendly figures could secretly hate us so much?

We never saw it coming. One day we all just woke up and realized that maybe all our coffeemakers and vacuum cleaners and dishwashers had suddenly turned human, bringing with this new order all the evils we naturals were capable of.

The ferry docked near the seaport and Arden filed out along with the rest of the Synthates. The Synthates moved toward the intake line and waited as crushers checked their work scans before they were allowed onto the island of Manhattan. Arden moved around them and passed through security with his NYPD shield.

Arden's parents had died on the Brooklyn Bridge that day. And that was the day he had also lost Night Comfort. He'd known she was involved with the Synthate rebellion and on the day of the attack he had come home in a rage. He had found her in his house making lunch for his daughter and had gone berserk. He smashed things and punched holes in the walls, but never touched her. Only told her she had to leave. And that if he saw her again, he would personally make sure she was handed over to the crushers.

At that point the rebellion was divided into many different factions, and later he found out Night Comfort had nothing to do with the attack. But by then it was too late. He had sought her out, but she refused to come back with him. And she would continue to refuse from that day forward.

Arden walked along South Street toward Battery Park. There he stood and looked across the water to where he could see the landmarks of the harbor: Governors Island, Bloomberg Island, and, near both, the Statue of Liberty.

Naturals never should have created Synthates, he thought. We never should have enslaved them like we have. But now they're tied to us and we to them, and so, together, our destinies will lead to an inevitable violent future.

Arden was certain of this. And he was just as certain that, in all the coming chaos, he would save his daughter. No matter what that required of him.

That evening as Arden drove past the broken form of the Brooklyn Bridge, he thought back to the day his daughter was born. He remembered having such an incredible feeling of dependence on the doctors and nurses, people he'd never met. He'd felt strange giving himself over to someone else's authority. He'd never felt more powerless in his life.

And years later when she'd gotten sick, when he found himself back in those same sterile rooms, this time the doctors and nurses had no answers. And the powerless feeling had come again. He hated the feeling. Almost as much as he hated what was killing his daughter.

They have a cure for Black Rain already.

Someone had lied to him. And his daughter was dying because of it. He felt helpless no longer. Inside now was only rage.

CHAPTER 20

Near the bar, Jack saw his brother and Lieberman deep in discussion. Phillip was stroking the bare back of a tall brunette in a skin-tight leather minidress as he listened intently. Out in the stadium, the announcer bellowed, "Today's competition, between the Atlanta TNT and New York's own Braves, is being brought to you by Golden Beverages, the Champion of Beers, and Nucleotech Genetic Pharmaceuticals. Ladies and gentleman, it's the Battle in New York!" There was a pause as the stadium lights flashed thousands of watts of brilliance. "Let's get ready to declare war . . . it's showtime!"

There was a rustle of interest around the room. Movement began in the direction of the window. Jack and Dolce took a seat.

"There was a time when our nation was locked in mortal conflict to decide its own fate!" boomed the announcer. "Now again, we are divided in civil war, as North and South, New York and Atlanta, meet on tonight's battlefield. We take you back in history, to September 17th, 1862, the bloodiest single day of battle in the entire Civil War. We bring you now to the killing fields of Antietam!"

Overhead a dazzle of fireworks exploded.

"McClellan versus Lee, Union versus Confederate. Twenty-five thousand men killed in battle. This evening, for your entertainment, we present again . . . Antietam!"

The noise was thunderous as the crowds below stood in their seats, applauding and then stamping on the bleachers. The eyeScreens 3Deed images of an incredibly thick-necked Synthate with a shaved head and gray eyes. He was Sky King, the grand champion of the battles, the most dominant Synthate ever to fight in the Games.

Since the beginning, Synthates had never received natural names, possibly because a Night Comfort, Rasputin, or Sky King was somehow easier to turn into a slave than one named Elaine, Robert, or Steven. Or maybe whoever was in charge simply liked the creative challenge. Whatever the reason, the end result was that all Synthates sounded less like humans and more like racehorses.

Sky King was the best of them all.

A siren sounded. The Games had begun.

Atlanta and New York were spaced about two hundred yards apart, with each one lying flat behind long stone fences and a few overturned horse carts, the scene exactly like the black-and-white Civil War 2Dees Jack remembered from textbooks. There was a booming sound and a flash of light inside a cloud of smoke. On the New York side, cannons placed behind an encasement of dirt and logs launched rounds of shot toward Atlanta. Teams of Synthates operated the guns, and flames burst forward as the giant iron frames heaved backward in unison.

The crowd whooped and hollered.

"This reminds me of your games," Dolce said. "The fans, game day, a whole stadium chanting your name. Sometimes I used to hate that."

Jack looked at her, surprised.

"I never told you that, did I?" Dolce said. "I worried it would take you away from me. But then I'd see you down on that field. And you were so good, so strong, so special, that I knew you were doing what you were meant to do. That nobody was like you. It was what God made you to do, and so I hated myself for wanting to take that from you."

He'd never imagined himself away from her, and no game could possibly pull them apart. But now that he understood what she'd been feeling during those years, he felt regret. On the field, Atlanta was getting the worse of the battle. Fires had broken out along their walls of defense. Trees burned, throwing sparks into the air. Dead lay behind stone walls, arms thrown backward at odd angles, faces singed and black.

Ten new Atlanta Synthates hunkered down behind the broken remains of a stone house. The structure had been struck twice by New York cannon fire, and bits of rock and broken timbers lay scattered across the field along with three dead Synthates.

Phillip rejoined Jack and Dolce, a glass of champagne in one hand, a cracker topped with black caviar in the other.

"Impressive so far, huh?" Phillip said as he popped the entire cracker into his mouth. "Atlanta's so weak this year. I'm embarrassed for them. I'm standing here, embarrassed for them right now." He downed the glass of champagne with a single tilt of his head, wiped his mouth, and patted Jack on the back. "Cheer up. You look like you're at a fucking funeral."

"Yeah, sure."

On the field, the eerie sounds of bagpipers began drifting up from the encircling clouds of mist. Drawn out by the pipes, the Braves emerged from behind their bulwarks. Together they ran forward, heads lowered, rifles raised. The bagpipes continued to sound as the crowd chanted, "Charge, charge, CHARGE!"

Facing their attackers, Atlanta's fighters sensed the oncoming wave of death running through the smoke. Their head coach, seeing them weaken, shouted out across the ragged lines, and Atlanta rifles fired a volley into the oncoming Braves.

"My God, this is terrifying," Dolce said, holding one hand over her half-open mouth.

New York faltered only slightly, and with a scream, they reached the low stone wall defense, hurled themselves over, and smashed into the Atlanta line.

"Atlanta is putting up some solid resistance, but at this point, they just don't have the numbers to hold back the Braves," the television commentator said on eyeScreens. "I'd be very surprised, too, if Coach Sharp committed any more Synthates to this battle. It's just too early in the season to lose so many fighters."

On the side, the Atlanta coach stared out across the field toward his line, three or four assistant coaches surrounding him. Shaking his head in disgust, he slid two fingers across his own throat.

An alarm sounded out across the field. The signal of defeat. Both teams dropped their rifles, and heavily armed crushers entered the field to keep the Synthates in check. The protective barrier separating the stadium seating from the field began to slide down, and heat poured out from still-burning cottages. Silhouetted against the rolling flames, the New York players turned their blood-and-smoke-smeared faces toward the crowd and raised their arms in victory.

The field was a ruined mess of mud and broken stone, flames and singed bodies. Synthates certainly died real enough.

Dolce touched Jack's shoulder. "I'm not in the mood to talk to anyone. Let's just go home." As they always were, the Games had been too much for both of them. He put his arm around her. "Sure, this isn't for us. Let's go."

CHAPTER 21

"Lights on. Dim." Jack closed the door to their honeycomb and poured a glass of orange juice. The eyeScreen flickered on and 3Deed silent images of tonight's battle.

"God, I don't know how people can stand that much violence," Dolce said as she unstrapped her shoes.

"People's appetite for it has always existed. People love the spectacle of violence. It's in our nature."

"So you're saying it's genetic?" Dolce asked.

Jack paused. "Maybe. I want to believe people are essentially good. Not that we're being held back from violent acts solely through fear."

"Fear? Fear of what?"

"Fear of going to prison. Fear of going to hell. I'd prefer not to think that the police department and God are the only things that stop us from killing one another."

"But if humans didn't believe in the presence of a soul, in some eternal life force, however you want to describe it, do you think we'd be more violent?"

"What do you mean?"

"Well, one might look at religion as our way of establishing checks and balances. Let's say, for example, that humans are indifferent to violence. That we're not naturally inclined toward it, but, in a race for scarce commodities, we'd use it as a means of getting what we wanted. If I have something you need, something in short supply, you'd be willing to kill me in order to get it. But the basis of religion is the presence of a soul, an eternal life within all of us.

"So when we place that soul within a religious framework that teaches us most forms of violence are wrong, we're suddenly faced with the idea of consequence resulting from our violent acts. Now, if you kill me, your soul's doomed to punishment in the afterlife. And perhaps this is what keeps humans in check."

"And you think that without the presence of a soul, humans would have no check against their baser tendencies, like violence?"

Dolce raised her palms. "I think humans, like almost all other forms of life, are essentially selfish beings. We're born knowing hunger, and we constantly strive to satisfy our own needs. Do I think without the presence of a soul we'd all end up killing each other? I'm not sure. But I do believe there is balance to the universe. Symmetry. An equilibrium will always be found. For humans to exist, we must live within a society. And a society cannot function with the presence of extreme violence.

"In my opinion our human moral code has less to do with a fear of punishment and more to do with our inherent need to maintain a stable society. A society filled with humans who cooperate with each other, rather than kill each other, will achieve far greater things."

On the eyeScreen, Jack watched as the Atlanta line was vanquished by the hometown New York Synthates. The camera panned the stands to show thousands of screaming faces caught in the frenzy of excitement over the victory.

"What about them?" Jack gestured toward the eyeScreen. "How do Synthates fit into our society?"

Dolce sighed. "I'm not sure. You know I'm not religious in a traditional way, but I do believe in the presence of a benevolent God, and so I don't know how Synthates fit. Something seems very wrong with how we treat them. But I also think everything happens for a reason, and that perhaps we don't yet know the role Synthates are to play. Whatever it is, I think it's certainly more than their slaughtering each other for the general amusement of the crowd. Such sadistic spectacle isn't what a benevolent God, what a benevolent universe, would want."

She sat next to him and Jack leaned back in to her, resting his head in her lap.

"I have to believe there is good in the world," she said as she ran her fingers through his hair. "Synthates were created for a reason. Sometimes we just have to wait to see what God reveals."

A seashell held to the ear produces the sound of the ocean. Night Comfort had told him that this was what it felt like to be a Synthate. You could sense this whole other world, this entire ocean of feeling, but inside was empty. Soulless. Lifeless.

The feeling was an illusion. Jack held Dolce against him. The ocean never existed. Jack had felt this his entire life. That something was different. In the stadium, before three hundred thousand pairs of eyes, two armies of Synthates had rushed to destroy each other.

Where did all the dead go?

Later, he couldn't sleep. He walked to the living room and the eye-Screen flashed old Warner Bros. cartoons, Marvin the Martian looking down at Earth through a giant telescope.

Mute.

He watched the silent images, then his eyes moved to the windows beyond. Outside, across the river, the city was dense with light. A Maglev train flashed by, crowded with people as it wound its way through the lights. There were vidBoards on every building through the conurb playing a silent looped commercial for the memory suppressant Samp Amnease.

Then the images changed, and Jack studied an advertisement for the Deco Casino in the Synthate Zone, featuring a Rudolph Valentino clone crooning before a backdrop of poker tables.

Crusher vehicles were lined up on the street outside Jack's building. Crime had been rising. It was the population density; it had to be. Everyone crowded together, no open spaces anymore. No wonder sometimes people went a little crazy.

"Can't sleep?" Dolce entered the room, her eyes not quite open. She yawned.

"No, I was just—"

Jack paused midsentence as something caught his eye. Through the window, the random flow of lights changed. The vidBoards outside had all gone blank, the arbitrary array of imagery suddenly shutting down and leaving grayness.

"What is it?" Dolce asked.

"I don't know," he said. "Look outside."

Something important must have happened. The vidBoards remained gray for a moment more, then a word flashed on each of their screens.

Wanted for Murder.

Jack's eyes widened. He watched as the lettering spread out, separated, and moved off the screen. Then another image appeared, rotating back and forth, giving a full dimensional view. This time it was a face.

Dolce grabbed his hand.

It was Jack's face.

On each of the vidBoards, Jack's face rotated back and forth. His name appeared alongside his picture, the lettering big and white on the vidBoards.

Wanted for Murder.

Jack's face stayed on the vidBoard, and beside it appeared the digitized image of a matronly looking woman. "This Synthate has murdered and is now hiding amongst you," she stated solemnly. "Under the

Fugitive Synthate Act, no one is to harbor this wanted Synthate. He is hiding under the name Jack Saxton."

What the hell was happening?

Jack removed his driver's license, the hologram image on its front flashing "Suspended, Warrant Outstanding."

He was being shut down.

"What's going on?" Dolce asked, her voice panicky.

There was a jangling noise outside. The sound of heavy footsteps moving down the hall. Jack strained to listen. Voices, hushed whispers, then a clatter of metal. He stared at the door, unable to move, unable to think. He had a moment more of indecision before the door exploded inward with a burst of white light and a shower of broken wood and plaster smoke.

Dolce screamed as a giant, black mass burst through the door. A dozen eyes of light shone and dipped and came toward them. Then the mass separated, the eyes stretched out across the room. The lights blinded Jack, and he shielded his eyes with a hand.

Voices screamed.

"Don't move! Don't move!"

"Hands up! Don't fucking move!"

Dolce was yanked from his arm and something punched Jack's gut. He gasped as the wind was knocked from his lungs.

Shadows stepped out from the darkness, men in black coveralls, bulky Kevlar tops and stubby-looking barkers. The pain in Jack's gut was so intense he could barely breathe. Dolce moved to help him but two men forced her back. Another blow to Jack's gut followed and he collapsed to the ground.

He saw Dolce slammed hard against the wall and a dark anger rose up inside him. He tried to pull himself upright again, but several sets of boots surrounded him and he was forced to the ground. He felt a band of cold metal along his wrists, then heard the sharp clink of handcuffs.

"Wait! This is a mistake!" Jack called out. The only response was the press of a boot against the back of his neck.

Hands grabbed beneath his shoulders and he was jerked to his feet. A light shone in his face. One of the figures, clad in helmet and goggles, stared at him.

"Open your mouth," a voice behind the helmet commanded.

He felt rough hands around his jaw, his mouth forced open. A set of hands appeared, shoving a single Q-tip into his mouth and scraping the bud along the inside of his cheek. Jack gagged, but the hands held his head in place. The Q-tip was removed and pressed into a small plastic DNA analysis tube. The tube processed the material, then flashed Jack's information on a small digital screen.

Two crushers did the same to Dolce, forcing her mouth open and pressing the Q-tip inside.

"Dolce!" Jack yelled and moved toward her. Again he was forced painfully back.

"Shh, shh." A voice called out from somewhere behind the line of men in combat gear. "This won't do at all."

Jack turned as the group of men split apart. From behind them walked a heavyset man in a suit. His face appeared to have been poured from pancake batter. Loose and pale with ripples of fat. Jack knew the face well. William Calhoun, Chief of the Synthate Fugitive Unit. The Synthate community was terrified of Calhoun and his crushers.

Calhoun waved his hand. "Sit him down."

A kick to the back of his leg forced Jack to the floor. One of the crushers checked the DNA reader, then turned to Calhoun. "It's him."

Calhoun studied Jack. "Did you really think you could live this way forever?"

"What?" Jack asked, confused. "What are you talking about?"

"Our code never lies," Calhoun said. "How long did you think you could hide the fact that you're a Synthate?"

Jack was stunned. Slowly he said, "A Synthate? I'm not a Synthate."

"You know what the penalty is for a runaway Synthate? Public shocking. One hundred times."

"Dolce, tell him I'm not a Synthate. This is ridiculous." Jack tried to rise, but the crushers held him in place.

"Ah," Calhoun said, as he turned his attention away from Jack. "And you must be Dolce."

One of the men spoke quietly into Calhoun's ear and showed the chief something on the DNA reader. Calhoun studied the reader. "It seems we have two Synthates here."

Calhoun advanced toward Dolce. She tried to pull her head away from him, but he took a handful of her hair and inspected it.

"Beautiful work," he said thoughtfully as he looked her up and down. "Who made you?"

"Get your hands off me." She lifted her chin away.

Jack felt a wave of anger ripple through his stomach. Dolce wasn't a Synthate. Neither one of them was. Calhoun pulled down Jack's shirt and inspected his bare shoulder. "No bioprint. All Synthates are required to have an exposed bioprint at all times."

"I don't have a bioprint because I'm a natural."

"A natural is born from a human mother and father. A Synthate is an artificially created humanoid, who is by law deprived of his or her liberty for life, and is the property of another."

"The codes don't apply. I am a natural. Why are you doing this?"

"Because runaway Synthates pose a threat to the structure of our country. And there is nothing so dangerous as a Synthate attempting to pass as natural. Mocks the work of God. Synthates are not godly creations."

"Listen, listen to me please, just listen," Jack pleaded. "Call my father. He'll tell you. George Saxton. Or . . . or my brother. Call my brother."

"I'm well acquainted with your brother."

"Then call Phillip. He'll tell you everything."

"I don't have to call him," Calhoun said.

"Why not?" Jack asked.

"Because . . ." a familiar voice said from the doorway, ". . . I'm already here."

A figure stepped forward from behind the wall of crushers. Jack squinted against the light as Phillip came into the room. Jack was overwhelmed by his relief at seeing a friendly face.

"Phillip, thank God," Jack said. "Tell them, tell them I'm not a Synthate. I'm a natural. Help me!"

Phillip cocked his head and said, sadly, "I'm afraid I can't do that, Jack."

"What? Why?"

"Do you remember what happened to my trophy?"

Jack knitted his eyebrows in confusion. "What trophy?"

"The trophy I won in music. For the piano."

Jack's brain worked slowly, bogged down by the confusion of everything happening. He tried to remember what his brother was talking about. He vaguely recalled piano lessons, maybe a recital competition, but no memories beyond that. Nothing about a trophy. And even if there had been one, he couldn't see how it mattered now.

"I don't know . . ." Jack said, cautiously. "What are you talking about?"

"The only fucking trophy I ever won!" Phillip exploded in anger. "He saved your awards. Your medals. But what happened to mine? I brought it home, and I never saw it again. I thought he'd put it on the mantel. Where people could see it. But it found its way to oblivion. Its proper place."

Something cold and tight pressed against Jack's chest.

"I won that fucking trophy. And he never cared. Just like he never cared about anything, all because *you* were so good. Because *you* always had to be the best. Had to win everything. And it wasn't fair. And it's still not fair. Because *you* had an advantage."

"What advantage?"

"A secret." Phillip held up one finger across his lips mockingly. "Shh, mustn't ever tell. Mustn't ever tell. Nobody can ever know. Once I asked Dad why you were so good at everything and I wasn't. Know what he did? He slapped me. He said never mention it again, and then he fucking slapped me across the cheek. So we tiptoe around it."

Phillip began pacing the room with exaggerated silent steps, like a cartoon cat burglar sneaking past a sleeping guard. Jack felt a seed buried deep inside him, a small bit of hibernating life all at once exposed to light and water and now suddenly growing. "Who told them I was a Synthate?"

"But he never asked how I was feeling. What I wanted in life."

"Who told them I was a Synthate?" Jack repeated.

"I did. I called the crushers," Phillip said, his chin jutting out.

The seed exploded with growth inside his chest, massive roots tearing through his heart and lungs. "My God, why?" Jack asked.

"You were always his favorite, and you weren't even natural. You're not supposed to be the one he thinks of as a son."

There it was, Jack thought, a lifetime of jealousy brought to bear in one sentence. "I think this conversation is over." Phillip turned to the waiting crushers. "You can take him."

"No!" Dolce shouted. Two crushers had her pinned against the wall. "Please, no!"

"So you're a Synthate, too?" Phillip walked toward her, bent down, and pressed his forehead against Dolce's. "I should have known. You two really are perfect together."

"Phillip, let her go," Jack pleaded. "Please . . ."

"Let her go?" Phillip considered the statement. "Let her go. Let her go."

"Please, Phillip, please . . ." Jack said. "You know her, we grew up together. Take your revenge on me. Not her."

Phillip turned to Calhoun and said, "He's right. You can let her go."

"I'm afraid I can't do that," Calhoun replied.

"What do you mean?" Phillip said. "She wasn't part of our . . ."

"No bioprint makes her a runaway. Synthate Code says any runaway is subject to one hundred stuns. Anyone who harbors a runaway is subject to imprisonment."

"But—"

Calhoun held up a hand. "That's the code."

Phillip looked visibly upset. He rubbed the top of his head and turned to face the window, confused suddenly. Then he looked back at Dolce. "I'm sorry."

"Fuck you," she said simply.

Jack tried to meet his eye. His brother had the power to do something. To get their father involved. Even the crushers would back down before George Saxton, but Phillip never looked at him. Instead, his brother looked blankly around the honeycomb before he turned and left.

Calhoun watched him go, then turned and addressed his men, nodding at Dolce. "I'm not finished with her just yet."

He ran a finger down the side of her cheek. She pulled her head away, then lunged forward and spit in his face. He wiped his eye and slapped her hard with the back of his hand. Her head snapped back.

"Don't make me break you down," Calhoun said.

Jack surged forward. With his arms pinioned behind his back, he struck against Calhoun hard with his chest, swung up with his head. Jack felt the top of his skull impact bone and Calhoun was knocked backward.

Hands grabbed him and the butt of a barker struck him in the chest. He collapsed onto his side as more blows fell on his head. He tucked his chin toward his chest and tasted blood as boots struck him hard in the face and neck. Finally, the beating stopped and he was hoisted back to his feet.

A trickle of blood streamed from Calhoun's nose. He wiped at it and spit on the floor. "The Synthate who, having struck any natural, to have produced a bruise, or the shedding of blood in the face, shall suffer capital punishment."

Jack charged forward again, but one of the guards swept his feet out from beneath him. Without his hands for balance, he fell forward and struck his chin on the floor. His body went light, then he rolled to his side and kicked hard. His foot impacted something soft, and Jack heard a grunt of pain.

"Brain blind him!" a voice shouted, and the weight of bodies fell on his chest, holding him in place.

One of the crushers held something that resembled a black motor-cycle helmet, forcing the contraption down over Jack's head and tightening it around his neck. Inside the air was hot. A visor slid down the open front of the helmet and shut Jack off completely into darkness. The helmet was padded and soundproof. He felt the grip of the gloved hands, but sound diminished to nothing.

A moment later his restricted perception flooded with soft white light. Then the light dimmed and turned orange, then red. A sunset appeared, falling over an ocean, waves rolling along the beach. Soothing music began to play.

Then a woman's voice: "Please cease your attempts to resist. You are under arrest. Please do not resist."

Somewhere outside, Jack felt his body lifted up off the ground. Cool air circulated through the helmet, relaxing him as the rolling ocean ebbed and flowed.

He felt movement below, a sensation of falling in his stomach. His mind tried to grasp what was happening. The elevator? They were taking him outside. The uncertain grip of hands around him was gone, replaced by a constant banded pressure around his chest and legs. He was strapped to something, a metal frame that slid beneath him, and then he felt himself being carried.

Maybe.

There was forward movement, but Jack couldn't decipher direction or speed. Around him was only the projected sunset over the ocean and the ambient music. Faintly, Jack thought he heard the sound of a truck engine and he tried to pull himself forward, but the bands of pressure tightened against his chest and held him in place. He screamed for help, screamed for Dolce, but only the faint, soothing sound of the ocean responded back.

CHAPTER 22

Light.

Jack blinked in the brightness, his eyes hurting. A crusher stood over him, the restraint helmet in his hands. Jack was seated before a metal table. The table was bolted to the floor, the chair was bolted to the floor, everything shining like surgical steel under the overhead halogen bulb. The room was chilly.

The crusher put the helmet under his arm and walked out of the room, the door slamming shut behind him. Jack was left alone. He shivered, then exhaled, a thin plume of cold steam issuing from his mouth.

As the Synthate population rose, the government, fearing a rebellion, had bestowed the crushers increasing amounts of power. Now they had an authority to search and detain even naturals that far exceeded the powers of any local police department.

Frightened, he closed his eyes and focused. His brother had betrayed him. His brother had lied and told the Synthate Fugitive Unit that Jack was a Synthate. And the crushers believed him. There must be a glitch in their database. Everything would straighten out eventually. For now, though, he had to remain focused in order to get back to Dolce.

A doorknob clicked and a section of the wall opened. Jack caught a quick glimpse of a second room, identical to the one he was in. Inside that room a man sat in an identical chair, behind an identical table, and in the moment before the door closed, Jack could see the stranger's hands and feet were bound. The man's head was down. A long train of sticky blood hung from his nose.

Suddenly the view was blocked by the closing door. Someone stepped into Jack's room.

There was a chair at the opposite end of the table, and the newcomer pushed it forward and took a seat. He wore a short-sleeved blue mechanic's shirt with jeans and boots. His hair was long and greasy and covered by a dirty white cowboy hat with the edges folded upward. He was thin but muscular, with veins like those of a heroin addict running the length of his forearms. He carried an old manila folder, which he placed on the table in front of him. He opened the folder and began to read, flipping pages back and forth. The cowboy looked up at Jack. "I know what you are."

Jack blinked once. "Excuse me?"

But the man was already looking back into the folder. "I'm known as the Overseer. I'm with the Synthate Fugitive Unit. And if you don't know what I am, I'm the only thing between you and a death squad."

"The death squad?" Jack said. "That's a sick joke."

"Do I look like I'm joking?"

"I've done nothing wrong. This is a misunderstanding."

"Misunderstanding?"

"Yes. A misunderstanding. I'm not . . ." Jack paused, thinking. "I'm not whatever it is you think I am."

The Overseer scratched the side of his nose, then flung himself across the table and punched Jack hard in the face. Jack's head snapped back and sparks flickered in his brain. The metal chair dug into his back, and his body slumped forward for a second. He shook his head and looked up, his brain still foggy. Stunned, he stared at the Overseer.

"Still think there's nothing I can do to you?" The Overseer took his hat off and regarded it. "I own you. I'm going to bend you, boy. Get you into shape. Just like I bend this hat. So don't you wind up on my bad side. I'll break you down."

Jack kept quiet. This man was insane. He was outside the constructs of society.

"Don't get me wrong. Personally, I don't have no problems with most Synthates. They work hard. They do their job. They respect authority. But I'm starting to have a problem with you. You don't seem to be following the program."

"I'm not a Synthate."

"I got my start in Texas," the Overseer said. "Catching illegals coming over the Rio. Mexicans. 'Course, after they opened the borders, I had to find another line of work. And I settled on this. The thing is, I'm good at my job. Damn good. And in this room, I'm about the closest thing to a God as you're going to know. You don't eat without me. Don't shit without me. Don't breathe without me. So if I say you're a Synthate, well, I guess that makes you a Synthate."

"But I'm not."

"No?"

The Overseer turned to the folder in front of him and pointed at it with his finger. "This here's the story of Jack Saxton. Cover to cover. I read it earlier tonight. Now, in this story, the white coats, our DNA lab here, detected some genetic anomalies in your blood."

"Anomalies?"

The Overseer held up a finger, then opened up the folder in front of him and read its contents once more. There was a minute of silence before Jack lost patience and asked, "What did they find?"

"Excuse me?" He smiled. "Right, I'm sorry. You know, I think this stuff is fascinating. I should have gone to medical school."

Jack felt the root of fear take hold in his chest but he tried to ignore it. "I asked you a question."

The Overseer smiled again, even wider, as he leaned out over the table. "You want to know what he found? Let me see . . ." He ran his finger over a line of text in the folder. "The subject's blood shows no indication of the Reverse Transcriptase protein, nor of any Retrotransposons, or their derivative LINE-I."

The Overseer looked at Jack meaningfully.

Jack stared back blankly. "I don't know what that means."

The Overseer laughed. "I don't know what the fuck it means, either! Until I asked . . . but wait, there's a little more. The lab goes on to say that, 'Upon further analysis, the subject's genome appears to be devoid of all pseudogenes and retropseudogenes.' So there, that's what his report says."

"I still don't know what any of that means."

"It means that your blood is missing a lot of shit that everyone else, us naturals, all have. None of it serves any purpose in the human body. If you were born without any of this genetic material, you wouldn't even know that it was gone. You could go through your life happy and healthy."

"And?"

The Overseer shook his head. "Fact is, even though we don't need it, it's all still there, in everyone. Gift from our mommy and daddy. Every natural has some of it, actually a lot of it, except you. There's only one group on the planet that doesn't have this junk DNA. You know what that group is?"

Jack already knew the answer, but he needed time to digest what was happening. "Who?"

"Synthates," the Overseer said. "Genetically engineered humanoids. When scientists created Synthates, they did it perfectly, down to the last detail. But then they went and eliminated all the junk DNA."

"So . . . what does that mean?"

"Well, that means that someone did a number on your genome, buddy. They built you up from scratch, then cut your DNA down till it was like a streamlined race car." The Overseer cut his hand through the air, making a whistling sound. Then he stopped, looked at Jack, and said, "You're a Synthate."

Leaning back in his chair, he folded his arms across his chest and stared.

"I'm not a Synthate," Jack said finally. "I've got parents, I remember them. I was a kid, played Little League, rode a bike. I don't have a bioprint."

"Hey . . ." The Overseer raised his hands up in resignation. "I don't do the tests. Not sure who genomed out your bioprint. You must have some friends."

"I'm *not* a Synthate."

"Stop jerking me around. You know damned well what you are. You don't get a lawyer, you don't get a trial. Synthates are property of the state from beginning to end."

"Listen, if I can just make a sync call. Let me call my father."

The Overseer reached into his front pocket, pulled a small photodisk from his pocket, and placed it on the table in front of Jack. The disk flashed blue then projected a 3Dee above the table of a room. A bed. Two dead bodies. Blood on the floor. The sheets.

"Is this a mistake?" the Overseer asked, indicating the pictures.

Jack cringed, disgusted. "What is this?"

"Two bodies. Pretty vicious even for a Synthate," the Overseer said. "Martin Reynolds and his wife. Believe he worked with you."

"He worked in the labs," Jack said. "What does that have to do with me?"

"Why'd you do it?"

"Do what?"

"C'mon, you know who killed Reynolds and his wife."

Jack shook his head, not following what the Overseer had said. "I don't understand . . . who?"

"You! You, you fucking savage. You fucking killed them, then snuck on home to your little life thinking nobody would know any different."

"Me?" Jack shrank back, horrified.

"Synthate cells under the female vic's nails. You worked with the male vic. And you're a Synthate. Sounds pretty good to me."

"You're crazy." Jack's voice sounded shrill, his throat tight. "There are thousands of Synthates out there. And the coding is proprietary. No reader can identify any particular one. Not that it matters, because I'm not a Synthate. I didn't kill them."

"Listen up. As a runaway, the SFU owns you now. We'll be selling you off to the Games, I expect. Maybe a death squad, but I doubt it. They'll find a use for you. You're too expensive."

This can't be happening, Jack thought. He had to get out of there. He had to get back to Dolce. She was what was most important now. Whatever had to be done, he swore he'd get back to her. It was all that mattered.

The Overseer stood and adjusted his hat. "You lived years in our world. It's time to go back to your own."

A door opened at the back of the room and two uniform crushers charged in with stun sticks. The blows came hard and fast. Electric pain tore through Jack's body and the world went black.

CHAPTER 23

Hidden below Wall Street, deep in an abandoned subway line, Night Comfort studied the Metropolitan Museum of Art schematic that 3Deed from her eyeScreen. Around her, the forgotten subway tunnel was filled with paintings and artwork. Rembrandt's *Storm on the Sea of Galilee* and Vermeer's *The Concert* hung from the faded brick wall, while a sculpture by Degas stood near the old token booths. An office had been constructed inside the former workers' lounge, and here Night Comfort had the plans spread out on what was once a break table.

She had come to believe the study of art was the study of the soul. They had all come to believe this. And the question of a soul was what differentiated them from naturals. If each Synthate also had a soul, it would make them the equals of naturals.

The problem was Synthates weren't permitted by law to own art. So that left them only one option. To steal it.

Gathered around Night Comfort, a half dozen Synthates studied the blueprint with her. Suddenly the door was flung open.

"We found him," War Admiral announced as he entered.

"Found . . . who?" Night Comfort asked.

"The one we've been hoping for."

She straightened. "Where?"

"He's here, in New York. Our monitors picked it up. Someone ran a scan of his DNA."

"A *he*?" Night Comfort asked with a hint of disappointment. Still, very little about this moment could be disappointing. They had been searching for years.

"He is. His name is Jack Saxton. He works for Genico."

Night Comfort looked at the rest of her council and smiled.

"But there's bad news," War Admiral said.

"What?"

"The crushers have him. They were the ones that ran his scan. That's when it popped on our screens. I checked their grid. Looks like they were tipped off about his location earlier today and picked him up at his residence."

"Oh no." She shut her eyes in frustration. "Do they know who he is?"

"I don't think so. Not yet, anyway."

The eyeScreen brought up a map of Manhattan. There wasn't much time. They had to act now.

"Where did they do the scan?" she asked.

"There were two. The first was in Brooklyn," War Admiral answered. "The second was in SFU headquarters."

"We have to try and get him before they transport to the Island."

"I don't think we're ready for that scale of engagement now," someone said. "He'll be in an armored carrier. We need more time to plan."

"I'll go," War Admiral said, stepping forward.

"Are you sure?" Night Comfort asked.

"I'm ready."

"Good, then let's get him back. We've looked for him for too long to give up now."

CHAPTER 24

Jack opened his eyes. There had been a sound. He lay for a moment more on the cold metal bed as he stared at the ceiling. His head still throbbed from the blow he'd taken . . . when? Yesterday? The day before? An hour ago? He rolled over on his side to survey the rest of his cell. No. He wasn't inside a cell, but in the back of a van. With him were three others, each in orange jumpsuits and white sneakers, seated on a metal bench.

Jack rolled himself up and onto his feet. He looked down, surprised to see that, just like the three others, he too was clad in orange. Beneath him, he could feel the bump and roll of the road. They were being transported somewhere. What had the Overseer said? He would be sold into the Games?

His trio of companions stared blankly at the wall. Bioprints marked them as Synthates, Guard class most likely. They had tough faces lined with old scars. None of them acknowledged his presence until Jack stood to stretch his legs, and then one looked over at him, shook his head, and hissed a quick, "No." Jack sat back down and the fellow resumed his vacant expression.

Once he was able to get to a sync, Jack would reach out to a team of Genico lawyers. They could order more tests. He had nothing to hide. The tests would prove he was natural.

Then it occurred to him. If he could be wrongly accused and imprisoned, how many others had been falsely accused as Synthates? Hundreds, maybe thousands. And some of these, he was sure, had to have died in the Games. Distracted by this line of thought, Jack barely noticed that their transport vehicle had stopped.

Simultaneously the three Synthates looked at each other. Some wordless message passed between them. Each bent over at the waist and tucked his head between his knees. The position was vaguely familiar to Jack. Outside their vehicle sounded the heavy diesel rumble of an approaching truck.

The noise grew louder, now bearing down on them. His fellow prisoners kept their heads tucked between their knees, and just as Jack thought, *crash position*, the rumble was on top of them. Something slammed against the van and then the world flipped.

Jack's body hit the roof of the vehicle hard and he felt the wind fly out of him, leaving him gasping. Then he was thrown against one wall. His arms still cuffed behind him, he couldn't protect himself, and his head struck the edge of the metal bench. Light and pain flashed in his brain and he struggled to stay focused.

Then everything stopped. He lay stunned and motionless, curled on what had been the side of the van. The three other men were sprawled around him. Two of them moaned, struggling to sit upright. The third wasn't moving at all. Somewhere outside the vehicle wall came the sound of running feet, then a saw whirred to life, followed by the screech of metal being cut. Sparks shot into the vehicle through the walls, and a spinning blade appeared. The doors were wrenched open and a black stretch of pavement became visible.

A face covered by a black ski mask appeared. Hands reached out and pulled Jack from the destroyed vehicle. He flopped down onto the pavement and rolled over onto his back. Through the pain in his head, he vaguely registered that it was night and he was on the edge of the FDR. He saw streetlights along the highway and the illuminated Williamsburg Bridge in the distance. He had just been pulled from an armored Synthate transport van, now overturned on its side, a tractor trailer rig almost embedded into its frame. Near the tractor trailer was a solar BMW.

Four figures, all in ski masks, worked to pull the prisoners out of the wreckage. One of the figures leaned over Jack and clipped his handcuffs loose.

The masked figure put a gloved hand on Jack's shoulder, and then a woman's voice said, "You're free, brother."

From behind came a gunshot and everyone ducked for cover. More shots rang out and the front windshield of the BMW exploded into fragments.

The two other rescued Synthates wasted no time, jumping the FDR guardrail and dashing off, each in different directions. The third figure still lay motionless. Forced backward by the gunfire, the figures in ski masks clambered back into the BMW. With a screech of tires, the BMW sped toward Jack and the rear door flew open. "Get in!"

Bullets continued to rain down on them. Someone inside the vehicle screamed in pain. An SFU helisquall skimmed low over the river toward him. As Jack watched, the BMW accelerated again out onto the FDR, the rear door still open, swinging wildly on its hinge before it slammed shut on its own.

And then Jack was alone.

Other vehicles had been stopped by the collision as well. Jack stood unsteadily and walked toward one of them, a silver solar with a young woman behind the wheel. He waved his hand to her, and she looked terrified for a moment before she pulled away and sped off. Jack looked down at his orange jumpsuit. Of course she was afraid. He looked like an escaped convict. Well, he was. Sort of. But it was a misunderstanding. The police would be here soon. He'd wait, and everything would be sorted out.

Something rustled behind him. One of the guards had pulled himself partly out of the overturned transport. Jack turned toward him and instinctively put his hands up.

"Don't move!" the guard said, breathing heavily. He was bleeding from his forehead and cheek, the front of his shirt soaked with red. He was still half inside of the vehicle's cab and appeared to be stuck. Jack took a step forward to help him.

The guard held out his barker, aiming it unsteadily.

"Whoa! Wait a minute," Jack said. Then the man fired. The sound of the shot seemed incredibly loud and Jack ducked. "Don't shoot! I'm giving up!"

The guard aimed again, but he was weak from the accident and Jack saw his weapon waver. Behind him, traffic accelerated away from the gunfire. Further up the highway, the red flashes of SFU cars quickly approached.

Glancing back at the guard, he realized the barker was now braced on the edge of the metal door, the hand holding it no longer unsteady. The weapon was aimed directly at Jack. Without thought, he turned and ran.

—m—

Night Comfort tore off her mask as the BMW sped southbound. Behind them, the chaos still visible along the edge of the highway receded into the distance. Barks sounded in quick succession.

A bullet had shattered the back window of the BMW and she had to shout to be heard above the rush of air that filled the car's interior. "We have to go back!"

War Admiral was bent over the wheel, his knuckles white as he skillfully navigated around traffic. "We can't. It's too late."

In the rear seat, Kentucky Morning groaned in pain. The front of his jacket was soaked a dark crimson, slick and shiny. Behind them came a final gunshot. Then the BMW crested a rise in the highway and the scene vanished.

"Are you okay?" Night Comfort asked.

Kentucky Morning pressed his hand against his shoulder. "Just get back. I'll be fine . . ."

The fourth Synthate, Outback, also had her mask off. Her face was streaked with sweat and she fumbled through a medical kit that she'd pulled from beneath the seat. Night Comfort reached through toward the back and pulled apart Kentucky Morning's jacket, revealing pale, torn flesh beneath, a round hole the size of a half dollar visible just below his collarbone.

She'd seen enough barker wounds to know Kentucky Morning would be dead before they reached safety. She reached out and took his hand.

The lights of SFU patrol cars flashed past them as they sped toward the accident, while across the water, a helisquall gunship was visible as it skimmed low over the river, its single searchlight cutting back and forth like a metronome. They had left Jack Saxton behind, after all the years they had spent searching. Now he was on his own. With no training and no direction, he'd be captured or killed within the hour.

And everything would be lost.

She felt a familiar anger and frustration build inside her, but another groan of pain from Kentucky Morning kept her focused. War Admiral exited near the old Brooklyn Bridge, the fragmented supports visible like jagged tree trunks against the night sky. He navigated the car beneath the bridge, toward South Street, then pulled it to a stop inside the abandoned warehouse of what had once been the fish market.

War Admiral exited, raised the door to the building, and then flicked on the electric bulbs overhead. Years after being abandoned, the huge space still showed signs of its former use. Empty wooden crates decayed in the far corner near a broken-down forklift while large fish hooks and fading signs hung from the walls.

"We need to get him out of the car!" War Admiral said. He opened the rear and grasped Kentucky Morning by the shoulders, slowly easing him off the seat and down to the concrete, his body completely limp.

"Too late," Night Comfort said, softly. She reached for War Admiral's arm. "He's gone."

War Admiral sagged to one knee and hung his head. Night Comfort stood and walked to the window, looking out across the East River toward Brooklyn. In the distance she could see SFU helisqualls as they circled over the accident scene. Somewhere to the north was Jack Saxton. And if he had any chance at all, he would be running.

CHAPTER 25

Back in his Miami days, Jack had always been known for his speed, and now he ran as fast as he ever had. He hopped the guardrail in a single fluid bound, then sprinted toward a row of tall brick honeycombs. He flattened himself in the shadows and, catching his bearings, realized he was just off 14th Street in lower Manhattan. NYPD and SFU patrol cars flew by down the FDR and screeched to a halt next to the overturned transport.

Near the building, in the dark shadow of a loading dock, was a dirty green dumpster. Jack used a touch bucks credit to open the lid and dropped down inside. Standing knee deep in garbage, he ripped open bags, looking for anything that he might wear. He found a checkered shirt streaked with grease that covered up most of the prison uniform. He could almost pass for some sort of starving East Village artist, temporarily at least. Thank God he had no bioprint.

He clambered out of the dumpster. The aging conurb buildings around him were all part of a complex that stretched five blocks north, with small parks and walkways running between them. As he reached the edge of the first path, he slowed. It was late, and very few people were out walking. He had to find Dolce. He believed that only an hour or so had passed since he'd left her at home. He hoped she was still there.

Ahead he saw the glow of an ATM and ran toward it. They hadn't shut down his touch bucks yet, but he wouldn't have much time before they did. Jack pressed his four fingers against the bioscan pad. The machine responded immediately and allowed him to get mao from his checking account. He withdrew the maximum, then, with bills in hand, he stepped out onto First Avenue and raised his hand to flag down a passing taxi.

Jack figured he had only ten to twenty minutes before his picture was broadcast again across every vidBoard in the city. A cab screeched to a stop as he flashed the fistful of mao and gratefully jumped in the back.

Jack gave his home address, then sat back and fingered Dolce's silver cross. The driver barely looked at him in the rearview as they sped down 14th Street. He would get Dolce, then they'd leave the city. Find a hiding place outside the conurb. Then Jack could contact his lawyer, arrange for another genetic test. He would prove he wasn't a Synthate. That he hadn't murdered Reynolds and his wife. That he was natural. Then he would arrange for his surrender. This running around was too dangerous.

The transport vehicle carrying him must have been attacked by the same rebels Jack had seen on the news. They'd been freeing Synthates all across the city since the beginning of the Games. As the taxi weaved in and out of traffic, Jack saw no flashing red lights behind him. He appeared to be safe.

When they pulled in front of his building, Jack threw the bills at the cabbie and jumped out. He rushed past the doorman and into the elevator. He had formed no plan, and when he stepped onto his hall, he acted only on instinct.

Two crushers stood outside his honeycomb. Jack sprinted forward quickly, closing the distance between them. One of them turned, surprise registering on his face before Jack buried his fist into it.

Just as the second crusher turned, Jack struck him hard with his elbow, knocking him back. His head struck the doorframe and the man collapsed. Stepping over the two officers, he entered the apartment. The living room was empty. Slowly he pushed the bedroom door open and was greeted by disarray. The mattress was turned over on the floor, a framed window broken, the condenser smashed and leaking water. Bloody sheets were balled in the corner of the room, and lying facedown on the hardwood floor was Dolce. Her feet were bare, her arms thrown out to either side, blood pooling around her body.

Jack felt his mind empty. He collapsed to his knees and reached out to touch the back of her head. His fingers came away bloody.

"My baby, my baby," he whispered. "Oh God, please . . ."

Footsteps sounded behind him. Jack turned and saw two crushers in the doorway, their weapons trained forward.

"Don't move!" one of them shouted. Jack's entire body was numb. Nothing mattered anymore. Slowly he raised his hands over his head.

"Step toward me!" one of the crushers commanded.

As he followed the instructions, his hands were brought behind him and metal cuffs tightened around his wrists. Jack sank back to his knees. There was nothing left. Everything slowed. Even his blood seemed to turn to ash inside his veins.

"What do you want to do with him?"

"The Braves always need bodies."

Jack was lifted up under his arms. His strength gone, he felt himself dragged out of the room. There was a sharp prick as a syringe pierced his shoulder. Instantly the blackness surged up around him and he fell into nothingness.

She's gone.

Jack opened his eyes but could see nothing. He lay on a hard bench, the feel of cool metal against his skin. Once again, the walls and floor rattled, the sound of a road passing underneath and an engine somewhere forward. The darkness was complete.

Dolce was gone. Only the rough sensation of the world around him was left.

He ran his cuffed hand along the wall, smooth and metallic. Wherever they were headed, this time, he doubted there'd be another escape. The past few hours replayed in his mind like a nightmare.

He pounded on the wall with his hand, trying to get someone's attention.

"I wouldn't do that," said a voice from the back. "If I were you."

Jack, startled, looked around, but could see nothing in the darkness.

"Just relax, we'll be there soon enough," said the voice.

"Who are you?" Jack asked.

"I am nobody," came the reply. "Just like you now."

CHAPTER 26

Phillip sat behind his Genico desk staring out across Battery Park. Hearing a knock, he turned as Amy entered. He was in a bad mood. She set his coffee on the edge of the desk. Her eyes were red and rimmed with tears.

"Thanks," he said, pointedly ignoring her obvious distress. The entire office had heard what had happened to Jack. And even worse, about Dolce's death. He'd never seen so many weepy faces. Dolce had been a mistake. The SFU had behaved excessively. But Phillip couldn't let himself feel bad about either of them. Mama would dull the pain and the guilt. She always did.

He turned back toward the window, but Amy remained paused in the doorway. He gave up on waiting her out. "You're like a tree, rooted to the ground. What's the problem?"

"Your father."

Phillip's chest constricted. "What about him?"

"He wants to see you."

"All right."

She lingered awkwardly. "I'm sorry about your brother."

"Listen, we got together a few times and I bounced up and down on you, and la-di-fucking-da. But let's keep this relationship a little fucking professional, okay?"

Amy turned and practically ran out of the room.

"Thank you for your condolences!" Phillip shouted after her.

Standing, he began to pace, muttering to himself. Finally, with a sigh, he gave a last glance out the window. "Daddy wants to see me."

The elevator opened onto his dad's floor.

"Yoo-hoo! Mr. Saxton!" Phillip called out as he popped a Vicodin and two red Euphorias. "Dad?"

The reception area was empty. The weapons hung silently behind their glass cases. Phillip entered the rear office. His father's chair was turned away behind the massive desk, New York City outlined beyond. A virtual fire raged in the fireplace while the giant grandfather clock tick-tocked resolutely.

Phillip entered the room quietly. His father remained still, even as he approached.

"Hey, Pop," he said pleasantly. No movement. Phillip reached out and tapped the back of the chair. Nothing. Then he twisted the chair around and his father revolved to face him.

The elder Saxton's skin was ash white, his mouth hanging open and eyes staring vacantly at the ceiling. Startled, the younger man took a step backward. He looked around the room to make sure he was alone, and then stared at his father.

Was he dead?

Through the window, lights flashed across the city. But on this side of the glass, there was an incredible stillness. Phillip pressed his fingers against the old man's neck. The skin was cold with the barest hint of a pulse. A flick of pain flashed through his chest, as infinitely precise as a paper cut. Even through the dullness of Mama, he felt its sharpness.

The old man was still alive.

He sat on the edge of the desk opposite his father. A sweet odor filled the room. Phillip had never experienced it before, but somehow he knew it was the scent of someone close to death. He held back a wave of anxious tears. And suddenly he was eight years old again, holding his dad's hand. There was a closeness he hadn't felt in years. He loved the old man. If only his father had felt the same.

He held two fingers over the old man's mouth. He felt the faintest whisper of breath. There was life in there still. And suddenly Phillip wanted desperately for the old man to live. If only to witness everything that would happen next.

Phillip turned on his sync. "Regal Blue. I need you."

CHAPTER 27

The light thrust itself into Jack's brain. He rolled over onto his back and the sun burned through his closed eyelids. His head pounded rhythmically with his pulse, his stomach stirred, and he retched violently.

"Jack," said a voice hidden in the light. "Time to wake up."

Slowly he opened his eyes. He lay on dusty ground. Standing above was a dark figure silhouetted by brightness. "Sleep well?"

Jack sat up, wiped his lower lip, and then rubbed his forehead again. He shielded his eyes with one hand and recognized a familiar face. Regal Blue, his father's personal bodyguard, stared down at him with his one good eye. Jack jumped to his feet. If Regal Blue was here, that meant his father was close by.

The sudden movement jarred Jack, and he pressed dusty fingertips against his temples as another wave of nausea hit him. "Where am I?"

"Training camp."

"Where's my father?"

The blow from the rifle stock struck Jack hard in the gut. "No talking," a guard snapped, interrupting them.

Regal Blue took an angry step forward, then stopped. His face melted back to complete calm and he stared into the distance. Jack gathered his breath and straightened himself up. He didn't meet the guard's eye. Instead, he turned to observe his surroundings. He stood with a small handful of Synthates at the edge of a promontory ending among cliffs. Below them was the wide expanse of the ocean. Waves broke apart against rocks, tossing foamy bursts into the air like sparks. Pale objects floated in the water, battered back and forth between the rocks. Jack focused his eyes on them.

Dead Synthates.

"Pay attention!" The guard pointed to the arid expanse that stretched out before them. Another transport van now pulled up, and, once its doors were opened, more Synthates were unloaded. Soon they stood together in a group, eleven in total, prodded forward into a ragged line. Like Regal Blue, each was a giant, thick with muscle and built for fighting. Many of them had long, ugly scars on their bodies. Diagonal slash marks across their arms or chest, star-shaped bullet wounds in their legs and abdomen. Their bioprints flared violence. The stifling afternoon sun was baking the ground to clay.

When Jack turned his attention from his fellow captives, it was to the wild confusion on the plateau. Beyond the newcomers, a mass of men stretched out in all directions, producing layers of movement and sound. Jack stared hard at the multitudes of arms and legs, listened to the grunts and screams of voices, trying to make sense of it all.

Yet a governing order was clearly in place. To his right, groups fought each other in timed rhythms with dulled ax blades, while ahead of him men fired rifles at round targets spaced fifty yards distant. Others pounded at each other with their fists while small bands of wrestlers grappled inside a sandy circle.

Coaches observed the figures, blew whistles and banged clipboards. As the afternoon heat grew steadily more oppressive, Jack saw several combatants collapse on the field. These Synthates were eventually dragged out of the way, but in the meantime they were simply ignored.

Jack looked out to the bleachers lining the far side of the field. In the stands, kids, moms, and dads were all absorbed watching the practice. Off in a corner he saw a golden retriever sniffing at a downed Synthate; beyond lay a parking lot filled with family transporters.

A golf cart glided across the field toward the newly arrived Synthates. The vehicle was driven by a leathery fellow in a Braves golf shirt, while next to him sat a beefy guy wearing a team tracksuit and baseball cap. The cart pulled up in front of the ragged line and the passenger stepped out. He had thick hands and features that looked slapped together from globs of clay. He inspected Jack along with the rest of the line. He didn't look pleased.

"I'm Samuel Sharp," he announced. "The head coach of the New York Braves and the closest thing to God that you sorry sacks of genetic slop will ever know."

Sharp clasped his hands behind his back and began speaking. "You are here to train and to fight and to battle in the Games. That is your one and only goal and, as easy as it sounds, many of you miserable Synths will fail to complete your mission.

"You are all genetic slop and have no rights as naturals. My mission is to get you ready for battle. For the Guard class, you've been made for this. For the rest of you runaways, you better pay attention or they'll be recycling you back to amniotic by the end of the month."

Sharp took off his hat, waved it back toward the fields. "You test babies may not know it yet, but this is the greatest moment of your miserable lives. We're gonna give you a gun. We're gonna let you use it. Gentleman, welcome to Braves training camp!"

They slept inside a long, concrete-block structure with bars over the windows and guards on the outside. The rooms were small, but the cots were comfortable. Jack was unpacking the small duffel of training gear each Synthate had been given when Regal Blue found him.

"Your father is dead," Regal Blue said.

Jack slowly lowered himself to sit on the edge of the bed. He stared at the cracked concrete floor. A full minute passed. The information seeped slowly into him, like water into dried wood.

Jack pressed the tips of his fingers to his eyebrows, then shook his head. He could not allow himself to mourn. Here, sadness was weakness, and weakness would destroy him. Instead he thought of the deposit box his father had left him. Jack had to find that box now.

"Thank you for telling me."

Regal Blue sat on the bed opposite Jack. "The day your father passed away, the crushers came for me. They knew I'd served in the Games before, but they sent me back, anyway. Just as well. The freedom I had is gone. I'm as good as dead."

"What happens now?" Jack asked.

"Now . . ." Regal Blue said slowly as he went out the door. "Now we get ready to fight." At that moment the dormitory's lights cut off and Jack was left alone in the darkness.

CHAPTER 28

In the camp, Regal Blue stayed near Jack's side, helping him along. He had never been a soldier, but the rhythms and mentality of the camp were already familiar to Jack from his football days. Their group was made up of twenty Synthates from different biotech companies.

All the naturals, even those who weren't fans, knew about the Games, which had become as much a part of American culture as the NFL. Even in his old life, Jack had always been aware of every season, but now he found himself in the midst of it.

The Games featured historical wars between two Synthate teams. Every week the theme of the battle changed, and could feature anything from the M-16 and the AK-47 of the Vietnam War era to the musket of Napoleon's time or the sword and shield of the Roman legion. Each week a new battle was announced, and the camps worked to train recruited Synthates on how to use the new weapons.

The Games season lasted for twenty weeks. During that time, each team was allocated a certain amount of Synthates to be used for the entire season. The new Synthates came in batches each week, some of them straight from the grow gardens, or others were recycled domestics who were thrown into combat to die as cannon fodder for the spectacle.

During the season, coaches tried to limit their losses each game so as to have enough Synthates left over by the end of the season. The winning team for the season was decided in a final enormous Super Bowl of battles that took place once per year with all the Synthates who had survived the season as well as whichever new Synthates a team might be resourced.

And training camp was how each new batch of recruits prepared for war.

Each week, Synthate teams representing major American cities battled each other with designated weapons. The weapons and theme of every battle were announced on Monday, with most battles taking place Sunday afternoons.

Training camp employed sports coaches as well as former soldiers and combat experts, most of them naturals, to train Synthates for the upcoming battles. Because the Games drew from all means of warfare spanning back thousands of years, combatants had a difficult time being truly prepared. Certain arms required a more advanced skill set while other battles focused more heavily on the brute strength and speed of edged weapons and shields.

Jack arrived in training camp on a Wednesday, and the upcoming week's battle had already been decided—a fight from the American Revolution, a conflict that in past Games had started off with line formations, then quickly devolved into brutal hand-to-hand combat between the two teams.

There were armed crushers everywhere in training camp. Most Synthates wouldn't be expected to last more than a few weeks in a season, so the crushers were always ready for escape attempts. But nobody escaped. Every Synthate in camp was fitted with a tracker. The tracker never came off, even in the battles, so the crushers always knew the location of every Synthate. Escape from camp or failure to show up for a battle meant guaranteed death.

For the Synthates who survived a season, there was a certain amount of freedom of movement within the Synthate Zones. The intensive opening training camp was for new Synthates. For the battle veterans the camp was optional. One of the only times Synthates were allowed to choose the course of their own lives. The naturals found that Synthates fought harder when they had something to fight for. And the freedom they received from winning was one of the biggest incentives. They only had to be briefed on the use of the new weapons for each battle. As long as they showed up for each new skirmish, they were relatively free. And the warriors who fought in the Games and lived were celebrities.

But Jack still had to survive. And surviving a Games was like storming the beaches of Normandy. Only the tough and lucky made it.

The first morning, the recruits viewed films in the darkened conference center from last year's Braves' season, learning line formations and weaponry. The films were brutal to watch. Countless Synthates being torn apart in battle after battle, left for dead on the stadium floor. None of the new Synthates had ever been inside Entertainment Stadium and couldn't even imagine the scale of what a battle was like. Jack had witnessed these miniwars from behind glass and had to manage the fear of what he knew was coming.

They didn't have much time to train before the Games, so every minute was filled, from learning new weapons to hand-to-hand combat. Synthates worked with weights and developed speed; the old strength and stamina of Jack's college days quickly returned to him. The regularity of drills, the blows of the whistle, all familiar from his time in football.

But every night in his bunk he thought of Dolce.

To break down now over her would mean death. Even the tiniest fracture would erode over time until everything crumbled. He lived now in a world of complete indifference, an indifference that he could not have even imagined in his previous time. An indifference toward life and death. He had grown up with love and support, and now to be surrounded by people who gave no care for his life and would find only good entertainment in his death was a shocking departure from his time as a natural. But this was the strange new world he inhabited. And while everything that had happened had all the hallmarks of a nightmare, the details were very real. He would have to persevere. He would have to find his own way. No matter what happened. He must go on.

Jack remembered Night Comfort, the pleasure parlor girl his brother had sent to his apartment. Maybe she'd been right. Maybe Synthates didn't have the luxury of peaceful protest. Before, Jack could never have supported a violent uprising. Now, though, his feelings began to change. Synthates comprised ten percent of the country's population. They were smart, strong, and angry. They could force a change soon.

Of his old existence, Jack had heard nothing, and soon his former life began to seem unreal. Not only his world of taken-for-granted privilege but his very identity had been stripped away. There had been no contact from the outside world. He had ceased to exist. Did anyone know he was here? Did anyone care? Did they all believe he was a murderer?

Jack had no way of knowing the outside world. Nothing filtered through to him through the security of training camp. He needed to question Regal Blue about his father's death. Something seemed wrong. But he had to find the right time.

The last day of camp, they were assembled in the locker room of the training facility. The room itself was modern and clean, one of the few luxuries afforded Synthates. Crushers stood watch around the edge while the team of assistant coaches huddled together reviewing rosters.

The crushers parted, and Coach Sharp entered the room. He wore a Braves sweatshirt and athletic pants. He was a big natural, fat in the gut, but with the rounded shoulders of a former athlete. His hands were thick and veined and he held them clasped behind his back as he walked the length of the locker room, inspecting each of the Synthates like a general at the front lines.

He stopped at the front of the room and turned toward them. "Many of you may know I was originally a coach in the National Football League. Now, football is very different from what we do. In football, you're facing a guy who wants to knock your head off. He wants to rip you apart, eat you for breakfast. He'd put a bullet in your head if he could. That's football. In this game you're about to play, the guy across from you actually can.

"Believe me, have no illusions, you are going into battle. As serious, and as real, as any battles that have ever been fought between men.

"That's what we've been training for. Good luck tomorrow. Make your makers proud."

CHAPTER 29

"Can Ralph come?"

"No, sweetie, Ralph has to stay here," Arden said, kneeling in front of his daughter. The vidScreen behind her played silently in the background, displaying Disney 3Dees. Arden barely noticed as he struggled with Maggy's pink pullover jacket. Maggy thought the jacket was too heavy and didn't want to wear it, so he had to coax the puffy garment over her shoulders using a series of distractions.

"What's Ralph like to eat?" he asked.

"Lettuce," came Maggy's cheerful reply.

He slipped the coat on a little more.

Ralph was a foot-long iguana that he'd bought for Maggy after she'd been sick. He thought she would have preferred something warm and furry that she could play with, but when Maggy had seen the iguanas inside their glass tanks, she'd immediately pointed at them in excitement.

On the drive home from the pet store, she was silent almost the entire way, so quiet, in fact, that Arden thought that the reptile with its bulging eyes and flicking tongue might be scaring her a little.

He was surprised, then, when Maggy suddenly said from the back seat, "Is he sick?"

"I don't think so. Why?"

"He's in a bubble. Just like me, when I was sick."

After that, Arden didn't feel right keeping the creature inside its glass enclosure. So Ralph was left to roam freely around the house. Maggy and Ralph soon grew close, the reptile seeking her out at night to sleep on her warm pillow and sitting at the breakfast table each morning while she fed him bits of lettuce.

"We can bring Ralph next time, okay, sweetie?" Arden said to Maggy, now fully inside her pink jacket.

"Okay. Mommy, too?"

"Well . . ." Arden replied hesitantly, ". . . maybe."

Arden's ex-wife, Sheila, was a lawyer who lived in a Battery Park City luxury condo with her boyfriend, Raoul, an asshole self-proclaimed post-modern painter from Brazil.

Once upon a time, she and Arden used to be happy. *Used.* That was a word that came up a lot in his life. A fucking curse, that word. He used to be a good cop. He and Sheila used to be a loving couple.

Maggy used to be healthy. Maggy. She was all that mattered now. Two years ago, when the white mist fell across New York, everybody was thrown into a panic. Arden still remembered the morning of the attack. Someone had infected the air scrubbers, and throughout the night the machines had quietly filled the atmosphere with toxic dust. That morning, New York City woke covered in a dark coating of ash. Six months after that, people started getting sick.

The newspapers called it the Black Rain. What it was, in fact, was a cancer-causing genetic mutagen. Black Rain occurred only a year after the virus El Diablo had struck the city, sickening and killing thousands, and a year before that the Synthate Liberation Front had blown up the Brooklyn Bridge.

Those were dark times.

Ralph sat on the coffee table and watched his mistress get ready. His tongue darted in and out. Maggy ran over to him, bent down, and kissed him directly on the nose with her tiny lips. For weeks after the attack, Arden had kept his daughter inside the house, but still the virus within the dust found a way to infect her.

"Say good-bye to Ralph," Maggy said as she took Arden's hand and headed for the door.

"Bye, Ralph," Arden said before shutting out the light, and Maggy echoed him. "Bye, bye Ralph!"

Twenty minutes later, Arden dropped off Maggy with Sanders's wife at their small honeycomb in the Brooklyn conurb. His partner's family lived in a relatively quiet block of tall honeycomb towers and micropod complexes, insulated from the Synthate Zones further to the east.

The passenger door opened and Dwayne Sanders sat down. "What're we doing out so late?"

"Going to the city."

Arden turned the car around and headed back toward Manhattan. "Why?"

"I think I got something on that Reynolds thing."

"Trying to earn your Junior G-man badge? They already got the guy for that, some undercover Synthate, worked at Genico."

"He wasn't just some guy. And he didn't just work at Genico. He was the head honcho's son. Doesn't make sense, a guy like that."

"The SFU says that's our guy, so that's our guy," Sanders said. "Whoever he is. Doesn't matter."

"And the SFU gets to tell the public they got another dangerous Synthate off the street. They get more funding for laser guns or whatever the fuck they use."

"Everyone makes out, what do you want to mess with this for?"

"It plays wrong to me, that's why," Arden said. "This Jack Saxton, everyone likes him. Former football hero. He gets up every day, goes to work, has a nice honeycomb, a car, plenty of touch bucks, then one day he just snaps and murders three people?"

"He's a Synthate. They don't think like you and me."

Arden drove across the Manhattan Bridge. Ahead, the Manhattan skyline stretched out, airplane warning lights blinking red atop the Genico tower. A helisquall hovered over the Synthate Zone to the north.

"That's my point. He didn't know he was a Synthate. This kid did everything right, had a ticker tape parade, for fuck's sakes. And now look at him. His wife is dead. He's bound for the Island, and we both know what kind of trip that is. So he destroys his whole life to waste some researcher and his wife at a costume party?"

"Yeah, yeah, yeah," Sanders said, playing an imaginary violin. "You got me all broken up inside. Now, let me tell you how I see it. You've got this young, up-and-coming executive, hot wife, nice apartment, no more honeycombs for him, maybe a few pleasure parlor trips, the whole fucking thing. Only trouble is, he's a Synthate. No problem, he's kept it hidden for the past twentysomething years, and he figures who's going to know? I've got my adopted daddy's mao keeping me safe. But then some snooping scientist, this guy Dr. Reynolds, is checking employee medical records—"

"Why would he do that?"

"Who knows? He's a good citizen, wants to catch himself a Synthate. And that's when he comes across Jack Saxton. He's got this guy cold, and best of all, it's the boss's adopted son. But before he can start blackmailing the dude, Jack offs both him and his wife."

"I don't buy it. Someone betrayed him. Someone turned him in to the SFU. And that gives him more reason for revenge than most people. But he didn't do Reynolds. No way. Doesn't make sense."

"Squad must have flaked a hundred Synthates for shit they didn't do. Maybe a thousand. Why are you taking this one so personally?"

"Because whoever killed Reynolds took out the one guy who maybe found a cure for Black Rain. And that pisses me off."

"Oh," Sanders said, understanding immediately. "So let's get the bastard."

"The SFU isn't going to like us meddling in their closed case."

"Fuck 'em. What you got?"

A burden lifted. Arden was asking a lot of his partner, but felt relieved to hear him say the words. He pulled over on the edge of Chinatown, took out the *Village Voice* and turned to the Adult Personals section. Small pop-up ads 3Deed in the car: Asian Escorts, Transsexuals, Teen Synthates . . . all danced and beckoned to them.

"Kinky," Sanders said.

"You remember Benny Zero?" Arden asked.

"Yeah, sure I remember."

Benny Zero was a hustler and pimp dealing mainly in Synthate whores and call girls. Night Comfort had mentioned his name to Arden, and the more he thought about him, the more Arden saw him as a possible link to whoever popped Reynolds and his wife. Back when Arden and Sanders had worked vice together, Zero was in the business of pimping only high-priced natural girls, but prison time and a brush with the Russian mafia had pushed Benny Zero underground. His trade was still whores, but strictly Synthates now.

With Zero's connections in the off-inventory Synthate world, he might be aware if someone had ordered a fucked-up psycho Synthate, the kind to undertake a contract murder. Problem was, before they could talk to Benny Zero, they had to find him.

Sanders picked out one of the ads at random. "Luscious Latin Escorts" featured a dancing vidImage of a raven-haired Synthate with big creamy tits and a pumpkin for an ass.

Arden dialed the number. On the third ring a woman answered.

"Hi, I'd like to place an order for delivery," Arden said.

"Sure," the woman responded, flirty but bored at the same time, as if her shift was almost over.

"I'm in town on business, staying at the Empire Hotel, room 3700."

"What type of food do you want? We have Asian. Spanish. Russian."

Arden thought of his ex-wife. "You have coldhearted WASP?"

"Uh . . ."

"I'm kidding. Surprise me."

"All right, thirty minutes."

The Empire Hotel was a rent-by-the-hour shithole on the west side of Manhattan underneath the abandoned rail line. The line had been turned into a park, which had been quickly taken over by junkies and crackheads and abandoned until it was filled with weeds, broken bottles, and heroin needles.

Arden parked two hundred yards from the hotel. Exactly thirty minutes later, a yellow taxi pulled up out front. A tall blonde stepped out, then disappeared through the lobby front doors.

"You're sure Benny Zero is still in business?" Sanders asked. "Thought he'd retire after the JFK heist."

Seven years ago, a container plane flying in from a Genico harvest factory in Malaysia had been hijacked at JFK Airport. Aboard were several hundred Synthates, stolen before they could be bio-tagged as Genico property. Over the course of the next year, the off-inventory Synthates kept turning up at Benny Zero whorehouses across the city. He was collared, did two years upstate for possession of stolen property, then got cut loose.

Now, as expected, the blonde appeared back on the sidewalk. She scowled as she stood and tried to flag down a taxi.

"No sucky, sucky," Sanders said. "Poor thing."

As she disappeared into a taxi, Arden pulled away from the curb to follow them. They headed uptown for about twenty blocks, and then the cab turned east and into Koreatown. The neighborhood's entire strip seemed like a single massive eyeScreen, each business's pulsing pixels of light merging as if somehow connected by more than proximity. BBQ joints and karaoke clubs and body art dealers, hundreds of them crowded together along the block. The whole placed flashed as if the entire space were tied together and powered by one electrical cord, and if someone accidently pulled the plug, all would go dark in unison.

The taxi stopped in front of a building in the middle of the block flashing eyeScreens advertised in Korean and English for a restaurant at street level, topped by a bioprint shop, topped by a pleasure parlor. Arden and Sanders double-parked and followed the blonde as she disappeared into the building. Inside was a narrow, shabby hallway, with a single elevator at its far end. The doors were already closing as they approached the elevator, and they watched the number display rise until the car stopped on the fourth floor.

Then it returned and opened for them.

The fourth floor was another narrow hallway, with a series of unmarked doors on either side. At the far end, a frosted glass door had the words "Trans Travel" printed on it in black letters. Sanders drew his weapon, then pushed it open. Inside was a small desk with posters of exotic travel locations on the wall. An old Korean woman sat at the desk, glancing up expressionless as Arden and Sanders entered the office. Silence descended on the room, then an old-fashioned telephone on the desk rang and the woman answered. She talked for a minute and wrote down information on the legal pad in front of her.

"Where's Benny Zero?" Arden asked.

The woman went back to reading a newspaper that she had spread in her lap.

"Well, we blew this case wide open," Sanders said. "We'll get departmental medals for this."

Arden went to the desk, and, ignoring the old woman, bent down and inspected the underside. Beneath was a large black button, which Arden depressed. There was a clicking sound, followed by the opening of a section in the wall. Visible beyond was a large lounge area with sofas and an eyeScreen tuned to glam rock. A half dozen Social Synthates of assorted flavors sat around on the sofa watching music 3Dees. The girls looked up at the detectives as they entered, but then quickly turned their attention back to the screen. Arden recognized one of them from the hotel. Beyond the lounge was another door. Arden pushed it open, and inside he found Benny Zero.

Zero sat at a cluttered desk. Behind him was a single window that looked out into Koreatown, while in front of him sat an Asian Synthate in a satin bikini, her bioprint a melting ice cream cone. Between the two of them, lines of cocaine were neatly arranged on a shiny glass mirror. Zero leaned back in his chair as the two cops entered.

"What is it with you cops?" Benny said. "You're like a fucking black cloud that follows me."

"Benny Zero, how are you?"

"Isn't there a parking ticket you should be writing somewhere?"

With his two-day scruff and bloodshot eyes, Benny looked like he was on the downspin of a two-day Euphoria binge.

The girl stared dumbly at them. She was beautiful, with waist-length black hair and bright eyes; to Arden she looked about seventeen.

"You have papers for her, right?"

Benny rolled his eyes. "Come on, what is this? Some sort of half-ass shakedown? How about you take her in the back and check her for papers, enjoy, then get the fuck out of my office."

"Hmm," Arden said, considering the offer. "That's an idea. Is that cocaine I see?" He nodded toward the desk. Benny Zero made a sour face.

"You missed some," Arden said, gesturing to the remaining lines on the mirror. "Go ahead, finish it. Then we'll talk."

"You want me to do fucking blow in front of you?" Benny Zero asked.

Arden smiled. "Sure, what's a party without good coke?"

Benny Zero raised his eyebrows. "Whatever. You guys are the weirdest cops I've ever met."

From his pocket, Benny produced a small plastic straw. Arden turned his attention toward the bookshelf opposite the desk. He ran his finger over the titles and pulled down a large, hardcover atlas. Benny slid the straw into his left nostril before leaning down over the mirror. He vacuumed up one line, his face two inches from the glass. As he moved on to the second one, Arden lifted the atlas and smashed it down on the back of Benny Zero's head.

Benny's face collided with the mirror, blood instantly pooling on its surface. His companion screamed and leaped up. She pushed past Arden, then stumbled out into the lounge, nearly tripping in her stilettos. Benny, shrieking in pain, fell backward in his chair. His nose was broken and bloody, the straw barely visible inside from where the impact had shot it up into his nasal cavity.

"God, that's disgusting," Sanders said.

"What the fuck did you do? My nose!" The powder on Benny's face made him look like a very unhappy clown.

Seeing Arden raise the atlas again, Benny held up his hands. "No more! Okay? What do you want?"

Arden reached into his pocket and passed over a large handkerchief.

"I want you to tell us everything you know about Synthate psychos running around New York killing naturals."

"Naturals?" Benny gasped as he tried to breathe, pressing the handkerchief to his nostrils.

"Yes, naturals. A Genico researcher and his wife."

"I don't know," Benny said between breaths. "Maybe. I sold one to a guy."

"When?"

"Around fourteen months ago. It was off-inventory Synthate, trained as a bodyguard and assassin. Real muscle for hire."

"Sold to who?"

"I don't know."

Arden shook his head, then tapped the atlas. Benny hesitated before saying, "I don't know, I swear. It was an anonymous buyer. I just have an address for the Synthate."

"Where?"

"I don't remember, uptown somewhere." Benny reached for the straw still in his nose and gently pulled. He gagged as it came out, bent and covered in blood. He dropped it to the floor, then opened his desk drawer and riffled through folders. He seemed to be having no success, but suddenly grunted. "Here," Benny said, dropping a scrap of paper on the desk. "That's all I have."

Arden picked up the tiny bit of paper. A Midtown address. He slipped it inside his pocket.

"You can keep the handkerchief," Arden said.

CHAPTER 30

Dolce was gone. But she had germinated a living creature, one that expanded inside Jack. His heart turned to wood, his lungs to hard branch, his blood became dark and solid. Pain was everything he knew. His body was only bruises. He was becoming a man made more of earth than flesh and blood. Knots formed under his eyes, dark mushroom brown. Fists crunched against his face, rendering his teeth and gums a rictus glued into place by sticky blood that thickened against his tongue like sap.

Training camp had turned him into oak. Yet inside was a fragile root. Inside was a bit of sun, a quiet westerly wind, a rolling hill and the little root. Outside he was hardened, but inside was Dolce, alive within him. She was the root from which grew his strength. Every blow he took in the training court, he thought of her. Every kick from every guard reminded him she had once lived. She was the reason he endured.

Death would have been easy. They had taken everything from him. But he still remembered. He kept her inside, sheltered from the rain, the tiny root of memory, the small inch of humanity left inside of him. He carried her with him. Kept her safe. Love could be a weakness. But it could also be a strength. Love coupled with hate formed a perfect whole. The yin and yang of his new being.

An armored train carried them to Bloomberg Island. Crowds surrounded the stadium and Jack scanned the frenzied faces through the bars, looking for someone he recognized from the old days. There was no one. Only the frightening anonymous crush of the mob.

To be a Synthate was to experience pain. They owned nothing, not even their own selves, and they could be bought and sold as easily as a Samp. Regal Blue had been born knowing nothing else. But Jack had experienced life as a free natural. He had been happy. And now, he could experience the loss that only someone who had once been free could feel. The pain that only someone who had once been in love could know.

Now as the moment of his first Games loomed before him, he followed his teammates into a concrete corridor beneath the stadium until the sound of the screaming mob outside faded to a low murmur. In practice, they wore team jerseys, but in the Games, they wore full historical uniforms. For this match, Jack and the rest of his team wore the uniform of the American colonial militia: black tricornered hat, chestnut-colored regimental coat and breeches, white shirt, black buckled shoes, and white stockings.

"The last time you were here you were on the other side of the glass," Regal Blue said and winked at Jack. "Tonight, you'll have a much better view."

The last time he was here, Dolce had been alive.

He remembered the feel of her hand in his. They had watched these same games from behind the glass, part of the last few hours he had spent with her before everything had been taken away. And being here now, even in the quiet before the violence, he felt reassured in that memory. He knew Dolce was on this field with him.

The corridor was wide and sprinkled lightly with sand. Behind them, black body bags were stacked in piles against the wall. As the combatants marched, they were each handed a regimental flintlock and a deerskin pouch filled with cartridges and lead balls. Jack remembered from his training that the flintlock was a heavy, awkward weapon, inaccurate at long range but devastating against troops in formation. Jack slung the ammunition pouch over his shoulder and watched as eyeScreens fixed along the hallway 3Deed demos of the correct loading technique.

"A skilled shooter can fire four or five times per minute," a monotone voice instructed. "As you fire additional rounds, your rifle will begin to foul with black powder residue. This will slow your loading ability and increase the chance of a misfire."

Jack touched the silver cross Dolce had given him. Already the rhythmic chant of the spectators began to seep into his consciousness. They were up there. The naturals. Waiting for him to kill. And he would kill for them. He hated everything about what was to occur, and he hated himself most for being forced into the position of giving them what they wanted. If it was death they wanted, he would give it to them. But he would never forget what they made him do.

Ahead now was a black metal gate. Beyond was the field of the battle. Coach Sharp and his staff waited near the door, headsets strapped on as they went over formation books.

Strains of music could be heard, and then the stadium announcer's voice. Suddenly the sounds of the crowd changed to low boos.

"Houston's heading out," Regal Blue said.

Behind them, a second gate rolled shut, trapping Jack and his team inside the corridor. The booing ceased, replaced again by the voice of the announcer heralding the arrival of the home team. Then cheering erupted amid the sharp blows of air horns and the shrill beats of loud dance music.

"Okay, get ready!" Coach Sharp called out.

With a rumble, the door slowly lifted upward. Light streamed down through the tunnel by degree and the crowd's multiple voices swelled and burst with increasing intensity. The sound of the stadium was tremendous. Fireworks exploded and sent showers of falling sparks around the fighters as they moved forward, filling their eyes and nostrils with acrid smoke.

"I'll see you on the field," Coach Sharp called out.

Jack followed his teammates onto the field. His equipment bounced and rattled as he emerged into the night air. The smoke had irritated his eyes, and the high-intensity stadium lighting made him blink.

Around him, everywhere, was the roar of voices, accompanied by the music's unrelenting throb. The team came to a stop at the far end of the field. Sky King, the grand champion of the Games, ran down the row of combatants, slapping each on the shoulder as he passed by. Opposite them were the Houston lines, their British uniforms red and threatening.

His body striped with war paint, the New York Braves' mascot rode bareback while gripping a long spear on a white horse across the field. When he reached halfway, he lifted the spear high as his mount reared up. Then he turned and rode hard toward the sideline.

Jack scanned the crowd above him, a sea of red-and-black jerseys. Thousands of frenzied fans. Gazing first at the press box, he turned his attention to the executive seating area. He could see people behind the long panes of glass, distant shapes that were impossible to recognize.

He reached into a narrow sack strapped to his shoulder and pulled out a spyglass. He aimed it up along the top edge of the stadium, toward where he and Dolce had sat together. The past had moved into the realm of the surreal. Restlessly, he continued to scan the crowd but saw nothing.

"The Star-Spangled Banner" began to play. Pulling his eye from the lens, Jack saw his fellow Braves at attention, hands on their hearts as they regarded an American flag waving in a floating hologram.

When the anthem's last bars had ended and the crowd's din was still suspended, the announcer continued to introduce the teams. The bagpipers sounded and a set of drums rattled in perfect time. Everything was happening quickly now and Jack felt himself pulled along, helpless against the inevitability of his situation.

"First team!" shouted Coach Sharp from the sidelines. "Load your weapons!"

At this, cheers exploded from the bleachers so deafening Jack barely heard the thud of fifty rifle butts striking the ground in unison as the teams began to load. Tearing open the small cartridge bag, he dumped powder into the pan of his flintlock.

Across the field, the Redcoats formed a firing line. Their flags rose up behind them, furling in the wind as their drummers beat. Overhead more flares erupted. Then a bugle, amplified monstrously, sounded the call to arms.

The battle had begun.

The 12-pounders roared as disgorged lead shot into the air. The balls screeched, built with the intensity of a kettle left on to boil, before they ripped into the field just ten yards ahead of the Braves' firing line. Chunks of dirt sprayed the faces of the men in the front line.

"Company! Attention!" Coach Sharp's voice rang out. "Forward march!"

Around them the drums and the bagpipes began again. The Braves marched into a field of waist-high grass. Around them, the artillery fire continued, tearing up the ground as the cannons closed their aim. A ball of grapeshot exploded on the right side of their line, felling two Synthates with splinters of shrapnel.

"March double time!" Coach Sharp's voice shouted.

The lines hurried forward, driven by the blow of the grapeshot. The Houston line was fast approaching, the gap between them narrowing until Jack could see each man's face in front of him.

There were thirty yards between them when Coach Sharp cried out, "Line, halt!"

The Braves stopped, rifles still resting against shoulders as they stood at attention. Jack felt his windpipe constrict, closing his brain off from air. The drums cut off, and the strains of the bagpipes died down with a last toneless wheeze.

The Houston line had also stopped, their flags and shirt collars rolled limply in the slight breeze. In silence, the armies waited. Even the stadium had grown quiet, every fan leaning forward in anticipation of blood.

"Line, make ready!"

Jack brought the butt of his rifle up and pressed it against his shoulder. The flintlock was five feet in length and extended between the heads of his own first line. Across from them, the Houston ranks did the same, the black, quarter-size holes of their rifle barrels showing clearly as the weapons were brought up and aimed. Jack cocked his rifle's hammer.

"Take aim!"

Scattered images flashed before him, snapshots in a picture book now torn out. The wind blew. The tips of the grass wavered. The silver cross felt cool around his neck. Dolce was dead. This is what the naturals made him do. They were turning him into a killer.

"FIRE!"

Jack eased his finger back on the rifle's trigger. The metal hammer made a click before it snapped against the pan. There was a burst of flame, then a blinding flash of light and the butt of the rifle kicked back hard against his shoulder.

Thick smoke was everywhere, stinging his eyes and leaving a dusty feel in his mouth with the heavy taste of ash. Through the smoke, Jack heard the thud of lead balls striking flesh in the lines around him. Men screamed. He was lost and alone in the white haze and waited for a lead ball to rip into him, but no impact came.

"Reload!" Sharp's voice commanded.

Jack listened to the scrape of rammers being pulled up. He reached into the pouch at his side, shakily pulled out another cartridge bag, and tore off the paper top. He poured the black powder into the pan. A lone rifle cracked on the Houston side and a lead ball whistled in the air.

Powder spilled from the pan and dusted the tops of the grass. On the Houston side, a second rifle ignited, then a third, sending balls rocketing toward the Braves. A voice cried out and a Synthate collapsed to the ground. Then another fell on his left.

There was a whirring sound above them, and the fog began to dissipate, sucked up into the exhaust at the top of the dome. Regal Blue was still alive. He stood further down the line. The muscles of his jaws bulged tight knots. His eyes looked strangely hateful.

"Fix bayonets!" Sharp ordered from the sideline.

Jack's bayonet hung from a loop on the belt around his waist. He lowered the butt end of the rifle to the ground until the barrel was just below his chin. Tearing the loop, he held the bayonet in his other hand.

The bayonet was long, three-sided, with ridged blood grooves. The bottom of the blade was swivel-locked with the top of the barrel, fixing the knife into position.

"Line, make ready!" Sharp called out.

Jack raised the rifle to his waist. The bayonet extended a foot and a half past the end of the barrel. His legs felt sluggish and weak. There came a steady chant from the stadium, "Charge! Charge! Charge!" From the massive loudspeakers came the sharp, piercing scream of a diving eagle.

Condensation from the fog machines beaded up into little droplets along Jack's rifle.

Jack inhaled once, long and steady, then readied himself.

"Charge!" Sharp cried. In unison the men on either side opened their mouths and roared. Jack joined them, the primeval sound coming naturally. They ran across the length of the field, bayonets extended. His legs suddenly felt incredibly powerful, his strides long and fluid. Everything melded together, the feel of the ground beneath his feet, the quickly approaching Houston line, and the roar of the crowd. Time stretched out. And snapped.

The two lines met with sudden and violent intensity, two waves smashing into each other. As they ran, Jack had chosen a target, a flat-faced Domestic-class Redcoat. The opposing Synthate had seen him as well, and they locked eyes from twenty yards away, each speeding to end the other's life.

As their bodies collided, the Redcoat head-butted him viciously and Jack felt his brain go light. He fell backward, the Redcoat on top of him, his hands wrapped around Jack's throat. His enemy's eyes were wide and dark, with flecks of tiny red veins that circled the irises. His mouth was open, lips pulled back against his gums.

Jack brought his knee up into the Synthate's groin. There was a bursting sound from deep within his opponent's lungs, a sharp exhalation, and he loosed his grip on Jack's throat, rolling over onto his side. Gasping for breath, Jack sat up, rolling away quickly through the long grass. He rose to his knees and, seeing his flintlock a few feet from him, picked it up.

The Redcoat had risen to his feet, knees pressed tightly together. They made eye contact once more. Jack swung the rifle around, still on his knees, and squeezed the trigger. The pan flashed as the powder exploded, while at the same instant, Jack saw the .69-caliber lead ball tear away half of the Redcoat's right arm. The Redcoat stood, staring down at the remains of the ragged stump. Jack charged forward and buried the bayonet deep into his enemy's chest.

The Redcoat twitched, more air escaped from his mouth, and suddenly the rifle became heavy in Jack's arm. The weapon slipped from his hands and fell to the ground, still protruding from the dead soldier's chest. The horror of the moment overwhelmed Jack in a dizzying wave. He stared at the destruction he had caused and felt his sanity slipping away from him.

A short alarm sounded from the loudspeakers overhead.

"What's that?" Jack cried. Regal Blue appeared next to him, panting and bloody.

"Houston's sending in more soldiers!"

Jack followed Regal Blue's gaze, eighty yards away to the Houston sideline. The large Plexiglas doors were sliding open. Something was coming out.

"They're coming!" Sky King shouted to the remaining Braves on the field. "How many of you are wounded?"

Several hands went up slowly.

"Take the rear line and reload weapons. There're only seventy yards between us and whatever comes out that door, so we won't be able to get off more than a few shots. We've got to make them count!"

One of them cried out, "We'll be massacred. There are only *eight* of us! Why doesn't Sharp send us more reinforcements?"

"You can't control what the coach does," Sky King said, his voice deep. "The only thing you can control in this life is what you do and how you choose to live the next few minutes. There is no place else to go but here. We are locked in this arena until the battle ends, and wherever you go on this field, they will find you. So we fight and gamble with our lives like men, or we run and let them hunt us down like animals. I choose to fight."

The door continued to open. In the stands, thousands stood upright, necks craned as they stared toward the opposite end of the field.

The heat from the battle had turned the fog to rain, cool, light drizzle that tasted of plastic. The eight Braves stood near the very center of the field, far from the cover along the sides. Sky King looked around them wildly.

"Grab as many rifles as you can hold, then fall back to the redoubt!"

Flintlocks lay everywhere in the grass, dropped by the fallen soldiers. Jack picked up two, carrying them awkwardly along with his own under his arms. The men turned toward the redoubt and Jack joined them, running through the high grass toward the log-and-dirt fort almost fifty yards away. As he headed there, Jack could see that the structure had been struck by artillery fire. A small fire burned along one side, the flames sizzling and crackling in the rain. The artillery on both sides was quiet now.

Reaching their goal, the team climbed over the wall. Inside lay a half dozen dead Synthates, most torn to pieces by shrapnel from grapeshot.

"Push the dead out, strengthen the wall with them," Sky King said as he grabbed one of the bodies and propped it against the broken front wall.

The fortification was small, about ten feet wide, enclosed by a camouflaged earth wall that reached up just past Jack's waist. Rain had turned the inside to slippery mud. The battle call sounded a third and final time. The crowd inhaled one massive breath, every eye glued to the end of the field.

Jack shielded his eyes against the rain. Something was coming toward them, breaking through the grass, moving over fences and stone walls.

Jack peered through his spyglass. The distant parts of the field jumped into focus inside the magnifying circle and he swept the view across the field.

"It's men!" Jack cried out. "Thirty of them! On horseback!"

Sky King snatched the glass from Jack. "Dragoons!"

Massive horses bore down on them, two long rows thick with muscle, flanks shining. Their riders had pistols slung across each shoulder and long cutlasses. Sweat showed on the beasts' flanks as their hooves pounded through the rain.

"Dragoons are coming! Form a line!" Sky King called out.

Jack crouched down below the wall, seven rifles lined up on his side. His vision blurred and danced with the falling rain. He swiped at his eyes. The black powder in the pan was growing damp. He could feel the mud that had seeped in through his pant legs, weighing down his uniform. Streams of water ran off of his hat and formed tiny rivulets that trickled coldly down his back. The horsemen galloped closer, then leaped the last remaining stone wall. They drew their swords.

"Wait . . ." Sky King's voice was steady. "Wait . . . wait . . . almost there."

Jack could see the approaching riders clearly now. Slowly, he took aim at the lead horseman. He heard nothing except the fall of the rain and the resonant beat of the hooves. He waited.

"Fire!" Sky King cried.

Jack pulled the trigger and the black powder flashed, igniting in the rain. He turned his head away from the explosion, but heard the whinny of horses in the distance. Jack looked back and saw animals bucking, riders thrown as the invisible wall of musket shot rushed up to meet them.

More riders followed and Jack dropped the empty rifle next to him, rapidly pulling a second from the row against the wall. He cocked the hammer and once more fired. The leaden ball caught one of the horsemen in the shoulder. The Redcoat twisted wildly in his saddle before he fell from his mount.

Jack took up a third rifle. Dead men lay around him. The lead horseman had reached the earth wall. Jack ducked into the mud as a giant black stallion cleared the mound over him. The small fort was filled with the sound of beating hooves. The dragoons had their swords out and they swung wildly down, hacking and cutting at everything.

In the chaos, Regal Blue pulled Jack's arm. "Time to go. Fall back."

Together they climbed up and out of the redoubt. Keeping low, they moved out quickly across the wet fields. Regal Blue led him toward one of the stone cottages that lay beyond. Thin trails of smoke rose from the single chimney and chickens lay huddled together under the dry eaves of the roof.

"There!" Regal Blue shouted.

Jack looked back over his shoulder as they ran, seeing the horsemen still inside the redoubt. They reached the front of the cottage.

Inside was empty except for a squat metal object the size of a furnace that made a humming noise and periodically loosed a cloud of steam up the fake chimney. There were four windows, one on each side of the building, and Jack could see six long pieces of two-by-four industrial timbers supporting the roof. The cottage was simply a prop for the field, part of a theatrical set.

"Get down! Get away from the windows!" Regal Blue hissed, as he crouched near the smoke generator.

Jack squatted next to him and together they cautiously peered through the window. The horsemen had scattered, three of them heading directly for Jack and Regal Blue. Jack ducked beneath the window and pressed his back tightly against the plasterboard wall.

Slowly, he reached down and pulled out a powder cartridge. Just above, Jack heard the snort of horses and a whisper of conversation. Two shadows fell across the window. The dragoons were hunting them now, and it was only a matter of time before they began checking the cottages.

Lifting his head, Jack peered out the window again. Close to his face was a long, fibrous horsetail swishing back and forth. A single Redcoat sat in the saddle, looking out at the field.

"We have to take him now," Regal Blue whispered.

Slowly Jack raised himself toward the window. The horse still stood in place, its rider checking his watch, anticipating the approaching halftime.

Jack raised the butt of his rifle and smashed the glass of the window. The effect was instantaneous. The horseman spun around in his saddle as Jack brought the rifle up through the broken glass, braced it against his shoulder, and fired. There was a loud crack, a flash of light from the black powder and a thud as the ball's force knocked him out of the saddle.

"Hit! Reload!" Jack shouted as he dropped down under the window.

Regal Blue stood immediately and propped his rifle against the sash. Jack quickly pulled a second cartridge from his pouch and began to reload the rifle. Regal Blue fired, then ducked down next to him.

Jack stood up again, taking his place. A second Redcoat lay in the grass where Regal Blue had shot him. This one was not yet dead and he rolled back and forth screaming, his hand over his abdomen. Two of his teammates ran through the high grass toward the cottage. Jack took aim. They were still forty yards away but moving quickly, their equipment jangling. A pistol shot smacked into the side of the cottage. Jack pulled the trigger on his flintlock and the ball caught one of the Redcoats just above the knee.

And then he saw Sky King.

The giant New York warrior rose up from where he'd been concealed in the tall grass, just in front of the still-running Redcoat. Spotting him, the enemy combatant tried to stop and raise his pistol in the same motion. But it was too late. Sky King grabbed his throat and brought up the short metal bayonet into the man's gut. The Redcoat's entire body shook before he dropped to the ground as Sky King released his grip.

"Houston!" Sky King shouted, raising the still-bloody bayonet. He pointed across the field. The last Redcoat halted on his mount beneath a large oak. Hearing Sky King's cry, the rider drew his sword, then kicking hard against his horse's flanks, he urged his steed forward. Sky King held steady, the bayonet drawn. As the horseman approached Sky King, Regal Blue's rifle exploded from the broken window. Just as the horse reared up, its nostrils flared in terror, Sky King sprung through the high grass, jumped onto the animal's back and buried his bayonet into the Redcoat's neck.

Horse and rider fell to the ground.

Slowly Sky King rose to his feet. Blood had stained his chestnut-colored uniform and almost obliterated its original color. Jack and Regal Blue left the cottage through the battered door and joined him.

"Kill outside," Sky King said, staring at the cheering crowd, "and they put you in prison. Kill in here, and they make you a hero."

CHAPTER 31

Arden had grown up in Brooklyn and remembered it fondly. The borough had real neighborhoods back then. There'd been crime, sure, but that was just New York; stray too far from home and you never knew what might happen. In those days, midtown Manhattan was a special, shining place to window-shop for luxurious goods, or sit, transfixed, in the upper balcony of a Broadway show. Then everything changed.

After the initial line of Synthates had begun rolling off the assembly line in faraway places like Malaysia and China, one of the first modification facilities was built in the center of Manhattan. Problem solving was behind certain critical decisions. For example, a family purchases a Domestic Synthate to take care of Granny, but then Granny dies and a geriatric caregiver is no longer needed.

No problem: The modification center would refurbish the Synthate, then sell him out to the DOT or Sanitation to pick up garbage or repair subway tracks or something similar. And of course, he needed a place to live, so he settled in the area around the modification plant. Synthates soon began to take over the area.

Most of them lived in poverty and thus crime started to rise. After tourists started complaining, the city took notice. Then came the effort to evict all Synthates from Midtown. Synthates rioted, set fires, and destroyed businesses. Realizing their mistake, city officials now regretted the earlier settlement policy.

The trouble was, by this point, the city had become dependent on Synthate labor. If the military was called in to solve the problem, daily life, with its need for sanitation workers, hospital orderlies, dishwashers, factory workers, etc., would grind to a halt. The solution arrived at in the end was the designation of a ten-block area as a Synthate habitation zone. Soon Midtown had the highest population of Synthates in the city, more even than Governors Island. They lived crowded on top of each other in vacated office buildings, leaving their zone only to travel to work.

The address Benny Zero had given Arden and Sanders was 30 Rockefeller Plaza, 65th Floor, the old Rainbow Room. A few vidBoards advertised sex shops, and prostitutes lingered around the chained and abandoned doors of the Rockefeller Center subway station. Where once had been glistening banks and restaurants now featured a few naturals who wandered in and out of seedy pleasure parlors. Arden and Sanders parked along the curb in front of Radio City Music Hall.

The hall's iconic sign had long since burned out, and a steady stream of addicts wandered in and out through the destroyed revolving door looking for Euphoria fixes. The homeless had encamped themselves with boxes and shopping carts inside the old ice rink of Rockefeller Plaza. Above everything the golden statue of Prometheus stood untouched in the center of the plaza, a monument to optimism.

The front lobby was gloomy, the fractured edges of lightbulbs visible in their sockets, like glass flowers in the dark. Sanders turned on his flashlight and swung the beam around, illuminating dusty display cases featuring advertisements of forgotten 2Dee television shows.

One elevator was in working order, and the detectives rode it up to the sixty-fifth floor. The double-frosted glass doors leading into the Rainbow Room were locked until a strong kick from Arden burst them open. Drawing their service weapons, the two advanced slowly into the darkened room beyond.

Sanders found a light switch behind an immense mahogany bar, and, an instant later, the chandelier over the dance floor flickered to life. Once the space had hosted dining and dancing, but it was now empty, filled with overturned tables and dusty booths. Floor-to-ceiling windows looked out across Manhattan. On the parquet floor stood a single bed, wooden chair, and table. The bed appeared recently slept in, while a lamp, some scattered papers, and a vidBoard sat on the table.

"What you got?" Sanders asked as Arden picked up the device. Through the window, the Genico tower loomed distant and dark against the night sky.

Arden glanced through the vidBoard. Some familiar faces appeared. He pushed the display tab and a holographic image of Mr. and Mrs. Reynolds hovered in the air.

"He's got images of our victims." Sanders poked through the papers on the desk and pulled out a yellowed architectural diagram. "And the layout of the murder location."

"Still think Jack Saxton is the right guy on this?"

"At least he had a connection to the victims. What's the motive here?"

Arden looked again around the sparse living space. A small plastic rectangle fell from the papers to the floor. Arden retrieved it. A Genico security pass. He held it up. "This is a start."

"You think someone in Genico was behind it?"

"I don't think *someone* in Genico, I think it's Genico itself."

"Why?"

"I think Martin Reynolds knew something about Black Rain that Genico didn't want released."

"Something worth murdering for?"

"Billion-mao industry. Murders happen every day for less."

Outside the doors came a humming whine as the elevator began to move. Arden put a finger to his lips and they both turned silently toward the closed doors leading out of the Rainbow Room.

Sanders eased his 9mm from his holster. The elevator noise grew louder, finally ending with a chime and the rattle of the car opening. They waited in silence, eyes fixed on the double doors. Footsteps sounded on the tile floor. Then there was silence.

Quietly, they moved across the parquet floor and pulled open the double doors. Outside the hall was empty. Rows of closed doors faced them. The Synthate Liberation Front was still active in the zones, and they had a distinct hatred for cops.

"We should get out of here," Sanders said.

Arden pushed the elevator call button and the doors reopened immediately. They only lowered their weapons when they were inside, the elevator car speeding back toward the ground floor.

"Want to have the crushers round this guy up?" Sanders said.

"I'd like to handle it."

The elevator reopened onto the main floor. The area was dark. A figure in a hooded sweatshirt walked toward them. The man noticed Arden and Sanders and stopped abruptly at a shuttered gift shop. His face was shadowed by the hood, but Arden saw a bioprint form into a serpent on the back of his hand. Then the bioprint was a blur of motion as the Synthate pulled a barker with incredible speed from his waistband. Shots echoed in the dim space. Arden and Sanders dived for cover against the elevator wall.

Arden fired back with his 9mm, one of the NBC display cases shattering into fragments of broken glass. The Synthate turned and broke into a run. Sanders and Arden followed, sprinting across 45th Street and through Rockefeller Plaza. The figure weaved in and out between small shanties and boxes, and then headed straight for Radio City Music Hall. Arden, who'd fallen behind Sanders, already felt a sharp stitch in his side. He was still trying to negotiate his way, shoving aside anyone in his path, as ahead the Synthate opened the doors to the theater and disappeared.

Inside, the hall was dark and musty.

Arden slowed, gripped his weapon and moved more carefully. The theater's grand atrium was empty, the atmosphere oppressive. The hall offered a heavy dose of the past, of a world before Synthates. Before Black Rain. Before the Brooklyn Bridge attack. Snack bars stood dusty and forgotten, glass shattered. Graffiti tagged up the frescoes on the walls. Euphoria droplet needles lying along the marble stairs shone like scattered bits of tinsel.

They moved up the steps and along the mezzanine hallway. The theater itself opened up in front of them, the stage below flanked by tiers of velvet seats. At the sudden sound of movement in the far balcony, Arden turned and fired blindly into the musty darkness. A second later he heard the echo of footsteps fading into the distance.

Arden and Sanders tried to find their way up to the balcony level. Most of the signs had deteriorated to illegibility or disappeared altogether, and the two quickly became lost in the stairwells and hallways that circled the interior. Eventually, Arden pushed open the right combination of doors and they found themselves in the balcony.

It was empty.

"This guy's long gone," Sanders said.

"Gone but not forgotten," Arden replied as he shone his light on a blood spatter on the balcony wall.

Arden ran his DNA scanner over the stain on the wall and collected a sample. They found their way out more easily than they had in. The sampling he'd scanned would tell him the make and manufacturer of the Synthate. In order to actually get a look at the guy's face, though, they'd need to crack the model code. The final one percent of any Synthate's genetic code was encrypted by the manufacturer in order to prevent patent infringement. Given the millions invested in R & D, companies liked to protect their product.

The detectives made their way back through the theater to their parked patrol solar.

"We need to get access to Genico computer systems. They'll be able to read this scan."

"They're going to fight a search warrant. No company likes to give up its patent secrets. These big companies, they can keep this in court for years before we get access to their records. Especially if they're involved in the Reynolds murder."

"I'm not talking about getting a warrant."

They had reached the car. Sanders stopped walking and looked around the empty street. "What are you talking about?"

"You know." Arden swung an imaginary baseball bat. "Swing for the fences."

"No. No. No. Breaking in? A company like Genico is going to have massive security in place." Sanders leaned against the car. "I'm your best friend and I would do anything for you, but there's no breaking into Genico. It's never going to work."

"It will work if I have help from inside."

"Nobody who works at Genico is going to help you."

"You're right. Nobody who works at Genico will help me. But someone who used to work there might."

"Who do you know that used to work there?"

"We've never been formally introduced. But I have an idea of some-one who might help. With the right motivation."

CHAPTER 32

Awake.

Eyes open. Breathe.

Musket fire echoed in Jack's ear, then faded to nothing. Overhead, a ceiling fan spun slowly. As he slowly sat up, his brain rolled inside his skull, creating waves of dizziness. He pressed the palm of his hand to his forehead and held it there.

He turned his attention to his surroundings. The room was small, four windows across one wall, bamboo-slatted blinds drawn shut and seamed with cracks of red neon light from outside. The walls were covered with peeling paper and a faded carpet bunched on the worn hardwood floor. Where was he? A potted plant in a corner had shed all its dried brown leaves on the floor. How had he gotten here? He swung his bare feet onto the rug.

The battle. They'd won the battle. But after that, only nothingness registered. A blank space in time until now. Until this room. This unknown room. They must have given him something. A memory suppressant of some sort. A spasm of nausea hit him.

Through the slatted windows came the sound of traffic. He wore only a pair of boxers. His leg throbbed, but clean white bandages were wrapped around his thigh. His arm had also been bandaged. The wound didn't hurt. Somebody had at least hired a good doctor.

Jack stood, slowly at first, keeping one hand on the bed for balance. He staggered to the windows but found the bamboo blinds wouldn't open. Beyond the thin seam of red light, he wasn't able to see what was outside. He moved to the door but found it locked. Next to the door was a small Automat window. He tapped the glass. Inside was empty.

What was this place?

Still exhausted, he collapsed back down on the bed and fell asleep.

He dreamed of Dolce. She had loved Naples, that ancient port along the Tyrrhenian Sea. She'd taken Jack there once, to the Aeolian Islands, off the coast of Sicily. He hadn't thought of that afternoon in a long time and now in his dream he returned to an old memory.

They sat on the terrace of her cottage that overlooked the sea, which itself overlooked everything and nothing at the same time. The house was faded pink in color, blending in with flowers that blossomed along the hills.

"These islands are named after Aeolus," Dolce said, turning to look out toward the sea. "The Greek god of the wind." The water's smooth blue surface was dotted with the masts of fishing boats. "He kept the winds of the world in a bag in his caves here. I can take you to them. To those caves."

"I would like that."

She wore a sundress almost the shade of the indigo sea. Her black hair was held back by a ribbon. She had the richest tan skin Jack had ever seen, like the sandstone rocks that edged the shore.

Above them, driftwood timber beams stretched out over the porch covered by a thatch work of sticks. Sunlight penetrated the thatch, projecting patterned shadows against the salmon-colored walls.

White and pink roses grew along the dried sticks above them, dropping their petals to the ground. One fell on Dolce, sliding down the length of her black hair, before curling into her lap. She inspected the petal, rubbing its softness between her fingers.

A cat emerged from the bushes beyond the terrace, silently stalking an unseen insect.

"Would you like to see Aeolus now?" Dolce said. "See the cave where he keeps the wind of the world?"

She leaned forward and kissed him, her lips like the cool adobe walls of the cottage. "I'll take you there."

When Jack awoke, he lay on his back and stared at the ceiling. He touched the bandages once more with his hand, then slowly unwrapped the white gauze with his fingers to reveal a dark black bruise on the skin. He pressed his index finger against his thumb. He felt the ridges of his skin, and thought of the deposit touch box his father had left for him.

The radio in the corner played big band music as Jack began an inspection of his space. He started in the corner near the Automat window and moved first along the baseboard, then slowly up along the peeled paper wall. There was nothing unusual.

He turned his attention to the door. He expected it to be locked as it was before. But instead, the knob turned and swung open. Outside was a long hallway papered in faded peach that matched the color of the rug. A man in a charcoal-gray suit sat in a folding chair against the wall. He was a natural, midthirties, with the still handsome build of an athlete just past prime. There was an almost tangible capacity for violence that hovered in place somewhere inside him, strong enough that Jack felt that if he reached out to touch this man, an electric jolt would pass through his skin. The man nodded at Jack and said, "Good morning."

"Morning. Who are you?"

The man stood and walked down the hallway toward an elevator. "Come with me."

Jack followed and together they stepped inside the elevator car. The man slid the gate shut and worked the operating lever. The car jerked and began to move upward.

"I imagine," the man said, "you must have many questions now."

"Where am I?"

"You are in one of the Synthate Zones," the man said. "My name is Charles Arden. I'm a detective in the NYPD."

The elevator stopped and they stepped out into an art deco office with rosewood furnishings and a gray sofa. Sectioned off by a silk panel Korean divider, the office was framed by sets of windows covered by venetian blinds. Arden slid behind the large polished desk and sat himself in a comfortable-looking leather chair.

"How did I get here?"

"After the Games, all the Synthates who survive are brain blinded and brought to the zone. Easier for them to keep an eye on you. You'll be here until the next Games," Arden said. "Then you'll fight again."

Arden pushed a button on the desk and leaned back in his chair. Behind him, the venetian blinds slid open and revealed the world outside. Through the glass was a city. A throbbing, pulsing city, alive with neon and smoke. The street below was crowded with human forms and lined with grease shops and pleasure parlors illuminated with the strobes of flashing signs. The burned-out shell of a yellow taxicab rotted slowly on the corner while torn-open manhole covers spewed thick steam. Tall, dark buildings rose up from the street and stretched far to the north. The only familiar presence, the ubiquitous eyeScreen behind a protective metal cage, flashed images of Bloomberg Island.

Then Jack's eyes settled on something he did recognize: directly across the street, broken neon tubes flickering bravely, the old Radio City Music Hall sign.

He was still in New York City. Still in Manhattan. But in Midtown now. He hadn't been here since the Synthates took it over. Not many naturals came up here. But he was no longer a natural.

"Not what you remembered, is it?" Arden asked.

"God, no," Jack said. He had no idea it was this bad. The censored news images everyone received showed small, orderly micro-pods. This place looked war ravaged.

"I came here as a kid," Jack said. "It was beautiful. Shows every night. Professionals in suits walking to work. Everything was bustling. This was Midtown Manhattan, the center of the universe.

"Twenty years of Synthates did this. It's not Midtown anymore. Now they call it Necropolis. City of the dead. Home to thousands of Synthates." Arden leaned forward. "I was the detective assigned to the Reynolds murders."

"I didn't kill those people."

"Did I say you did?"

"But if you were the detective assigned to the case, then what am I doing here?"

"Because you're an easy mark."

"And who are you? The cop with the heart of gold?"

Arden shook his head. "Not exactly. You'll always be a Synthate, there's nothing I can do about that. But what I can do is help you find the people who put you here, the same ones who murdered Dr. Reynolds. And the ones who murdered your wife. And in return, you can help me with a problem I have."

Jack's hands tightened to fists. He thought of his brother. Phillip had not acted alone. He was sure of that now. He had needed the support of others at Genico and inside the SFU. There was a depth to what had happened to him that Jack didn't understand yet, but he didn't know if he wanted a cop involved.

"Why do I need your help?"

"Come here," Arden said. "I want to show you something."

Arden opened the glass sliding door and street noise assaulted them. Horns and cries dueled over the constant hum of released steam. Arden stepped out onto the balcony, twenty stories high. Evening was falling, streaks of red burning across the darkening sky. Around them the zone stretched out its electric painted landscape. Traffic was light. Gasoline-powered public buses, dredged up from thirty years ago, hauled their metal bodies slowly up the avenue. The blue neon of a restaurant across the street advertised cheap steak dinners, a few forms hunched over on bar stools while the owner wiped down the counter.

In the distance to the north, high over the street, the Maglev streaked by, a single thin line of light that traveled down toward lower Manhattan. Jack watched the train as it moved into what had been his old life.

Arden lit up a smoke stick and glanced toward lower Manhattan. "Without me, you will never make it out of the Synthate Zone. How's your arm?"

Jack felt the tenderness in his right forearm. "Sore. Why?"

"Tracking chip. Every Synthate in Necropolis has one. You leave here without authority, they know."

"Who are they?"

"The Synthate Fucked Unit," Arden said, calling the SFU by their not-affectionate nickname. "Only Synthates with valid work permits can leave here. Every morning the Maglev carts out construction workers, maids, dishwashers. All the jobs naturals don't want to do. It all falls on you. The grease that keeps the natural machinery working.

"I can get you out of here. But freedom has its cost."

"What cost?" Jack asked warily. He could no longer trust naturals. They were the master and did what was necessary to protect their power. But because Jack was so powerless, he had nothing to lose.

"I don't think we're there yet. Neither one of us has reason to trust the other."

"So it's something illegal?"

"Would breaking the law stop you from your revenge?"

"Nothing would stop me," Jack said evenly.

"This is why I chose you. Free will is a powerful thing. You'll help me with my problem because you want to. Because of what I can give you in return. There's no loyalty with someone who kills for mao. They can be bought and sold. But you, you're powered by something that can't be bought. Just as I am. That's what's important to me."

Arden produced a small business card from his pocket and handed it to Jack. "I want you to go see somebody at the old Carnegie Hall." Jack took the card and Arden continued. "It's a casino and a nightclub now. Sort of has a 1920s, 1940s theme. It's the only business that's profitable here. Naturals actually come in to play. Nobody wanted to risk their lives to come up here for classical music, but they'll sure make the trip for a spin at the roulette wheel. There's a Synthate there you can see. I've spoken to him already. He'll give you what we need."

"Why don't you see him?"

"He doesn't trust naturals."

"He'll help me?" Jack asked.

"Oh yeah." Arden smiled. "He's going to love you."

CHAPTER 33

There were several sets of suits in the closet of his living quarters. Jack chose a charcoal-gray pinstripe. Outside, he kept his head down and walked north toward where Arden had said the casino would be.

Jack was amazed by how quickly the city had fallen apart. Homeless and addicts lay passed out along the street corners. The small shops and restaurants were crowded as evening fell, and Synthates still in the uniforms of their day jobs filled the streets—maids and construction workers, nurses and cleaners. A crusher surveillance drone sped by overhead, a black camera eye gleaming as it hovered over the remains of a health club before the craft turned and headed west down 54th Street.

He had lived just on the outside of this world, but Jack had no idea of the squalor most Synthates were forced to live in. He could never have imagined the pressure of this constant surveillance, the daily desperation involved in just surviving.

The casino was visible from blocks away, the old Carnegie Hall transformed into a gaudy gambling and entertainment complex called the Deco. The clientele outside were all well dressed and looked like big-city types—Samp brokers, politicians, tourists and visitors who took the Maglev from lower Manhattan for a night of blackjack, and Synthate whores. A security team of massive Synthates guarded the street outside, ready to push back any invaders from the impoverished zone a few blocks away.

Across the front entrance, letters spelled out "The Deco" in white and silver neon, flanked on either side by illuminated palm trees. A billboard near the street advertised shows starring Synthate-cloned versions of Humphrey Bogart, Lana Turner, and Rudolph Valentino.

Jack made his way to the front door of the Deco and showed the business card to one of the Synthates, a hulking giant with a long scar running down the side of his neck. The doorman waved Jack through, and inside the casino opened up around him. The original structure of Carnegie Hall had been preserved, with its massive open ceiling and wide balconies rising up like layers around him. But the seats had been removed and the machinery of the casino filled the floor.

Once people had sat here for Tchaikovsky. Now slot machines whirred and blinked while dealers presided over card tables and roulette wheels. A bustling crowd sat around tables and slots and stood packed together near roulette wheels and the green felt of craps stands. vidBoards strobed jackpot mao amounts, while voices in Chinese and English advertised games and shows and restaurants, rallying people to a frenzy.

At the front, on the old stage, was a thick redhead Synthate in a tight blue dress that showed off her legs and well-rounded hips. Jack gave his hat to the hatcheck girl, and then he stood at the rear champagne bar between two rows of video slot machines as the redhead began her number.

He waited a moment, then headed up a back set of stairs and out onto a balcony. Below him, the line was boisterous. People talked and laughed. To the north, what had been Central Park was now dark and overgrown, zoned off by the contaminant dome.

"Hi there," a female voice said. He turned to see a tall, strikingly beautiful woman in a fitted black dress. She had black hair and perfect eyes. Something about her was immediately familiar.

"You must be Jack."

"What makes you so sure?"

"Because you don't have the look of a natural."

"What look is that?"

"You know, that asshole look of entitlement," she said. "And we've met before."

Suddenly Jack remembered. His father's apartment. She was the Synthate Social girl. She extended her hand. "Night Comfort. Pleased to meet you again."

Her palm was warm.

"I remember you," Jack said.

"And I remember you," she said. "So what do you want here?"

"Arden sent me," Jack said, confused.

"I know he did, but what do you want here? You looking to get killed in the Games? I only ask because, if your life continues on its current path, you stand a pretty good chance of getting your head blown off. So tell me, what is it you want?"

"Revenge," Jack said.

"And you think this will make you feel whole again? This will be worth your life?" Night Comfort said.

"You can't understand."

Night Comfort stared at him. "You think because you were sent here, you know anything about loss. About real loss. Look around you, at the thousands of faces. Synthate faces. At least you were able to live out there and have feelings none of us will ever have. You know how much I would have given to feel what you feel?"

"Then you don't have any idea how hard it is to have it taken away from you," Jack said.

She considered this, and said, "I guess I don't."

She took his arm and led him back inside to the edge of the balcony. Below them the casino floor chimed like a jukebox. The music onstage was going strong and the air was heavy with the smell of smoke sticks and alcohol.

"Welcome to the Deco," she said.

Below them stretched an expanse of people. A living, breathing thing that seemed to ripple and move as a single massive creature. Natural men in expensive suits, Synthate women slung over them like colored scarves. Tables lined the floor, padded velour furniture behind them, some separated by thick velvet curtains the color of burgundy.

The main bar stretched out in the middle of the floor, glass bottles of alcohol glistening under the lights in perfect rows while bartenders served the throng of patrons along the marble bar. Cocktail waitresses flitted in and out through the crowd between the card tables, delicately formed glasses stacked precisely on circular trays held in front of them as they moved from table to table.

"Prostitution here is legal. Drugs are legal. Gambling is legal. Any vice you can name thrives in the Synthate Zone. There are no rules, no laws, no consequences," Night Comfort said. "So be careful. Remember, this isn't your old life. A murder here won't even make the grid."

Below them, the band had a good rendition of Duke Ellington's "Take the 'A' Train" going, the Duke and his musicians never sounding so good. The lead performer, a Synthate with a saxophone bioprint, looked just like Ellington, like a picture ripped from a book.

"It's the celebrity genetic reconstitution program. Something just for the casino. Part of the entertainment," Night Comfort said. "The band leader looks like Duke Ellington, because he is Duke Ellington. Genetically speaking, anyway. The casino hired one of the big genetic groups to tailor for them a group of Synthates modified to look like celebrities from the twenties to the forties. They perform all the shows here, the attractions. The Mirage casino had Siegfried & Roy, we've got Duke Ellington, Humphrey Bogart, and James Cagney. Among others."

"Their Duke is excellent."

"He was made to be excellent."

"And what were you made to do?"

Night Comfort smiled slowly. "Depends who you ask."

"What if I ask you? What do you think?"

"I think Synthates are better than naturals. Smarter. Stronger. I think it's only a matter of time before the revolution begins."

Jack remembered now her revolutionary talk. Then a more obscure memory popped unbidden into his head. Her voice. He had heard it before, under different circumstances. She had been the woman in the mask, the one who had freed him from the crusher transport.

"You were there," Jack said, amazed. "You knocked over the SFU transport. Your voice."

She looked at him thoughtfully. "Synthates need a voice."

"Take the 'A' Train" was dying out, the music giving way to the melodic sound of conversation throughout the club.

"So you work for Arden?" Jack asked, still trying to figure her out.

Night Comfort laughed. "I work for an organization. We've been looking for you for quite some time now. That's why we broke you out of SFU custody. Unfortunately, you managed to get yourself arrested again."

"Looking for me? Why?"

"All in time. But for now, you're here to meet Rudolph Valentino, correct? He runs the zone. He's a Synthate, but everything that comes through here, he gets a piece of. Sex. Drugs. Gambling. If anyone would know about what happened with you, it'd be him."

"Is he dangerous?"

Night Comfort smiled. "This is the zone. Everyone here is dangerous."

"Does that include me?"

"Depends if you think you have anything to lose. Most of us here have nothing. That's what makes us dangerous. We're all slaves. How much worse could death actually be?"

"Everything I have was taken from me. Sometimes it's worse to have a thing and lose it than to never have it at all. Makes you hate the ones who took it from you."

"You're going to need that hate. All of it. Hate will give you something to live for. Make you strong." Night Comfort looked down to the crowd below. "The one you're looking for is down there."

Below them, Jack could see into the dark recesses of the casino floor. Night Comfort pointed to a circular table on the far side of the club facing the stage. The table was backed by a cushioned booth in which sat a group of five or six Synthates talking in clouds of thick smoke. A man in the center of the group was wearing a white linen suit, striped shirt, and high-waisted trousers. His necktie was pulled down a few inches off the collar. His shoes were black and white two-tones, his hair slicked back with brilliantine. Jack studied his face. Something about it looked familiar.

"Rudolph Valentino," Night Comfort said. "That's Genico's version sitting over there. The reconstituted DNA project. They took the real Valentino's DNA and made a Synthate with it."

The resemblance was amazing.

"Should I go talk to him?" Jack asked.

Night Comfort pulled on her smoke stick and smiled. "He's going to love you. But be quick. The Games begin again soon. And you'll be due back in battle. You don't have much time."

The table was littered with empty glasses, bottles of champagne, and smoke stick trays. The Synthates laughed and conversed amongst themselves. As Jack approached, he saw that all five seated around the table were men, Valentino in the middle. They were dressed sharply, most in linen suits, their hair slick and shining. Onstage a shapely blonde was singing something low and sweet, the men at the table mostly ignoring her.

Valentino barely looked up as Jack approached. He waved his hand dismissively. "We're all set on drinks. A pack of smoke sticks would be nice."

"Are you Rudolph Valentino?"

Valentino turned at this, looking up at Jack, his eyes flickering down the length of his body.

"Maybe." Valentino smiled, leaned back in the chair. Jack noticed the eyes of the other four men on him as well. They were all handsome, high-cheekboned models with soft lips. Valentino turned his head to the figure next to him, a delicate man in his early thirties. "Well, this one is certainly bold."

"I need to talk to you," Jack said.

Valentino waved his hand again. "Sit down with us. Have a drink and maybe later I'll give you my autograph."

The rest of the table broke into laughter.

"It's not about that."

"Oh please, sit down and have a drink," Valentino said, exasperated. "Don't be so serious."

Jack sat down at the end of the table, crammed next to a thin black Synthate with a white V-neck sweater and pinstripe shirt and tie. He smiled at Jack. "You fought in the Games?"

"That's right."

"So you're one of our conquering heroes? Cheers," Valentino said, leaning in toward Jack. The smell of brandy was heavy on his breath. "Look at that face. You're beautiful, passionate. Please don't ever get dragged into the Games again. I don't want anything to happen to that face."

The men at the table laughed.

"You should sing for him," someone called out.

Valentino smiled. "You want to hear me sing? I did shows, twice a day for the casino."

"Well, actually . . ."

"Then I will!" Valentino stood up unsteadily, slicked back his hair with one hand, and moved toward the front. The blonde had finished her number and Valentino stepped onstage, shielded his eyes with one hand against the lights, and made his way to the microphone. Around him, the crowd cheered in a soft wave, raising martini glasses up to him.

Valentino looked out at the audience. "This song is inspired by the great Rudolph Valentino movie *The Sheik*. 1923."

Music started behind him and Valentino began singing, a wavering version of "Kashmiri Love Song." The tune was slow and sad, familiar to Jack in the dim recollection of memory. Valentino sang well, his voice tremulous with feeling.

The men left at the table gazed openly at Valentino onstage. One of them leaned in toward Jack. "He did so many silent pictures, people never knew he had such a wonderful voice."

Jack scanned the club. Smoke wreathed everything, leaving a pale haze over every lamp. Through the open doors to the terrace he saw Night Comfort. She turned from the lights of the city and met his eyes. Onstage Valentino continued to sing.

And Jack felt the loneliness of this place; this city of the dead, filled with empty people lost like seashells among the sand of glamour and light. Valentino ended the song, bowed once to the crowded room, then wordlessly stepped from the stage and returned to his seat. The men with him laughed and patted him on the back, but Valentino's mood seemed to have changed. He waved them off and looked at Jack and said, "You wanted to speak with me? About what?"

"Arden sent me," Jack said, unsure of how to respond.

Valentino was playing with two speared olives, rolling them around in the clear liquid of a martini glass. He pulled the olives out and slid one into his mouth, chewing thoughtfully. Then he turned to the man next to him, a tanned Brazilian-looking Synthate with jet-black hair. He offered the other olive to the man.

Valentino turned back to Jack. "Let's go. You and me. I'm tired of this place. These slot machines give me a headache. I want to go home. Will you take me home? I need attention tonight."

Jack leaned back slightly. "I'm not . . . um . . ."

"A fag?" Valentino asked. "Believe me, if I'd wanted that from you I could take it." Valentino stood up, the men at the table watching him, waiting. "Well, I'm leaving. Julian, give me a hug."

Chosen, the Brazilian stood and Valentino hugged him, then kissed him on the cheek and pulled away. "You're killing me."

Valentino turned, patted Jack on the back, and walked out of the casino. Jack followed him across the floor, past blackjack tables, then down the long marble staircase and out onto the warm street. Valentino's automobile, a cream-colored Avions Voisin convertible with big, shining silver headlights, was parked out front of the Deco.

"Get in," Valentino said, opening the driver's door.

Valentino was quiet during the ride, the sweet smell of alcohol lingering in the pools of stagnant air inside the car. He lived in a penthouse in the old Ritz-Carlton, directly on the park. The building had long been abandoned by naturals and now housed only the most influential Synthates. Valentino left the car out front and they passed through the main lobby, heading up in a marble-covered elevator.

The elevator doors opened and Valentino staggered out. A manservant in a tuxedo stood in attendance at the edge of a long black-and-white-tiled hallway.

"Mrs. Valentino is awaiting you in the library, sir," the butler said.

Jack wasn't sure if the butler had seen him yet, but if he had, he gave no indication of surprise.

"Fine, Edward, tell her I'll be in," Valentino said.

"Very good, sir."

The butler disappeared behind a door at the far end of the hallway and Valentino turned back to Jack, indicating a room off to the side. "Wait in there if you like. The reception room."

Then he headed off after the butler. A door closed. After that came voices, angry voices, male and female, a subdued argument taking place somewhere in the penthouse. Jack stepped into the dark reception room. He flicked on the light switch and two gas lamps behind colored glass sparked to life.

The reception room was large and luxurious. Two leather sofas formed an L in the center around a glass table topped with picture books on New York City. A large bay window across the front looked out on Central Park. A big electric crystal radio sat in the corner of the room, framed in mahogany wood.

The walls were hung with various arms, an Indo-Persian round shield and battle ax, a spiked Iranian war helmet, and an eighteenth-century English smallsword. Seeming out of place hung a reproduction of Renoir's *Dance at Bougival.* Jack remembered seeing the same reproduction from one of his tours of the Roosevelt Island Genico Grow Garden.

Alongside the painting were clippings from the front pages of various newspapers, each from the summer of 1926, set in frames and placed along the wall.

U.S. Commander Byrd First to Fly Over North Pole

Gertrude Ederle First Woman to Swim English Channel

Rudolph Valentino, 'The Sheik,' Cinema Heartthrob, Dies of Perforated Ulcer at 31

Jack sat down on one of the leather sofas and picked up *Motion Picture* magazine from off the glass table, the cover fronted by an illustration of Rudolph Valentino wearing a long desert turban from the movie *The Son of the Sheik.* Jack opened the magazine, becoming so engrossed in flipping through old articles that he didn't hear Valentino come back into the room. The Synthate walked to the liquor cabinet, poured a drink, went to the window, and looked out across the park.

"Genico is making a theme park in California," he said. "Old Hollywood. They'll populate it with Synthates like me, have the public come. Charge for tickets. There were twenty thousand one hundred and twelve trees of thirty-seven different varieties in Beverly Hills in 1929," Valentino said. "You know how many trees the Beverly Hills section of the new Genico park has? Twenty thousand one hundred and twelve with thirty-seven different varieties. The exact number. It took them eight years to get that right."

Valentino swirled his drink, then sipped again.

"Listen, I need to talk to you about things that have happened to me," Jack said. "My name is Jack Saxton, I—"

"I know who you are," Valentino interrupted. "What's happened to you."

"That's why I came to see you, because I don't know. I don't know why I'm here. What happened to me. They said I murdered all these people, but I didn't. And then they said I was a Synthate, which I'm not. I'm natural."

"And what am I?" Valentino said, turning away from the window. "I'm a Synthate. So, if I'm not natural, then who am I?"

He moved to the front-page newspaper headline. *Rudolph Valentino Dies at Age 31.*

"Am I him?" Valentino asked, looking at the headline. "Is he me? Are we the same person, just ages apart? I turn thirty-one in two months. Genico runs this place. Do you think they're going to let me live to see thirty-two? That would be factually inaccurate. These people know the exact number of fucking trees in Beverly Hills. Do you think they would let their biggest star be older than thirty-one?"

"I'm sorry. I didn't know."

"Rudolph Valentino made thirty-two movies between 1917 and 1926. Do you know how many movies Rudolph Valentino, me, how many I have made?"

Jack shook his head. "No."

"None. I have never made a movie in my life. I am indistinguishable from Rudolph Valentino and all I am is a living picture in this history book they call Necropolis. That's all I am. A picture in a book. And when I reach thirty-one, they'll tear out the picture and throw me away.

"Valentino had a wife, so that means I must also have a wife. So they marry me to a woman I have no feelings for. I do have feelings, desires, but not toward my wife. How do I explain that to the governors? I am the same genetically as Valentino, so he must have had these feelings and desires, the ones that I have, but in public life he was married. So I too must be married and carry on this pretense."

"I'm sorry," Jack said again.

"Yes, well, the show must go on. And you . . . you, my beautiful boy, this is your first time in this fabulous staged production. You're the main character. The controversial male lead. You were born to play this part."

"No . . . no . . . this is a mistake."

"Twenty thousand one hundred twelve trees. Not one more, not one less. These people do not make mistakes. You are here for a reason, whether you know it or not."

"But I didn't kill those people."

"I believe you."

"So why am I here?"

"They want you here." Valentino smiled. "This city is a glimmering illusion, built around wealth and power. It's a deception that hides a very dark and lonely place, my friend. Perhaps the darkest and loneliest city in the world."

"And you've been here your entire life?"

"I was made to live here. That is my role in this production. You need to find out yours."

"How?"

"You were arrested as a Synthate and charged with murders. You're biotech property so were never tried. Just assumed guilty. This has been going on for years. We make the easiest targets because we have no rights. But the question is, what do you want to do?"

"I want to prove my innocence. I want revenge on the people that did this to me. There was a woman I loved. They took her."

"Did you know Martin Reynolds?"

Jack thought of the murdered scientist. "Very little. I knew he worked at Genico."

"He was a good man. He was there at my birth." Valentino rolled up his sleeve, exposing his forearm. On his skin was a bioprint of a single staff of sheet music. "I'm a Synthate mimic. I was allowed to have a bioprint in a less conspicuous area."

"What's the music for?"

"To always remember the creative spirit. It's 'Ode to Joy,'" Valentino said. "And that's why he gave me that." Valentino motioned to the reproduction of the *Dance at Bougival* painting that hung from the wall. "Do you know that painting?"

"I've seen it before."

"How far are you willing to take this?"

"I've got nothing to lose. I'll take it all the way."

"You're still alive, aren't you? That's something. They will not hesitate to take that away from you. Safe as long as you don't question. That's the rule of the zones. When you don't follow the rules . . ."

"I'm ready."

Valentino walked to a large art deco cabinet covered in mosaics beneath the Persian helmet. He opened one of the drawers, took out a leather-bound portfolio, and put it on top of the cabinet. Then he turned back to his guest. Jack took a step forward and Valentino hugged him tightly, resting his head on Jack's shoulder. "I love you, Jack. I love you inside and out and would never do anything to hurt you."

"You just met me."

"I know you more than you could imagine. My time here is almost gone. I'm scared and I'm pathetic. But you have given me hope."

Then Valentino kissed Jack on the cheek. "Everything you need is in that portfolio. Arden will know what to do with it."

"Why are you helping me?"

"Your father was a great man. Not the man who raised you. But your real father."

Jack blinked. No one had ever spoken of his real father before. "You knew my father?"

"We've all heard the stories. If you want to know about your father, there's someone you should see."

"Where?"

"There's a village deep in the park. My butler knows the way." Valentino sat on the edge of the sofa and pressed his fingers against the bridge of his nose. "Tomorrow the Games begin again. Good luck in battle."

CHAPTER 34

During the housing crisis, Central Park had filled with the homeless and addicts. As a result, few had complained when large portions of the park had been purchased anonymously by a private corporation. After the dirty bomb left the entire southern section contaminated, a clear containment dome was constructed and the area was left abandoned. A single red metal door was cut into the wall, and from his pocket, the butler produced a large key.

He turned the key in the lock and the sound of a deadbolt clanked loudly. The butler pushed open the door to reveal a concrete corridor beyond. Masks hung from the wall. The butler indicated one. "You might be more comfortable with one, sir."

Jack strapped the mask over his face. Inside, the air stunk of plastic. "Shouldn't I be wearing a suit or something?"

"Stay briefly and you'll be safe. The Ramble is through here. They're expecting you."

"Are you coming with me?"

The butler shook his head. "I'm afraid I'm not invited."

Jack stepped through the doorway and the butler shut the door behind him. The key turned and the deadbolt sounded again, locking

Jack inside. The corridor was lit by a series of overhead bulbs that extended the entire twenty feet of its length. At the far end was the edge of the dome. The surface was clear and strong with a door cut in the middle. Jack wondered how much radiation could actually penetrate the dome. He could be exposed right now and not even know it.

The dome's door slid open and Jack paused. The mask he wore seemed like a Cold War relic and he wasn't sure how much protection it would actually offer. The butler had told him to stay only briefly, but he didn't mention how long "briefly" actually was. Jack inhaled a last final breath of clean air and stepped through the open doorway.

Beyond was a strange sight.

The lights of a small village lay along the banks of a pond ringed by trees. The village was composed of two dozen small whitewashed cottages illuminated by waxen lanterns, lit brightly in the darkness. Above the line of the forest towered the dome, and through the clear surface was the Manhattan skyline.

But the surface wasn't completely clear. Instead an image was projected onto the dome itself, a 3Dee of an abandoned park thick with wild growth.

A gravel path wound between oak trees and snaked around the edge of the pond toward the village. Night Comfort stood at the edge of the path in a white cotton dress. She wore no mask. She smiled at him. "Welcome to the Ramble."

CHAPTER 35

The bathroom stalls were the size of phone booths, with no locking doors and white frosted windows the color of the exotic substance that fellow broker Mike Gorfinkle had neatly tucked away inside small paper envelopes hidden in the change pocket of his jeans. Phillip was inside the phone booth with him, one of his Ferragamo loafers propped up on the side of the clear glass toilet rim.

The blackish skin of the Ferragamo was very lightly dusted with white powder. Seeing this, Phillip carefully undid his shoe, held it up to his nose, and vacuumed his nostril across the smooth alligator surface. The door to the bathroom opened, revealing the dark, anonymous throb of the nightclub, before a girl with a small dog tucked inside her shirt appeared. She stared at Phillip and Gorfinkle with a shocked, vaguely disgusted look before Phillip pushed her back out into the belly of the club and pulled the telephone booth door shut. Through the thin frosted glass, A Flock of Seagulls blared, circa 1982, "I Ran (So Far Away)."

They were somewhere deep in the beating heart of Club USA. It was three a.m. Work was four hours away. Mama Blanca, your mind, only faster. The door to the phone booth opened again. This time a man appeared on roller skates in an all-white suit that glittered in strobe, seemingly in time to the Tommy Tutone song that started across the floor. He eyed Phillip, then Gorfinkle, then the small packet of Mama Blanca, and took a step forward. "I'll suck your dick for a bump."

Phillip pushed him back with a quick, "Do you mind?" before slamming the door shut and focusing again at the task at hand.

The task, somehow obscured by the pounding music and the phone booth and the strobe lights, was to put as much Mama into his nose as humanly possible.

"We are the backbone of society," Phillip said as he focused carefully on unwrapping the small white paper. "The backbone. I mean, look at us, what we do . . . am I wrong in wanting to drive a Ferrari? Is that a wrong thing? I mean we save people's lives. Shouldn't I at least have a Ferrari, or a honeycomb in Tribeca? Fuck a honeycomb, an actual apartment. I mean, am I off base here?"

Gorfinkle shook his head.

"People buy what we sell them, and it saves their lives and makes everyone mao, and there's no downside, and I don't understand how shit like this can even be printed." Phillip pulled a folded *Wall Street Journal* from his back pocket and waved it too quickly in front of Gorfinkle's face. *Heartless Samp Industry of Wealth.* "I just want a Ferrari."

"We all want a Ferrari."

"I'm Ivy League educated, I'm handsome, in great shape . . . I mean, since when are we supposed to be punished for being successful? What, I should be poor and degenerate and work like a fucking Synthate so liberals don't force their guilt on me?"

The Mama Blanca took effect suddenly and Phillip reeled back. He closed his eyes for a moment and reopened them, energized. Without further word, he kicked open the telephone booth bathroom door and emerged roughly into the crowd, pushing people aside as he headed for the throbbing dance floor.

Gorfinkle followed behind, almost overpowered by Exposé's "Let Me Be the One" that boomed out of the speakers hoisted around them. Phillip hit the dance floor like a force, his body thrusting in hyperactive action. Above him, four too-perfect Synthate Socials danced together on mirrored pedestals. The dance floor was crowded, but Phillip pushed toward them. Taking off his tie, he twirled it over his head before he snatched a wad of mao from his pocket and threw it up to the women. Gorfinkle reached out to pull him away from the crowd, but abruptly Phillip's face went red, then white, and he collapsed backward, striking his head against the mirror side of the pedestal. There was the loud clunk of bone, and Phillip deflated as he stared wildly around at the crowd, a trickle of blood forming at the base of his nose.

And Jack was there. But Phillip knew he couldn't be there. He smiled slyly, another one of Mama's tricks. He focused on Jack, recognition bubbling up from somewhere deep inside. The trader reached up and grabbed the lapel of his brother's suit jacket. Phillip's mouth opened as he tried to speak, tried to impart some final wisdom before Mama Blanca closed the curtain.

Phillip pulled Jack down toward him. "I . . . just . . . wanted . . . a . . . Ferrari."

Then Jack morphed back to Gorfinkle, and Phillip's eyes glazed and he turned to face the lights and the dancing girls. He opened his mouth to speak again before his words dissolved into the mumbling mantra. "A Ferrari, Ferrari, Ferrari . . ." as hundred-yuan notes fell around them like ticker tape.

CHAPTER 36

The afternoon was warm when Jack finally awoke in the village in the Ramble.

He lay on his back and looked up at the crisscross pattern of dried wood that layered the ceiling. His head felt mercury filled, but slowly the night came back to him. He was inside one of the small cottages. Warm sun streamed through windows on the far wall and the open door, casting bright rectangles of light on the floor in front of him. Behind him was a small cot, to his right a wooden desk topped by a vase filled with wildflowers.

His wounds from the battle had healed to dull black blotches that covered his body like smudges of charcoal. He pushed himself upright, stood, and walked to the open doorway. The cottage was on the rise of a hill overlooking a pond, the tops of Upper West Side apartment buildings visible in the distance through the 3Dee projected onto the dome.

Night Comfort was sweeping the front walkway. She stopped when she saw Jack and nodded up at the dome. "There are four eyeScreen projectors that 3Dee the abandoned images against the inside of the dome. From the outside, looks just like an empty park."

"But the dirty bomb attack? The radiation?"

"There was never any attack. There was never any radiation. It was all your human father's idea."

"My father?"

"He wanted to create a haven for Synthates. Someplace outside the zones where the crushers couldn't go." Night Comfort paused, correcting herself. "Where the crushers wouldn't go. He invented the dirty bomb scare to keep away the naturals."

"But there was radiation," Jack said, remembering images of Geiger counter needles swinging wildly and entire blocks being evacuated.

"A little. Carefully controlled at harmless levels. The scientists were all Genico employees. They advised a quarantine and it was Genico who built the dome. Outside, the world thinks there will be toxic radiation levels for the next three hundred years. But inside, we're quite safe."

"And the projectors 3Dee the park slowly going wild."

"If we're to live here, we need people to believe this is all abandoned. We 3Dee images and hide beneath the canopy. We have no other technology here so our power levels never register on the grid."

"What about the trackers? I thought Synthates all had one."

"The projectors reflect the signal, put the tracker position just outside the dome in the Synthate Midtown Zone. Won't work if the crushers are really looking for you, but it's a good temporary measure."

"My father did all this?"

"Your father always believed Synthates needed a home."

A fieldstone path led down the slope toward the water, running between cypress trees and fragrant herb gardens. More cottages dotted the hill, each of them made from a cream-colored adobe tiled with faded red clay and outfitted with bleached-blue windowsills.

Synthates of varying ages and classes worked in gardens that lined the edges of the algae-colored pond. They wore simple clothes. Jack saw no syncs or eyeScreens.

"If you really want answers, I can take you to see someone."

"Who?"

"His name is Alphacon," Night Comfort said. "He's one of the oldest living Synthates. He can tell you much about everything."

The sun was beginning to set, the air still warm, the woods buzzing with insects as Jack and Night Comfort made their way along the gravel path. Alphacon lived north of the pond in what had once been the Central Park Zoo. Most of what remained of the original structure was still present, faded and crumbling now after years without upkeep. A wide brick entrance was topped by a clock and surrounded by fantastic animal sculptures. A glass display case covered with lichen advertised the menu at a snack bar now closed for years.

They walked through the main gates, passing empty ticket booths and lion cages and concession stands. She led Jack down a glass arcade. Much of the glass had been broken, leaving bare metal frames that looked up to the sky. On either side of them was murky water, areas that had once been home to various wild creatures now left vacant and molded with leaves.

At the end of the arcade was an octagonal building of brick and glass. A small pillar of smoke rose from a chimney in the center. Illuminated paper lanterns fluttered in the breeze. Outside stood a man.

He was not old, exactly, but not young, either, his age almost indiscernible. Somewhere perhaps in his late fifties, but with the strength of a much younger man. His skin was tan and shining, his hair white, his body still muscled from a youth of heavy activity. He wore a charcoal-colored suit with a white panama hat. He took Night Comfort's shoulders and kissed her on the cheek.

"My girl, it is good to see you." Alphacon smiled.

Night Comfort returned a genuine smile. "I want you to meet someone."

"Of course." Alphacon took Jack's hand warmly. "I know who you are."

Night Comfort left them and sat on a shaded bench beneath a stand of oak trees. Behind her, long fields of hay grass had reclaimed the tiger habitat, giving off the sound of cicadas.

Alphacon studied Jack. "To find you here, after all this time."

Around the outside of the building were old carousel animals: A brightly painted tiger snarling. A horse rearing its wooden body, white and blue. A zebra twisting its head and looking skyward. Alphacon sat in a green-and-red wooden chariot, two cherubs painted on either side, the chariot's front fashioned into a dragon head. Jack leaned against a white swan.

Alphacon's knuckles were covered in the deep scars of a Guard class. Of someone who had fought in the Games. His bioprint was an open field in summer. "Alphacon, my name. Do you know what it means?"

"No."

"Alpha is the first letter in the Greek alphabet. My name was given to me because I was in the first Synthate harvest."

Alphacon removed from his pocket a 2Dee image of twenty or so Synthates grouped in two rows on a stone stairwell.

"That is me, years ago." Alphacon pointed at a much-younger face. "That was the group I trained with. All of those men are now dead. Killed in the Games. Your father was one of them."

Alphacon touched a face in the back row. The Synthate in the 2Dee was tall, handsome almost to excess, to the point of appearing cruel, and yet he was the only one in the photo who smiled. That smile made him kind, his eyes not yet darkened by what the Games were sure to show him.

Slowly Jack began to see himself in that face. The curve of the chin, the shape of the eyes all somehow familiar to him. The small points that combined together to form a whole, to give a sense of a person, he shared with this stranger in the 2Dee.

Jack's throat went dry. "My father?"

"He was the best friend I had," Alphacon said.

And Jack's own fragmented past, always filled with blank spots, suddenly presented itself in one complete whole. Jack understood where he had come from. How he had come to be. He was part of that man in the 2Dee. His connection to the past. And suddenly he felt an anchor with life.

"What was his name?" Jack asked.

"Titus."

"What happened to him?"

"It is a Synthate story," Alphacon said. "We fought together for many years, not just in the Games. They sent us secretly into Iran. Syria. Saudi Arabia. Your father saved my life many times. He was very brave. Very fierce. And then he met your mother.

"She was one of the doctors who tended to wounded Synthates. Back then, medical students worked on Synthates during their schooling. That's when a miracle happened."

"What?"

"She became pregnant."

"I thought Synthates couldn't have children," Jack said.

"They can't. This is why your birth was a miracle. I don't think you realize how important you are. You're the only one of your kind. Half-Synthate. Half-natural. You are proof that we are as human as they are. That we're their property no longer. And this gives us all hope."

"So my stepfather knew I was a Synthate?"

"Of course. Your stepfather did what he could for us. But he was still a natural. We need to be led by a Synthate. We need to be led by someone like you."

Jack shook his head. Now was not the time. He wasn't ready to give up his hate. All he had left was his hatred. That's what made him strong. And that's what he needed now.

"My wife was taken from me. Murdered. When the men responsible for her death are also dead," Jack said, "then we can talk again."

"I understand." Alphacon grasped Jack's shoulder. "Your stepfather created your genetic line. The same line your Synthate father passed on to you. So in some ways, the head of Genico was as much a father to you as your Synthate father. He did everything he could to protect you. But now he's gone. And everything he feared has happened."

"How did he die?" Jack said.

"We don't know that."

They walked back down the arcade to where Night Comfort waited for Jack. As they reached the end of the path, Alphacon said, "If you continue with this investigation, they will kill you eventually. Maybe here you could find peace."

"I will have no peace until this over."

"Take this." Alphacon handed Jack a sync. "You can always reach me. Genico seeks to enslave even naturals themselves. Enslave them with disease."

"What do you mean?"

"Look at their Ituri project. Something there is making naturals sick," Alphacon said and shook Jack's hand. "Good luck. It has been good to see you. It is like seeing your father again."

Jack rejoined Night Comfort, and they walked together between the cypress trees down the length of the dirt path. The air was warm as the sun dropped toward the horizon, a shimmering ladle dipping down between distant buildings beyond the dome.

Together they sat on rocks by the edge of the pond.

Night Comfort turned to him. "The greatest trick the genetic industry ever pulled is convincing the world that Synthates don't have a soul. If you believe that, you'll never feel equal to naturals."

Valentino had been right. If Synthates weren't human, then what were they? Certainly something more than reflections on water, something that dissolved at the touch.

"You know . . . I haven't much time here," Jack said slowly. "Tomorrow the Games begin again."

"You could stay here. With me."

Jack shook his head. "I have to go. Eventually the naturals will win. They always win. And I'll be dead. I just want to make things right before that happens."

They were all dying, a little bit each day, and there never seemed to be enough time. For *them*, for the naturals, maybe there was a heaven. But for us, Jack thought, there was what? In time, death comes for us all, but it only takes *them* to that place beyond. What was left for Synthates? And if Dolce were truly a Synthate, then where had she gone in death? Jack could not imagine her in a cold place. Dark and lonely forever. He would not believe it.

After a time, they walked back to Night Comfort's home. The cottage was cooling in the evening air and she hung paper lanterns until the trees glowed with candlelight. They sat together on steps that led down toward the lake. The water was quiet and shimmered with moonlight. Boats were moored along the edge, and further back lights in windows reflected out over the water.

"It's strange," Night Comfort said. "My life has been filled with such horrible moments that I've learned how to tune them out. Like I've taken a dose of Amnease. But now the only thing I want is to stay here, soak myself in this moment of peace, like a tree putting its roots to water.

"The water flows through the roots into the leaves, like I want this moment to flow into me. But if I have no soul, then I have no place to store these times. Everything flows out of me."

And when you leave, will I be able to remember these feelings?

Night Comfort closed her eyes and rested her head against his shoulder.

In the dawn, she walked him to the gateway out of the Ramble.

"The Games are tonight," she said. "It's going to be a tough battle. They made the announcement, fourteenth-century weapons. That favors the heavier, more physical Synthates. You're not favorited to win."

From a canvas bag slung on her shoulder she pulled a sword, a long, heavy blade almost three feet in length. Patterns were engraved on the metal, with an inscription in Latin.

"And so I seek justice," Night Comfort read aloud, and passed the sword to Jack. She also presented a helmet, beautifully crafted, embossed with scenes of a battle between a fierce tribe of ancient Greece and their mythical half-man, half-horse enemy. "These were once worn by great kings and warriors."

"How did they end up here?"

"Liberated from museums." She closed her arms around him and put her mouth to his ear. "May God protect you."

"I thought there was no God for Synthates."

"There is. And he knows everything."

"You sound like Dolce."

Night Comfort took his hand. "A transport will take you back to the Synthate holding zone on Governors Island. Arden will meet you there. You must survive. Whatever it takes."

"I will see you again. I promise," Jack said as he returned the sword and helmet to the bag. "In this world or the other."

CHAPTER 37

In the Synthate Zone on Governors Island, the air was cooler along the harbor, the water crowded with wave farms and slowly moving aqua bots. Arden waited for Jack near the harbor's edge, as a storm broke over the water and heavy thunderclouds sailed across the sky like ships. A deep gray hung over Wall Street. The Games were tonight.

Jack handed the leather-bound portfolio to Arden. "This is from Valentino. I did my part. Now tell me how to get back to the natural world."

The detective handed binoculars to Jack and pointed across the water. They were slightly south of Manhattan. The line of the collapsed Brooklyn Bridge and the jutting piers of the Seaport wave farm jumped into view.

"Look north," Arden said. "See anything familiar?"

Rising above the Manhattan skyline was the slowly rotating sky turbine of the Genico corporation.

"We're going to break in," Arden said.

Jack lowered the binoculars and looked at Arden. "Why would I do that?"

"I think Reynolds's murderer was a Genico Synthate. The only way to prove that is to access the Genico vidDrive, inside the building."

"Why would you help me?"

"Because I need to get into Genico, too. And I need your help to do it. You've been inside before. You know your way around. My daughter is dying. I think Genico has the cure."

"How do we get inside?" Jack asked. "I don't have access anymore."

Arden held up the packet Rudolph had given them. "Everything we need is in here. Access codes. Security details. Collected by Synthate cleaners and construction workers who make the building operate."

"But I can't leave this island. I'm restricted."

"I know a way. During the battle with Baltimore tonight, look for the black stone castle. At its base you'll find a gate. Beneath the gate is a tunnel. Someone will meet you there."

"And the tracking chip?" Jack said. "They'll know the moment I leave the island."

"So we'll take the tracker out."

"But I thought it never came out."

Arden sighed. "That's not exactly true. There is one time . . ."

"What time is that?"

"When you're dead."

Long armored transports brought Jack and the rest of the Synthates into the stadium. Lines of crushers formed as they exited the vehicles deep below the structure and entered the armorer's room. From above, the sound of the crowd pulsed through concrete like distant waves. Regal Blue walked with Jack past the line of crushers. "Cowards," Regal Blue said. "All of them. Think they're big men with their stun sticks and their armor. Let them go in and fight."

The armorer's room was a vast open space filled with medieval weaponry displayed on heavy wooden racks. Swords of all lengths were surrounded by maces, crossbows, and bows. Nearby, lined along the floor, were helmets, shields, and chest plates.

Coach Sharp stood with the team of armorers. A map of the field 3Deed in space from his sync.

"Take your pick. Synths trained as archers take bows, everyone else hand weapons," one of the armorers called out. "Step up now."

The Synthates moved in a line, taking up weapons from the rack and testing them out with a few short swings or pulls of a bow. Jack saw Sky King heft a large ax, too heavy for any normal man, and swing it easily in a long arc, the blade whistling through the air. Jack moved to the corner of the room, removed the equipment and weapons Night Comfort had given him and set them carefully to the side. One of the armorer assistants moved through the crowd, passing out blue coats of thick wool, the Braves emblem emblazoned on the front. Regal Blue joined him. He carried a heavy, spiked mace in one hand, a long, battered shield in the other.

From above, an air horn sounded.

"Let's go now. Be brave. It's almost over," Coach Sharp called out. The armed Synthates moved at a double-time step to the base of the entrance ramp leading up to the field. The noise of the crowd was thunderous. Jack felt the familiar butterflies in his stomach. He gripped his sword to stop his hand from shaking.

Around him were a hundred Synthates. Jack wondered how many of them would die out there. He scratched the tip of his sword blade across the concrete. Soon the weapon would be red with blood. Tonight they fought the Baltimore Raiders, the only undefeated team in the Games.

A priest walked the ramp, sprinkling the Synthates with holy water, giving benediction in Latin.

"They say I have no soul," Regal Blue whispered as the priest passed by. "So what then are they blessing?"

Jack put on the helmet Night Comfort had given him, raised the visor, and looked out between the iron eyeholes. Sky King met Jack's gaze.

"If I knew of a way to escape, would you come with me?" Jack whispered.

Sky King looked at him. "That's impossible. There's no escape from here."

At the front, the big door began rolling open. Light and sound streamed down. Then a whistle sounded and the Braves moved up toward the battlefield.

The noise outside the gates was now deafening.

To their left rose a large sandstone castle, five stories in height, a city block in width, with six turrets. Atop them, Braves' banners whipped in the wind. The New York mascot rode hard toward the center of the field, waving the Braves' flag overhead as the crowd cheered. Coach Sharp and his assistants jogged toward the sideline bunkers. Jack scanned further across the field. On the Baltimore side, two hundred yards distant, rose another castle. This one was black. Black stone, like Arden had said. That was how they would escape.

The escape route was on Baltimore's side.

As the loudspeaker announced the arrival of Baltimore, the Raiders poured out onto the field. Both teams took off their helmets as the first notes of "The Star-Spangled Banner" sounded.

Then the lights went out. Jack looked up through the open dome, considering the night sky, still peaceful. There was a burst of sound, the call to battle, harsh and irrevocable.

The Braves ran over the grass, mounted ladders up the side of their own castle and ascended the walls. Directly below, at the base of the wall, were large pools of water.

"Watch the surface of the water," Regal Blue said. "If it ripples, a tunnel is being dug beneath us."

From the top, Jack could see the breadth of the battlefield. On the opposite side, their opponents mounted the black castle. Each Raider held a flaming torch, making their position on their wall resemble a trail of fireflies moving across the rough stone. A Baltimore drum played, its beat deep and insistent across the dark field.

Jack felt nauseous warmth spread through him. He dived deep inside himself, swam into the black hatred. He needed it now. He thought of Dolce, alone in that dark place. Dying because of them. And this fed his anger.

Torches were spread along their walls along with large cauldrons filled with black oil. Handed a long bow, Jack took it and tested the strength of the line. The ends of the arrows were wrapped in rags and soaked in gasoline.

Everything around Jack seemed to be rolling. The shadows on the walls undulated in the flicker of the torches. The crowd rose and fell in waves of color. The smoke wafted and spread across the field. Everything moved with flames and sound and the furious preparation of violence.

"Ladies and gentlemen of New York . . ." The announcer's voice pierced the darkness. "Are you ready for war?"

There was no turning back. It was what the crowd demanded, and their thirst for brutality flowed into Jack like electricity. A buzzer sounded.

Jack saw a mass of movement on the Baltimore side. The Raiders streamed down the side of their castle wall. Their torches advanced over black ground.

"They're going to attack," Regal Blue said.

The crowd cheered, "Defense! Defense! Defense!" Inside the chain of torches, a long dark shape stretched out menacingly. Then slowly the mass began to move across the field toward them.

"What is it?" Jack asked.

"Battering ram," Regal Blue replied.

Soon its outline was clearer to discern. Jack saw that the weapon had two parts. First was a long wooden shed, topped with animal skins and mounted on wooden wheels. Beneath that defensive structure hung the smooth trunk of a massive tree. Its end had been tapered to a point and capped with iron, then suspended by thick chains from a support beam running lengthwise on the shed's roof. Pushing together, twenty Synthates, straining against the weight, edged the weapon over the field toward the Braves.

"When they get within a hundred yards of us," Sky King instructed, "fire flame the arrows and use the longbows. Burn them!"

A sense of suspended time now took over, with the New York Synthates leaning against the parapets watching the attackers' progress.

"Here they come!" Sky King shouted.

The giant ram picked up speed. The rest of the Baltimore cohort, behind on their castle wall, cheered while the drums beat faster.

"Archers ready!" Sky King shouted.

Jack took up the longbow and notched one of the arrows.

"Flame your arrows!"

Small flames from the fifty bows lit up all along the New York castle wall.

"Aim!"

Jack pulled back on the longbow, felt the wood go tight against his hand, bending against the force of the line. The arrow was notched and against his ear, the flaming tip hot against his gloved hand. He sighted down the shaft, aimed high over the approaching enemy. The battering ram moved up an incline and he could see the attackers looking up at the rows of archers' flames. Moving in tighter against the ram, they gathered under the protective roof of the shed.

"Fire!"

The air filled with the whisk of arrows. Flames cut across the darkness like tiny meteorites, trailing smoke and fire. Jack heard cries and calls of "Take cover!" from the crew of the battering ram below them, now only yards distant. Stopping short, the Raiders sheltered beneath their massive burden. Rapt, the crowd rose in expectation as the arrows reached the pinnacle of their ascent and began to fall back to Earth.

Waiting. Waiting. Now!

The arrows pierced wood, earth, and flesh in an assembly of sounds, the ground lit with the flames of burning points. Then the ram began moving again, even as small fires broke out across the top shelter.

Jack and the rest of his team notched flaming arrows and fired once more. The fiery points again breached the night. Still the battering ram came forward until the heavy wood structure settled against the castle's two doors. Jack could see the opponents massing for their assault.

Cauldrons of heated oil on the Braves' wall began to boil. From below came the first crack of the ram against the wooden doors. As the assault gained in force, the impacts became louder, followed by the creaks of timbers beginning to snap.

"Give them the oil!" Sky King said.

The cauldrons went over, spilling blackness down the wall and onto the already-burning battering ram. First came a rushing explosion as oil turned to flame when it struck wood. Molten liquid fire spread out across everything below. Then came the screams. Fire was everywhere below, and even five stories up, Jack could feel the heat against his face.

Now the booming sounded again. The remaining Raiders still manned the battering ram and pounded again at the castle doors.

"No matter what we throw at them," Regal Blue said, "they'll come at us, again and again. They'll break the door down before we can burn them out."

On the sidelines, one of Sharp's assistants waved a yellow flag overhead, the signal to descend the castle wall and attack on foot.

"We're going to the ground," Sky King ordered, and a dozen ladders went over the side. The ground seethed with fire far below them, a terrible storm of screaming men and burnt flesh. Jack and the others began their descent down the ladders. From the ground came the sound of pulled bows. Arrows fired from below hummed past Jack's head, snapping violently as they struck the wall. Some of them hit their mark, burying deep into flesh as Synthates screamed and fell from the ladders. Finally, Jack reached the ground and unsheathed the long sword Night Comfort had given him.

He ran over the hot ground, its surface like slow-burning charcoal. As he moved, he swung the long sword, feeling it meet flesh and armor. Screams and cheers surrounded him, the Braves still on the wall above shouting their encouragement.

The enemy was less resilient than they had seemed from atop the wall. Fallen Raiders were everywhere, and soon Jack had nothing left at which to aim his sword.

Sky King held his sword up, first toward the cheering crowd and then across the highlands to the Baltimore castle. Sparks and smoke swirled around him as he stepped over the burning timber and past Jack and Regal Blue. "Nothing but death awaits them here."

Yet as Jack watched the burning ram, doubt grew in his mind. Something was wrong. Where were the archers? The foot soldiers? Once the ram had battered down the castle door, there would have been no one to follow the attack. No archers to give cover. This seemed less of an attack, and more of a . . . *what*? Suddenly the word burst on his mind.

A diversion.

This wasn't an attack at all. It was a distraction.

Sky King and the rest of the Braves were still going over the Baltimore dead, checking for survivors and gathering the weapons of the fallen. Jack ignored them and looked back across the field. The grass stretched out before him, still and dark. Much of the crowd was up from their seats, stretching in the lull of battle. Jack, watching, saw the usual lines of people heading for the bathrooms and the concessions. Nothing there.

As his eyes moved down from the seating, they passed over the pools of water spaced evenly around the castle. Bits of ash and dust clung to the surface, moving in slow swirls around each other like dancers across a polished floor. Then the water rippled once, a perfect circle that spread from the center of the pool, ballooning out and out until it hit the rounded edge. Then again, the same slow wave.

"The water ripples!" Jack said. "They're coming in tunnels!"

Sky King looked at Jack and turned his head to gauge the water's speed. The crowd sensed the air of oncoming menace and returned eagerly to their seats.

"Up the ladders," someone called out.

"No time," Sky King said. "They'll be here too soon. Everyone, backs against the wall."

Obeying his command, the Braves moved quickly to the castle, their swords ready. The battering ram continued to burn, throwing ash into the air. The Baltimore dead lay around them, flaming arrows sprouting from their flesh like candles.

The spectators continued to wait expectantly. Jack gave a second's thought to them, with their beer and hot dogs, and, if only for an instant, remembered what it had felt like up there, with no blood in his nostrils, no soot coating his tongue. He imagined what they must look like from the other side of the barrier. The hard plastic seats, cold plastic cup of beer against the hand, and in the distance a castle, a group of Synthates standing and waiting for an attack.

A geyser of soil exploded into air.

Raiders, soiled black and screaming horribly, flooded out of the gaping hole. Some of them carried long ladders and raced to place them against the wall.

The Braves launched a frantic march to meet the dirt-smeared enemy. Jack joined his teammates, dodging arrows raining down from their archers on the castle walls. A Raider stabbed at Jack with a short blade. Jack swiftly pivoted and the blade caught him on the side of the ribs. He butted the Synthate with his elbow, drove him back, then swung the great sword over his head and caught his assailant full in the chest.

Around him were the distorted shapes of men, their faces emerging from the darkness. And there was Jack himself, slashing and screaming for his life.

CHAPTER 38

High above the field, Night Comfort watched the Game. Her perch was one of the few Synthate-only areas, where servers and culinary workers prepared food. Behind her the kitchen was in full swing, plates of food being readied for the naturals below. She hated seeing Synthates killing each other for their masters' entertainment, yet had to know what happened to Jack.

From behind her came a voice.

"I didn't think you would come."

She turned as Arden approached.

"Nor did I," she said. "But I was wrong."

He joined her at the window and together they looked down at the grim spectacle. From this height, it had been difficult to find Jack, but he was down there still. And alive, she could feel it.

She noticed Arden staring at her. "You have a plan to get him out?"

"Yes, there's a plan." He checked his watch. "I don't have much time."

He looked at her, hesitated, then said, "When this is over, when Maggy is well again, could you see yourself coming back?"

Night Comfort responded sadly. "Don't ask me that. I don't want to have to say no to you."

In the beat before Arden spoke, the sound of the crowd cheering filled the entire stadium.

"Yeah, well . . . maybe you'd think about it?"

"Maybe." She gave a faint smile. "But now you should go."

On the field, Sky King turned to Jack. "It's not over yet."

Jack regarded the wound he'd sustained, a gash just below his armor. Blood was flowing freely down the side of his abdomen. From the crowd, a deep moan began to swell. A cadre of forty Baltimore Raiders ran out onto the field to reinforce the line. Climbing up their ladders, they reentered the safety of their castle's bulwarks.

Jack wiped his hand, now slick with blood, against the front of his armor. From behind the enemy castle, he heard the slow creak of timber. Slowly, emerging from the Baltimore castle, a five-story wooden structure came into view, pulled by twenty Synthates. A long single arm the size of a telephone pole extended out from the base, where rings and rings of leaden weights hung past a pivot point on the opposite end. Wooden wheels screeched in resistance.

Jack peered at the device. "What is that?"

"Trebuchet," Sky King said.

Slowly, the great throwing arm began to descend as forty Synthates in unison heaved ropes attached to giant pulleys. Overhead the flags snapped in anticipation as, foot by foot, the timber arm was lowered and then locked in place by thick chains. Soon, its ammunition would also be in place.

The Braves ascended their own ladders once more.

"It has been decided then," Regal Blue said. "We are to die today. They give *them* the trebuchet. We can't fight such odds."

In the distance, a giant clay pot the size of a boulder was being fitted inside the trebuchet's sling. Someone moved forward with a torch, touching it to the black oil inside the vessel, and immediately eager flames erupted. Quickly the blaze grew inside its cradle.

The command to prepare themselves echoed through the Braves' ranks. Jack ducked below the stone parapet. Across the sideline, he saw Baltimore's coach holding his hand in the air. A second later, it fell. The firing pin was pulled and the trebuchet's arm sprung forward, its massive counterweights descending and propelling the flaming meteor up. The spectators caught their breath, the missile highlighted against the night sky.

"Here it comes!"

Jack pressed himself as tightly as he could against the stone wall. There was a rushing sound of air before the moment of impact. The pot exploded, spraying flaming oil on the New York defenders. Jack's face was scorched by burning air. Then Sky King wrenched him away from the heat's growing intensity.

The entire far side of the Braves' castle was engulfed in flames. Oily black smoke clouded the sky, the crowd barely visible through its swirling, angry curtain. Synthates leaped off the walls, jumping for the pools below, the water hissing as it swallowed up fire and scorched flesh.

The trebuchet arm began lowering again for another attack, another lethal missile placed inside the sling.

Calls of "Down!" erupted through the Braves ranks, as the combustion spread.

"Evacuate the castle!" Sky King ordered. "Spread out on the field!"

Ladders once again were dropped over the castle walls and Jack found himself sliding down one. His footing slipped and then he was falling. The ground rushed up to meet him and drove the wind from his lungs. He lay on the grass, stunned, the flaming structure above him, the orange and red perversely beautiful against the night sky. Then he was up on his feet, putting distance between himself and the castle, spreading out from his fellow Braves. Sky King turned to the sideline and pointed his sword toward Coach Sharp.

"Give us more men. We can take the castle now!" he shouted.

The fans also screamed for reinforcements. Sharp looked at Sky King, before, slowly, he turned his back to the Braves.

No one was coming to help them. A decision had been made. The battle was already lost and no reinforcements would be sent in to be killed. Simple strategy. The season was long. Don't waste all your Synthates in one battle.

Jack heard a cry from the far side and saw the enemy castle gates slowly opening. The portcullis was being raised, and from the opening Raiders in orange and black were running toward them. Baltimore was attacking. They were trying to take the field of battle. They intended to kill them all.

Sky King's shoulders sagged. He turned toward Jack. "I will kill for them, but I will not die. You leave tonight?"

"We try."

"Then I'll try with you."

The Raiders onslaught was closing quickly. Another flaming cauldron broke against the walls, spreading a vertical cascade of fire.

Sky King looked slowly up at the Baltimore Synthates rushing them. "It may be too late."

Jack looked around the field. His teammates were massing a defensive line in front of the burning castle. Smoke was everywhere, choking and burning the eyes of every battling Synthate. There were no choices, only the imperative to struggle on, to defend, to kill or be killed.

Then he saw something.

"The tunnels. Baltimore's tunnels. They lead directly back. We must try to take them," Jack said.

In the midst of chaos, Jack found Regal Blue and pulled him back from the front. More smoke had filled the battlefield, obscuring everyone in thick clouds. Baltimore swept into the Braves, the smoke filling with clanging metal. In the chaos, Jack, Regal Blue, and Sky King made their way to a tunnel opening.

The Raiders had come up from the earth through a hole about five feet wide. Taking the torch from Sky King, Jack waved it down into the hole, seeing only dirt and the corpse of an enemy Synthate, three arrow shafts protruding from the front of his chest. Jack jumped down into the hole. The tunnel loomed up before him.

"Move quickly," Sky King said from above.

The walls of the passageway were smooth and symmetrical. Too perfectly formed. Synthates with shovels could not have done this. The construction crew must have come through here yesterday and dug it out with heavy equipment. All the Raiders had been required to do was dig the last few feet.

Jack set off down the tunnel, the torch alternately sputtering and blazing in his hands. Sky King and Regal Blue followed, keeping watch behind them as they went. They could hear the sounds of fighting over-head and clumps of dirt fell from the ceiling. Jack feared the roof might collapse, but then the battle noises faded as they moved further on.

Their route stretched across the entire battlefield, almost two hun-dred yards in length. They covered the distance with increasing speed. Ahead was a single square of light cut in the earth above. Jack turned back to his companions, and then, holding a finger to his lips, he extin-guished his torch in the dirt.

They crept toward the square of light until they were beneath the opening. They were inside Baltimore's castle. Stretching above him were its black stone walls. Cautiously, he raised his head through the open-ing. High on the castle walls, three Raiders stared out across the field, watching the battle.

Jack ducked back down.

"Three guards," he whispered. "Up top."

Jack eased himself up and out of the hole, then crouched. Inside the castle, the framework of the walls was visible. There were pools of water and a large oil pump just to the right of the gatehouse. The three guards atop the wall continued to look out toward the field. Their backs were turned as Sky King and Regal Blue followed Jack.

Keeping low, he crept along the inside wall.

"Where now?" Sky King whispered.

Jack scanned their surroundings. Nearby a metal grating covered another hole in the ground. He pointed and they crept forward. Regal Blue kept his longbow out, an arrow notched and aimed upward toward the guards.

A lock on the grate came apart under Jack's sword, the noise of the battle masking the sound of steel on steel. Sky King lifted up the grate and set it aside. They looked down into the opening.

This time the walls were slick rock, a shaft sliding down about seven feet before bending back underneath the battlefield and off toward the harbor. The trio lowered themselves down and began to move again. As they proceeded, moving as rapidly as possibly, the men heard voices ahead of them in the blackness.

Jack gripped his sword. The voices had to be off somewhere to their right in an adjacent tunnel. To their relief, the voices faded away as they got closer. The Raiders must be moving in the opposite direction. Silence had enveloped them when suddenly they reached a break in the tunnel. Open space extended out indefinitely in front of them. Faintly they could hear the sound of running water. With their eyes adjusted to the darkness, they saw they were coming into a Maglev track.

They'd reached one of the line's tunnels as it moved from the island onward to Lower Manhattan. The track passed just below where they stood.

A large spotlight flashed on, blinding them.

A figure stepped from behind the spotlight and then dimmed the light. He was a slender natural with a gold NYPD detective shield around his neck. He held his hand up. "My name's Detective Dwayne Sanders. I work with Arden. Let's get going. There's not much time."

He held a small, gun-shaped device in his hand, pausing as he saw Sky King and Regal Blue. "There was only supposed to be one."

"The plan's changed," Jack said.

Sanders shook his head. "Not for me it hasn't."

"My friends come out with me. Or I don't leave. Understand?"

After a long moment, Sanders finally shrugged. "Okay. As I said, there isn't much time. Give me your arm."

Without waiting for Jack to comply, he pressed the gun-shaped device into the underside of Jack's wrist.

"What are you doing?" Jack asked.

"We have to remove your tracking device." Sanders pressed the trigger. Immediately metal prongs circled Jack's wrist as a needle jabbed his skin. Further back down the tunnel came the sound of voices and a flash of light. Sky King turned toward them. "We've got company."

The pain spread down Jack's arm as Sanders worked to remove the tracking chip. Jack could feel the needle as it probed the tissue. Regal Blue and Sky King were poised now in positions of defense. Torchlight flickered against the stone surface, and Jack saw a small band of Raiders approaching. Sky King loosed an arrow, catching one in the chest and felling him. The Raiders stopped and spread out quickly in the tunnel.

In the distance, Jack heard the whir of the Maglev train approaching. Sanders had begun to sweat as he worked the extracting device over Jack's arm. There was a sharp pain and Jack saw a small chip being pulled, finally, from beneath the skin.

"Is that it?" he asked.

Sanders nodded. He placed his trophy inside a small metal case.

"The case shields the chip from being tracked. Later we'll plant it on one of the Synthate dead. They'll assume you were killed during the battle."

The rumble of the train grew louder. At tunnel's edge, Sky King and Regal Blue continued to exchange fire with Baltimore. Sanders looked at them, then at the approaching beam of the Maglev.

"Your friends," Sanders said, "had better hurry."

"I'm not leaving without them."

Jack drew his sword and ran back. Sky King turned toward him. He grimaced in pain, and Jack saw an arrow protruding from his right thigh.

"No!" Sky King shouted. "There's no time!"

Jack shook his head. "We go together."

"Tonight, you go alone. We'll hold them as long as we can."

Further down the tunnel, more Raiders appeared. Too many to fight. Sanders tugged Jack's shoulder. "It's time," he said. "It's now or not at all."

"Go." Regal Blue echoed Sky King.

Regal Blue clasped Jack's hand, and then Jack turned and ran toward the Maglev line.

"The train will stop for twelve seconds. No more than that," Sanders said. He threw a bag toward Jack. "Clothes in there. Put them on."

Inside the bag were heavy work pants and a shirt, as well as a battered hardhat and boots. Jack stripped off his armor and began changing. The Maglev train pulled along the tracks underneath them, its brakes screeching as it rolled to a stop. "Go now," Sanders said. "Jump. Get inside the last car. Arden's meeting you there."

With a last look back at Regal Blue and Sky King, he jumped. The roof of the train was slick, and his momentum caused him to slide out toward the edge. His legs lifted off the side of the train, and for a moment his body dangled in the air. Then his hands and fingers found a safety lamp affixed to the car's side, and his body jerked to a stop. His knees struck the side of the car and new pain jolted through him.

The train began to move again, slowly at first, then gathering speed. Jack felt a rush of air as he was pulled forward. Soon it would descend beneath the harbor. If he was still on the roof, he would drown. Ignoring his throbbing knee, he pulled himself forward. With the train reaching top speed, the wind now began to pry him off his perch.

Carefully he inched his way toward the gap between cars and dropped down between them. A whir sounded as the waterproof sheathing surrounded the train. A moment later, the Maglev veered sharply downward. It vibrated slightly as it entered the water and the white froth of the disturbed East River slid past the clear shield.

Jack pulled open the door to the car and stepped inside.

Inside, the train was crowded. With his head down, Jack continued toward the rear. The wound in his side ached and he pressed one hand against it. To bleed now would draw attention. He made for the train's last car reserved for his kind. Finding an empty seat next to a Synthate in a Sanitation Department uniform, he sat down and waited for Arden. He lifted his shirt slightly. A ten-inch slash mark ran across the line of his ribs. The wound had begun to clot, the blood caked in dried rivulets that ran down his skin. Later he could be stitched up, but now there was nothing to be done.

He lowered his shirt and looked through the window. The blue darkness of the harbor was visible outside and a stream of bubbles slid along the length of the glass. Seconds later, the train broke the harbor's surface, emerging into the night air. Rapidly approaching was the Genico tower, the elevated Maglev rail cutting through the center of the building.

Ahead, Jack saw Arden, bag in hand, walking the length of the car toward him. The detective passed by Jack without a word. Jack stood and followed him. Arden stopped at the rear of the train, and as the Maglev entered the Genico building, elevated five stories up, he pulled the emergency stop lever. Red lights flickered as brakes screeched, throwing everyone forward. An alarm sounded. Arden pushed open the rear door of the car and together he and Jack jumped down onto the rail.

The track was surrounded by a clear tube that cut through the interior of Genico's sky turbine tower. The train had halted in the open space high above the atrium. The two men crouched on the rail, the floor a dizzying fifty feet below. The alarm went off, and the train began to power forward until the two were left alone in the tube.

Arden moved to a maintenance access door on the side of the tube. He pulled an acetylene torch from his bag. Around them, the Genico building was still except for a giant hologram strand of DNA that twisted around itself in slow, constant motion over the atrium. The floors were open to the atrium, so anyone walking along the hallway would have a clear view of them inside the Maglev tube. They were completely exposed.

"Watch for guards," Arden whispered.

Torch flames sparked against metal as Arden went to work cutting open the maintenance door. The lock was thick and the torch cut slowly through it. Jack crouched down next to him, surveying the atrium. The white glow of a flashlight appeared from one of the hallways.

Jack rapped Arden on the shoulder. "Guard!"

Arden cut off the torch, pitching them back into darkness. They crouched in the tube, keeping still and watching as a single guard appeared, making a slow walking tour of one of the hallways. The guard was two or three stories above them, his flashlight beam cutting over their location.

They held their breath and waited. In the distance, Jack heard a faint shriek of metal from further down the tracks, back toward the island. He felt a breeze against his cheek. Next to him, Arden's body went rigid. He reached for the torch and ignited the blue fame.

"What about the guard?" Jack said.

"Do you hear that?" Arden glanced back toward the distant sound. "That's another train coming."

Sparks fell fifty feet to the ground, easily visible in the darkness. The guard continued to walk along the hall. Somehow he hadn't seen them yet. The rumble of the train grew louder and the tube filled with wind. Beneath them the track began to vibrate.

"C'mon, cut, cut!" Arden whispered.

Lights bore down on them as the train rocketed out of the river.

"How we doing?" Jack said.

"Almost there . . ."

There was a clang as the metal access door fell away and struck the ladder below. "I'm through, let's go!" Arden said.

The train rushed toward them, the tube filled with the high shriek of metal. Arden was already through the access panel and Jack pitched himself toward the opening as the Maglev rushed by with an explosion of wind and sound.

They clung to the access ladder, the metal vibrating violently as the train sped by overhead. Then it was gone. Jack exhaled. Underneath them, the ladder ran the length of a support column to the lobby floor. Together they began their slow descent. The guard was gone, having walked off around a corner, and the building had returned to darkness. Everything was silent except for the gurgle of water from the fountain below.

They reached the end of the ladder and stood near a food court, stacks of trays piled at the edge of long metal runners leading past cafeteria-style serving areas. Tables and neatly stacked chairs were spaced across a tile floor.

"Where to?" Arden asked.

"Top floor. My father's office. He had access to everything. If the Samp you're looking for exists, that's where we'll find it."

They moved quietly across the food court toward the large glass elevator in the center of the atrium. Parts of the building would still be unlocked. Genico employees often worked late. The danger was bumping into someone who recognized Jack.

The elevator took them to the small foyer outside his father's office. The entrance was blocked by security doors, a touch reader set on the wall nearby. Arden pulled a flat polymer screen from the package Valentino had given Jack. He placed the unit over the surface of the security panel. There was a flash of green and the door to the office clicked open.

Ambient lights flickered on as they entered. His father's office had changed. The room was filled with new furniture, his brother's, most likely. Even the falcon's old perch was gone, replaced by a liquor bar near the balcony where Jack and his dad had last stood. Only his father's desk and the wall of weaponry remained.

Jack pointed down the long corridor. "You'll find what you need down there."

Arden moved off quickly down the corridor. Jack waited until he was alone and then brought the Genico mainframe to life on the desktop. Jack inserted the flash of the Reynolds DNA data that Arden had given him.

"Analyze code."

The monitor flickered and then displayed lines of genetic code. The data moved across the screen, forming up pairs and bonds, as a slowly revolving DNA helix appeared. While the computer worked to decode the information, Jack opened and flipped through the 3Deed contents of an eyeScreen virtual filing cabinet. A folder labeled "Ituri" attracted his attention. He opened the folder and scanned the contents.

"Who's there?"

The sudden voice startled Jack. His heart dropped and he turned, ready to run. The room was empty.

"Who is it?" the voice called out again.

Jack said nothing, standing fixed in place behind the desk. Slowly in the corner of the room, an image began to materialize. Vaporous at first, then growing stronger. A face appeared, hovering near the weapon's case. The image was an eyeScreen 3Dee, but with a bad connection. The 3Dee flickered, threatening to fade away, and then finally grew sharp enough until Jack realized he was looking at his father's face.

"Jack?" the 3Dee asked, the eyes squinting as if trying to find someone in darkness.

"Dad? Is that you?" Jack replied. "My God, they told me you were dead."

The image flickered again, then held strong. "Come closer so I can see you."

Jack felt strangely cautious. He wanted desperately to believe that his father was real, but this felt like a Genico trick. The apparition could be some kind of artificial intelligence modeled after his father. A trap designed to slow him down. He listened carefully, trying to hear the approach of crushers or the ring of an alarm. The building was silent.

Jack approached the 3Dee of his father. "Where are you?"

"I don't know where I am, exactly. I remember a little. I had a stroke. It's dark where I am now. But my mind is clear. Your brother went after Reynolds, was responsible for his murder."

"Why?"

"Reynolds's work was dangerous to Genico. He was going to liberate the Synthates. Make them totally free and the equals of the naturals."

"How?"

"There was something Reynolds called the 6th Day Samp. It would make the genetic code of Synthates indistinguishable from the naturals. It was going to make all Synthate tests obsolete. All means to differentiate between Synthates and naturals would be removed."

"Why would he do that?"

"Because he had fallen in love with his own creation. He wanted to save Synthates."

"What about the bioprints?"

"He'd developed a new skin spray. It would cover the bioprints completely. Perfectly blending with their own skin. Think of it, Synthates could live as naturals. They wouldn't be slaves anymore."

Jack checked his watch. He wondered how much time they had left. "So what happened?"

His father shook his head. "Reynolds was killed and the 6th Day Samp vanished. I think Reynolds knew what was coming. He hid the Samp somewhere to keep it safe."

"Where?"

"I don't know. But your brother has been looking for it. Genico's survival is based upon the current . . ."

The 3Dee flickered then went out.

"Hello?"

The room was empty and dark. The elevator rumbled to life, rattled in the silence for a few seconds, then cut off again. Jack wondered if security made their rounds into the office.

His father's image reappeared in a new corner of the room. "It's hard to keep a connection," George said. "Genico's survival is based on Samps and Synthates. Your brother is polluting the Samp market, too."

"What do you mean?"

"Look at this," his father said. A folder 3Deed suddenly and opened, documents floating across the space of the room. "These are all Samps developed by Genico Pharmaceuticals and shipped to Ituri, delivery taken by the Italian government."

"Phillip did this?"

Jack studied the Iturian Samps closer. They'd been sent out in two batches of one thousand each. Both were delivered to one of two Iturian villages, followed a month later by a separate batch. The first one to be dispatched had been a cure for mesothelioma.

That was very strange.

"Mesothelioma is caused by exposure to asbestos. Why would Iturian villages need a thousand of these?" Jack asked.

"Keep looking."

Confused, Jack pushed aside more 3Dee documents and skipped down to a separate batch of Samps that had been delivered to the same villages. These had been developed for the treatment of acinic cell carcinoma.

Acinic cell carcinoma was an even rarer form of cancer, occurring in the salivary glands. It was so uncommon, in fact, that Jack found it hard to imagine why Genico had developed a related Samp.

And then Jack noticed something unusual.

These cancers actually were occurring there. Or had been. The data was confusing. All at once, he knew the answer. There was only one logical conclusion. He suddenly felt sickened.

"Genico has been using Ituri to test new Samps," Jack said.

"Very good."

"Ones that cure a disorder, but at the same time infect the host with another," Jack said. "A Samp meant to treat mesothelioma, but that would also modify the genetic structure to produce acinic cell carcinoma."

If a Samp could modify genes to affect cures, they could also do the same to trigger disorders. Jack had never considered such a hideous possibility, because why would Genico want to create disease?

But the answer was suddenly obvious.

"Genico is becoming *too* successful."

"Exactly," his father said.

"If all genetic disorders are eradicated, there's no need for a Genetic Samp Exchange. The whole system falls apart. Phillip was creating Samps that guarantee future illness. Repeat customers. And he was experimenting first on Ituri villagers."

"You have to find the 6th Day Samp."

"Where would I even look?"

"Reynolds hid it. Try Beach's Road, there's . . ." His father paused, cocked his head. "Someone's coming." His voice cut out as his 3Dee flickered and faded away.

"Wait, not yet!" Jack called out.

Where was Beach's Road? Jack reached toward the vanished image. There was still so much more he needed to know about everything. His watch chimed.

As if summoned, Arden appeared from the back hallway. "Time's up. We have to go. Did you find what you needed?"

The flash of the DNA data from the Reynolds murder beeped. The mainframe hadn't found a match.

"The Synthate that killed Reynolds isn't in the system," Arden said.

"What does that mean?"

"Means Genico didn't build it. Or someone went in and deleted the record." The two made their way to the elevators. Arden pushed the elevator call button, but the car held at the ground floor.

"What about your daughter?" Jack asked.

"She'll live."

With a slight hum, the elevator finally began to move, the numbered display rapidly ticking upward. Arden glanced at Jack. The detective gave a tight-lipped smile. His forehead crinkled. He seemed uneasy.

"I've been thinking about Dr. Reynolds's last words," Arden said.

Jack narrowed his eyes in surprise. "I didn't know he had any last words." Jack had assumed the doctor was already dead when they found him. "What were they?"

"The pain passes but the beauty remains," Arden said. "I didn't really understand that before. Now I think I do."

Something about Arden wasn't right. Jack turned away from his companion, toward the security eyeScreens that 3Deed images on the wall. Night views around the building appeared in random sequences. All except for one. The camera mounted inside an elevator, the car crowded with choppy black forms.

"Screen focus," Jack said. The 3Dee sharpened and revealed an elevator crowded with armed, uniformed men. The Synthate Fugitive Unit.

Jack spun back toward the elevator, now rapidly approaching the top floor.

"I'm sorry," Arden said. "This is the only way to save my daughter."

"Trading me for her," Jack said.

"I had no choice."

"There's always a choice."

"You're right," Arden said. "There is. I give you up, my daughter gets the Black Rain cure."

Arden's hand tightened his grip on his service weapon, and then he drew the Smith & Wesson. Jack lunged forward, knocking the gun to the floor. He struck Arden hard in the neck, causing him to gasp as he fell backward. Picking up the Smith, he aimed the barrel back toward its owner.

"How many are coming?" Jack asked. He kept the Smith trained on Arden.

Arden looked confused. Then said simply, "Everyone."

In a panic, Jack scanned the office looking for some way out. It couldn't end now. He wouldn't let it. Jack lowered the Smith. He needed a way out now.

"What are you going to do?" Arden asked.

"I'm going to run," Jack said as he took a step toward the back stairwell door.

"Jack!" Arden called out.

Jack hesitated.

"Good luck," Arden said.

Jack looked at him. The cop's eyes studied him sadly. Jack felt no hatred toward him. They were all part of the same game. "You did what you had to do to save your daughter," Jack said. "I understand. I do the same for my revenge."

And then he ran.

CHAPTER 39

Jack moved quickly down the fire stairs. He would not live if the crushers found him. And if that happened, Dolce would never be avenged. He had to find the 6th Day Samp. His father had mentioned something called Beach's Road. That was where he could start.

Footsteps clattered far below. The crushers were coming up, trying to trap him. Contain him. But they could not contain where he was going.

The door to his old floor pushed open easily and Jack jogged down the darkened hallway past the familiar offices of coworkers from a lifetime ago. *If you ever left*, Cindy had said, *I'd keep everything of yours and take it out once a week to remember you.* Her storage closet, he knew, was carefully concealed behind dark walnut panels.

Inside were cardboard boxes filled with possessions from his old life: framed 2Dees, a University of Miami pennant, several pairs of sneakers.

He didn't find what he was looking for until the third box.

Inside, carefully packaged, was his base-jumping gear. Thank you, Cindy. Moving quickly, he stepped through the leg straps and adjusted the parachute onto his shoulders and back. Completing this, he took up a box labeled "2Dees" and, on top, as he knew there would be, was a snapshot of him and Dolce. This picture, too, he tucked in his pocket.

Helmet in hand, he took a last look at the familiar space, then exited the office. At the stairwell door, he paused to listen. Nothing. He pushed open the door. Above, he could hear mute voices and the subdued squelch of SFU radios. They were in his father's office. Silently he made his way up the stairs.

As he reached the next landing, the door leading to his father's office opened and a crusher stepped out. Jack swung his helmet up and caught the man beneath the chin. There was a loud crack as the soldier collapsed. Through the open door, he glimpsed a team of crushers before he took the stairs to the roof at a gallop.

The roof was two flights up, and he heard his pursuers behind him. When he pushed open the final door, he fell panting onto the roof. The colored spires of buildings rose up all around him. In the distance a vidBoard 3Deed advertisements. Jack ran to the building's edge, the ground seeming to sway far below him. He had completed base jumps before, but never with so many obstacles. He wasn't even sure the parachute was packed correctly. If not, this would be a short jump with a painful end.

"Don't move!" an angry voice called from the stairwell.

Jack sucked in his breath. A barker fired; red-hot pain burrowed into his side. And then he jumped.

Trajectory angles, wind speed, gravitational pull, lines of vectors drawn out on chalkboards by chute designers . . . everything moved together, and he fell down, the panic in his stomach churned by the flash of Genico metal and glass along his periphery. The chute opened with a whoosh. His body jerked vertically, then swung like a pendulum beneath the fulcrum of his harness. A gust of wind pushed him away from Genico and he sailed between the ravine of skyscrapers that cut channels over concrete rivers.

A line of parked cars rushed toward him and he hit the algae fin of a livery cab. He felt an incredible jolt in his left leg. His ankle bent inward and something popped deep in the joint. His hand loosened on his weapon and it clattered somewhere off ahead of him. He bounced off the algae fin and landed on his shoulder on the pavement. The chute billowed down around him, momentarily obscuring his vision. He pulled the lightweight material from his face and then disconnected the harness.

The pain from the gunshot was intense and he pressed his hand against his side. His fingers came away bloody. His legs went weak and he staggered a few steps forward before he collapsed to one knee. The crushers would reach street level in a minute, maybe two. Agony flared in Jack's ankle like the strike of a hot poker and he sucked his breath, closing his eyes and waiting for it to pass.

Behind him, tires screeched on pavement and he turned to see a black Audi accelerate toward him. The car braked hard and the passenger door flew open.

And then he blacked out.

CHAPTER 40

The room slowly appeared . . . table . . . dresser . . . closet rising out of a fog. Jack lay on the bed for a moment, looking around, taking in the feel of the place. He was in a hotel room. He was sure of that. *But where?* His eyes adjusted from the darkness, absorbing the details now. The drawn curtains the color of sandstone. The faded whitewashed walls, cracked with spidery veins. A desk and chair, a pair of sunglasses folded on the desk, a terrycloth bathrobe draped over the chair. A long, black, coffin-size box sat in the corner.

The scent of aerosol hung in the hair.

To his left, on the table beside the bed, was a business card, lettered in gold. *Times Square Hotel, New York City.*

He was on the edge of the Midtown Synthate Zone. He closed his eyes and the world faded to familiar blackness. From the hall, footsteps and angry voices rushed past the door. Then outside, a deeper sound, a low rumbling. Tanks? A short staccato burst of gunfire rattled, then an explosion. In the darkness, the room trembled.

Jack opened his eyes again. The world returned.

Who had done all this? How had he gotten here?

This was all too real to be a dream, and yet, he felt disconnected.

The room trembled again; the lamp by the bedside flickered. He looked down at himself and saw black bruises that stretched along his chest, his ribs sore to the touch along the slash. Beside the table sat an antique landline phone. Jack reached for it, lifted the receiver off the cradle. He needed to call for help. There were two clicks on the line, then a long buzzing sound.

A voice came on the line. Female.

"Stay off the hotel phone . . ." the voice hissed, startling Jack.

"Who is this?" Jack asked.

"Never answer the phone, Jack. They can track through the phone."

The line clicked dead. Jack listened to the hiss of static, then the dial tone.

Never answer the phone, Jack.

The voice knew his name. Who would find him? The crushers? His brother? Fear spread through Jack, radiating out from his stomach, out along his arms to the tips of his fingers.

The bedside phone rang again.

He looked at it. Another ring.

Never answer the phone, Jack.

But he had to answer. He was stranded here. He needed to find a way out. Slowly he reached for the receiver.

"Hello?"

A dial tone sounded. Nothing. Someone checking to see if he was awake?

Outside the window, another explosion rocked the room. Across from him, the bathroom door was shut, a seam of darkness running the length of the bottom. In his bare feet, he went to the door, the knob cold against his skin. He had to focus. He had to get oriented. Outside the hotel, machine-gun fire popped again. Jack pushed against the knob and the door swung backward into shadows.

Without thinking, he stepped into the black, found the faucet, pressed down and in the darkness heard the sound of water sloshing into the bowl. He dipped his hands into the water, splashed it against his face, and wiped away the sweat that had collected. He ran his hands along the wall, pulled a towel down from the rack, and buried his face in the cloth.

An intense wave of dizziness overtook him. He steadied himself. Since he was a kid he had suffered from these spells. He waited a moment and the feeling passed.

The last thing he remembered was landing hard on the street beneath the Genico building. There had been a car screeching toward him. And after that a long stretch of nothing.

Jack took a step back toward the doorway and felt for the light switch. His fingers brushed the hard knob of plastic and he pushed up. Immediately bulbs overhead flickered to life, cool light filling the room, shining over porcelain and tile. He squinted for a moment in the light. Dazed, then focusing.

What was happening here? Why had he been left alone?

A mirror on the wall held his image. And above his face, on the mirror itself, words in red had been scratched upon the glass.

They are coming for you! Leave now!

Jack spun away from the mirror. Angry voices sounded in the hallway. He opened the room door a crack and peeked out. A long hallway stretched down and, at the far end, crushers, bulky with Kevlar body armor and carrying Galil assault rifles, were systematically knocking down hotel room doors.

They were looking for him.

A telephone rang. A high musical pitch. Not the room phone, a sync, the tone muted. Jack turned from the door and focused on the sound. The ringing melody continued, "London Bridge Is Falling Down." Jack followed it across the room, the sound coming from around the bureau. Jack pulled open the drawers. Inside one was a plain T-shirt, and under the T-shirt he found a handgun. He put the

T-shirt on, then inspected the weapon. Beretta, 9mm. He looked at the weapon for a moment before he dropped it on the bed.

Beneath the gun was a small black bag. Inside the bag was a small sync and a generic hotel key numbered 214. Jack took the sync out gingerly. Still in his hands, the sync rang again, a tinny rendition of "London Bridge" playing out. Jack slid the sync behind his ear.

"Jack, you're in danger." Night Comfort's voice sounded panicked. "Look outside the window."

"Why am I here?" Jack asked.

"There's no time. If you want to live, do as I say."

Jack moved to the window, threw back the curtain, and looked out. He was on a high floor overlooking the ruins of Times Square. Below him, chaos. Broken glass and twisted metal lined the area. A fire raged inside a rusted acid scrubber. The windows of souvenir shops were blown out, broken glass in the street.

There was a low groan of metal as an Israeli-made Merkava tank turned the corner at the edge of the hotel, two lines of crushers following behind in full riot gear. A helisquall swept over the street, side door open, machine gun pivoting over the terrain.

This was a full-scale incursion. The crushers were moving into the Synthate Zones. War in the streets had arrived.

"This morning the crushers raided each of the zones. We can't get to you."

Static crackled on the line and the sync went dead. In the hallway, soldiers quickly approached, the sound of their boots kicking down room doors getting louder.

They are coming for you.

A second explosion sounded off just outside his window and the entire room shook. The antique television set flickered to life in a flash of color and sound. Through the window, Merkava tanks gunned at something down the street. Synthate snipers had taken position atop the old ESPN building. A brief answering round of machine-gun fire rattled in short staccato bursts.

His sync rang again.

"We have a tracker on you. I can get you a way out but you have to listen to everything I say. Go to the door," Night Comfort said.

Jack swept up the black bag and held it against his side. He took a last look around the hotel room. His fingerprints were everywhere, but there was no time for a cleanup. He had to remain focused. That was the key. That was how he survived. Stay calm. Look for opportunities.

If he stayed in the room, the crushers would break the door down. There was no other choice. He listened to Night Comfort's voice.

Clutching the bag, he moved to the room's door. He turned the knob and stepped out into the hall. At the opposite end, crushers were still kicking down doors, breaching each room as they pulled out Synthate occupants and laid them facedown on the carpeted hallway.

"Walk to the end of the hall. There's a fire exit there."

Jack turned quickly away from the scene, walking as calmly as he could toward the end of the hall where he could see an illuminated fire door. Behind him, a voice called out sharply. "Stop!" Jack kept walking, raised his hands and placed them palms down on the top of his head. The command came again.

"Stop. Now!"

He continued to move, keeping his back to the crushers. He prayed they wouldn't open fire.

"Stop now, or I shoot!"

Almost there, five steps. He heard the sharp metal click of the Galil assault rifle as it chambered a round. Booted footsteps fast approached, three sets of them. Jack broke right suddenly and hit the emergency release bar on the fire escape door. The door swung backward into the stairwell, accompanied by the piercing shriek of the fire alarm.

Gunfire sounded, partially muffled as the door closed behind him.

"Move down the stairs, move quickly!"

Jack ran down concrete steps. Behind him, the door banged open as soldiers followed him into the stairwell. He moved quickly down the flights and pushed open a door into the hotel lobby.

The lobby was in disarray.

The front windows were shattered. Broken glass lined the inside marble foyer. A potted plant lay on its side, dirt spilled out in brownish clumps while large red and purple flowers were strewn across the floor. The concierge, a natural with no bioprint, stood behind the front desk, keeping his head low, watching through the glass doorways as outside on the street the giant Merkava tank dieseled by.

"Past the elevators is a service door. Go through the door now."

Jack looked, seeing a metal door next to a row of elevators. He moved toward that, pushing through the doorway. Beyond was a narrow corridor, tightly packed with empty fabric laundry dumpsters and a small security room. The security office was vacant, sectioned off from the rest of the room by glass windows laced with chicken wire. Through the windows, a desk sat beneath a wall of security camera screens. One of the screens offered a view of crushers moving out into the lobby.

"You're in the security office. To your left is the service elevator. Push the call button."

Jack did as he was told, and immediately one of the doors opened.

"Reach in and push the button for the tenth floor." He reached in, pressed the button, and stepped back as the doors slid shut.

"Behind you, you'll see a rack of suit jackets. Take one. Put it on."

Jack turned. Next to the security office, a rack was lined with dark blue suit coats bearing the hotel insignia. Jack pulled one of the suit coats off the rack, throwing it over his T-shirt and buttoning it up the front.

"Move into the security office."

Jack reached for the office door, but the knob wouldn't budge.

"It's locked," Jack said.

"What?"

"It's locked. The door won't open."

"Try again."

Jack tried, the knob still not giving. "I'm telling you, it's locked."

Outside, he could hear the squelch of radios as crushers moved through the hotel lobby. A heavy fire extinguisher hung from the wall, next to the office window. Jack tore the extinguisher from the wall. Then, wielding the end like a battering ram, he slammed the metal edge down onto the doorknob. After two hits, the knob snapped, and, working his fingers into the opening, Jack pulled back the latch.

There was a click as the simple lock opened and the door swung open.

"Okay, it's open," Jack said.

"Go into the office and sit behind the desk. Pretend you're the hotel guard."

Jack moved into the security office, shut the door behind him, and slid into a chair beneath the main desk. Through the glass were the two service elevators and the laundry area. He took two deep breaths and steadied himself. A moment later the service door ahead of him swung open and four crushers pushed their way into the service corridor. Their guns trained toward him, they called out as they cleared the room.

"Don't speak," the voice in his ear warned. "They'll have voice stress detectors. They'll know you're lying."

The troopers loomed up in front of Jack. He pushed himself forward, trying to get his lower body beneath the desk. His feet were bare and he wore sweatpants.

One of the soldiers banged on the glass with the barrel of his Galil. Jack's fist clenched, but he said nothing.

"Point toward the elevator," the voice in the earpiece said.

Jack pointed to the elevator and the crushers turned to watch the illuminated dial rise up toward the tenth floor. Jack's eyes left the soldiers for a moment and floated back to the bank of security screens.

There, next to him, in sight of the entire room, was the camera view of the elevator's interior, the same one he'd just pointed to.

The car was empty.

More crushers found their way into the room, the squelching of their radios filling the small space. The crushers had turned back toward the security desk and faced Jack again.

"Don't move. Just sit," the female voice commanded. "You don't have a bioprint. Security here are naturals."

One of the crushers spoke quickly into his radio, then pressed the elevator call button. As the elevator doors opened, four crushers stepped inside the service car. A moment later, the doors shut, and the soldiers disappeared from view.

Jack was alone.

Breathe.

"When you think you're ready," Night Comfort said, "move through the rear door."

Jack continued to sit for a moment, collecting himself. The crushers hadn't recognized his face. They'd walked right by him. That was good. For now. There was a metal service door in the rear of the security office.

"I'm going out," Jack said, pushing the door open.

Outside, behind the hotel, the night air was warm and dry. The faint scent of rotting garbage and concrete dust hung in the air. The hotel was backed by a block of modern honeycomb apartments. They reached up twenty stories above him, each with a metal, gate-lined porch. Synthates leaned over their railings, watching the crusher incursion deeper in the zone.

"What now?" Jack asked.

"Step into the doorway, don't move."

Jack stepped back as a helisquall swept low overhead, its searchlight running the length of the apartment building. The shadowy figures along the railings disappeared back into the darkness as the massive searchlight swung over them. Jack kept his head down, moving along the length of the hotel. From overhead the retort of a pistol sounded as a gunman hidden inside one of the honeycombs fired at the helisquall.

The helisquall swung in a low arc around the side of the hotel, then the 30mm chain gun open fired into the apartment complex. Shattered glass cascaded down to the street below. Someone screamed and the building went dark. The helisquall swooped, hung for a moment in front of the silent apartment building, then swung toward one of the Broadway theaters.

"To your left, at the far end of the street is a car," Night Comfort said.

Jack turned to look, seeing a car flash its lights at him.

Jack cut across the vacant street and headed behind crowded Synthate housing developments. The neighborhood was empty, voices and 3Dees faintly audible through closed metal doors. A dog buried its nose in overturned garbage on the street outside a restaurant.

A Synthate restaurant owner with a thick mustache, his front covered by a large apron, stood in an open doorway surrounded by barrels, arms folded across his chest as he watched the helisqualls in the distance.

More gunfire erupted in the distance.

The car was an old Mercedes, dusty, with a bullet hole in the driver's side panel. Two Synthates with beards stood on either side of the car, antique pistols hanging from their belts. Jack approached slowly. One of the men tossed away a smoke stick and waved his hand for Jack to come closer.

"Who are these two?" Jack asked.

"Synthates from Genico's Qatar plant. They'll take you where you need to go."

The Synthate waved his hand again at Jack. They both looked Guard class.

"Come," he said as he stepped back and opened the front passenger door for Jack. With an industrial factory bioprint, the first Synthate was bigger, thick around the waist and chest, his black hair long and curly. The other one was thinner, with a scraggly beard, dressed in a dirty brown-and-white checkered sweater with elbow pads.

Jack slowly advanced toward the Mercedes, bent down, and looked through the open door. The inside was worn, the leather on the seats torn, deep scuff marks appearing along the base of the console. There were empty bullet casings on the floor.

"Come," the bigger man said, and smiled, waving again for Jack to get in the car.

"You sure about this?" Jack said to Night Comfort.

"No choice."

Jack moved to get in. Then the smaller man touched his shoulder from behind, held up a small burlap sack and indicated that he wanted to put the sack over Jack's head. A blindfold.

"No, no, no," Jack said as he stepped back, shaking his head.

"Yes, is necessary."

"No, not necessary," Jack said to the man, then talking into the sync, "They want to blindfold me? Are you fucking crazy?"

"You wanted out, this is out," Night Comfort said. "This is the only way. You have to trust me."

Jack turned back to the car. The two men still stood on either side, watching him.

"Let's go," Jack said, walking quickly back to them.

The smaller man held up the burlap sack again, indicating that he had to put it over Jack's head.

"Fuck you," Jack said pleasantly as the man pulled the sack down and everything went black.

CHAPTER 41

Jack could see nothing. His senses were limited to the bump of the road beneath the Mercedes, the smell of cologne, the voice of Synthate resistance on the radio.

They were driving fast over rutted streets, the windows open as the rush of air fluttered the hood over Jack's head. There was a fourth man in the car, seated in the back. They had stopped a few moments before, and Jack heard him step inside the car.

The Mercedes came to a sudden stop, gunfire ahead of them. A rapid conversation in Arabic passed around the car as the three men argued. Then the Mercedes turned and the big engine groaned as Jack accelerated blindly. The car moved jerkily, slowing at times to a crawl, then speeding up again, possibly moving through the debris-covered streets of the Zone.

Abruptly they stopped.

Doors opened and the men stepped out. Moments later, Jack's door opened and a hand came to rest on his shoulder. He was lifted out of the car, guided forward across smooth pavement, then into a faintly air-conditioned space and up a flight of hard concrete-like stairs. He heard the ping of an elevator door opening. He was pushed inside and heard the metal rattle of the door as it closed.

The elevator moved, carrying him upward. Then a pause. A jerk. The doors opened again.

And nothing.

Jack stood, waited for someone to guide him forward, but there was no one, the only sound the faint rumble of tank shells in the distance.

"Hello?" Jack asked.

No response.

"Hello? Anyone?"

Jack reached for the bottom of his hood, slipped his finger under the fabric and slowly lifted it off.

"I'm taking this off. If there's anything I shouldn't see, let me know now . . ."

He lifted the hood up and blinked in the light. He stood alone in the center of an open elevator car, looking into a hotel hallway lined with doors. The building had been elegant at one time, but had since fallen into disrepair. A worn Oriental carpet covered the floor. He saw peeling wallpaper and a cracked vase filled with wilted flowers, everything in the hallway slightly faded. Tarnished bronze number plates adorned each door, and under each plate, the words *The Big Apple Hotel, New York City* were inscribed in cursive scroll.

The Big Apple Hotel.

The name was familiar to Jack. The Big Apple had been one of the new hotels, elaborately furnished for the hordes of tourists the city thought would come for the Synthate Zone gambling and pleasure parlors. The tourists had never arrived, but the city's newly renovated buildings remained, waiting with unrequited bank accounts, slowly deteriorating into a faded jewel.

The hallway was silent. Jack walked slowly down the line. All of the doors were closed. Jack fished from his pocket the key he'd found in the duffel.

A black tag affixed to the key read 214 in the same cursive scroll.

Room 214 was last in the hall, nothing to distinguish it from any other door. Jack fitted the key in the lock and turned. There was the snap of a bolt and the knob turned in his hand.

Jack slowly opened the door, making sure to close it as soon as he entered the space. Beyond was a small space with bare walls and a single paper lantern hanging from the ceiling. There were two beds and an antique, box-style television set. Footsteps sounded in the hall behind him. The room door swung open and Night Comfort entered. She hugged him hard.

"You made it," she said as she reached into a duffel bag she carried and pulled out a battery-powered saw with a razor-thin circular blade. She pushed a switch on the base and the saw whirred to life, the blade spinning in a blur of metal.

"What's happening outside?" Jack asked.

"Crusher incursion. They're looking to take out the resistance." Night Comfort brought the saw down onto the edge of the television set. The blade tore into the plastic, the electric motor whining as she cut a circumference around the screen.

She followed the exposed antenna line, to which she attached a quarter-size disk. She turned on the television.

"What are you doing?" Jack asked.

"Intercepting the satellite signal. The crushers transmit a live satellite video image from their incursion teams," she said as she bent down and flipped the channel on the television. Jack watched her, still trying to get his mind moving fast enough to keep up with everything happening.

"They broadcast the feedback to Calhoun, the head of the crushers. But if you know how to look . . ." she said, pausing on a station and taking a step back, "you can intercept it."

The television screen flashed. An image appeared from a handheld camera at eye level inside the passenger seat of a car. The automobile was moving quickly, bouncing over narrow roads in Midtown.

Night Comfort pulled out a mini-machine gun and a large British Army SA80 from her bag. She laid the weapons on the floor.

"Do you see that?" She glanced at the television. Onscreen, a car navigated fast through a burned-out road. Honeycomb buildings were crowded tightly together, small alleyways visible in flashes as the vehicle passed.

"Yes . . ." Jack said.

"Recognize it?"

Jack looked closer. The car hit a pothole. The view bounced wildly, then re-centered. The roads were paved but rugged, jutting out in uneven cracks. A series of vacant buildings passed across the screen, then a row of concrete block pods fenced in by barbed wire moved into view.

"The Midtown Synthate Zone," Jack said.

"One block away. They're coming!"

"What happens when they get here?"

Night Comfort stood, holding the British Army SA80 in one hand. "They try and kill us."

Jack ran to the window. A black Audi pulled up to the corner. The doors opened and four armed naturals stepped out.

"Who are they?" Jack said.

"Crusher hit squad."

"Hit squad for who?"

"For you. They're coming for you. Go to the closet," she yelled at Jack. "Get the bag in there."

He retrieved the bag and handed it to her.

The television screen showed the hallway outside. The incursion team was fast, as they'd already made their way up the stairwell. Night Comfort reached behind the screen, unclipped the satellite transmission interceptor, and threw it into the bag along with everything else. She rushed to the door. "Go. Quickly. Across the hall."

Jack threw open the door and stepped out. Night Comfort followed after him, dropped the duffel, and produced a key. Around the corner, obscured from view, the sounds of booted feet quickly approached.

"Hurry," Jack whispered.

Night Comfort pushed the key into the lock of the room across the hall. Nothing happened. She pushed again, jiggling the handle. The footsteps had almost reached the corner of the hall, with both of them still in plain view. The lock clicked and the door swung open. Picking up the duffel, she flung it into the darkened room and shoved Jack in, following behind him and slamming shut the door.

Jack pressed his eye against the keyhole. The hallway outside was empty, stretching out in fish-eye distortion. Suddenly the area filled with men advancing fast and silent.

There were four of them, all wearing black, each one heavily armed. The men flanked either side of Jack's previous room. One of the men whispered something into a radio headset, then knelt in front of the door lock and pulled out a plastic card the size and shape of the hotel room key. The card was attached to a phone-size electronic lock decoder. The man fitted the key into the lock and looked down at the decoder.

A moment later the lock to 214 clicked.

The man pushed down on the door handle and the armed squad exploded into the room.

"They're not wasting time," Night Comfort said. "We have to go out the balcony."

The balcony of their room was high above street level. Jack closed his eyes as he swung his legs over the rusted metal rail. Slowly he lowered himself down until he hung suspended from the bottom edge. Swinging his body, he could barely reach the railing of the balcony below, just grazing the metal with the tips of his toes.

"Let go," Night Comfort hissed.

Jack let go with one hand, his body swinging outward. Far below, the ground swung like a pendulum.

"Hurry," Night Comfort called out again. "They're in the hall! They're kicking down doors!"

Night Comfort swung her leg up over the railing, lowering her body down toward Jack. She hung from the same balcony, then dropped, landing gracefully one floor below. Standing up, she turned, reaching for Jack's legs.

"I've got you," Night Comfort said. "Just let go."

Jack heard a clicking sound from inside room 213. He pulled himself up until his eyes were above the level of the balcony, looking back into the room. The door opened, four crushers coming into the room, each heavily armed. One of the crushers locked eyes with Jack. Without pause, the man raised the barrel of his machine gun.

Jack let go.

He felt his body freefall for a moment, then his feet hit hard, catching on the railing of the balcony below and pitching him forward. He landed on his elbows on the concrete, stunned for a moment. Above him came the sound of running footsteps, then the clink of metal as someone above leaned over the side of the railing. Jack felt hands underneath his chest as Night Comfort picked him up.

Gunfire came from above. The concrete floor of the balcony fragmented into shards of stone. Jack pulled his feet in tight and pressed himself against the glass of the closed balcony doors. Night Comfort swung her bag forward, the heavy gun metal inside smashing the glass.

They passed quickly through the vacant room and into the exterior hallway.

As she ran, she unslung the bag again from her shoulder and retrieved the SA80. They pushed open the stairwell door. One floor above, they heard the crash of a second door opening, the crushers following after them. Night Comfort paused, turned, and fired a machine gun burst into the concrete wall.

They reached the ground floor and rushed out into the street. Outside the chaos of battle still sounded. Night Comfort hid the machine gun back in the duffel bag and together they fled east, away from the fighting.

"How do we get out of the Zone?" Jack asked.

"Synthate resistance hit the grids that control the wall. All power is down. We can move freely. For now, anyway."

They headed two blocks east before they hit the massive wall that separated the Zone from the naturals' area. The wall was fifty feet high and layered with Synthate graffiti, like old 2Dees of the Berlin Wall. Two Synthates stood waiting near a boarded-up brownstone. Night Comfort greeted them, and the Synthates guided her and Jack into the building.

Inside, a stairwell led down to the basement.

"We built this tunnel years ago," Night Comfort said. "But when power is on to the grid, movement sensors in the wall make it impossible to use."

She opened a heavy metal door, and beyond was a narrow hallway cut into the ground and lined with hanging lanterns. The tunnel threaded its way between old Con Edison pipes and hundred-year-old water mains. The two moved quickly until they reached a metal stairway leading up.

"Where did you learn all this?" Jack asked, amazed at her special ops skills.

"I've been training for years. The Synthates from the Games, those who survive, they teach some of us about weapons and combat. We have others who have gained access to tracking technologies. We study how the crushers operate so we know how to fight them."

The stairs ended in the basement of an abandoned store. They made their way onto an empty street. Behind them loomed the Zone wall. They were on the natural side.

They walked fast, trying to distance themselves from the Zone. Jack turned toward Night Comfort. "Do you have your sync?"

"Sure, why?"

"My father mentioned something called a 6th Day Samp. Said it would change everything for Synthates and that it was hidden near Beach's Road."

Night Comfort flipped open her sync. A small map hovered over her palm. "There's a Beach Road in Staten Island."

"Doesn't sound right," Jack said. "Beach's Road doesn't have to be in New York City. It might not even be called Beach Road. It might just be near water somewhere."

"There are thousands of roads like that."

"Can you get me to the Bank of New York?" Jack asked, thinking of the promise he'd made to his father.

"What's there?"

"Something my father left me. And I need to find it."

CHAPTER 42

The Wall Street branch of Bank of New York rose like an Egyptian monolith from the busy downtown streets. While the Synthate Zone burned and hundreds died, down here, life went on as normal for the naturals. Most had no idea what was happening on the other side of the wall. And as long as their streets got cleaned and someone made their food, they didn't want to know.

"My father knew what was coming," Jack said. "He planned for it. I have to believe that he left something to help."

There was no hiding inside the marble-lined bank lobby. Naturals milled around, waited in line for the teller, or deposited cash into touch buck card refills. A Synthate musical trio played a cello, a violin, and a grand piano in the far corner. When Synthate labor was free, why not have it played live? Two Synthate waiters in black tie stood behind a refreshment bar, serving lemon meltwater to customers. In the midst of this, Jack, dirty and bloodied, and Night Comfort, an obvious Synthate Social, her bioprint of a pacing tiger flashing on her skin, quickly drew attention. Within moments, a bank manager scurried over to meet them.

"I'm here to pick up a deposit box," Jack said. He pressed his thumb against a touch scanner. The machine blipped green. The manager's eyes narrowed, hesitant to let them deeper into the bank, but he turned on his heels. "Right this way, sir."

Jack and Night Comfort were led to a sealed metal door with a second keypad. The manager punched in a code and then heavy bolts clanged as they unlocked. The metal door swung slowly open.

"Follow me," the bank manager commanded, and together they stepped through the doorway. As they entered, overhead lights illuminated a classroom-size room with a maple table and stuffed leather chairs.

"Well, sir, I'll give you your privacy," the manager said, and then he was gone. The metal door closed behind him.

An eyeScreen in the corner flashed to life. The Genico logo twirled, and then a 3Dee of Jack's father appeared, standing life size in his old office. The prerecorded image was clearer than in Genico.

"My son," his father began, his eyes fixed forward onto the recorder. "If you're watching this, then you know the truth of your life. I am sorry for what I had to conceal from you, but for your safety, I thought it necessary. A lie is easier to live if you believe the lie to be true.

"By now you must know that you are the son of a Synthate and a natural. Synthates were never designed to be able to create new life on their own. And so you are beautifully unique, Jack. A child that science held to be an impossibility.

"My entire life I have been a scientific mind. A mind bound by rational ideals. I have lived in a world set forth by immutable laws. But as I advance steadily toward my own passage from this world, I have come to realize that to truly expand, the scientific mind must come to understand the possibility of something more than natural law. Some great life force that binds us all, natural and Synthates. And with the existence of this greater being, there is no impossible.

"What makes naturals different from Synthates? Some would say it is the presence of a soul. Of an everlasting life force within naturals that Synthates will never know. But I have seen things. Synthates who put paint to canvas in beautiful ways. Composed music that moved anyone who listened. Creation. Your father was a Synthate. Your mother was natural. And yet they loved each other more deeply than anything I have ever experienced, and in this love, they created you. And this is the greatest proof of a soul that I know. This is the truest miracle I have ever seen.

"But perhaps naturals are not yet ready for miracles. Perhaps the marvels of rational science have dulled their capacity to understand what is beyond science. And we always fear what we don't understand. Naturals may fear you, Jack, and in fear, there is danger. By now, I'm sure, you have become aware of this. The part I have played in enslaving something as great as Synthates has brought me great shame. I could never have conceived of the ways naturals would find to torment and abuse my life's work.

"And for that I am truly sorry.

"I have created for you a new identity. I have left you everything that was mine. And with this I hope you can find freedom.

"I am sorry, Jack. I am sorry for having lied to you. I am sorry for having lied to Dolce. But what has brought me great happiness is watching the love that you two have grown to share with each other. If you should ever doubt yourself, if you should ever question your own humanity, you need only look at this. Humans are selfish creatures. But love is the selfless act we are all capable of. And it is beyond the scientific mind to ever understand.

"Good luck, my son."

The image of his stepfather blinked out. A door hidden in the wall at the end of the room swung open, revealing a hallway.

Together Jack and Night Comfort walked through the open doorway. Beyond was a small elevator car with an ivory-numbered panel.

"What now?" Jack asked as he looked at the panel. According to the elevator, they were on the bottom floor. "The car doesn't go any lower."

A set of gears cranked, the doors closed, and the car jerked downward. They were going beneath the street.

"Guess it does," Night Comfort said.

The floor vibrated beneath Jack's feet and the air grew cooler, offset by the continual clank of the elevator motor.

After a minute, the car slowed, then stopped abruptly. The doors slid open and the light from the small overhead bulb in the elevator illuminated the first few feet of a marble-tiled floor.

They stepped out of the car into darkness. Night Comfort spoke. "Where do you think we are?"

"No idea."

She pulled a flashlight from the duffel bag. A brilliant stream of light shot out and illuminated the open space before them.

They stood at the edge of a long, elaborately furnished underground subway station. The floor was mosaic marble tile, which stretched back to giant decorative planters that Jack imagined must have at one time held high-reaching palm plants. In the center of the room was a wide fountain, now dried and filled with plaster dust, and beyond that was a colonnaded wall spaced with marble statues. At the edge of the tiled floor was a five-foot drop-off, rail tracks visible below.

The station had been remarkably preserved. The walls looked freshly scrubbed and the floors still shone like they were newly waxed. A small section of the ceiling had collapsed over time, littering the inside of the fountain and a portion of the marble floor with plaster dust, but the rest of the station was in pristine condition.

Jack followed Night Comfort toward the end of the tracks, past an old ticket booth, the glass still intact and perfectly clear. A single yellowed ticket lay on the floor in front of the booth. Jack bent down, picked it up, and inspected the face.

THE BEACH PNEUMATIC TRANSIT CO
1ST OF MARCH, 1870
260 BROADWAY, ENTRANCE UNDER DEVLIN BANK AND TRUST
OPEN FROM 10 TO 5
FOR THE BENEFIT OF THE UNION HOME AND SCHOOL
FOR SOLDIERS' AND SAILORS' ORPHANS
ADMISSION, 25 CENTS.

"Beach's Road," Night Comfort said, as her sync 3Deed a moving image of the subway station in its prime. "This was built by a man named Alfred Beach in 1870. It was the first underground transit system in New York City."

Beyond the ticket booth was a set of new glass doors. Lights flickered on as they moved forward, revealing an underground Genico lab of shining metal and glass, everything meticulously recreated. They walked through the lab inspecting everything.

"You could design any Samp you wanted down here," Night Comfort said.

"This was where Reynolds was working. This is where he designed the 6th Day Samp. This was why they killed him."

They jumped down onto the old rail tracks and walked up the line past the lab. Over one hundred years ago, New York's wealthiest walked this same path to be marveled by Beach's creation. And now there was a new technological creation.

After twenty feet, they passed out of sight of the subway station and the laboratory, and entered into the tunnel. Around them, the walls were brick and mortar and rose up to form an arch some fifteen feet overhead.

Out of the shadows loomed the blocky form of a subway car. Their lights reflected off the windows, the brass bell that hung from the front, and the gold-plated strips that lined the red wooden frame. The car was about twenty feet in length, constructed neatly of wood and brass, with sets of windows, lightly dusted with age.

Along the side was printed in gold leaf, "Beach Pneumatic Transit."

Night Comfort reached up and pulled on the brass-fitted handle, and one of the double doors swung open with a creak of old hinges. She stepped up inside the car and shone her light around. Inside were seats composed of thin wooden slats. Beneath the seats were hinges that allowed them to fold up and down. The forward section of the car had a seat for the conductor, in front of a panel of knobs and levers and highly polished brass fixtures.

"It's amazing," Jack said slowly as he surveyed the inside of the car. "That all this was forgotten for so long."

A map was posted on the wall of the car. It showed a network of subway lines that stretched beneath the city. They were all old tracks, ones Jack had thought were abandoned. Genico must have refurbished them somehow, and together the lines formed a hidden transportation network that ran beneath the city. The tracks ran up to Central Park and linked each of the Synthate Zones together before funneling down to the Beach subway station and the hidden laboratory.

Jack stepped back onto the tracks. Nearby, a ladder had been bolted into the brick wall.

"Any idea where this goes?" Jack gripped the ladder and began to climb.

Night Comfort followed, and soon they began to hear street noise above. The ladder opened into a small, bare room with a single door. They could hear a murmur of voices, the low sound of Muzak and the long whoosh of the Maglev.

Cautiously Jack pushed open the door and they stepped into the garish light of a Synthate retail shop, featuring white walls trimmed with Lucite and matte butcher block tables with eyeScreens 3Deeing various Synthate designs. Naturals walked through aisles shopping for servants and laborers and comfort workers, while through the front panel glass, Jack could see the iconic Wall Street Bull.

The door closed behind them, and Jack turned to see the words "EMPLOYEES ONLY" stenciled on the front.

"There was no Synthate attack here," Jack said slowly.

"What?"

"There was a bombing at the Synthate store nearby Genico. Supposed to have been a Synthate resistance attack. But it was just an excuse to shut the place down and finish the tunnel."

Jack surveyed the store. Naturals streamed in through the front, many of them walking with their personal Synthates.

"This place is perfect," Jack said.

"Why?"

"Synthates come and go without suspicion. My father knew this. That's why he built the tunnel here," Jack said. Together they left the Synthate store and stepped out into the sunlit plaza. Across the plaza, the Genico sky turbine slowly turned. Phillip was in there somewhere.

But here in the sunlight, Jack thought of a different time.

"Dolce and I used to walk through here," Jack said as he and Night Comfort headed past the National Museum of the American Indian.

"I'm sorry for your loss," Night Comfort said. "The pain passes, but the beauty remains."

Jack's fists tightened in surprise. Night Comfort saw his expression. "What's wrong?"

"The pain passes, but the beauty remains," Jack repeated. "What is that?"

Night Comfort replied, "It's just something Synthates say."

"Where does it come from?"

"We learn it at the grow gardens. It's supposed to give us hope, I guess," she said. "It's a famous quote."

"From who?"

"Pierre-Auguste Renoir."

"The painter?" Jack said, feeling a rising excitement. Jack raised his hand to his forehead. Everything had suddenly become clear.

He knew where Reynolds had hidden the 6th Day Samp.

CHAPTER 43

The Maglev let Jack and Night Comfort off at Fifth Avenue and 79th Street. They each carried one of the knock-off DNA rings that Arden had given Night Comfort. The scanners read them each as Chinese naturals, and none of the transit crushers even looked their way on the ride up.

A few blocks south, the Central Park dome rose up over the pond and the Ramble, protecting the Upper East Side naturals from the supposed radioactivity beneath. Jack thought of Alphacon and the Synthate village hidden beneath the camo dome. He wondered how long they would remain safe. So much had been revealed to Jack in such a short time, his mind still struggled to grasp it all. Was he one of the only few who knew Synthate secrets? How many were out there who knew what he did?

And he knew nothing about the oddities of his own timeline. His wounds from the battle seemed to have all healed. Even with his Synthate ability to repair faster, such a feat still seemed impossible to explain. And the blackout before waking in the hotel room . . . what was behind that?

There were still so many things that he couldn't piece together. Life was moving so fast that the edges had become a confusing blur. But he had to keep moving forward.

"Where are we going?" Night Comfort asked as they walked past the expensive park conurbs.

"My brother told me that Reynolds had turned into something of an art collector before he was murdered. The prizes of his collection were Renoir's painting, *Dance at Bougival,* and an extremely rare eighteenth-century Guarneri violin," Jack said. "Valentino mentioned the painting. He said I would do well to remember it."

"Why?"

"I think Reynolds left something in the painting that will get us to the 6th Day Samp."

Night Comfort shook her head. "How could you know that?"

"It just makes sense. I think Reynolds was a good man. I think he wanted what was best for Synthates."

"But why hide secrets in a painting?"

"Because he knew Synthates were naturally drawn to art. He gave you all a genetic predisposition to be artists and musicians. He felt that creativity and culture would help define a people."

"Maybe," she said.

"And in his death, he made sure that the painting would be kept safe."

"So let's go take a look at this painting and see if there's anything."

Jack stopped walking and sighed. "Well, that's the thing. According to Reynolds's will, after his death, the Renoir and the Guarneri violin were both bequeathed elsewhere."

"So we'll track them down. Where are they?"

Jack pointed to the massively secure building across the street. "Unfortunately the painting and the violin are both there now."

Night Comfort followed the line of Jack's finger until her eyes rested on the massive beaux-arts–styled Metropolitan Museum of Art.

Stretching five city blocks, the building stood like a fortress on the edge of Central Park.

Night Comfort looked confused. "I'm sorry, you said what we need is in there?"

"That's right."

"That's the Metropolitan Museum of Art. One of the most highly guarded buildings in the world."

"I know. That's probably why Reynolds thought the 6th Day Samp would be safe."

"It is safe. There's no way we can get to it."

Jack smiled. "I'm sure we can figure out a way."

From inside Genico, Phillip watched a solar island float slowly down the Hudson as it headed toward its anchorage in Jersey to power down for the night. The last loop of a Genico ad 3Deed along the front of the island; a pregnant mom talked and smiled with a genome technician, while below scrolled the words, *Now your child's potential has no limit.*

That wasn't actually true. There were careful limits set on human growth and natural modification. Legally, as long as you still wanted to be considered a natural, there *were* limits. So you could become smarter. But never brilliant. A better athlete, but never godlike. Too much genetic modification and you might no longer scan human. And that was why Jack had always been better. He was stronger and faster and smarter than anything nature had intended. He wasn't human. He was a fake.

And he was still alive. He was still out there. And as long as that was true, Jack would always be better than his brother.

The Genico turbine continued to slowly rotate and the view changed toward the north, the electric neon glow of the Synthate Zone casting a halo toward the sky. Phillip's office was empty now, but Jack had been here. Somehow he had escaped the battles and made his way home. Back to Genico. Even now, even with Phillip's complete control of the company and Jack fighting in the pits of the Games, Phillip still felt the familiar haunt of inferiority. And he realized with sudden, sharp clarity that it was impossible to enjoy his success as long as he felt this way. Feeling less than was sometimes worse than actually being less than.

But it didn't have to be that way.

Now your child's potential has no limit.

Phillip ran a company whose entire specialty was making people better. Making them stronger. Faster. Smarter. More beautiful. He could be better, too. No crushers were taking his scan. And whatever happened, it would be worth beating his brother. Just for once in his life. To exist on that higher plane. To know that you were better than everyone around you. Not just because you had more money. Or had a faster car. Or a better-looking woman. But that you were fundamentally better, in a deeper evolutionary way. You were literally a better, more evolved human being.

In their liquid form, Samps were actually quite beautiful. Phillip held the vial in his hand up to the soft white of the city skyline. Inside, the liquid rolled like quicksilver. Genico had designed plenty of Samps to make you better, but none to make you go back to the way you were. Because who would want to be worse? So if he took this Samp, there was no going back. His old life would be gone forever, replaced with this newer, shinier, stronger one in which he might finally become the star and Jack a supporting player.

He would no longer be human. But people said that like it was somehow a bad thing. He would be more than human.

"Fuck it," Phillip said, then injected the Samp. The liquid was cool, then burningly cold. He felt the coldness spread through his arm, slowly filtering through the rest of his body. Like an entire colony of worker ants, the Samp went to work on his body on its most basic level, changing him, making him better, making him more like Jack.

The controlling dynamic of this new Phillip would be stronger, faster, smarter. The new human. As a kid he had loved comic books. He took to the superheroes who started off as ordinary and then were exposed to some reactant, their lives thus changed to something extraordinary. Peter Parker wasn't born as Spider-Man. He had to be bitten by a radioactive spider. The Flash had to be exposed to chemicals. And Steve Rogers was the biggest faker of them all with his Super Soldier Serum. Born too sickly to be accepted into the Army, he cheats, takes a drug, and becomes a superhero. And not just any superhero. Captain America.

So what's the lesson there? If you could take something to make you better, it wasn't cheating. It was being an American. It was making your own limits. Steve Rogers was human. Captain America wasn't. But did we penalize him? No. We named him after our fucking country.

But that was comic books. This was real. And just like the Super Soldier Serum, a Samp could override the natural in any of us. Phillip had always wanted more. And now he was going to do what it took to get it. And just like Steve Rogers, he would become the new super soldier.

CHAPTER 44

William Calhoun watched his interview on the eyeScreen, then turned as the office door opened and his assistant entered. Calhoun hushed him with a single finger.

"Of course we will track them down with vigor," the eyeScreen image of Calhoun said. "Synthates are a threat to the national security of this country. Soon there will be a time when the population of Synthates is equal to the population of naturals, and we must consider the consequences of this. Lawlessness. Riots. Killings. The Synthate is not a child of God. He is a wild creature. An animal. He must be controlled. Monitored. And those that escape will be tracked and punished by the SFU." The eyeScreen image of Calhoun turned and stared deeply into the camera. "And I give my word of honor on that to every American."

Calhoun clenched his fist in support of his eyeScreen counterpart. His timing had been perfect, but more than words had made the American public love him. Audiences adored his feeling. The depth of his feeling. His loathing for the fugitive Synthates. The ones who tried to live outside the bounds of law. Who turned their backs on their masters.

"The Synthate is a coward. They do not have the same strength of spirit as we naturals. He lacks our fortitude of character, our notions of honor. But this does not mean he is not dangerous. But the weak are his prey. His device is intimidation. This is why we must be strong. Vigilant. And let all Synthates fear the SFU."

The interview ended and Calhoun's assistant Mr. Minton cleared his throat.

"Yes, what is it?" Calhoun asked, turning from the vidScreen toward his assistant.

"A gift arrived for you today, sir," the assistant said as he held out an envelope. "From the Genico Company."

Calhoun took the envelope and opened the flap with a flick of his boot knife. Inside was a small card with a handwritten note.

Thank you for your consideration. Enclosed is a token of our gratitude.

Calhoun had found that his rewards for service had risen commensurately with his rise in the SFU. And now, after his promotion to sector chief, he was able to more fully enjoy the small tokens of gratitude his hard work and service had provided.

"And the gift?" Calhoun asked.

"Is in the next room," Minton said. "But I must warn you, since the C-16 provision, it has been more difficult to attain your exact request."

"Meaning?"

"Meaning," the assistant said apologetically, "she may be a bit older than your usual."

Calhoun clasped his hands behind his back. "Oh . . . I see."

Synthates allowed a man's actions to reflect the full range and desire of his taste. An act that might be considered immoral with a natural could be considered quite normal when done with a Synthate. Calhoun had always experienced an attraction, an irresistible force, that drove him toward young girls. It did not seem unnatural to him to desire smooth, tight skin. But of course, with naturals, to take a fifteen-year-old to bed was considered a perversion under the law. He could be arrested and imprisoned for merely acting on what he deemed a natural impulse.

But Synthates allowed freedom. A female Synthate aged to appear in her fifteenth year was an acceptable outlet for his drives. And many men felt the same way, so that the Synthate 14-16 Age class had become quite popular. But soon various groups began to complain that this might encourage that same interest toward naturals of a similar age. Calhoun thought this was ridiculous, since allowing the use of a Synthate 14-16 gave him an outlet for his desire. Still, many felt uncomfortable with the idea of a female in her fifteenth year being taken sexually by a man, regardless of whether she were born in a laboratory or not.

So the C-16 Bill was passed, which made it a finable offense for a company to produce a Synthate that appeared to be less than sixteen years of age. As a result, many of the reputable labs ceased their production of these Synthate models.

"Shall I ask her to come in?" Minton ventured.

Calhoun laced his fingers together. "Of course. Let's hope she is acceptable."

His assistant opened the door and motioned to someone in the hallway. Calhoun stared, and then slowly a smile crept across his face. A creature of amazing beauty stepped into his office. She was tall and blond, with a curving physique accentuated by the black silk dress that clung to the contours of her hips. In one hand she held a black handbag, which she rested against the side of her leg.

She smiled demurely at him and said, "Thank you for seeing me."

She was older than he usually requested, but she had a flawless beauty never found in the natural world. Genico had done amazing work. Her genetic structure must have taken years to develop, and was perfectly expressed in the Synthate female before him.

Calhoun cleared his throat. "Mr. Minton?"

"Yes, sir?" his assistant asked from the open doorway.

"Bring around my car," Calhoun said. "I have business to attend to and I'll be out of the office for the rest of the afternoon."

"Very well, sir."

Calhoun turned his attention back toward the woman. "You are marvelous looking."

"Thank you, sir."

"Who made you?"

"Genico."

"They've done well."

Overcome with lust, he approached her and wrestled his hand through her hair and forced her head back. Her eyes flared with surprise. He kissed her roughly, awkwardly on the mouth, then on the neck and chest.

"Wouldn't you rather be in private, sir?" she said.

"I can't wait to open such a generous gift as you," he panted.

"But your reputation," she said.

Calhoun hesitated at this, pulled back and wiped the back of his hand across his wet lips.

"When we're alone, I'll make you very happy," she said, and ran a finger down his chest. "I promise you."

He stared at her greedily. "I guess I can wait to unwrap you a little longer."

Minton appeared again in the doorway, keeping his eyes on the floor. "The car is ready, sir."

"Yes, yes, let's go then, shall we?" Calhoun said. He placed his hand against the Synthate's back and together they walked out of the SFU station. Calhoun's black Mercedes was parked by the curb in the front of the building; the darkly tinted windows reflected the mass of concrete and glass of the SFU headquarters. Minton stopped on the sidewalk, as Calhoun opened the rear door of the Mercedes and ushered the Synthate inside.

She sat next to him on the vehicle's leather interior. The tinted divider between the passenger seats and the driver rose as the car pulled away from the curb. Calhoun placed his hand on her knee and then awkwardly rubbed the inside of her thigh. She smiled at him and said, "I have something for you."

"Another surprise?"

"Something like that."

The Synthate moved with incredible quickness. Something sharp pressed against Calhoun's neck. Surprised, he looked down to see a knife held to his throat. He smiled.

"You dumb Synth," Calhoun said. "You're dead."

"We're all dead eventually."

"What do you want?"

"Genetic handscan IDs. And before you open your mouth and say something stupid, I know you have them, and I know you sell them."

"You think that will save you? We'll still find you. All of you."

With an almost casual motion, she brought the knife up and sliced Calhoun's cheek. He felt a searing pain, and then the wetness of his blood as it ran freely down his cheek. Instinctively he reached up toward the cut, and the knife sliced his other cheek.

"Let it bleed," she said. "Move your hand again and you'll lose an ear."

Calhoun shuddered. The Mercedes continued to drive. He wondered who was behind the wheel. Then the edge of the knife was at his throat again.

He knew exactly what she wanted. And it was going to be of no use to her. As soon as she let him go, he would shut down all handscan IDs on the grid. If she impersonated anyone's DNA, the crushers would know.

"I'll give it to you." Calhoun reached into his jacket pocket and removed a black neoprene glove layered with genetic line scans.

"How does it work?" She took the device from him.

"Put it over your hand. It layers your palm with a temporary natural skin spray. Can fool any crusher touch screen. Only lasts a few hours."

The woman turned away from him and reached into her purse. Her hand moved quickly toward her mouth, and then she turned back. Strapped over her face was a small black mask. Calhoun recoiled in surprise.

In her hand was a white metal canister that began to hiss a plume of white gas.

"What are you doing?" Calhoun said in stark terror. "What is this?"

She didn't answer, and instead tilted the canister so that the gas hit Calhoun in the face. Immediately he felt his head go heavy. He swiped at the canister, tried to knock it from her hand, but his movement was weak, inaccurate.

She looked at him closely and he felt a prick in his arm, surprised to see she had stuck him with a needle. She patted his hand and smiled.

"Don't worry," she said. "You're one of us now."

He turned to open the door, to escape the blackness that crept in on him, but everything folded over. Something seemed to shut down, trapping him, the air heavy and close with nothing but darkness.

SFU Chief William Calhoun awoke on hard concrete. He was in a small cell with damp floors and a door of iron bars. A wooden table stood in the corner, on top of which was an old rotary phone. Somewhere metal clanged, and someone screamed in pain. A pile of clothes lay on the floor in the corner. He stood unsteadily, bracing himself against the wall.

Where was he?

He closed his eyes and the world faded to familiar blackness. His head throbbed with pain. Slowly he began to remember what had happened. There had been a Synthate female. A gift sent over by Genico. She had come to his office. Then his car had picked them up. The knife to his throat. And the gas. The sweet tingling odor of gas. Calhoun opened his eyes, furious now. Outside he heard a low rumbling explosion.

He would find them. He would destroy them all. Even if a hundred thousand Synthates expired in the process. The genetic companies were enormous; profits could suffer.

Calhoun looked down at himself, surprised to see he was wearing some kind of military uniform. The outfit was a drab green, with a darker green collar and shoulder straps with some sort of insignia over his chest. On his feet were black, military-style boots.

He looked closer at the insignia. It was a stylized eagle, both wings stretched out, its fierce-looking beak caught in profile. Below the talons, a familiar symbol.

A swastika. He was wearing the uniform of a WWII-era German infantry soldier.

The cell trembled again from some outside explosion. He heard a deep roar that sounded like ocean waves. The overhead lamp flickered. The telephone rang. Calhoun held the receiver to his ear. A voice came on the line. Male. Unknown.

"Hello, William," the voice said.

"Who is this?"

"You once took someone very important to me. Her name was Dolce. And you killed her. And for that, I'm going to kill you."

"Who are you?"

"My name is Jack Saxton."

The name was familiar. Calhoun's mind retreated back in time. Back to when Calhoun and his crushers had entered an apartment and found a Synthate impersonating a natural. He thought of the woman they had found as well. He couldn't remember her name anymore. But he knew they had been doing their duty.

"Wait a minute, I never touched her," Calhoun blurted out.

"You took everything from me. I want you to feel what I have felt."

Calhoun's chest tightened in anger and fear. "Now you listen to me! I was doing my job. And when I get out of here, everyone you know, everything you love . . . I will make it my mission to hunt them down and kill them. Do you understand?"

"Look in the mirror. Welcome to your next life."

The phone clicked and went dead.

"Hello? Hello?"

Calhoun listened to the hiss of static, then the dial tone. Fear spread, radiating out from his stomach, out along his arms to the tips of his fingers. He glanced around the cell again, this time seeing a small mirror that hung from the concrete wall. Slowly he moved to stand in front of it. Someone else's reflection stared back.

He moved toward the reflection. Then he pulled back in confusion. The face in the glass was not his. He touched his nose, his cheeks, his chin. All different. He had been given a new face. Now his skin was tighter. He looked younger. His eyes had changed from hazel to blue, his hair from brown to dusty blond. And above this new face, on the mirror itself, words in red had been scratched upon the glass.

You are one of us now.

Someone had changed his code. They had modified him somehow while he was unconscious. Given him a genetic facelift. Angry voices resounded from the hallway. Calhoun moved toward the door of his cell and peeked through the bars. A long hallway stretched down and at the far end SFU troops, bulky with Kevlar body armor and carrying Galil assault rifles, were systematically opening up cell doors and pulling out Synthates dressed in Nazi uniforms.

"Let's go, time to fight," one of the crushers said.

"Hey! Down here," Calhoun called out.

Immediately one of the soldiers responded, turned toward Calhoun, and raised his Galil rifle. Calhoun took a step back, surprised. "I am Section Chief William Calhoun. Put that rifle down, soldier."

"Don't speak to me," the crusher said as he advanced toward Calhoun.

"Now wait a minute here, soldier," Calhoun said, "you don't know who you're talking to."

The cell door opened and the crusher advanced.

"Shut your mouth. Do not speak unless spoken to!"

The rifle butt struck Calhoun hard, just below the rib cage. The blow knocked him backward; air vacated his lungs. He staggered and dropped to one knee. Hands grabbed him roughly by the neck and slammed him against the wall. He opened his mouth to protest, but he could do nothing but gasp for breath.

He was surrounded by crushers, their hostile stares foreign to him now. A lieutenant kept one hand wrapped around Calhoun's throat. Then, with the other, he jabbed a genetic marker test into Calhoun's mouth. Calhoun gagged as the cold metal snatched a layer of skin from inside his cheek.

The lieutenant checked the marker monitor and turned to one of the crushers. "Synthate 3420394."

The crusher checked a small vidBoard in his hand. "He's on the list."

The lieutenant pulled his hand away from Calhoun's throat. "Put him in."

Soldiers grabbed Calhoun under his arms and dragged him off the wall toward a line of waiting Synthates. Calhoun jerked his body, caught his breath and yelled, "Wait a minute! I'm Section Chief William Calhoun."

"And I'm fucking Abraham Lincoln," someone said with laughter from behind, just before a hand smacked Calhoun hard on the back of his head.

"This isn't right!"

Calhoun and the Synthates were forced to shuffle walk down the long hallway before being crowded into a freight elevator. A line of crushers held the mass of men at gunpoint.

"Time to fight," one of the crushers said. He held a large duffel bag, which he threw into the car. The bag struck Calhoun in the chest, then fell to the ground. The doors of the freight elevator closed and immediately the car began to carry them upward.

"Get that bag open," one of the Synthates said. Hands reached down and unzipped the bag. Weapons appeared. Luger pistols, blunt-nosed submachine guns, rifles, even a flamethrower. Someone began distributing the small arsenal around the elevator car.

"What's happening?" Calhoun asked a Synthate nearby with an elephant bioprint wearing the same uniform, the German eagle bearing a swastika stitched to the chest.

"Reinforcements."

"Reinforcements for what?"

"The Games. We're the cannon fodder," the Synthate said.

They really thought he was a Synthate. His own crushers didn't recognize him. The genetic reader had marked him as a Synthate. Someone had modified his genetic code. Someone had changed his DNA and now he was completely unrecognizable.

Around him, Synthates loaded their weapons and began to shift uncomfortably. Above them sounded machine gun fire, then another explosion. An enormous crowd cheered. The elevator car jerked to a halt. A siren blared and the doors opened. There was a push behind him of men and Calhoun was forced forward into the open. He squinted in blinding light. Slowly his eyes refocused. He stood at the edge of a gutted wasteland. The shells of buildings stretched ahead of him, brick structures whittled down to frames and piles of crumbling rubble. Roads had been turned to dirt and mud, pocked with craters the size of automobiles.

An explosion sounded terribly loud and Calhoun cringed, covering his ears with his hands. To his right, a dusty metal tank, a black swastika imprinted on its side, fired into the rubble of buildings. Its squat body shook as fire tore from the single turret. Figures in faded gray-green camouflage, armed with machine guns, huddled beneath cover.

In the distance, men in brown ducked between buildings, approaching under the protection of gunfire. The corner of a building burst into flames, and the low thunder rolled across the field of battle. Calhoun turned away from the men and stared into a massive crowd of people that stretched out of sight behind a thick wall of Plexiglas. The crowd responded to the rolling fire on the field as they rose to their feet and cheered. Overhead, a massive eyeScreen cut to an image of the building as it collapsed into rubble.

Terrified, Calhoun ran across the field and dived behind the corner of another structure. Three dead Synthates lay in the crater next to him. Calhoun shrieked and pulled himself away from the bodies. He stared wildly around. His analytical mind clicked into place and he recognized his location. He was on the German side during the fall of Berlin. Gunfire fire minced the dirt around him and he screamed as pain exploded in his right leg. Blood poured from the bullet wound and he clenched his teeth.

Above him, booted feet scraped against the rubble, and he turned to see a massive Synthate in a Russian infantry uniform silhouetted against the stadium lighting. The Synthate held a rifle, a long bayonet affixed to the end. Expressionless, the Synthate took a step toward Calhoun.

Calhoun held up his hand. "Wait, there's a mistake. I'm a natural. I don't belong here."

Without a word, the Synthate thrust the bayonet forward. Calhoun felt incredible pain in his gut and looked down to see the metal knife pushed into him up to the barrel of the rifle. The Synthate twisted the rifle and Calhoun felt his insides turn. Then the bayonet was yanked out, bits of flesh and blood still clinging to its shiny metal side.

Calhoun stared at his destroyed body. Then he burped warm blood and collapsed to his knees. The pain was unbearable. Then it gradually faded. All senses flowed out of him, through his belly and onto rough ground. Everything he'd ever known, his entire life, slowly caked the earth red, to the roaring applause of the crowd.

CHAPTER 45

A fleet of yellow taxis made slow progress along Fifth Avenue. The evening air had grown cool, the ambient heat from the sidewalk already siphoned off by the grid to illuminate the street lamps that hung along Central Park near the edge of the dome. Night Comfort's silk dress fluttered against her body as she stepped from a taxi. The driver had been a Synthate, his bioprint a clipper ship, sails billowing along his neck.

Her own bioprint was concealed with skin spray. In the Synthate code, this was an action punishable by fifty stuns. But if she were caught tonight, that would be the least of her problems.

Ahead of her, the Metropolitan Museum of Art was long and tall, its elegant limestone façade a beacon of humanity. Whatever that was.

"Without art," Jack stood next to her, looking up at the museum, "the crudeness of reality would make the world unbearable."

"The world has certainly become unbearable."

"Time to get some art," Jack said as he handed her an invitation. "Are you ready?"

Night Comfort nodded. "Are you?"

"We all are."

She turned and kissed him on the cheek, then quickly crossed the street.

A large crowd had gathered on either side of a red carpet that extended down the stairs. She joined the throng and lost herself in the stir of people, slipping into the anonymity of the crowd. Her invitation had been paid for with a generous donation to the evening's fundraising cause, and layered over the skin of her palm was a forged touch ID they had gotten from Calhoun.

The guard scanned her palm and the information returned came back natural. Night Comfort stepped inside the soaring neoclassical Great Hall. Inside the lobby, waiters were circulating glasses of champagne. Night Comfort took one, then headed through a set of doors. Pausing to admire a set of Egyptian sarcophagi, she took a sip of her drink, bent down, and placed on the ground a modified bottle cap. She stood, moved further down the hallway, stopped again in front of a set of papyrus pages, bent down, and placed a second cap on the polished wood floor.

She continued to move quietly and efficiently through the Egyptian wing. Here was the party's central area, where more waiters courteously plied the chattering crowd with canapés. Nearby, a chamber ensemble played, their music filling in the spaces of the general din.

Along one length of the room stretched a giant wall of glass, the abandoned section of Central Park visible beyond. Night Comfort surveyed the scene before proceeding toward the Asian galleries.

Her purse had been filled with caps. By the time she reached the top floor and the Impressionist Hall, it was almost empty. She paused before a colorful work by Gauguin, then walked past Monet's 1905 *Water Lilies* before she stopped at her destination, Renoir's *Dance at Bougival.* An hour had passed since she'd entered the museum and she'd managed to cover most of the floors. She still had a few minutes to admire the objective of her efforts. She studied the painting. One of the artist's more ambitious works, oil on canvas, painted in 1883.

Night Comfort had stared at a reproduction of it for hours while she prepped for tonight. She had felt a compulsion to reproduce the painting in her pod on Governors Island. But she had never seen the work like this. In person, close enough to admire each brushstroke, the colors, the engraving on the frame itself. The work was breathtaking.

And she was going to steal it. The thought thrilled her.

Around her the gallery was crowded, but still no one seemed to notice her. From her purse she retrieved a plastic tube the size of a ChapStick container. Inside was an iron-and-salt compound combined with petroleum, a faintly gray mixture the consistency of lip balm. She pulled off the top and a few moments later felt the tube grow warm, the iron oxidizing in the air and producing a low heat. Tube in hand, she bent down and made a small, four-inch streak along the wall just below the Renoir's frame, outlining the bottom left corner.

Then she stood, capped the tube, and slid it back into her bag as a tan-suited guard walked briskly toward her, telling her to, please, keep clear of the exhibits. She apologized and thanked him. Satisfied, he turned and returned to his post.

One of the natural guards stared at her, then smiled flirtatiously when she made eye contact with him. She smiled back. Inside she felt nothing but disgust. God, she hated them. She dialed Jack on her sync.

"See you soon."

Night Comfort left the museum, walked along Fifth Avenue and entered the lobby of their new rented honeycomb. Upstairs, Jack stood in the living room, pulling on a tan jumpsuit over his tuxedo.

"How'd you do?" Night Comfort asked.

"We're set," Jack responded.

Hearing this, Night Comfort took a second tan jumpsuit from Jack's hand and reached for the zipper of her dress. As she was about to drop the dress, she looked at him. He returned her stare, and she shrugged, letting it fall from her body. Standing there, she met Jack's eyes, then slowly pulled the jumpsuit on. She tossed a radio transmitter to Jack. "Don't get too distracted."

They walked down the back stairwell to the parking garage beneath the building. At its edge stood a large metal cart, the words "Carlotta Ice Design" printed on its side. Together, they began to push the cart along Fifth Avenue.

Ahead of them, the museum was outlined sharply against the night sky, lit by two dozen or so halogen lamps along the base of its walls. The crowd at the front doors had thinned considerably, with the party inside now in full swing.

The duo moved to the rear service entrance. The oil-stained, concrete loading dock was empty except for two natural security guards who burned smoke sticks at the top of the ramp. As Night Comfort and Jack drew closer, the guards turned their attention toward the cart heading in their direction. Night Comfort was designed too beautifully to ever be from the Domestic line. She kept her eyes to the ground, trying to conceal her face beneath her hair.

As they drew close, one of the guards flicked away his smoke stick in a long, burning arc.

The guards stepped forward and blocked their path to the service door.

"For the banquet," Night Comfort said.

"Late." The guard stepped aside, neither of the guards noticing that both Jack and Night Comfort wore latex gloves.

"Little bit," she replied.

Past the service entrance was a wide storage area with a blue metal door labeled "Electrical Closet."

Moving quickly, Night Comfort opened the blue door and stepped into a small room lined with silver metal circuit breakers. At its far end was a ladder leading up to a trapdoor in the ceiling. From beneath the cart, she retrieved a blowtorch and then climbed the electrical closet ladder. She twisted the torch on and put the hissing blue flame to the padlock securing the trapdoor. Quickly the lock fell open and Night Comfort pushed the door upward.

"All set," she said.

Jack pulled a black duffel bag from beneath the cart and handed it up to her. Holding the bag, she climbed up through the hole in the ceiling and shut the trapdoor behind her. The space above the electrical closet was dark and cramped. A metal I-beam stretched out ahead of her, bundles of thick wire reaching along it like vines as they threaded their way out through the museum and powered the exhibit lighting. She was now between the first and second floor, and, according to the architectural plans, the space ran directly over the Impressionist exhibit.

Night Comfort retrieved a small headlamp. She switched it on and a dim arc of light penetrated the darkness of the crawl space ahead of her. Fitting it over her forehead, she removed four metal poles, each an inch thick. They opened to form a rectangular sled of black mesh three feet long and two feet wide. The sled had titanium wheels, which she affixed on the far side of the I-beam, allowing the unit to slide along.

Slipping the bag over her shoulders, she lay down onto the sled, the mesh shape extending from her chest to just below her knees. As she began to pull herself forward, the wheels rolled silently along the ridge of the I-beam. A small digital odometer affixed to the sled ticked off numbers as she advanced.

The Impressionist gallery began one hundred and eleven feet from the electrical closet. The gallery extended for one hundred and eighty additional feet, with the Renoir being hung at approximately the ninety-third foot, or a total of two hundred and four feet from her starting point.

She turned on the sled's small electric motor, its low whir barely audible as it powered the strange vehicle. The ride continued smoothly, and a dusty breeze spilled against Night Comfort's face as she traveled above the coat room, the Exhibition shop, the American wing, the Frank Lloyd Wright room, and two 17th-century Dutch galleries before she finally felt herself begin to slow. The odometer counted past two hundred feet as she passed silently over the Impressionist gallery.

She slowed as the sound of the motor died off until finally she bumped to a stop. Below her, through the plaster ceiling, she could hear the faint murmur of conversation and the even fainter sound of music.

It was time.

She took a small electric winch and nylon rope from the duffel and attached the mechanism with four screw bolts to the I-beam. When it was secure, she used a hand-powered drill to bore a hole into the plaster ceiling below her.

She turned off her headlamp. The immediate area went dark except for a small circle of light that radiated up through the hole below her, illuminating swirling white plaster dust.

Next to emerge from the duffel was a handheld LCD monitor the size of a paperback book. A thin fiber optic cable snaked out from the end, and Night Comfort fitted the cable down through the hole in the ceiling. When she turned on the monitor, a black-and-white image of the gallery below flickered into view.

The view the screen relayed was of the milling crowd ninety feet below. She moved the camera in a slow swivel, inspecting the gallery. Two security guards were visible as they lounged against doorframes, lazily eyeing the assembled twenty or so people. Then she turned to the paintings. The Renoirs hung on the far wall nearest the door. Next to them, was the Van Gogh. And there, in the center of the gallery, was Monet's *Water Lilies*.

She had always thought *Dance at Bougival* was Renoir's finest work. Tonight, though, what was most important to her was this exemplar's weight.

Weight of the paint. Weight of the canvas. Weight of the frame.

The canvas itself was double-primed Belgian linen, 78 5/8 inches tall, 38 5/8 inches wide. Moderate in thickness, Belgian linen weighed just over one ounce per one thousand square inches, making the Renoir canvas itself, free of paint, approximately 2.9 ounces, or just under one-fifth of a pound.

The canvas's four stretcher bars were made of maritime pine, a light wood found in the Landes de Gascogne region of France. The stretcher bars would contribute more of the canvas's weight, adding another eight pounds.

Night Comfort's true fascination with art had always been about color. Color created with paint. The master's paint, heavy by today's standards, would have been made by boiling linseed oil, then adding ingredients such as yellow ochre, red and white lead, and pulverized cochineal, a type of insect dried and ground into a fine powder. Based on the specifics of Renoir's style, anywhere from five to six hundred milliliters of paint, about eight ounces, would be required to fill the canvas with color.

The bulk of the weight of the masterpiece, however, had to do with the frame. It was made from two-inch-thick gilded white oak, with a five-inch molding of applied ornament. A dense wood, white oak weighed 4.2 pounds per board foot, making the total weight of the frame alone approximately 74.2 pounds.

She checked her watch. Twenty minutes remained. She looked back at the monitor and passed her hand over the surface, over the image of the Renoir, readying herself to touch it for the first time.

Still where she had left him, Jack laid a linen tablecloth across the cart's top and let it drape over the sides. He then placed two trays of hors d'oeuvres on the white fabric. Pushing the cart from the electrical closet, he crossed through the service area and out into the Great Hall.

The Synthate named Grand Bleu stood on the other side of the doorway regarding a Max Ernst. He wore a well-tailored tuxedo, a cloth napkin over his arm. His body was athletic, not quite the pure bulk strength of one of the Games warriors, but conditioned to be in the Guard class. His face was handsome and unmarked by scars, a Synthate designed to blend in with the naturals, a product for those who wanted their security to be discreet. Nodding wordlessly to Jack, Grand Bleu took the cart. Jack watched Grand Bleu push it down the straight gallery hallway, past the chattering partygoers as he headed toward the musical instrument gallery.

Up in her hidden perch, Night Comfort felt her watch vibrate silently against her wrist. Five minutes to midnight. She inched forward and clipped a metal carabiner to a harness around her belt, then snapped the other end to a loop in the winch's nylon rope. The winch whirred one complete revolution and released a foot of loose rope that coiled on the sled next to her. The wireless operator on her harness controlled the winch and allowed her to regulate the desired speed.

She adjusted an infrared spotting scope over her eyes, the lithium battery power supply humming quietly inside the unit. From the bag came a rounded metal handle, jagged points on both ends. She pressed it into the plaster ceiling below her and turned the handle, locking it in. Taking a small handsaw, she slowly began cutting a five-foot-long rectangular section out of the ceiling around the handle. The saw was slightly sticky on its side and bits of plaster dust adhered to it before they could fall to the gallery floor below.

The handle gripped the plaster as she cut away the rectangular piece. Carefully she lifted up the section of the exhibit ceiling and placed it to the side.

Through the opening, the gallery lights illuminated the small crawl space in which Night Comfort hung, yet no one sensed her presence, nor did any alarms sound. She checked her watch again. Thirty seconds.

She slid a pneumatic dart pistol from the holster strapped to her leg, each dart loaded with 5cc of the powerful tranquilizer Telazol, used in the Games to operate on the wounded and more than enough to immobilize anyone. Keeping the pistol in her left hand, she checked her watch once more and gripped the side of the sled. She imagined the small detonator charge that Jack, then in his Con Edison uniform, had planted on the museum's power tubes beneath Fifth Avenue. There was no way to cut the museum's power entirely, only disrupt it momentarily. But that was all Night Comfort required.

Her watch ticked down to midnight. Underneath the street outside, the charge detonated, destroying the conduit tubes. Below her, the lights in the gallery went dark. Abrupt cries of surprise from the assembled New Yorkers filled the darkness. A moment later the emergency lighting came on. The guards moved quickly to the center of the room, talking into their radios and looking unsure how to respond. Night Comfort still waited, watching the confusion below her.

CHAPTER 46

An entire wing away and up one level, Grand Bleu pushed the linen-covered cart quickly down the long open hallway overlooking the Grecian marble statuary. Reaching the musical instruments gallery, he glanced at his watch and saw he was now twenty-five seconds behind schedule. He could see Outback waiting, a glass of champagne in her hand. She wore a black cocktail dress that accentuated her slim figure as she looked down at a West African balo xylophone.

Just beyond Outback was a single guard.

Grand Bleu pushed the cart against the wall, next to a fifteenth-century Irish harp. Walking swiftly up to the guard, he pressed his right palm hard against the man's face and pushed him backward. Holding the fellow down, he injected the guard's shoulder with Telazol, waiting until he was unconscious. When Grand Bleu felt the guard go limp, he dragged his body across the floor, opened a supply closet door, and pushed him inside.

Outback was there to greet him when he turned around. She kissed him on the cheek.

"Problem?" she asked.

"Not yet."

She straightened his bow tie. "You look very handsome in your tuxedo."

He checked his watch again. There was time.

Invisible now to the disrupted cameras, he took a step toward his prize: an eighteenth-century Guarneri del Gesù violin, in mint condition with its red-gold varnish still shining. Night Comfort had already briefed him on its history. Most critics acknowledged that the sound quality of Bartolomeo Guarneri was superior to the work of his Italian peer, Antonio Stradivari. This particular violin had been long held in a private collection in Warsaw before becoming a Nazi prize, seized during the invasion of Poland.

From beneath the cart, he removed a roll of clear plastic, eighteen inches square and sticky on one side. Outback helped him apply its adhesive surface to the display case glass, the plastic adhering tightly to the protective casing. The case was wired with a shatter alarm that would sound the instant the glass was broken. This alarm would send a signal to the security desk, alerting guards throughout the museum that the Guarneri violin had been compromised.

The response: A team of shotgun-toting guards would be heading straight for Grand Bleu.

That is, unless the security system had reason to believe more than just the violin was being stolen.

Grand Bleu gripped the wireless detonator in his hand, keeping a close eye on his watch, the seconds ticking by. The detonator would trigger the sixty small flash-bang explosives that Night Comfort had planted around the museum. All the units had been molded inside generic bottle caps, and as each went off, they would cause no damage to the museum or any artwork. Yet the result would be a concussion wave large enough to trigger any vibration alarms within a twenty-yard vicinity. So instead of the security system registering just the danger to the violin, it now had the chaos and confusion of many compromised areas.

The real target, then, could be any one of thousands of different pieces. The security system would light up each one, leaving the guards having to track down the single priceless needle in the haystack.

In the largest museum in the Western Hemisphere.

Grand Bleu wasn't going to circumvent the alarm system; he was going to use it.

He depressed the trigger with his thumb. Immediately the floor vibrated as the detonations were felt throughout the museum. There was an instant of quiet, and then the alarms sounded.

Grand Bleu took a ball-peen hammer from the cart and shattered the glass case with short, even strokes. He followed a path around the edges of the clear plastic, which held the shattered glass in place and ensured none of the fragments fell backward and damaged the delicate instrument.

When he'd carefully broken a complete square, Outback took hold of one edge of the plastic, quickly pulling down and away from the case. The entire square section of plastic came free, the shattered sections of glass still clinging to it, creating an eighteen-by-eighteen-inch opening. Grand Bleu reached in and removed the violin from its stand, holding it gently but firmly in his gloved hand.

He retrieved a black case from its hiding spot beneath the cart and placed the purloined treasure inside its velvet interior. He locked the case and handed it to Outback.

"You're sure you want this?" Grand Bleu asked.

"Of course," she said. "I always wanted to play the violin."

From above the Impressionist Galley, Night Comfort continued to watch the disturbance below. The area was protected by a SmokeOut alarm, a system that produced an enveloping and visually impenetrable cloud of harmless smoke designed to confuse intruders and prevent theft and escape. The mist was pumped out by four jets and infused with helium, giving it buoyancy and allowing it to spread more easily through the room.

She saw the white smoke billow out to each corner of the gallery and quickly envelop the surprised crowd. From inside the thick whiteness came frightened shouts as people lost in the smoke tried to find their way out. The jets continued to work, and quickly the fog rose up the wall of the gallery and headed toward the ceiling.

Night Comfort flipped down the infrared eye lens. The view relit in swirls of red and yellow as the imager picked up the heat in the room. At each of the exits was a large mass of pulsating red, barely distinguishable as individual bodies. She gripped the pistol tightly, rolled off the sled, and fell through the opening and into space. There was a tug as the winch began to lower her smoothly down into the smoke-filled gallery.

A figure, visible only as a warm glowing blob of red, stood ten feet to the right of her descent path. Night Comfort sighted the tranquilizer pistol, pulled the trigger, and watched the blob stagger back before it collapsed to the ground.

The smoke was thicker as she descended, visibility without the IR imager reduced to six inches, everything blanketed. She continued to descend, gradually slowing as she neared the museum floor.

The red blob she'd struck with the pneu-dart lay immobile on the ground to her right. In an hour or so she or he would begin to wake. The winch stopped suddenly. In front of Night Comfort was only white fog. Even without being able to see, she knew she should be only a few feet off the ground. Cautiously she swung her lower body down and felt the hard floor come into contact with her knee.

She placed a hot pad on the floor, then stood and surveyed the room. The pulsating reds and yellows were still visible while an automated voice instructed the crowd to head toward the exits.

Night Comfort turned her gaze now and concentrated on the details: the bright yellow of the emergency lights in the ceiling, the slowly fading pinks of the turned-off gallery lighting, the greens of the backup alarm system and, straight ahead of her, a four-inch line of red: the mark she had left earlier, the warm line of iron oxide streaked on the wall underneath the Renoir.

She moved quickly through the smoke and headed toward the treasure, her harness still attached. When she reached the red line, she slid her hand up along the wall until she felt the corner edge of the frame with her hand, the ornate beauty of it barely visible through the smoke. She took the wood firmly in both hands and lifted it up off the wall. A separate, more urgent, alarm sounded in the gallery.

The painting was heavy in her hands. She carried it awkwardly back through the smoke, guided toward the heat pad, which glowed a dull yellow in the infrared. When she reached her target, the winch smoothly pulled in the slack until the harness tugged against her back. A moment later she was in the air as she moved steadily up through the fog.

Grand Bleu and Outback kept moving. They traveled the long gallery back toward the rotunda. As they passed a fire alarm pull, Grand Bleu knocked out the glass and yanked down the lever. Immediately a siren sounded. By the time he reached the rotunda, the party was in chaos as people made their way toward the exits. The security team ran the perimeter of the rotunda, fingers pressed against earpieces, as they tried to determine what the hell was going on.

Directly below, the conductor was rounding up the tuxedo-clad men and black-dressed women of the small orchestra. Grand Bleu, in his tuxedo, and Outback, in her black cocktail dress, mixed in with the orchestra and let themselves be swept along toward the exits.

The alarms were still erupting as hordes of people bunched up before the exits where security checkpoints had been hurriedly set up. A metal detector had been placed to the rear of the exit, a final precautionary measure before the guests reached the outside world. The musicians, too, were being searched, their instrument cases inspected. Grand

Bleu and Outback followed the line to the checkpoint. A stocky guard with a black mustache pointed at Outback. "Open your case, please."

"Of course, but what's happening?" Outback asked.

"There've been some alarms set off," he said as she opened the latches on her violin case. "Security checks for everyone leaving the building."

Calmly, Outback opened the violin case and exposed the Guarneri. At an adjoining table, a tuxedoed man had been told to open his viola case, and Grand Bleu watched a guard poking around inside the instrument with a metal rod and a flashlight. In fact, all around them instrument cases were being opened and prodded, exactly as he had planned.

The guard picked up the Guarneri roughly, inspected the bridge and the ribs and tried to peek down into the F-hole.

"I hope nothing's been stolen," Outback said.

"I don't think so. Our security is excellent here."

"I've noticed that."

The guard sighed, put the violin back in the case, and closed the lid.

Outback took the handle in a firm grip and hefted the case off the table. Grand Bleu had reached the front of the line and was holding his arms up as another guard ran a metal-detecting wand over his body. She was already out in the night air before he received his own grunted dismissal. Behind Grand Bleu another violinist was being patted down. Tonight, Outback would make one more musician leaving than had arrived, with the extra violinist carrying an especially old and especially rare violin.

Night Comfort was ninety feet in the air as she rose up through the hole she'd carefully cut to accommodate the painting. Below her, the museum gallery was still filled with fog. She unhitched herself from the harness, then rolled over onto her back on the sled, the Renoir resting heavily on her chest. The sled began to move, carrying her back down the length of the girder, its motor humming.

When the sled had traveled forty feet, it stopped again at the second premeasured distance, the access ladder. Gripping the painting, Night Comfort rolled off the sled, crouching in the small crawl space. She turned on her headlamp. The bulb melted away the darkness and revealed the skeletal structure of the ceiling, the steel support beams, the lengths of wiring and, only a few yards away, a single metal ladder.

According to the schematics, the ladder ran the entire height of the building, between the galleries of Chinese Art and 19th-Century American, before it exited on the museum's roof near the ventilation systems, forty yards from the Cantor Roof Garden. Removing a custom-made backpack from beneath the sled, she slid the Renoir inside and strapped the bag to her shoulders. Picking her way over the lengths of cable to the ladder, she slowly climbed up. Below her, she could still hear the ongoing shriek of the alarms.

The ladder ended with a large trapdoor. She cut the lock with her torch and pushed the heavy panel upward. Cool night air flowed through the open space. She climbed out onto the moonlit roof of the museum, the Central Park dome reflected the street lamps, and in the distance, the lights of Manhattan stretched before her.

By now, the museum guards would have formed a perimeter around the museum. Police sirens approached from all sides. The entire museum would be shut down. She flicked off her headlamp, the moon and the skyline providing her with light. The roof was lined with square ventilation fans that formed a single column, pale like a row of metallic gravestones. She counted the third one in from the northern side of the wall. Crouching down next to the fan, she unzipped a side pocket of the carrier and emptied its contents onto the roof.

Spread before her was a lightweight polyester composite balloon. She rolled it out to its full length, fourteen feet with an opening at one end connected to a compressor valve and a two-foot-long flexible tube. She affixed the tube's open end to the lip of the fourth exhaust fan, then checked her watch and waited.

The ventilation fan was connected by a straight duct to the Impressionist gallery, now filled with the helium-infused smoke. Helium naturally comprised only .06 percent of the Earth's atmosphere, but levels of the gas's concentration inside the gallery had quickly reached seventy percent when the alarm was triggered. To prevent hypoxia of museum guests and to allow the authorities to enter the room and assess loss, the alarm system was set to a timer, with the room automatically cleared of smoke in exactly nine minutes. As the smoke was pulled through the overhead ventilation systems, the helium naturally separated itself and was then released through the exhaust fans on the roof as a ninety-eight percent pure gas. The released helium would rise from the ventilation system and disappear into the Earth's atmosphere, unless something was placed over the exhaust fan to catch it.

Something like a balloon.

Night Comfort watched the timer. Down at street level, the sirens grew louder. Tires screeched as black-and-whites pulled into the circular museum driveway far below her. A police helicopter would be in the process of being scrambled now from the NYPD Aviation Center in Brooklyn.

The exhaust fan was still quiet. It was getting late and she couldn't wait much longer. Without the helium from the gallery below, she would have to leave the Renoir behind. From her spot on the roof, she could see across to the side-facing wall of the museum's east wing; museum and police units moved through the rooms, appearing from window to window. Enough alarms had been triggered that security units would be spread out thinly through the building, trying to ascertain what exactly had happened.

Suddenly she heard the fan beginning to move. Slowly but steadily it pumped out the helium and smoke from the gallery below. She turned on the small compressor, forcing the helium-filled air from the museum into the balloon.

Its design was similar to a full-scale blimp. Interior ballonets worked like the ballasts of a submarine, deflating or inflating with additional air as the balloon needed to rise and fall, while air scoops, valves, and flight control surfaces all served to guide the direction and angle of movement. Two battery-powered engines were at the base, smaller versions of turbo-propeller airplane models, each about two and a half feet in length and giving the balloon a top speed of twenty miles per hour.

In place of the gondola were a series of metal fasteners that clipped lengthwise along the carrier.

The necessary diameter of the helium-filled balloon had already been calculated in order to ensure there was enough lift to pull the weight of the bag, painting, and frame off the roof. The gallery below carried a helium capacity far beyond what was necessary for launch.

A beacon located northeast of the museum on City Island in the Bronx sent out a cellular homing signal every twenty seconds, which was received by a small transponder located on the balloon itself. Once airborne, the engines powered themselves automatically, the balloon rising to two thousand feet before propelling itself up over Manhattan toward the homing beacon.

The balloon was rapidly filling now, tugging at Night Comfort as she held it in place. In the visible section of the museum's east wing, the flashlights still crisscrossed over the walls and floors as security personnel made their way through the Greek and Roman exhibits.

Night Comfort wondered how long it would be before they discovered the Renoir was missing.

The exhaust fan still whirred, and the balloon, almost completely full now, was pulling away. A tightly rolled 100-yard length of nylon rope was attached to its side. She untied it, letting out slack until the bulk of the coil rested on the roof. If the balloon got into trouble during the first hundred yards, moving toward trees or electrical lines, Night Comfort would still be able to keep control manually. Beyond one hundred yards, it was on its own, following the signal being emitted from the final destination point.

She sealed off the air envelope, pulled away the filling hose, then in one motion released the balloon from her grip. It rose quickly into the air, becoming a vague smudge high over the museum. In a few minutes, its efficient turbo-propeller engines would begin to power forward.

She disconnected the hose from the air exhaust fan and heard a noise at the rooftop's edge, twenty yards behind her.

The sound of booted feet on the metal rungs of a ladder.

Then a voice, surprised and overaggressive. "Hey! Police! Don't move!"

Night Comfort kept her back to the speaker as she slowly stood, raised her hands to the black ski mask on her head, and unrolled it until it covered her face, single holes for her eyes and mouth.

"Don't move! Show me your hands!"

She did as she was told, raising her hands over her head. Behind her she could hear the screech of a police radio, then the excited chatter of voices.

"Turn around . . . slowly . . ."

Night Comfort turned and stared into the barrel of the SIG Sauer the young NYPD cop was aiming at her chest. He stood about twenty yards away. It would be a difficult shot for him to make if she moved quickly.

"Nobody has to get hurt tonight," she said steadily.

"Stop talking. Don't open your mouth."

On the far side of the roof, she heard shouting and new footsteps as four more cops climbed up onto the roof behind her.

"Down on your knees! Hands behind your head!"

Night Comfort slowly lowered herself to her knees, clasping her hands behind her head. The young cop moved forward, gun raised, chin down, as he talked into the radio on his left shoulder. Somewhere above, the balloon continued to rise, the control rope quickly uncoiling.

The officer, ten yards away now, reached toward his belt and removed a set of handcuffs. The rope was almost completely uncoiled, stretching a full hundred yards above Night Comfort, just a few feet to her left.

"Don't move . . ." the cop warned again.

"I'm not going with you," Night Comfort said. She turned, grabbed the very end of the nylon rope, and ran toward the back edge of the museum roof. The cop froze for a moment, then lowered his gun and chased after her. She reached the rooftop edge, and, still in stride, leaped out into space, nine stories up. The world became a spinning, blurry thing of passing images and sounds. There was the wail of police vehicles, the hard, flat pavement, and dark grass, everything swinging back and forth below her.

Then the rope pulled taught in her hands, and she felt her body swing as she was lifted up and over the street.

The rope oscillated wildly before she swung her legs and steadied herself. Above her the balloon had already begun to power forward, giving her momentum from the jump as she sailed away from the immense building. Her weight was too much for the lift to carry and she slowly felt herself sinking back to Earth, falling in a long arc from the museum's roof.

She began to fall faster as she sailed across the line of squad cars parked at jagged angles below. Moments later, her feet skimmed the top brush of the elm trees that lined Fifth Avenue. She began to float downward until she hit the solid, grassy ground just before the park. She rolled, and let go of the rope. The balloon rose up again, carrying the line with it. She was a hundred yards down from the museum.

Night Comfort turned from the shadow and ran, quickly swallowed up by the city.

CHAPTER 47

Night Comfort had gotten out of the city. After meeting Jack in a parking garage, they had picked up the Guarneri Gesù violin from Grand Bleu and Outback, then she and Jack had driven the rental van north while the painting floated somewhere overhead. Now, an hour later, Night Comfort lay alone in the center of a small wooded field on City Island that stretched down to the edge of Long Island Sound.

Wind carried with it the smell of the ocean. Sometimes she thought there was so much beauty in the world that all the canvas that had been painted and all the stone that had been sculpted since the beginning couldn't possibly come close to capturing it all. Sometimes she almost couldn't breathe, so saturated was she with beauty that her lungs filled up and every pore was blocked.

She thought of Arden, how she could feel no love for him. She felt maybe she had been created wrong. Created with a faulty vessel inside her, a leaky soul that let the beauty slip through and left her helpless and empty as so much seeped out of her, evaporated through her skin like a sheen of water in the hot sun while she struggled vainly to keep it all in, to remember it all. What would it be like to hold on to those little moments of beauty, this field at night with its hay grass and fragrant trees, to keep this place inside of her forever, carry it with her, keep all these places with her until she swelled with the joy of it like a woman carrying a growing child? What would it be like to have this as her soul?

The homing beacon in her hand continued beeping with the steady regularity of a metronome. The Renoir was high above her, sailing among the stars, a black void against the night sky, difficult to see even with her amplified Synthate vision. The balloon began its descent, growing larger and larger until it sank into the tall grass off to her right. She kept her eyes on the stars above, and listened to the sound of crickets.

Finally, she stood. Across the water, Manhattan's lights stretched out like a distant sun dipping below the horizon. The big balloon was slowly deflating, collapsing in stages to the ground like a dying animal.

Slowly she bent down, unzipped the carrier, and opened it.

Inside Renoir's *Dance at Bougival* glowed in the moonlight.

On the top of the frame, a small red light blinked once. Then again. Curious, Night Comfort bent down to examine the point of light. Her heart plunged.

A tracking device.

"Jack! Get over here," she called out.

Jack came at a run and she pointed to the flash. "They put a tracker on it."

"How much time do we have?"

"Not much." Night Comfort took a corner of the painting. "Let's get this in the van."

In the distance, they heard the low hum of rotors. Out across the water, two helisqualls skimmed the surface of the bay, heading toward their location.

"Too late," she said. "Here they come."

Night Comfort navigated the wheel as the van sped south back toward the city. Jack sat in the back with the Renoir, bracing himself against the door as the van bounced over roads. Through the rear window, he could see the lights of the helisquall gunships.

Jack scanned the back of the frame, looking for anything out of place. If Reynolds had hidden something in the painting, the frame would be the easiest place to do so.

"I don't even know what I'm looking for," Jack said.

"Find something. We're running out of time. Half the cops in the city will be headed our way."

The van passed over the RFK Bridge, water turbines blurring by beneath them. In his hand, the tracking device continued to blink red. Even if they got rid of it now, the helisqualls still had them in sight. The van took a hard turn, and Jack was thrown against the rear doors.

"Where are you going?" he called out.

"Don't know yet," Night Comfort answered.

Jack focused back on the painting. The canvas was flat and blemish free. There was no place to hide anything there and for a moment, Jack began to doubt his theory about Reynolds. What if the scientist hadn't hidden anything in the painting?

"Check the frame," Night Comfort called out.

The frame was solidly constructed of several-inch-thick oak. The wood seemed smooth and completely seamless. Jack began slowly running his fingers over the back. He had almost tracked the entire length of the frame when his skin brushed against an inconsistency in the wood.

He bent down and saw a hairline seam in the wood.

"Hey, I think I've got something," Jack called out. He dug his fingernails into the seam and slowly worked out a piece of wood. One six-inch segment of frame slid out, and from inside, a Samp cylinder popped into Jack's hand.

"Find it?"

"Got it. Reynolds hid something in the frame. Looks like a Samp."

"Samp for what?"

Jack studied the liquid as it rolled inside the clear container. "Don't know."

The van passed through an acid scrubber mist cloud, then bounced over a pothole. A brilliant white light flooded the interior. One of the helisqualls covered them with a searchlight.

"We're never going to be able to outrun those things," she said.

"We have to get out of sight."

The van screeched and narrowly avoided a parking taxi. "I'm open to suggestions."

Jack thought for a moment. "Remember the map we saw in Beach's subway station?"

"So?"

"The tunnels extended all over the city. They must have openings somewhere. We just have to find them."

"How do we do that?"

Jack quickly pulled out his sync. Trying to maintain his balance in the rear of the bouncing van, he did a quick search for Alfred Beach. He then cross-referenced the search with all of the holding data that Jack had downloaded from the Genico mainframe. In a moment, the search came back with the results. A single, ten-story granite office building 3Deed inside the car along with an address.

"Think I got something," Jack said. "Head to 9 West 20th Street."

Night Comfort turned the wheel of the van, and the tires screeched as they exited the FDR and began to head west through the Park conurbs.

Keeping her eyes on the road, she asked, "What's there?"

"That was Alfred Beach's home address the year he died."

"So?"

"The entire building was bought by Genico a few years ago. If there's going to be a tunnel entrance somewhere, that's where my father would have put it."

Rotors whined overhead as one of the helisqualls buzzed over the top of their van and moved ahead of them. "Hang on," Night Comfort called, before she turned the wheel hard. The vehicle spun around a corner, then she accelerated past traffic and headed west on 47th Street.

"Where are you going?" Jack gripped the Renoir tightly, trying to keep the canvas from banging against the van's interior.

"Park Avenue viaduct. We'll lose them there."

The viaduct was an elevator roadway that cut around Grand Central, then passed directly through the interior of the old Helmsley building. The helisqualls wouldn't be able to follow them through the building. But as they sped down Park, there was something about the plan that bothered Jack.

One of the helisqualls struck a low wind farm, knocking the turbine against the side of an office building. Sparks and broken glass rained down on the sidewalk. Naturals scattered. Night Comfort accelerated, and the big engine roared as they jumped the curb around a garbage truck. Synthates in khaki-colored uniforms dived out of the way.

Jack realized what was wrong. The viaduct split as it entered the Helmsley building, and they were in the oncoming lane. Ahead loomed the massive 35-story building. Each of its two circular road entrances gaped open like mouths.

"You're going down the wrong way!" Jack tried to pull himself toward the front, desperately grabbing at a seatbelt.

"Hang on," Night Comfort said.

Seeing the approaching buildings, one of the helisqualls banked sharply. A burst of gunfire sounded from its mounted machine gun. The back tire of the van exploded, and the vehicle lurched forward, metal rims thumping against the pavement as they entered the darkness of the tunnel inside the building. Headlights bore down on them, and Night Comfort turned the wheel sharply.

The van impacted against the curved tunnel wall. Jack was thrown forward against the front seat. The Renoir frame slammed painfully against his leg. The van spun once, then came to a rest inside the tunnel. Somewhere a horn blared.

Night Comfort was out of the front seat in an instant. A yellow taxi had come to a stop just feet from their van. She ripped open the front seat of the taxi, then pulled out the startled natural driver.

"Come on, let's go," she called out to Jack.

Jack's head was ringing from where he'd struck it against the back of the seat. He staggered toward the sliding door of the van, then turned and saw the Renoir. The painting lay undamaged on the floor of the van. He hesitated, looking at the priceless work of art.

"Just leave it," Night Comfort said. "We have what we need."

Jack knew he should leave it, but to be in the presence of that beautiful work of art had changed him inside. When he looked at the painting, he felt somehow free. And he didn't want to just walk away from that.

"Jack," she called out again. "Come on."

"Synthates aren't even allowed in museums," Jack said. "This is our chance. We may never get this moment again."

"Let it go," she said softly. "Jack. Let it go."

All the hatred built up over time suddenly seemed to explode. The naturals had taken everything beautiful from his world. He wanted to take something beautiful from theirs. Outside the sounds of sirens were fast approaching. Jack flipped open a gravity knife from his pocket and carefully cut along the frame until the canvas fell free from the wood. The tracking device imbedded in the frame continued to blip its red light.

"Sorry, Pierre," Jack said as he rolled the canvas into a tube. "But our people need this more than yours."

With the roll of artwork in hand, Jack jumped from the van and joined Night Comfort in the taxi. Cautiously she pulled out from the tunnel and back into the night air outside the Helmsley building. Overhead the sky was clear. Jack imagined that both helisqualls would be hovering on the opposite end of the tunnel, waiting for their van to appear. They didn't have much time before cops and crushers entered the viaduct, found the smashed van, and realized what had happened.

"We need to get underground," Jack said, clutching the painting in his lap, the 6th Day Samp still in his pocket.

"We can't go to the Ramble," Night Comfort said. "We can't take the chance of leading the crushers there."

"And anywhere near Genico is going to be crawling with crushers now after Calhoun's disappearance. We'll have to try Beach's home. Hopefully we can find a tunnel entrance."

CHAPTER 48

The building at 9 West 20th Street was closed for the night, but a scattering of lights in the higher floors showed the edifice wasn't completely empty. They left the taxi parked on the street outside. Jack pulled on the single glass door and found it locked. The front lobby was dark.

"We could break it," Jack said, knocking on the glass.

"No." Night Comfort shook her head. "There would be an alarm."

Jack saw a touch screen mounted on the wall near the door. He pressed his palm against the screen and the door lit green and swung open.

"Looks like someone left you the keys," Night Comfort said.

They entered the building cautiously. Beyond the doors was a small, anonymous lobby, with a single elevator and an empty doorman's desk. The acid scrubber churned quietly in the corner. A metal door opened into darkness. Jack found a switch, and lights flickered on to reveal a set of metal stairs leading down.

"Another gloomy tunnel underground. Great," Night Comfort said as she stepped past Jack and began walking down. "That's just what we need."

After ten feet, the stairs leveled off to a flat concrete hallway that stretched beneath the building. The hallway was lined with eyeScreen pedestals that flared to life as they moved forward. Each pedestal 3Deed a human form, which revolved in space along the edge of the hall. There were dozens of 3Dees featuring both men and women. Some were muscular, some beautiful, some short and stocky, all varied impressions of the same form.

"What's happening?" Jack asked as they walked down the hall.

"They're all Synthate Design classes. From the inception of the Synthate program." Night Comfort walked slowly down the line. "Each class has slight modifications so they can be differentiated from one another. But this is an entire history of a people."

Jack could see how the first Synthates had gradually been divided into the four classes: Social, Domestic, Industrial, and Guard. Night Comfort stopped before a 3Dee of an athletic young man, constructed with the perfect proportions of a Michelangelo statue, but built from flesh and bone. "This is the male prototype for my class," she said. "This is our Adam."

"What happened to him?"

"Who knows? Probably extinguished in some pleasure parlor somewhere."

Beyond the Social Adam were more pedestals with 3Dees of other Synthates. Jack walked slowly down the line, taking in each one. They were all variants of one another, like the stencil drawings of Darwin's finches. Or the ascent of man from the apes. Each prototype was another variation on evolution, all carefully constructed in a lab.

And then Jack felt his heart drop. The world seemed to shift and move forward in one jerky motion, like the gears of some terrible machine clicking into place.

"My God," Jack said.

"Find something?"

Jack couldn't answer. Could barely speak.

What is this?

Jack *had* found something. He had found Dolce. And she was standing in front of him.

Jack reached his hand out for his wife. His fingers passed through her, as if she were made of mist. *Am I hallucinating?*

Night Comfort squeezed his arm. "She's a 3Dee. She's not real."

Jack look down and saw the eyeScreen base at her feet. Her image projected upward into space. He reached out once more, and again his hand passed through her body. Then Dolce looked at him. "Can I help you, sir?"

That was her voice. But there was something creepy about its sound. Something empty.

He turned toward Night Comfort. "What's happening?"

"This must be a showcase model," Night Comfort said. "For Synthate stores."

Dolce bowed slightly. "Maybe I can be of service. Do you have any questions?"

This wasn't his Dolce. This was just a shadow. A puppet with her face. But she stood before him so full of life. So real. "Who are you?"

"I am Synthate model 5300. I'm happy to serve a variety of home and relaxation needs."

Jack wanted to feel doubt. "Dolce wasn't a Synthate."

Night Comfort frowned, and studied the 3Dee. "She may have been."

"But she had no bioprint. She had a childhood. I grew up with her."

"She might have been a prototype."

"So you're saying my wife was what, like a test run of some new Synthate model?"

"We had heard stories of a new design. More like a natural than a Synthate. But still from a grow garden."

"She was pregnant with my child," Jack said. "How do you explain that?"

"I have been designed to be fully reproductive," the 3Dee of Dolce said. "I will be the perfect companion for those naturals seeking to start a family with a loving partner."

Jack felt suddenly sick. "You're saying you can give birth?"

"Yes. I will be designed to be as fully reproductive as a natural."

Jack turned to Night Comfort, his face white. "Who am I talking to right now?"

"It's a Synthate display model. Most of the answers are prerecorded. Some interaction is possible, but basically you're talking with a Genico mainframe. It's a Synthate advertisement."

"Who designed you?" Jack asked the 3Dee.

"Genico Industries."

The excitement he had felt the day Dolce had told him she was pregnant suddenly faded away. Everything felt empty and contrived, part of some Genico master plan.

"Will you know you're a Synthate?" Night Comfort asked.

Dolce looked down at her. "I do not understand your question."

"After your inception, will you know you're a Synthate or will you think you're human?"

"That is determined by my mate or those naturals who choose to adopt me as a parent. I will be told the truth after my inception. I will be aware that I am a Synthate. But if my mate or my parents so choose, I can be given Amnease Samps and my memory modified so that I have no recollection of my beginnings."

Her voice was hollow. Empty of emotion. Like she was reading from a script. He tried to reconcile the Dolce he remembered with this lifeless image that now stood before him.

"Have we met before?" Jack asked.

Dolce studied Jack, her eyes heartbreakingly blank. She shook her head. "I don't believe we've met before, sir."

An intense wave of sadness flooded through Jack. He reached again for Dolce, but pulled his fingers back before he touched her. God help him, but he wanted to hold on to this illusion for a few minutes more. He couldn't bear the sight of his hand passing through her projection.

"I'm so sorry," Night Comfort said to him.

"I don't understand. I've known this woman my entire life," Jack said. A thought occurred to him. "How many of you are there? How many were produced in the first inception?"

"The first inception occurred twenty-nine years ago. In that inception there were two Synthates with my exact coding produced."

Two. My God. Somewhere in the world was another just like his Dolce.

"What happened to those two?"

"One of the engineered Synthates has been retired."

"And the second?"

"The second currently habitats a residential community east of here. I can send an address to your sync."

"Is she living as a natural or a Synthate?"

"I do not know."

Jack tried to absorb this information. He imagined this alternate Dolce and what life she might be living.

"Were there any Synthates of your design class produced with a male coding?" Night Comfort asked.

"Yes. There was one Synthate male produced."

Jack looked up sharply. He hadn't even considered such a possibility. There was a male Synthate. Would that mean Dolce had a brother?

"Do you know his location?" Jack asked.

"I have no knowledge. He was removed from the database after his inception date."

"Can you show me what he would look like?"

"Of course." The 3Dee of Dolce flickered, then shifted to display a new image of a fully grown man. The man rotated over the projection pad and gave Jack the shock of his life.

Above him, rotating in 3Dee over the projection pad, stood Phillip Saxton. Jack felt a chill run the length of his body. He struggled to understand. "My brother is a Synthate?"

"That's not possible," Night Comfort said. "Your brother is so average. No Synthate is genomed to be that way."

"So what is this? Why am I looking at him?"

"I'm not sure," she replied, then turned toward the man. "Do you have a name?"

The 3Dee of Phillip turned to look at her. "I am Synthate model 5300m. I'm happy to serve a variety of home and relaxation needs."

"How many in your production class?"

"There was one of my model in production."

"Where is he currently?"

"My information does not contain that record."

"When was your production date?"

"Five years past."

Jack turned back to Night Comfort. "So Genico made a perfect model of my brother. For what purpose?"

She shook her head. "I don't know."

"I don't know, either. But I can't stand to look at him anymore. Let's go." Jack turned and began to walk away from the pedestal.

Night Comfort caught up with him. "I know how hard this must be for you."

"To see that my whole life and every person in it has been a Genico lie?"

"I'm sorry."

From behind them came a voice. "Wait. Please."

Jack's heart accelerated. Slowly he turned back. Dolce stood again on the pedestal. But now she seemed to stare with increased alertness. "I do know you, Jack Saxton."

"You remember me?"

"*Remember* is not the appropriate word. We have never met."

"So how do you know me?"

"Your face is familiar to me. I was instructed that you might come."

"Instructed by whom?"

"Dr. Martin Reynolds. Do you know him?"

"I know him," Jack said, thinking of the murdered scientist. "He told you I would come?"

"He said that you were very special. And one day you might come. And that if you did, I was only to talk to you."

"Talk to me about what?"

"Do you have the key?"

Jack glanced at Night Comfort. "What's she talking about?"

She shook her head. "No idea."

Jack walked back and stood before the 3Dee of his dead wife. "What key?"

"I have access to many things. If you have the right key."

"Access to what things?"

"Not before the key."

"Where would I get the key?"

"I cannot tell you that."

"But Dr. Reynolds told you to talk to me."

"He told me to do so only if you have the key. He was going to give you the key and then I would know if you were to be trusted."

Jack understood. Reynolds had planned to find Jack and to give him this key, whatever it was. But Reynolds was murdered. And the key was lost.

"Reynolds planned to give me something," Jack replied.

"He already gave it to you," Dolce said.

Jack turned back toward her. "What?"

"I see that you have already been given the key."

Jack shook his head. That was impossible.

"Wait a minute," Night Comfort said. "We're thinking of locks and keys. But I think she's talking about keys in music."

"A musical key? Where would that be hidden?"

Night Comfort pulled something from Jack's backpack. "Somewhere like this, maybe?" In her hand, she held Reynolds's Guarneri Gesù violin they had taken from the museum. She held the violin up to Dolce's 3Dee. "Is this the key?"

"I cannot help you," she said.

"Fair enough," Night Comfort replied. She bent down over the violin and began to inspect the antique instrument. It was constructed of a varnished wood, with the typical long neck and S-shaped body. She shook the instrument gently, hearing nothing rattle inside. Then she peered down through the F-hole near the bridge.

"Can't see anything inside," she said. "But I'm not even sure what I'm looking for."

"What if the entire instrument is the key?"

"No. She would have told us," Night Comfort said. "It has to be something else."

"If it even has to do with musical keys."

Night Comfort frowned and ran her fingers over the peg box and scrollwork at the end of the neck. "Look at this peg. It looks different than the others. Newer."

The tuning pegs were constructed from rosewood. Three of them were uniform in color. The fourth was lighter, the edges more defined. Definitely newer. Night Comfort began slowly unscrewing the peg, which soon came free in her hand.

The rounded wood straightened to a metal-colored key that had been concealed inside the peg box. She held the peg up to Dolce.

"You have found the key," Dolce said.

Dolce flickered and then vanished. Then the entire room filled with light as a map of New York City formed in the center and slowly began to spin around them. The map was overlaid by a series of grid-like networks that crisscrossed the entire island.

Dolce's voice narrated as the map revolved around them. "This map shows a network of acid scrubbers that have been installed throughout the city. These scrubbers were funded and controlled by Genico following the acid rain waves of many years ago. All air is scrubbed with cleaning compounds, eliminating acid rain and synthesizing clean, breathable air."

"What does this have to do with us?" Jack asked.

"The acid scrubbers are controlled by a single system accessible from the top floor of the Genico building. Any substance introduced into this system can be dispersed throughout the city."

Jack thought of something immediately. "Could a Samp be dispersed in this way?"

The map flashed, vanished, and Dolce reappeared. "Yes. A Samp would be made airborne and spread like a mist throughout the entire city."

"How many people would be affected?"

"Given infection rates of Genico-devised Samps, this system would cover ninety percent of the population. Over ten million."

Night Comfort turned toward Jack. "This was how Reynolds was going to spread the 6th Day Samp."

Something bothered him. There was something so familiar about this conversation. A thought that sat just on the edge of his consciousness that he couldn't quite rein in.

"Have the acid scrubbers ever been used before in this way?" Jack said.

"Once. There was a test run to see if the system design would be capable of distributing an aerosol contaminate."

"And was it successful?"

"It was successful. I believe it was referred to in the media as the Black Rain infection."

Of course. That made perfect sense. "You're saying that Genico engineered the Black Rain attack? We were told it was from the Synthate rebels."

"Genico created an aerosol contaminate to allow them to track the efficacy of the acid scrubber system as a dispersal unit. They did not realize that the contaminate, or Black Rain, would cause such severe illnesses in people. The Synthate rebellion story was created as a diversion."

"Who programmed you to tell us all this?" Jack asked.

"I have access to Dr. Reynolds's journals and correspondence, and video archives of his research. His personal thoughts indicate that he felt a great deal of responsibility for having caused so much unintended pain to naturals and Synthates. He felt that the increasing commercialization of the genetic industry was to society's detriment. In his later years, he became determined to allow more open access to the benefits of the genetic industry."

"That's why he created the 6th Day Samp," Night Comfort said. "So we would all be equal."

Jack was lost in thought, his eyes fixed on the 3Dee of Dolce. So eerily familiar. He realized that none of this really mattered to him. In the end, he just wanted revenge against those who had taken her from him. He turned to Night Comfort. "I have to see her."

"See who?" Night Comfort asked.

"Dolce." Jack pulled out his sync. "We know where she is. I have to see her."

Night Comfort turned toward him. "I don't know if that's a good idea."

"You didn't lose her. You don't know what that's like."

"I've lost almost everyone I've ever known. But the Dolce you knew is gone forever. Whoever is living out there now, the second Synthate in her production line, she's not going to know who you are."

"Don't say 'production line' like she's some vidScreen. She was my wife."

"She was. And she was taken from you. And whether she was a Synthate or a natural, that pain will always be there."

"When I see her, she will know me. I feel it in my heart."

Night Comfort turned toward the 3Dee. "Synthate model 5300, is there a shared consciousness between two production models?"

"I do not understand."

Night Comfort thought for a moment, and said, "Is there a way for one production model to know what the other production model is experiencing without direct communication?"

"No. That is not possible."

Jack turned away. He wanted so desperately to believe.

"Synthate model 5300, give us a moment," Night Comfort said.

"Of course."

The 3Dee vanished, leaving Jack and Night Comfort alone in the hall. She turned toward him. "We can find her. But she won't know you." She indicated a door at the end of the hall. "Through there we can get back to the Beach lab. If we're successful, we can liberate an entire race. That way, Dolce will have died for something."

"We're two people. What possible difference can we make?"

"We're not just two people. We are every Synthate ever produced. There are thousands of us. Trained. Battle hardened. Ready."

"You can get Synthates to fight?"

"They've been waiting for someone like you to lead them. They've been waiting for someone half-natural half-Synthate to show up and speak out. They will follow us. They will fight. I promise you."

Jack thought for a long moment, then turned and began to walk back down the hall.

"Where are you going?" Night Comfort called after him.

"You're right," Jack said. "We're going to that lab. We're going to free the Synthates."

"We'll need help to do all that."

"Help from who?"

"The naturals," Night Comfort said.

"Why would the naturals help us?"

"They will when they find out who their true enemy is."

CHAPTER 49

She would live. The doctor said there was no trace of the Black Rain illness inside Maggy's body. She was cured and no one in the hospital could explain why. But Arden knew. His daughter was cured because of a choice that he had made. A choice to give up on the investigation into the Reynolds murder. A choice to turn away from the truth and betray Jack.

One of Genico's own had approached him first. A guy named Lieberman had synced Arden days before he and Jack had broken into the Genico building. Arden had been asked to drop the Reynolds investigation and turn in Jack. In return, Lieberman promised that Arden's daughter would be cured. When it came to Maggy, he had no choice.

And so he made the phone call when they reached the Genico building. And the crushers had come for Jack. And Arden had gotten his cure.

Arden placed his hands on his lower back and stretched. He was in the waiting room of Bellevue Hospital, the plastic chairs around him filled with family members of patients. On the walls, plastic-coated posters warned of choking hazards and the first signs of Black Rain fever.

Jack had escaped.

Arden had watched him base jump away from the building, then vanish into the night. But they would still be looking for him. They would always be looking for him. As long as he was a Synthate. For Arden, the story had found an end. His daughter was cured and he was a natural. There was nothing to run from anymore. He lived in the safe world.

"Is she better?"

The familiar voice came from one of the plastic chairs behind him. Arden spun toward the chair as one hand reached beneath his jacket and touched the butt end of his service weapon.

Night Comfort was dressed like a pleasure parlor girl. Her bioprint of dark clouds sailed across her shoulder. She stared at Arden. The detective kept his hand on his weapon. "She'll be fine."

"That's good," she said. "You can take your hand off your pistol. I'm alone."

Slowly Arden removed his hand and slid it back out toward his side. "Does he know you're here?"

Night Comfort shook her head. "No. Jack doesn't know I came. I know what happened between you two in Genico. He doesn't blame you."

"I'm not asking his forgiveness. Nor yours," Arden said. "So you're with him now?"

"I'm working with him, if that's what you mean," she said. "To make things right."

"I offered you a safe home."

"I don't belong in your world. I don't know why you can't see that. I'm a Synthate. Not a natural. We cannot coexist now, no matter your feelings for me. I must find my own way." She frowned and shook her head. "I didn't come here to fight with you."

"Why did you come?"

"To tell you the truth about Black Rain. Where it really came from."

"It was a Synthate attack."

"No. It wasn't," Night Comfort said. "Genico created it and released it." She handed Arden a sync flash.

"Why would they do that?"

"To keep people sick."

"Then why not release the cure? Sell it on the open market, they would make a fortune."

"The business of healthcare isn't to heal naturals. It's to make them just sick enough that they'll always need Genico. But not so sick that they die. That's what Black Rain does. Think about your daughter's treatment. How long it's lasted. How much money it's cost. That's where fortunes are made, not in the healing, but in the treating."

He thought of the endless doctor's visits he'd had with his little girl. All the Genico treatments barely keeping her alive, spending every dime he'd made just for a little more time with his daughter. Arden looked at the sync she'd handed him. "What's this?"

"Information. You might think differently about who you're protecting. Lot of cops' families got sick from Black Rain."

"Yes, they did."

Night Comfort stood to leave. "You know, I shouldn't be surprised that you turned on Jack. Naturals are all the same. They'll always betray you in the end."

She turned and walked from the waiting room. Arden watched her leave, part of him wanting to go after her, but the rational side kept him in place. She was right; they did live in two different worlds. He had saved what was important, and if she wanted to go, there was nothing Arden could do. Nothing except learn to forget her.

CHAPTER 50

They came from all over the city. Night Comfort had spread the word through her network to Synthates of every class. And they all responded. The muscular, hardened Guards with the squat Domestics and Industrials standing side by side with the beautiful Socials. Thousands of them, filling the space beneath the Central Park dome. They stretched along the pond, figures visible between the trees. Behind them, the Midtown Synthate Zone continued to burn, black smoke rising from Rockefeller Center. A helisquall cut through the smoke, heading south toward the Gendustrial Zone.

They had come from Midtown and Governors Island. They had walked out of factories and day cares and training centers and pleasure parlors and found their way to the Ramble beneath the camouflage canopy. Some of the Guard class had raided the Games armories on Bloomberg Island and arrived wearing a strange assortment of military uniforms. Synthates were now clad in gear that included the plate armor of the Middle Ages, the crimson uniforms of British Redcoats, the deep blue of Civil War Union soldiers, the horned helmets of samurai, and the green-and-brown camouflage of the modern military.

They carried with them every manner of weapon ever devised—long swords and axes, blunderbusses and rifles, machine guns and barkers. The Domestics had long butcher knives; the Industrials carried giant wrenches and fire axes. Each class had armed itself as best it could. Even the Social classes carried brass knuckles and small derringers.

They were here to fight and, if necessary, die.

"Quite a sight," Night Comfort said. She stood with Jack on a rocky outcropping at the crest of a hill that surveyed the entire crowd. "Must be thousands here."

"The naturals will be ready. Their city is shutting down without our help. They'll know something is happening."

"They've grown weak from relying on us for years."

Jack shook his head. "They still have the crushers and the police."

"The cops won't be a problem."

"How do you mean?"

"Many of them lost family in the Black Rain strike. They won't risk their lives for Genico."

"I don't want there to be bloodshed," Jack said. "After this is done, we need to live together in peace."

"I can't promise there won't be blood." She frowned. "I can't promise we'll even be able to do what's necessary. I just know we can't go on living like this."

Another helisquall appeared on the horizon, swooping low over Columbus Circle.

"We don't have much time," Night Comfort said. "The crushers will be coming soon."

They would take the tunnels below ground, running along the length of the island, then surface near the Genico building. If they could take down the building, they could erase the Synthate records. They would become indistinguishable from the naturals.

Jack looked out across the mass of expectant faces. He felt afraid. All these lives were looking at him to lead them. What if he led them to nothing but their deaths? Could he live with that?"

"There's no going back," Night Comfort said. "We're committed now. The crushers have made certain of that."

There was no going back. All that was left was to see the thing through.

"Let's go."

CHAPTER 51

He'll be coming.

Phillip sat in his father's office and looked out across Lower Manhattan. Fully armed helisqualls circled the building, their blowers rocking the wind farms and rippling the air. Far below, hundreds of crushers surrounded the building.

The elevator opened and Lieberman appeared. He looked flustered, his tie undone and hanging loose, his hair a wild mess. "The Synthates have gone underground. Completely off the grid."

"How many?"

"We're still trying to figure out. Looks like thousands."

Phillip felt a sudden rush of excitement. This was all coming to an end. Whatever happened, winners or losers, the world would never be the same after this. The revolution was here.

"We've got crushers," Lieberman said.

"Not enough."

"What about the police?"

Phillip shook his head, turned back toward the window. Across the city, lights were going out. Synthate Industrials had turned off the machines. Without them, the naturals had become almost helpless.

"The police won't be coming," Phillip said.

"Why?"

"Because Genico created Black Rain. Because of us, thousands of naturals got sick. Little kids. Mothers. Grandmothers. And if Jack is smart, the naturals will find out about this," Phillip said. "Would you help us?"

"But we have the cure now. We can help them," Lieberman said. "If the Synthates tear us down, they'll lose everything."

"I think they'll just be happy to watch us burn."

"There's still time to leave," Lieberman said.

Phillip surveyed his father's office. He had always lived in his brother's shadow. And if he ran now, nothing would ever change. He shook his head. "I've been running all my life. I've been scared as far back as I can remember. Today that changes."

"They're going to kill us all," Lieberman said. "Jesus, I've been going to the Games for years. I've seen what they're capable of."

"We've had this coming for a long time."

CHAPTER 52

The Synthates streamed down into the subway station by the thousands. They were less than five miles from the Genico building, and in the tunnels they could travel undetected beneath Manhattan. Jack and Night Comfort stood in the conductor's car, an old Industrial Synthate sitting in the operator's chair. When the cars were packed, the doors pinged closed and slowly the train began to move forward on the ancient tracks.

"Your brother has to know we'll be coming," Night Comfort said. "He'll have the building surrounded by crushers."

"I know."

"If your brother fights?"

"I'll handle him."

The subway car picked up speed, heading south down the old abandoned rail line. An empty station passed, dead leaves littering the platform, the window of a token taker dusty and cracked. When they reached the Gendustrial Zone, Jack would split the Synthates into two groups so they could flank the Genico building. He hoped the crushers had enough sense to run. He wanted this to be peaceful, but he knew that wasn't possible. There was too much hatred. Too many had seen fellow Synthates killed by the crushers. Once they hit the streets, armed and angry as they were, Jack couldn't predict what would happen.

The train began to slow as they reached Beach's pneumatic station.

Someone handed Jack an M-16 taken from the Games armory. He gripped the weapon and headed toward the tunnel exit. Night Comfort led the last half of the Synthates back toward the second station, down the long tunnel that led toward Murray Street. They climbed the stairs and poured out of the station onto Broadway. The sun was bright and the metal of a hundred different types of armor and weapons glittered.

To the east was City Hall, ringed by New York City police officers. The cops stood still as Synthates filled the street. They made no move to intervene. One of them even waved toward Jack. Night Comfort was right. Arden would have told his fellow cops. The naturals knew what Genico had done. They would not protect the Gendustrial power anymore.

They continued south, past Zuccotti Park, the slowly revolving Genico turbine ahead of them. The streets were empty of naturals and soon they approached the wide pavilion that fronted the Genico building near the edge of Battery Park. Broadway forked around the iconic Wall Street Bull, and the Synthates pushed forward, filling the entire Bowling Green space. The crushers guarded the front entrance of the building, rows upon rows of naturals in black uniforms. Helisqualls hovered in the distance, and two armored transports rumbled up over the sidewalk. Beyond them, the waters of the bay lay still.

Jack craned his head back toward the massive pinnacle of the Genico building and its ninety stories. Somewhere up there was his father's office. Somewhere up there, Phillip was waiting for him.

"You are not authorized to be here," a megaphoned voice boomed out from the crusher side. "All Synthates currently here have broken curfew and are in violation of genetic law. Synthate code prohibits you from bearing arms of any kind and from leaving your assigned work area. The penalty is capital punishment."

The lines of Synthates held, one hundred yards distant from the Genico building. Jack stepped forward.

"What are you going to do?" Night Comfort asked him.

"I'm going to talk to them. See if they'll stand aside."

"They won't."

"Then it will be a short conversation."

Jack and Night Comfort left the Synthate lines and headed across the open plaza. Ahead of them, the crushers stood five deep. A familiar face stepped from behind the ranks. The man who had interrogated Jack on the night of his arrest appeared, the man known as the Overseer.

He wore military fatigues and a battered cavalry Stetson. A Colt revolver hung at his waist. He sauntered toward Jack, cracking his knuckles as he walked.

"Jack Saxton," the Overseer said. "Didn't think I'd see you again. Should have killed you when we first met."

"Nobody has to die here."

"No naturals have to die, maybe. But you and your kind. All of you have to go to black. We'll expire as many Synthates as we can. There's no other way to deal with an uprising. A slave has got to know his place."

Jack looked around the open square. There wasn't a cop in sight, only the crushers. "Do your men feel the same? Are they ready to die for Genico's greed?"

"My men know their place. This has nothing to do with Genico. This is about preserving a way of life."

"Your ways are over. We can't be contained anymore. There are too many of us."

The Overseer shook his head. "You have no idea. An old union breaker said once, 'I can always hire one half of the poor to kill the other half.' But the beauty of Synthates is that we can always just build one half of the slaves to kill the other half."

The head of the crushers raised his hand. Two wide doors in the front of the Genico Synthate shop opened, and out streamed hundreds of Synthates, each fully armed. Their bioprints flared violent images. In the front of their group was Rasputin, Lieberman's battle-hardened Synthate.

"Fresh from the grow gardens." The Overseer smiled. "So, as I said. No naturals have to die today."

The new Synthates took position in front of the crushers. Jack felt himself deflate. These Synthates were new to the world. They didn't know what kind of life they were destined for and, if Jack could take down Genico tonight, how much better their lives would be. They would fight as they had been ordered.

Jack turned and walked back toward his lines. Night Comfort fell in next to him.

"What do you want to do?" she asked.

Jack sighed. "I don't know."

"You must know. They are looking to you to lead. Whatever you think is right, you must make a decision."

Jack surveyed the faces of the old Synthates who crowded the square in front of them. Even if they gave up their arms, and went back to work, what would that serve? They would still be dying in the Games. They would still live as slaves, subject to the whims of the naturals.

"None of them have ever had a choice about anything," Night Comfort said. "And now they're choosing to follow you. Don't take that choice away from them."

"Send the word," Jack said. "We will fight."

CHAPTER 53

High above Battery Park, Phillip walked slowly around the perimeter of his office in time with the sky turbine, looking down at the crowd of Synthates that filled the park below. All of them had been constructed from birth by the naturals but had gone on to develop in ways none could have foreseen. And yet, it was only a matter of time before the naturals were confronted with this moment. A people couldn't be enslaved forever without a reckoning.

"Whatever happens, the Synthate industry will never be the same again," Lieberman said. "People will want to know how we ever let things get this far. There'll be oversight and committees and more regulations. I think we're witnessing the end of our glory."

"We should have dealt with this a long time ago." Phillip felt remarkably clearheaded. In the end, Genico would survive. Greed always survived. But the truth of what had happened here, what had caused all this, might never be known. "Tell the crushers to do what's necessary."

CHAPTER 54

Overhead, the helisqualls circled away from the Genico building and swooped down low over Battery Park, machine guns extending.

"Here they come," Jack called out. "Take cover."

Synthates scattered for the open doors of the buildings that lined Broadway, finding safety in the office buildings and shops of Lower Manhattan. The helisquall guns fired, mini gun rounds tearing away façades and blowing out the glass of buildings along Broadway. The Guard Synthates, vanishing into heavy stone buildings, had been trained to stay calm in battle. They would make the crushers come into every building and hunt them down one by one if they had to.

Jack turned and ran with Night Comfort back north up Broadway. One of the helisqualls peeled off from the main group and accelerated after them. Jack could hear the roar of its turbine, then the whir as the mini gun opened fire. They ducked for cover beneath the stone overhang of the American Express building, chunks of concrete and stone splintering down on them as the helisquall passed overhead.

They watched the machine skim across the side of Trinity Church in the distance before it banked sharply and headed back in their direction. Jack fired his M-16 at the attacking aircraft, but the armored plating deflected the rounds. The helisqualls were designed to be almost impenetrable to ground fire. Jack took Night Comfort's hand and pulled her across Broadway until they were running down the narrow footpath of Exchange Place.

The helisquall roared after them. The walkway was narrow, and Jack turned back to see the craft miss the turn and slam into the edge of a Chase bank building. The craft righted itself, then the nose dipped and it propelled forward.

"Down here," Jack yelled, pulling Night Comfort up the narrow confines of Broad Street. The helisqualls were fast and agile, but the machine was having difficulty navigating the carriage streets of old New York. Even so, every minute the two were in the open, the helisquall was able to close the distance. They wouldn't have much time.

Ahead was the iconic structure of the New York Stock Exchange, the familiar Greek Revival columns stretching the length of the front. They raced toward the main entrance. A cyclone of trash kicked up around them from the helisquall's rotors. The Stock Exchange stood shadowed in a valley of taller buildings, each rising high above the helisquall. Jack and Night Comfort flung themselves through the unlocked heavy metal doors of the exchange. The helisquall struggled to keep level in the narrow Wall Street ravine. Jack looked through an impact-proof window cut into the thick granite of the exchange.

The helisquall leveled off outside, still buffeted by the turbulence inside the narrow space. High above on the roof of an adjacent building, two Synthates appeared, each bearing rocket-propelled grenade launchers. The weapons were antiquated and any helisquall, under normal circumstances, would easily be able to outmaneuver an RPG attack. But in the tight confines of the narrow street, the craft was vulnerable. With a white flash, two grenades streaked down from the adjacent roof, struck the helisquall, and tore through the machine's armor. The craft went down in a fireball burst, sheering off the George Washington statue in front of Federal Hall before bursting into flames.

CHAPTER 55

Phillip stopped the Genico sky turbine rotation and watched with Lieberman from high above as the Overseer led an army up Broadway. Gunfire erupted from windows on either side of the walkway from the Synthate mob who had taken refuge inside the buildings. Minutes before, a helisquall had skimmed up Broadway, then a massive explosion had followed near the Securities Exchange. The Overseer hadn't planned on the Synthates being this well armed. Or this well organized.

Intense fighting erupted outside the Custom House at the edge of Bowling Green. The solid-looking beaux arts building stretched for three blocks, and Synthates had taken position inside the building, firing down with a variety of weapons at the crushers. The Overseer's men had taken cover behind armored personnel carriers and he had sent the new Synthates forward toward the building. The new batches, just out of the grow gardens, were inexperienced and rushed forward, cut down by the gunfire from the Custom House.

"We've got the grow gardens pushing new Synthates out as fast as we can," Lieberman said. "We're trying to grow an army."

"If they get into Genico, Jack is going to try to upload the virus into the scrubber system," Phillip said.

"How do you know that?"

"Because I know my brother. The only way to help the Synthates is make them like us. So can we take the system offline?"

Lieberman shook his head. "There's no way to do that without severing Genico from the system."

"How would we do that?"

"We'd have to destroy the building."

"No matter what happens, we can't let my brother succeed," Phillip said. "My father forced us into this position. If we have to destroy the building, that's what we do. We can rebuild again."

"I don't see how we can lose. We have the crushers. We have weapons. We have new Security Synthates. They've got a handful of kitchen maids and whores patched together with some stolen relics."

"They have anger. And they have nothing to lose."

An explosion outside the Custom House caused a shock wave against the Genico building. Even ninety floors up, the windows rattled in their frames.

CHAPTER 56

Jack and Night Comfort ran the few blocks back to the Custom House. The building housed the National Museum of the American Indian, and they ran up the stone steps beneath a fluttering banner advertising a Hopi exhibit. Statues that flanked the exterior entrance had been knocked from their pedestals and lay in broken fragments. Scattered marble heads and limbs littered the ground. Inside, the building was filled with smoke and rattled by gunfire. War Admiral met them, dressed in Desert Storm–patterned camouflage, wearing a heavy flak jacket and a helmet, and carrying an M-16. Part of his ear hung in bloody tatters.

"We've got a few hundred crushers outside. They're rolling in armored carriers," War Admiral said as he led them deeper into the museum, past Indian exhibits, their glass cases shattered, tribal relics scattered across the floor. The group entered a collector's reception room with oak-paneled walls, then stopped inside the building's magnificent central rotunda, an enormous open space of white marble with a glass skylight that spread above them. The walls were adorned with murals depicting the exploration of early New York.

"How long can we last?" Jack asked.

"Depends how much damage they want to avoid," War Admiral said. "We've taken over the buildings, like you said. Right now they're the only things keeping us in this. Nobody wants to take out half the real estate in Lower Manhattan. Not until they get desperate, anyway."

"They'll have to come after us building by building. Floor by floor," Night Comfort said.

"How are we with ammunition?" Jack asked.

"Good. Problem is we've got weapons throughout centuries. Everything from machine guns to crossbows. None of what we carry is interchangeable."

"So what do you think?"

"If we've got any chance, we need to take a unit to the Genico building. We can keep the crushers occupied out here while an advance team moves into Genico."

A helisquall engulfed in flames roared overhead, visible through the rotunda skylight. The aircraft spun wildly out of control, then crashed into the top of the rotunda dome; massive pieces of mortar rained down on them.

A whistle blew from the front lobby, the sound of machine gun fire suddenly louder, followed by the drone of machinery.

Two Synthates ran through the rotunda entrance. "The crushers are coming!"

Through the open door of the rotunda, a team of a dozen crushers appeared. War Admiral fired his M-16, forcing them back into the lobby.

"We need to get you out of here," War Admiral said.

They fell back deeper into the museum. Synthates moved past them to guard the rotunda entrance from the crushers. The warning whistle continued to blow.

"You can get out through the rear of the museum. There's a second door leading onto Bridge Street. From there you can try to make your way to Genico."

They followed War Admiral through the remainder of the exhibits, then down a narrow corridor that ended in a heavy bronze door. War Admiral pulled the bolts open on the door, then heaved on the handle. Slowly the door swung open into a small alley behind the Custom House building. War Admiral held out his hand.

"Good luck. Don't make this all be for nothing."

Jack shook War Admiral's hand. "I won't."

Night Comfort hugged the big Synthate. "Thank you."

War Admiral bowed, then vanished behind the heavy metal door. The locks swung back into place, and they were alone in the alley.

CHAPTER 57

Jack and Night Comfort moved quickly from the alley onto Bridge Street. They passed along a series of loading docks, heading south toward Bowling Green. In the distance, a crashed helisquall lay on its side, the front windshield cracked, the dead pilot visible inside.

"Do you know how to operate one of those things?" Jack asked.

Night Comfort studied the helisquall. "Sort of."

"What does 'sort of' mean?"

"I've done a simulator," Night Comfort said as she reached the downed aircraft. The pilot's face shield was smashed, his body limp and slumped over against the seat. Jack unbuckled him and dragged him from the helisquall.

Night Comfort slipped behind the flight controls. Jack sat next to her. The front console seemed undamaged. She swiped her hand over the power grid and the turbines whirred to life.

"You sure this thing can fly?" Jack asked.

Night Comfort lifted back on the controls and the helisquall began to unsteadily lift upward. "Fifty-fifty."

The right wing was badly damaged. Strips of armor plating hung down near the turbine. Black smoke poured from one of the engines, but the machine slowly rose off the ground, then hovered ten feet in the air.

"Looks solid," Night Comfort said, testing the tilt. "Where to now?"

"Think you can land this on the Genico roof?"

She lifted back on the controls and the helisquall jerked upward. Jack's stomach lurched as the ground fell away quickly beneath them. "Guess we'll find out," she said as the machine banked sharply and skimmed out across Bowling Green toward the Genico plaza.

Below them, a mass of crushers moved toward the Custom House building. Gunfire poured down on them from both sides of Broadway. The helisquall sputtered as something gave way with a metallic clunk in one of the engines. The entire craft lurched to the right, the ground a dizzying blur far beneath them.

Jack gripped the edge of his seat as Night Comfort shoved the controls hard left to compensate. They spun counterclockwise, the turbines whirring as they narrowly avoided a wind farm that floated off toward Battery Park.

"Trouble coming," Night Comfort said, and glanced toward the north. Two helisqualls skimmed down Broadway toward them, moving fast between the valleys of buildings.

"What do we do?" Jack asked.

"Try to make it to Genico. They won't want to damage the building."

The helisqualls separated, skimming across the plaza. One of them opened fire, the twin guns blazing starbursts of flames. Metal impacted their craft, and Night Comfort banked the machine down. The ground seemed to bound upward toward them. Jack let out a startled choke before they leveled off and whisked along the plaza.

The two helisqualls followed behind. They banked sharply upward again, the façade of the Genico building sliding past them at an alarming rate. Their craft climbed vertically, the glass side of the tower blurred past.

"Why aren't they shooting?" Jack asked over the roar of the damaged turbine.

"They can't. Like I thought, they don't want to damage the Genico building."

They soared up past the line of the roof, the Manhattan skyline a panorama around them. Then the craft twisted and stalled as its engine finally gave out. Night Comfort fought with the controls as a warning alarm sounded inside the cabin.

"I'm going to try to land it there!" Night Comfort indicated the gardens that layered the Genico roof. The craft dropped quickly and hovered for a moment before the engine died and they plummeted down. Their helisquall crashed through a solar panel, black glass splinters flying away, then severed a stand of cherry trees along the edge of the roof before burying itself in the base of a statue. The belt pulled tight across Jack's chest, as the helisquall spun, its momentum carrying it toward the edge. They teetered for a moment, ninety stories above the pavilion, before finally coming to a rest.

Overhead, the two helisqualls circled the roof.

"Anything broken?" Night Comfort asked.

Jack rolled his neck. "Not so far. You?"

Night Comfort unbuckled her belt and rolled out onto the roof. Jack followed her. As their weight left their helisquall, the aircraft tilted forward. Then, with a shriek of metal, it fell over the edge of the roof.

CHAPTER 58

Phillip had watched the damaged helisquall rise up from outside the Custom House and then be attacked by two other craft over the pavilion. The machine had risen up the side of the Genico tower, and as it turned, Phillip had caught sight of his brother in the passenger seat. Then the craft rose out of view, the sound of an impact coming minutes later from the roof. His brother had arrived.

"He's here," Phillip said, turning away from the window.

Lieberman's face was pale. "We need to get some guards up now."

"I'm not hiding anymore. I'm better than him. I can beat him."

"No. You can't." Lieberman backed slowly away, then turned and rushed out the door.

Phillip watched the man go. Below, another explosion rocked the Custom House, two columns collapsing from the front of the façade. This was going to change everything. The naturals would never again trust the Synthates. They could no longer exist as a species together.

He turned from the window and slowly walked along the edge of his father's artifact display cases. Weapons stretched back to the beginning of man. The first in the case were two of the Schöningen Spears, over 300,000 years old, the oldest known weapon ever found. Next to that, a pair of Sumerian maces, then another case with Khopesh swords and Mamluk scimitars and Greek tridents, each in sets of two.

Every weapon was in a pair. And for the first time, Phillip knew why.

CHAPTER 59

Jack and Night Comfort ran toward the elevator. Overhead, the two helisqualls hovered like giant dragonflies before they turned and spun back toward the pavilion. Jack watched them fly off, as below, a detachment of crushers turned and headed back toward the Genico building. They didn't have much time before the place was crawling with crushers.

"Lieberman's office is below," Jack said. "Take the elevator."

"Where are you going?"

"After my brother."

"Need help?"

Jack shook his head. "This I do by myself."

They stood in the center of the rooftop garden. Manhattan spread around them, pillars of smoke still rising from Midtown. Light from the setting sun glittered on the Hudson. Jack couldn't help feel how much change this island had experienced. Long ago there was nothing here but farms and woods and settlers as far as the eye could see, and now the city was burning and its inhabitants were sick.

Night Comfort took his hand. Then she kissed him.

"Good luck," she said.

"I'll see you soon."

She stepped into the elevator and disappeared from view. Jack took a last look across the skyline, then headed toward the stairs down to his father's office.

CHAPTER 60

The door was already open. Quietly Jack stepped into the familiar space. The sky turbine had begun to spin again, and through the windows, the view slowly rotated. The office was clear, segmented by a wall that closed off the rear of the space. Centered in the wall was a large oak door, a single tree carved in the center. The door opened and his brother stepped out.

Phillip wore a dark blue suit. His eyes looked sober.

"Welcome back, brother," Phillip said. "You've had quite a journey."

Jack stepped into the room. He expected some kind of security. Some for-hire Synthates lurking in the corner waiting to attack. But the room seemed empty.

"There's no one here except you and me," Phillip said. He slipped off his jacket and folded it onto his father's desk.

"You would face me alone?"

"The great and powerful Jack Saxton?" Phillip said. "You think I'm that afraid of you?"

"You've always been afraid."

"Not anymore," Phillip said. "Have you made your decision?"

"About what?"

"If you're going to kill me."

"I don't know. Maybe. Now that I see you, I don't know if it's worth it."

Phillip shook his head, then rolled up the sleeves of his dress shirt. His forearms were bulbous and muscular, with veins running their length. Jack was taken aback.

"You see this room. Our father's museum?" Phillip indicated the glass display cases. "All these weapons. There are two of everything. Did you ever stop to think why?"

"It's just a collection."

"No. It's not. These are real weapons. One for you. One for me. It's always been this way. Our father always planned this moment. Planned for us to end things this way."

"That's your imagination."

"You think our father was a good man? You think he was a kind man?" Phillip said. He pushed a button beneath the desk and the fronts of all the glass cases in the room slid open, exposing the weaponry inside. "Our father was evil. He was twisted. You had no idea who he was. What he was capable of."

Phillip moved toward one of the weapons cases. Inside were two wicked-looking Gladius swords. They had sharp-edged metal blades about two feet in length with white bone handles. Phillip took one of the swords and tossed it toward his brother. Jack snatched the blade out of the air and gripped the handle.

"What if I don't want to fight you anymore?" Jack asked.

"Yes, you do," Phillip said. "That's who you are. That's who you've always been."

"You made me this way when you sold me out. When you took Dolce from me."

"I didn't make you this way. Our father did," he said.

Phillip advanced with surprising speed, spinning the Gladius around and driving the blade down with tremendous force. Surprised, Jack stepped to the side, brought up his own blade, barely parrying the blow. The metal clanged loudly. Phillip stepped back, circling his brother.

"Be careful," Jack said. "You might get hurt."

Phillip thrust the Gladius forward. Jack sidestepped and the blade shot past him. Phillip quickly recovered, dropped low, then brought the blade up in an arc. The edge of the sword sliced toward Jack's head. Jack brought his own blade up and the two swords slammed together. He felt his arms vibrate from the blow.

"I've made some enhancements," Phillip said.

"You've taken Samps!"

"Just trying to level the field between us."

Phillip lunged forward; his Gladius cut through the air. Jack stepped back, the blade whistling past his face. Their blades clashed again, and Phillip brought up an elbow, catching Jack in the face. Stunned, Jack backed up, his eyes watering. He could feel a trickle of blood from his nose.

"You know, you've killed before," Phillip said.

"Only when I had to. You forced me into the Games."

"No," Phillip said. "You were the one who killed Reynolds and his wife."

"That's a lie," Jack said, and attacked. The two swords met as the brothers swung viciously, moving in a circle around the floor. Jack could feel his arms beginning to weaken. His brother seemed unmoved. His swings were measured and powerful, with no sign of faltering. Jack wondered when Phillip had developed such skill and assurance. Their weapons met overhead, and Jack felt his wrist give way as his sword shattered. Jack backed up, still bearing the handle, a jagged shard of metal protruding like a small dagger.

Phillip turned his back to Jack and returned to the weapons case. He dropped the Gladius to the ground and pulled a pair of bronze Greek tridents from their mount. Phillip flipped one toward his brother. Jack caught the weapon.

"You think I took Dolce from you?" Phillip said.

"You brought the crushers down on us. They took her from me because of what you did."

Phillip advanced toward Jack, the evil-looking trident extended in front of him. "The crushers didn't kill Dolce. She took her own life."

Jack felt a surge of anger. He charged Phillip and thrust the trident forward. His brother moved quickly, but not fast enough, and the edge of the blade caught his shoulder, slicing through fabric and skin and drawing blood. They separated again. Phillip finally appeared to be breathing heavily. He glanced down at the gash on his arm.

"I deserved that," Phillip said. "I know you loved her. I am sorry for her death. But she took her own life over what you had done. What our father had made you do."

"Enough lies!"

"Our father chose you."

"To run the company, and that made you jealous. You couldn't bear it."

"No, not to run the company. To lead the Synthate revolution. He used you from the beginning. He knew all about you. He wanted you to suffer. He wanted you to go to the Games. He wanted you angry. Because he knew this is how things would turn out. I didn't turn you in to the crushers. It was our father."

"What?"

"Our father was a god. He gave birth to a new species. He created Synthates. Created new life. And he was determined that his creation would rule the Earth."

"How?"

"Genico designed the Black Rain attack. It was a test case. To see how many naturals we could infect. Reynolds was working on the project. He developed it, along with our father, in a lab underground somewhere. A secret lab."

An image of the underground laboratory in the old subway station flashed in Jack's mind.

"Reynolds wouldn't do that. He was working to help Synthates."

"Our father pressured Reynolds into the Black Rain project, but Reynolds wanted to back out. Wanted to expose everything. And our father had him killed. Had you kill him."

In a rage, Jack pressed forward with the trident. They clashed across the length of the floor, swinging the long blades at each other. An explosion on the street below rattled the building, throwing Jack off balance. Phillip jabbed the trident forward with murderous intent. Jack barely parried the three-pronged spear, but couldn't step away fast enough and the weapon buried into his thigh. A flash of pain shot through him as his leg went numb.

Phillip pulled the bloodied trident away, then moved back to the weapons case. He tore a Frankish throwing ax from its placement and whipped it overhand toward Jack. Jack saw a flurry of metal in motion and ducked down. The ax buried itself into the wall behind him. Jack dropped the trident and pulled the ax from the wall. He hefted it back and forth.

"The only person from Genico I've killed will be you," Jack said.

Phillip backed up, the other ax in his hand. "Think back. Try to remember a black box. A coffin-shaped box. About the size of a man."

Jack did remember such a box. He had seen it twice. Both times it was as if he had awoken from a dream. He thought back to the hotel during the crusher attack. A box had been in the room with him. He remembered thinking it was strange. But he hadn't had time to think on it. His only thought then was to escape.

"You're a Genico product. Part natural, part Synthate. But did you ever look at your code?" Phillip said. An eyeScreen flashed in the corner. A series of DNA coding flashed on the screen. "Your code is defective. Your mind is destined to break down over time. To become violent. And that's what it's been doing. You killed Reynolds."

"That's insane."

"You just don't remember it."

"How could I not remember murdering someone?"

"Because you died, too."

CHAPTER 61

The elevator doors opened and Night Comfort moved silently onto the Genico trading floor. Rows and rows of eyeScreens sat blank and silent, filling the large space. She hated these men who bought and sold life. She hated their sense of entitlement. She burned to be the instrument of their destruction.

A single light was on in the rear of the floor. An office door was open, and someone passed in front of the doorway. Night Comfort shouldered her M-16 and moved quietly down the hall. Something smashed and broke inside the office, and she heard the sound of furniture being overturned. She reached the open doorway.

Inside was a wood-paneled room with leather-bound chairs and oil paintings on the wall. One of the paintings was swung away from the wall, revealing a wall safe hidden behind. The safe was open, and a man was busy pulling out stacks of currency and stuffing the blocks into a duffel bag.

Quietly, Night Comfort placed the M-16 on the floor, then flicked open a wicked-looking blade of a knife.

"Hi," she said.

Harold Lieberman spun around, a terrified look on his face. "Who the fuck are you?"

"You don't remember me?" Night Comfort asked. "I'm not surprised."

Lieberman glanced down at the knife. "What do you want?"

"I'm going to cut your balls off with this knife. Then I'm going to slit your throat. And if I can break the glass, I'm going to throw you out the window."

"Jesus. Who are you?"

"Your reckoning. Look down there." She glanced out the window. "A plague has arrived for your sins."

Still clutching the bag, Lieberman glanced back toward the elevator.

"Nobody is coming to help you," Night Comfort said.

"There's millions in this bag," Lieberman said. "It's yours. Take it."

"I don't want your money. I can't be bought off. I'm going to kill you. And there's nothing you can do about it."

Lieberman backed up. His foot caught on an edge of carpet and he tumbled backward. He scurried along the floor, crab like, before he backed himself against the wall.

"The feeling you're experiencing now, that mix of fear and power-lessness. An overwhelming sense of dread. Of death," Night Comfort said as she advanced toward him with the knife. "Now imagine that feeling every moment of your life. From the instant you're born until the instant someone else chooses for you to die."

Lieberman shook his head. "Please . . ."

"Now you can almost begin to feel what it's like to be a Synthate."

Night Comfort stood over Lieberman, then slowly bent down toward him with the knife and began to cut.

CHAPTER 62

Because you died, too.

"You're a clone," Phillip said, still brandishing his ax. "Father never told you."

"That's impossible. You're the clone. I've seen it. You're a Synthate."

"I'm not," Phillip said. "Genico cloned a Synthate model of me. It's true. In case something happened to me, there was someone else with my face who could step in. But I'm still me. I found that Synthate and I removed him. You are the clone. Not me."

"You're lying."

"Father picked you to lead the Synthates. But you're too unstable. You become violent too easily. He had you kill Reynolds and his wife. Only Reynolds was ready. As he was dying, Reynolds shot you. You died too that night in the mansion. And your father's trusted Synthate Regal Blue came and got you.

"Your clone was prepared. Memories downloaded into your brain. You were left at your apartment and you awoke with no recognition of what had happened. No knowledge of the shift in time. The blips. Remember your dizzy spells? They said it was from your car accident when you were sixteen. What do you think really caused that?"

"You're telling me you knew about this?"

"I suspected. But Dolce knew. She knew you weren't the man she'd fallen in love with when we were kids. A clone is never perfect. Oh, it can pass superficially. But someone that really knows you. Someone you share a bed with night after night. Imagine what a torture that must be for them. She married you the first time, even after you were killed in the car accident. But I guess she couldn't take it anymore. And after you killed Reynolds, well . . . that's why she did it."

"Did what?"

"Took her own life. The crushers didn't kill Dolce. She was pregnant and she killed herself. She couldn't accept what you had become. And what you would become. Because with each cloning, your brain degenerated faster."

"You mean it happened before?"

"Your car accident. When you were sixteen. You died that night," Phillip said. "That was the first time. And then again, after you murdered Reynolds. Your memory was modified. Your mood swings were erased, your 'tendencies,' you used to call them. Genico had developed the Samp years ago. It was used to cure and treat post-traumatic stress disorder."

"Why did you never tell me?"

"It wasn't part of the plan. Father wanted you to be taken into the Synthate camps. He wanted you to get involved with the rebellion. Everything led to this moment. He sacrificed you for the cause."

"Don't lie to me, you called the crushers. You identified me. You were there when they took me."

Phillip hung his head sadly. "I was there. I knew you had murdered Reynolds. I knew what you were capable of. I thought you had to be stopped. And to my shame, I didn't have the nerve to do it myself. But I do now."

"Stop me from what?"

"The Samp you have, the 6th Day. You believe it's going to help Synthates. Make them indistinguishable from naturals. But it won't. It will change the balance, but it's going to kill thousands of naturals. Father thought naturals had become a plague on the Earth. And the only solution was to rid the planet of them. Let the Synthates inherit the world."

"No," Jack said. "I don't believe you."

Jack advanced with his ax. Phillip moved out of the way as Jack swung. The weapon swooped through the air, then buried itself into the edge of a desk. He tried to dislodge the blade, but it was embedded deeply into the wood.

Phillip lifted his ax but Jack tackled him. The two brothers fell to the ground in a flurry of punches. Phillip drove his knee into Jack's stomach and rolled free. Jack grabbed a rapier from the display case as Phillip launched the throwing ax end over end. Jack fell flat as the weapon spun overhead, cracking the glass wall at the end of the office. Jack pushed himself upright to find his brother pulling a curved scimitar from a jewel-encrusted scabbard.

"I'm going to use the 6th Day Samp," Jack said. "And I will go through you to do it, brother."

"You're not my brother," Phillip said, hefting the curved blade. "My brother died years ago."

They crossed weapons again in the center of the office. Phillip was tiring quickly now, his mouth hung open, and thick beads of sweat fell down the sides of his face. Sensing the end was near, Jack moved faster, his Games training keeping his body moving. Through the window, two helisqualls roared by, spinning off toward the Custom House. He wondered how the battle was going. But soon it wouldn't matter. When the 6th Day was realized, there would be no Synthates. No naturals. Only one human race.

Phillip's foot caught on something and, exhausted, he stumbled backward. Jack pushed the advantage, the rapier blurred the air, and he buried the blade deep into Phillip's side. Phillip roared with pain as the sword pierced his gut. He swung his blade up, catching Jack across the shoulder and slicing into skin and muscle. Phillip pulled away, staggered for a moment and then collapsed to his knees.

His hand reached up to the wound and he pressed against it, blood pouring around the edges of his fingers. The color drained from his body, leached out into the ground. He looked down at his destroyed body, then up again at Jack. Behind him, setting sunlight burned across the river, and in the distance, the towers of Manhattan sparkled with infinite promise.

"Where's your humanity now?" Phillip asked.

"I'm a Synthate. You didn't give me any."

Jack turned his back and headed toward the elevator. He would find Night Comfort and then they would access the scrubbers. Synthates would finally be free. Behind him, Jack heard the rasping final breaths of his brother.

"Jack," his brother called out.

He turned and saw Phillip standing at the end of the weapon display.

"Look." Phillip pointed a bloody finger. "Your shoulder."

Jack looked down at himself. His shirt was torn open where the scimitar had cut him. Blood flowed from a gash across his shoulder, his skin hanging loosely from the wound. Something moved, a quick flash of something beneath his skin.

Jack took hold of the loose skin and began to pull. Slowly, the skin peeled away from his shoulder, coming off in a single rubbery adhesive piece. Disgusted, Jack gave a quick jerk, and the skin segment pulled completely off. Beneath was new, pale skin, and across his shoulder, a bioprint of a three-masted warship crashed through churning waves with cannons blazing.

"They covered it with skin spray," Phillip said. Jack's brother pulled an old flintlock pistol from the case and aimed it unsteadily at Jack. "You know, you can't always win in everything."

The weapon boomed with a burst of smoke and flame. Pain punched its way into Jack's right shoulder, just over the bioprint, and he fell backward. A crimson flower of blood welled up beneath his clothes. Shocked, Jack looked up as Phillip carefully lifted the second pistol from the case.

Jack held up his hand. Phillip ignored him. His brother looked wildly out across the room and called out, "Father! I want you to see this. Where are you?"

Jack turned toward the empty space, seeing nothing. But then, slowly, came the faintest shimmer of movement. And as if rising from inside a mist, his father's face appeared, 3Deeing in space in the center of the room between bursts of static.

"I wanted you to see this," Phillip said, still holding the revolver. "I wanted you to see what you've done."

Jack started toward him. "Phillip, no!"

Phillip turned the pistol, placed the heavy barrel in his mouth, and then pulled the trigger. There was the loud clap of the weapon, and the back of his head erupted. The body collapsed to the ground.

Jack was frozen by the pain in his shoulder, and he reached for the wall to steady himself.

"You've been shot," his father's voice sounded from the 3Dee. "Are you injured?"

Jack turned toward his father. The 3Dee flickered strangely.

"I don't understand," Jack said. He could feel the blood draining from his body. "The things my brother said."

"You were never meant to hear any of that."

"But are they true?"

"Yes," his Father said. "You died when you were sixteen years old. But I couldn't bear that. So I brought you back. I created your memories as best I could. And you lived. And thrived."

"And Reynolds?"

"Reynolds had to be dealt with."

"I murdered him?"

"You did what had to be done," his father said. "No more. And you took no joy in it."

"My God." Jack felt sick. His entire world was off balance. He wanted to lie down, close his eyes, and forget all this. "Why did you do this to me?"

"Because you are meant to be a king. Synthates will rule this world. Your kind will rule. And the naturals have no place left."

"But we can live together," Jack said.

"No. The naturals will never accept you as equals. They will never be able to be trusted. There is no place for them."

"So the 6th Day Samp?"

"It is designed as a plague for naturals. Synthates will not be harmed. And in only a few days' times, maybe weeks, Synthates will have the city to themselves."

"But that's never what I wanted."

"It's not about want. It's about necessity. And we all do things that are necessary."

"And if I refuse?"

"I will find someone who will do this."

Jack looked down at his body. Blood dripped steadily on the floor. He wondered how long he could even stand. "I'm dying, anyway. It doesn't matter."

"You can never truly die," his father said. "I've made sure of that."

The elevator pinged and the doors slid open. From inside came Regal Blue pushing a cart with a coffin-size black box. The box had a power source at the bottom that glowed a rich green. Regal Blue pushed the cart to the center of the room and then stepped back, arms folded behind him. Jack staggered to the box. The last time he had seen Regal Blue, it was inside the tunnel, Baltimore Raiders coming to kill them.

"You survived the Games?"

"Sky King saved me."

Jack touched the lid of the black box, and with a hydraulic hiss, the top slowly slid open. Inside was a full-grown man, naked and pale, feeding wires rising from his navel, a thin coat of amniotic covering his skin.

The man's face was Jack's own.

Jack turned toward Regal Blue. "This is my clone?"

"He is."

"So you wait until I die, then you replace me with him?"

"I do."

"Jesus," Jack said.

"You don't die," his father said. "This way you can live forever."

"But this thing isn't me." Jack indicated the man in the black box. "I'm not him. We're separate. This is some artificially created man. He doesn't know my life."

"He will be you exactly. He has your same DNA. Your same memories. He will be you."

Jack turned back toward Regal Blue. "Have you done this before?"

"I have."

"When?"

"The first was when you were only a boy. Then you were shot by Mr. Reynolds. You died on the floor that night in the library just feet away from Reynolds and his wife. I removed you and placed a second you in your bed. You awoke that morning as if from a bad dream and went to work without any knowledge of what had happened."

"When else?"

"Later, when you escaped the Genico building, you bled out and died. I placed a second you in the hotel room. Again you awoke, evaded the crushers, and made your way on as if nothing had happened."

Jack remembered the bad dreams. He remembered the moments of waking up. The feeling of strangeness, of still being caught in some dream world. And he remembered now how Dolce had changed around him. Her distance. Her look of fear. Now he understood perfectly. She had taken her own life. She had known what was happening around her, and had felt powerless to stop it. The crushers hadn't killed her. It had been Jack. And his father.

Even if what he was hearing was true, then Night Comfort must have been in on it. There was no one he could trust. Not even himself.

Jack turned back toward the 3Dee. "What are you?"

"I am your father."

"No, you're not. I don't know you at all. I don't know who you are."

"I have done all this for you. To change the course of history and to make you a king. The Synthates will follow you and you can rule them."

Jack staggered forward, walking slowly toward where his father 3Deed. He passed through the projection and kept moving. Ahead was a large oak door with the image of a tree carved on the surface.

"Where are you going?" his father asked, a slight note of hesitation in his voice.

Jack pushed open the wooden door and stepped through the frame. Inside was a hospital room. A sleek, black, polished floor, white walls, and a bed surrounded by medical equipment. In the bed lay his father. He had grown so thin he was barely recognizable. His skin was translucent, and cool to the touch. Wires and tubes covered his body. His head barely made a dent in the pillow. He was a living corpse.

Regal Blue stood at the edge of the room, watching carefully.

"His brain is still sharp," Regal Blue said.

"What's wrong with him?"

"He's dying."

"He can hear me? Understand what I'm saying?"

Regal Blue nodded.

"I understand," his father's voice said, a new 3Dee appearing in the hospital room.

"Good." Jack bent down near his old man's ear. "I forgive you." He reached out and took his father's hand. Jack took the 6th Day Samp from his pocket and showed the tube to his father.

"What are you doing?" his father asked.

The liquid inside glowed. He pressed the injector of the vial against his father's arm. "But I can't accept what you've done."

The Samp injected the liquid into his father's arm. Trapped in the prison of his failed body, his father remained completely still. But Jack saw the faintest glimmer of movement in the old man's eyes. A slight narrowing of recognition.

The 3Dee began to flicker, then faded away. His father was gone.

Exhausted, Jack slumped down against the bed, then slowly sat. His back rested against the bed frame, the beep and whir of medical machines around him. From the corner, Regal Blue watched him impassively, like a vulture waiting for the end to draw near.

"I'm dying," Jack said.

"Shall I call for help?"

Jack shook his head. There was a war going on outside. Nobody would come to help him. And maybe that was best. Jack had been created with lies and had lived with falsehoods. Maybe what he needed was something new.

"When I die, will you replace me?"

Regal Blue bowed. "That has always been my job."

"And my memory?"

"Will be altered. You will forget what has happened with your father. You will awaken only knowing that you must help Synthates. That the revolution must come at all costs."

Jack shook his head. "I want you to promise me something."

"If I can."

"I know I'm dying. I know you will replace me. But please, leave my memories as they are. I need to remember the past. I need to know the things that have happened. It's important."

Regal Blue looked thoughtful. He tapped the black box with his fingers, then glanced toward Jack's dead father. Finally, he nodded. "Your memory will stay."

"Thank you," Jack managed. He looked out across the room. A vidImage 3Deed in the corner. Some lingering memory of his old man, perhaps. It was Jack, Phillip, and their father. Taken long ago, when Jack and his brother were boys, their father a much younger man, years of life still left ahead of him. Jack was smiling, Phillip had a slightly worried expression, and their father grinned, his arm around both of them. Behind them, rising into the sky, was the skeletal framework of the not-yet-constructed Genico building.

Soon there would be a new world. A better world. Without naturals and Synthates. But only men and women and the ways they choose to live.

EPILOGUE

Awake. Eyes open. Jack lay on the sofa in his father's office. His father was dead. Phillip was dead. Dolce was gone. Time is a careless hand, stretching roughly forward, destroying everything until all is lost but memory. The memory of this place. The memory of her. In time even these moments begin to fade, distant parts of the mind that grow dim with disuse. He would come here often to remember how it had been.

Night Comfort sat on the edge of the sofa, her hand on Jack's shoulder. Regal Blue stood in the corner. Jack was the son of a Synthate and a natural. He was Genico's legacy. That was the past and now the future stretched forward as vast and blank as the ocean.

The wind changes the face of the rock one grain of sand at a time. Too much time for any one man's life. Today was Friday. Somewhere the crowd had cheered and battles had taken place.

But not here. Here, there was only the beginning of the new world.

ACKNOWLEDGMENTS

Thank you to my amazing agent, Kimberley Cameron, for staying the course and believing in this project from the beginning. Every writer should be so lucky.

MDi